IN OUR OWN
BACK YARD

In 2016 Anne Kayes won the Storylines Tom Fitzgibbon Award for her first book: *Tui Street Tales*, a collection of inter-linked stories for 8–12-year-olds, published by Scholastic. The sequel, *Tui Street Heroes*, published by Wildling Books, received a 2020 Storylines Notable Book Award. *In Our Own Back Yard* is her first Young Adult novel.

After combining tertiary teaching and writing for many years, Anne now divides her time between writing and author visits to schools. She also runs writing workshops for students and teachers.

Anne lives with her family in Auckland. Anne can be contacted through her website: www.annekayes.com

If you're a teacher, I can visit your class or whole year group to read, discuss and answer questions. Contact me through my website: www.annekayes.com

Also, there are Teachers' Notes on *In Our Own Back Yard* also available on my website: www.annekayes.com

IN OUR OWN BACK YARD

ANNE KAYES

BATEMAN
BOOKS

For my dear friend, Tivinia Ngauamo, who, among many things, taught me how to plait hair. 'Ofa lahi atu.

And for Paul Douglas, my old friend.

Typographical design © David Bateman Ltd, 2021

Published in 2021 by David Bateman Ltd,
Unit 2/5 Workspace Drive, Hobsonville,
Auckland 0618, New Zealand
www.batemanbooks.co.nz
ISBN: 978-1-98-853874-7

A catalogue record for this book is available from the National Library
of New Zealand.

Cover design by Keely O'Shannessy
Typesetting by Tina Delceg
Printed in China by Everbest Printing Co. Ltd

CONTENTS

LOCKDOWN

It's the second week of lockdown and my fifteen-year-old daughter is doing her schoolwork online. I can hear her tapping away at her laptop as I pass her room with the washing basket in my hands. My seventeen-year-old son is in the room next door. He's still asleep and it's 10am. I wonder whether I should wake him but then decide to leave him. We've all been hit with a tiredness since the Covid-19 virus lockdown.

When Jesse finally does come out of his room at midday, he rubs his droopy eyes. 'Where's Eva?' he asks.

'Studying in her room,' I answer. I smile to myself. His hair is sticking up in all directions.

'Here I am,' Eva says. 'Study break. I need food.' She saunters into the kitchen and nudges me. 'What are you making, Mum? Something we can all eat?'

'It's a sandwich for me,' I say, stepping away as she makes a grab for it.

'Where's your motherly instinct?' she asks, following me to the table where she reaches again for my sandwich.

I slap her hand away. 'There's food in the cupboard. Make your own.'

Eva laughs, walking back to the kitchen bench.

'Eves,' Jesse says, sitting beside me at the table, 'can you flick the kettle on?'

'Yep, but just notice how I do things for you, Jesse. Maybe you could try to do something in return some time.'

'What?' Jesse looks at her and then at me, rolling his eyes. 'That's a bit extreme,' he mutters under his breath.

For a minute or so, we're all quiet. I munch on my sandwich, looking out at a fantail on the tree. A pīwakawaka visiting us is a pretty rare thing, but I've been noticing more birds around and hearing them more since we've all had to stay at home. Under Alert Level Four lockdown, no one can drive unless they're going to the supermarket, pharmacy or petrol station. Essential service workers can drive to work, otherwise everyone is supposed to work from home.

Eva hums to herself while the kettle boils, and Jesse leans on the table, his head on his hands.

'You okay?' I ask him.

'Just wondering when this will end,' he says. 'Dad reckons it might go on for longer than four weeks.'

Our prime minister, Jacinda Ardern, has told us on nationwide television that the lockdown will be for about four weeks if everyone does it properly. We have to keep a distance from others, apart from those we live with, to help stop the virus from spreading.

'Think positively,' I say.

Ross walks in. 'Lunchtime?' he says. He's been working from home at a desk he's set up in our bedroom. 'Making me a coffee, Eves?'

Eva sighs. 'S'pose so, Dad. Guess I'll make yours too, Jesse, while I'm here.'

Ross pats her on the back. 'Nah, I'll make them. You go and eat that sandwich you've made.'

Jesse stretches beside me. 'This lockdown is hard on us teenagers.'

'Did you ever have anything that affected the whole country like this when you were a teenager?' Eva asks, plonking herself down at the table.

'Hmmm, not like this, no,' Ross says, stirring his coffee at the bench.

'We *did*,' I say. 'The Springbok Tour! That affected the whole country.'

'I was in Singapore.' Ross's dad was in the New Zealand Air Force, stationed in Singapore for some of Ross's teenage years.

'Well, I was here,' I say, 'and I'll never forget it. I was your age, Eva.'

'Yeah, but did it affect the whole country, Mum?' Eva asks, while stuffing her sandwich into her mouth.

'It had a huge effect on the whole country.' I stand up and take my plate to the sink and run it under cold water. 'It was like the country got turned upside down. People either wanted the Springboks to come because they wanted to watch rugby, or they felt it was wrong because black people in South Africa were denied basic human rights. New Zealanders were really divided.'

'You went on anti-tour protests with Uncle Rewi, eh?' Jesse asks.

'Yep. You've seen the photos of us.' There are photos in an album of me and Rewi marching together. He's my oldest friend, but I haven't seen him for a while. He's busy with his work and family in Wellington and I'm the same here in Auckland. It feels impossible to explain to my kids what that time was like for us.

'You should write about it, Mum,' Eva says, 'while you've got no work.'

I wipe the bench. 'That's a thought.'

'And, if we have to write Lockdown poetry for English, then you should write something about the Springbok Tour,' Eva says. 'Not fair otherwise.'

I smile. 'You're at school. There's a difference.'

'You're a freelance journalist with no work due to this virus,' Eva says. 'You should make the most of this time and write about something like that.'

'*What affected my nation as a teenager,*' Jesse says. 'That's the topic for the females in this house today.' He's beside me at the bench now, tipping some of his coffee into the sink and putting more milk in it. 'Dad never puts enough in,' he says.

I shake my head at him.

'But, back to you, Mum,' he says. 'Sounds like a good way to spend your time. Just don't stop all the baking you've been doing. Been enjoying that.'

Ross looks up from the table where he's smearing peanut butter on some bread. 'Yep, that's been one of the positives about Covid.'

'Well, I'll think about it,' I say. 'I'm used to writing with a purpose and for a particular audience, so I might not be very motivated by your Springbok Tour assignment.' I head out of the kitchen to empty another load of washing from the machine.

'You can give us little readings,' Jesse calls after me. 'Every night, we'll expect a new instalment. *We're* your audience. *We're* your purpose!'

'Maybe,' I call behind me. 'Let's see.'

The washing machine creaks as I pull the wet towels out and throw them into the basket. I'm too hurt to write, I tell myself. Magazines and newspapers that I regularly wrote for have told me they can only afford to pay their full-time staff now. Basically, I've been fired.

For a few days, I cried and cried. Ross told me not to worry, because he's earning. He teaches at the local secondary school, so that's consistent, ongoing work. It still hurts whenever I remember I'm effectively unemployed though.

At the washing line, I think about Eva's idea. It would keep me busy, but would it be too painful? There had been so much going on for me back then. Too much for a teenage girl to manage really. Writing about it might stir it up.

Later in the afternoon, I sit at the table and turn on my laptop to answer some emails. From Jesse's bedroom, I can hear him doing his online lessons. There's a cicada outside the window rubbing a discordant sound from its wings, like a child learning the violin.

I scoop crumbs off the table into my hand and throw them out the window, then sit back down, staring at the screen. Instead of clicking on my emails, I find myself opening a Word document. I don't need to think too hard. My fingers are on the keyboard. I know where the story begins.

CHAPTER 1
THE SOCIAL

When Ursula reached over and tapped his shoulder, I hadn't expected his green eyes. He was sitting with his arm around a girl, who was talking to someone beside her. The disco lights flicked over him so, for a moment, he was lit up.

'Liza, this is Harry,' Ursula yelled over the music, putting her arm around my shoulder. 'Harry, this is Eliza, but *we* call her "Liza".'

I smiled and shouted, 'Hi.'

He lifted one eyebrow. 'You go to Saint Theresa's?'

'Yeah,' I said, but the tinge of sarcasm in his voice made me take a step back. Ursula had turned away and was talking with Josh, who couldn't possibly need her as much as I did at that moment.

'I'm at the very forward-thinking Newton Grammar School.' Harry's top lip curled upward into a smirk.

'Up the road from us?' I yelled. It was hard to talk over the music.

He nodded and lifted his arm from the girl next to him, who turned and looked me up and down. Sliding her arm around his waist, she continued her conversation with the girl at her side.

'I've seen you walking home from school,' he shouted.

My cheeks were warm. Think of something to say, I told myself. I put my hands in my jacket pockets and felt for my cigarettes. If only we could smoke in these church halls.

'Are you in fifth form too?' I yelled.

'Sixth.' His top lip was still curved into that smirk, and it occurred to me that this may have been the way he was born. An image of Mick Jagger flashed through my mind. Harry leaned forward and gestured for me to come closer. I bent towards him.

'So, do you believe in all that Catholic stuff?' he shouted.

'Some of it.'

'What, like virgin births?'

His warm breath was on my ear. I stepped back again. 'I, well, I haven't thought about it too much.'

Ursula was dancing with Josh in the space that had been cleared into a dancefloor. Her blonde hair fell around her as she moved. Josh was her third boyfriend and I'd never even had one. I'd kissed some boys at parties, not because I'd liked those particular boys, but because I'd just felt I should. Some of my friends said they'd gone way beyond that already.

'I need to find my friends,' I yelled.

'Eliza,' Harry said, glancing back at his girlfriend, then leaning towards me. 'Liza.'

I looked right back at his green eyes. 'Yeah?'

'I won't forget that name,' he said.

His girlfriend swivelled around and looked at me, more intensely this time. Maybe she'd heard what he said. Reaching up, she took his chin, turned his face towards her and kissed him. I guessed she was trying to make me feel uncomfortable, to show me he had a girlfriend. I didn't blame her. He shouldn't have said that to me.

I thrust my hands deeper into my pockets and walked away. The hall was suddenly too hot. Something sad swelled in me and I wanted to run outside into the cool air. I blinked away the image of Harry's Mick Jagger lips and looked around.

Rewi was dancing with some friends on the edge of the dancefloor. I mimed to him that I was going outside for a smoke and he made his way over to me. Ursula and Josh joined us, sweaty from dancing. The sadness was still hovering, and I decided I'd head home after my smoke. The Presbyterian church holding this social was only a street away from my house.

Ms Jefferson was standing near the door, talking to some students from our school. The church only held socials if teachers from local schools agreed to help supervise. Ms Jefferson smiled at me as I passed her. She was wearing jeans and a T-shirt and her hair was up in a ponytail. She could almost have passed as one of the students. Ursula and I called her 'Starship', after the band 'Jefferson Starship', but only between us, never to her face, although she probably wouldn't have cared. She was pretty cruisy.

When we stepped outside, kids were crowding the steps. Rewi grabbed my arm and told me to go back inside. I craned my neck to see what was going on.

In front of us, a group of guys was facing another group. They seemed older than us and were wearing black boots with narrow-legged jeans. A few of them had shaved heads. One of the skinhead guys leaned forward, jutted out his face and sneered at a boy with an afro in the other group. 'What you gonna do, hori boy? Do a little haka?'

I reached for my ciggies, but my hand froze in my pocket. The skinheads were all white and the other group were all Māori and Polynesian. I looked around. Where were the teachers? Someone needed to tell them to come out here.

'It's getting aggro,' Rewi said, gently nudging me behind him, so I had to stand on tiptoe to see over his shoulder.

I recognised some of the boys. They went to Newton Grammar and their kapa haka group had joined up with ours for the Polynesian Festival last year. Two of them walked the same way to school as me. My fingers were tight around my cigarette packet.

The boy with the afro didn't say anything. He just stared back at the skinhead guy, who stepped forward and stuck out his tongue, jumping up and down, like a clown. 'Ka mate! Ka mate! Hori, hori!' he yelled, spit flying from his mouth, as he lifted his hands and slapped at his thighs. The guys around him started to laugh.

The boy with the afro stepped forward. 'Better stop doing that, or I'll smash you,' he said.

The skinhead guy dropped his arms and was still for a second before he ran at the boy with the afro and rammed into him. It was like a high rugby tackle that sent the boy backwards into the wire fence behind him. He bounced clumsily off it.

As if a whistle had just blown in a sports game, both groups lunged at each other, swearing and pounding their fists and feet into stomachs, thighs and faces. One of the skinhead guys fell to the ground in front of us. He had blood all over his face. I didn't see him fall, but I heard the crack of his head on the concrete step. I felt as if I was going to vomit.

I turned around but there were people crowded on every side of me. From the hall behind me, The Swingers' 'Counting the Beat' belted out into the warm night. People were still dancing in there!

Parents, teachers and church members began to push their way out of the hall, shoving us aside and yelling at the boys to stop. Someone got straight in between them and pushed them apart. I heard her voice, that firm certainty that it had. Breathless, I shoved past Rewi, who grabbed my arm. 'Don't!' he said, but I had to stop her. She could get hurt.

I pushed down the steps and walked towards the heaving mess of boys pounding into each other. 'Ms Jefferson!' I yelled. 'Ms Jefferson!'

She was standing between two boys and yelling at them to calm down. 'Do you want to spend the night in a cell?' she shouted over the noise. 'Go home! Get out of here!'

Other adults began to do the same, getting in between the boys and pulling them apart. Sirens screeched and, moments later, police cars were in the church driveway. I'd never seen police with batons before. I should have stepped out of the way, but my legs wouldn't move. Somehow, I was closer to it all than I'd meant to be.

The police strode into the chaos. One policeman dragged out the boy with the afro. His arm was bleeding badly, like someone had cut him. The policeman pushed him, face first, hard against the wire fence, so that his cheeks and forehead must have been dented by the wire. The boy kept telling him that it wasn't his fault, that he hadn't started it, but the policeman clicked some handcuffs around his wrists.

Then Ms Jefferson was pulling my arm. 'Come on, Liza, go home,' she said. It was impossible to stop watching though. Two guys were locked together, rolling around on the concrete. One of them yelled, 'Fucking black coon!' He said it over and over while they punched, kicked and kneed each other.

Two policemen began to force their batons between them. 'Break it up!' one shouted. He lifted his baton and hit one of them on the leg. 'Separate now!'

Ms Jefferson turned me away. She took my arm and led me up the church driveway. 'Liza, where are your friends?'

I looked around. Rewi was walking towards me. He called out, 'Liza!' I couldn't see Ursula and Josh. Maybe they'd gone back inside.

Ms Jefferson stopped and patted my arm, waiting for Rewi to catch up. She must have felt me shaking. My teeth chattered as if it were winter, but it was a week before Easter, early autumn, and mostly warm. I still felt like I was going to vomit.

'Go straight home now, you two,' Ms Jefferson said. 'I'll see you on Monday, Liza.'

Someone had turned off the music and I could only hear yelling now.

'Let's go,' Rewi said.

We began to walk away, but I couldn't stop myself from looking back. The policeman was shoving the boy with the afro into the back of a police car.

Rewi stopped and lit two cigarettes, passing one to me. We were quiet most of the way home, puffing smoke out into the still night. When he'd finished, he stubbed his smoke out on a brick wall and tossed the butt into a bush. 'Don't know if you noticed,' he said, 'but that skinhead dude climbed over the fence into someone's back yard. Cops went over after him, but the rest of his Pākehā mates got away.'

I nodded, dragging on the last of my ciggie so that it sizzled right up against the butt and almost burned my nose. I thought of the policeman's hand pushing down hard on the boy with the afro's head, forcing him into the car.

Rewi only spoke again when we were outside my front door. Our dog, Sal, had heard us and she whined and scratched on the inside of the door. 'I didn't want to get arrested,' he said. 'I'm on their records anyway, cos of Mum. That's why I kept out of it.'

'You did the right thing,' I said.

My older brother, Pete, opened the door. I could hear the *Goodnight Kiwi* theme tune, which played on TV when all the programmes had finished for the night. Someone switched off the television. I knew it wouldn't be Dad, because he was a reporter at the *Auckland Star*, and he didn't come home from work until after midnight.

Mum and my sister, Jo, came into the kitchen with plates and cups in their hands. They were both in their dressing gowns and, with their brown hair and brown eyes, if Mum had been younger, they could have passed for twins.

We told them about the fight. Mum switched on the kettle, and Rewi and I made some toast.

'One of those skinhead guys goes to Newton Grammar,' Rewi said. 'He's a dick.'

'How come?' Mum asked.

'He just is.'

'Well, that wouldn't stand up in court,' Mum said.

'He called me a "coon" once,' Rewi said, 'when I was walking past him in P Block to get to maths. I bumped into him and he said, "Watch where you're going, coon." I pretended I hadn't heard him. Should've told him to get his ethnicities right and use the correct offensive term.'

'Good you ignored him,' Mum said.

'I don't know. Mum thinks I should've confronted him or gone to the principal to make a complaint.'

'What do you think?' Mum asked.

Rewi shrugged. Sal started to bark at something outside.

'Shush, Sal,' Mum said. 'Must be a possum out there or a hedgehog.' She reached over and pulled Sal over to her, telling her to sit. When Sal was quiet, Mum looked at Rewi. 'Just keep away from that boy at school. Keep right away from him.'

A bit later, Rewi left to walk home. He lived three streets away from me. Mum told him to stay at our house, but he said he wasn't tired yet and that he felt like walking.

CHAPTER 2
A DRINK WITH
A NEIGHBOUR

When Mum woke me to go to church the next morning, I felt like I hadn't really slept. I'd woken during the night, feeling clammy and hot, so I'd kicked my duvet off onto the floor. I lay back with only a sheet on me and listened to the drone of a lawnmower next door. My eyelids sank.

'Eliza, this is the second time I've had to wake you. We'll be late for mass,' Mum called from my doorway.

I groaned and forced myself to sit up. 'Can I miss mass today? I feel a bit . . .'

'Get up,' Mum interrupted. 'No excuses. You can pray for the people who got hurt last night. Ten minutes and then we start walking.'

I swivelled and put my feet on the floor, my soles soaking up the coolness of the wood. Anger prickled under my skull. Mum was probably halfway down the hallway when I yelled, 'I'm sixteen in October! Old enough to make my own decisions about religion.'

'Stop wasting time arguing and get out of bed!' Dad called from the kitchen.

I pictured him leaning against the bench, showered, drinking strong coffee and tired, but still coming to mass with us. Sometimes, he fell asleep in church and Mum had to nudge him if he started snoring.

The sound of a radio discussion came from the kitchen. Dad liked to listen to not only the news, but also discussions of the news.

If I suggested switching the radio to a music station, he'd raise his eyebrows and shake his head, saying, 'And you want to be a journalist!'

I sighed, picked up my duvet and dumped it on the bed. The single bed on the other side of room was neatly made up. It had been Jo's bed when Pete still slept inside. After he'd left school, Pete got a job at the gas station over the summer and bought an old caravan that sat in our back yard. It wasn't linked up to electricity or hot water or anything. He just slept in it. At night, through his caravan window, his torch light made patterns on my bedroom wall.

It was a relief not to be sharing a room with Jo. She was always telling me how I should spend more time doing homework and work harder at school, and that I needed to do more to help Mum. She once asked me if I smoked. I told her I didn't, but I don't think she believed me. She said she thought I was weak and easily peer pressured. Rewi secretly called Jo 'the good girl'.

The thing is, I *did* work hard at school, I *did* help Mum and Dad, so I *was* trying. It was just that my oldest friends, Rewi, Ciara and Stella, had started smoking. Then Ursula was moved up to our class in the hope that she'd work harder away from her old friends. The way Ursula smoked had been the tipping point for me. She curled the smoke slowly out of her mouth, and her lip balm left a smudged, dented ring around the butt. Ursula made smoking look sexy. I wanted to look like that.

Jo was right about the smoking. I *was* easily peer pressured, but she wasn't right about school. I wanted to pass my exams. Yes, I'd laugh at Ursula's pranks and her almost-rude comments to teachers, but I wanted to be a journalist, like Dad, except maybe not dealing with news events like he did. I liked the idea of interviewing interesting people and writing about them.

I took my time getting dressed, mulling over more things I could say to Mum about why I shouldn't be forced to go to church. I'd recently watched a documentary about how women had been priests in the Anglican church since 1976. Five years ago! The Catholic church still didn't allow women to be priests. At school, I'd asked Sister Agnes why this was, and she'd rambled on about how all the disciples were men and a whole lot of other stuff that wasn't very convincing.

Pete came to my bedroom door and told me to hurry up. 'Just pretend,' he said. 'You don't have to believe it all, just do it to keep Mum and Dad happy.'

'That's fine for you,' I said. 'You can be a priest!'

'What? I don't want to be a priest!'

'Well, you could if you wanted!'

'Do you want to be a priest?' Pete asked.

'No, but it's the principle,' I said, furiously wrangling a brush through my hair to wrestle it into a ponytail.

Pete rolled his eyes. 'Your English teacher, Ms Jeffries . . .'

'Jefferson,' I corrected him.

'She's turning you into a man-hating feminist.'

'Get out of my room!'

'Leave her alone, Pete!' Mum called down the hallway.

We ended up driving to church because I'd made everyone run so late. Usually we walked, because Saint Theresa's Church and the school Jo and I went to were only three streets away.

One thing I did like about church was the statue of Mary at the entrance. That morning, she glistened with dew and, when I looked up at her, I wondered if she'd ever felt a bit shaky, a bit tearful, the way I did that morning. She was calm though, as always, her eyes gazing down at me, as if to say that things were going to be okay. I thought of the sandy-haired Harry, with his green eyes and his scathing tone, asking me if I believed in the virgin birth. My face felt hot and I looked away from Mary's reassuring face.

We were a few minutes late and the entrance hymn had begun, so we slipped into a pew at the back. Sitting between Pete and Jo, I began the ritual of kneeling, sitting, standing and speaking at the elderly priest's signals.

When he began the sermon with his usual, 'Brothers and sisters . . .', I closed my eyes and thought about the night before. The boy with the afro had probably spent the night in a police cell. The skinhead guy might have too if the cop had caught him. Television shows depicted prisons as filthy, grimy places with concrete floors stinking of urine and with dirty blankets on stained mattresses. Did they leave lights on so prisoners could see or was it completely dark? What if some older, greasy-haired guy on the bed opposite sat sharpening a knife he'd kept hidden under his mattress? I pictured the boy with the afro trying not to watch this, burrowing down under the blanket, wishing his mum or dad could come and get him.

Pete shifted his position beside me. I opened my eyes and tried to focus on what Father Luke was saying. He leaned over the lectern, looking over the top of his glasses. Usually he ranted on about the gospel, but today he was talking about the Springbok team who were booked to come to play a series of rugby games here in July. It had been in the news, but I also knew about it because Rewi's mum had been photographing protests against the tour.

Father Luke's voice increased in volume. 'Letting the South African rugby team come here to play is like having a beer with your neighbour on a Friday night, when all week long you hear him beating his wife.' He took off his glasses and waved them at us. 'If Jesus were on earth now, he'd be deeply concerned that black South Africans cannot vote and are treated as second-class citizens. Our country needs to show disapproval at these injustices by *not* playing rugby or any other sport with South Africa.'

My brother played rugby and he was leaning forward, listening.

When we'd finished saying hi to all the other teenagers who'd been forced to go to church too, we made our way out to the car. Mum and Dad were talking about how our school, also called Saint Theresa's, needed money for more sports equipment. They said there was a car-washing fundraiser coming up, which we could all help with.

Jo and I rolled our eyes at each other and, seeing us out of the corner of her eye, Mum said, 'It doesn't hurt to give time to help . . .'

'That thing about stopping the Springbok Tour,' Pete interrupted, pulling hard on the car door that jammed. 'I agree it's not okay to have apartheid, but it hasn't got anything to do with rugby.'

Mum turned the key in the ignition. I always held my breath when my parents did this, as sometimes our old Holden Kingswood didn't start, and we had to get out and rock the car from side to side. Miraculously, that would make it kick into action. Dad reckoned the starter motor just needed a bit of a shake-up. Thankfully, that morning, the car started without our assistance.

A year ago, Mum had gone back to work for two days a week. She'd been a social worker before she got married and her old boss had phoned and asked if she wanted a part-time job. I'd hoped, with the extra money, that we might get a new car, one that didn't embarrass us. So far, it hadn't happened.

'The All Blacks weren't allowed to have Māori players when they toured South Africa in 1960,' Dad said. 'Lots of people protested, carrying signs saying, 'No Maoris, No Tour'. The team went anyway. This issue with South Africa and rugby isn't a new one.'

Dad knew about historic events. He could remember dates without checking encyclopaedias. His long legs jiggled in the front passenger seat.

Pete didn't say anything.

'When South Africa finally did allow Māori players to play there in 1970, they called them "honorary whites",' Dad continued. 'Must've been hard for the Māori players.'

No one talked for the rest of the short drive home. For once, mass had given us something to think about.

CHAPTER 3
KALĀSIA

At school on Monday, Ursula walked into form class with pink streaks in her long blonde hair, which was tied up in a ponytail. We weren't meant to dye our hair, but Ursula never took any notice of school rules.

Sister Agnes was marking the roll and looked up at Ursula. 'What a shame to do that to your pretty hair,' she said. 'You're on detention and you'll need to wash it out tonight.'

'It won't wash out for ages, Sister,' Ursula said. 'It's semi-permanent.'

'Well then, you'll be on detention for a week,' Sister Agnes snapped. 'You know the rules.'

I watched Ursula sway past Sister Agnes and plonk herself down at her desk. Sister Agnes pursed her lips.

From two rows behind, I could see Ursula's hair and, as if sensing I was watching, she turned around and smiled at me, her black eyeliner accentuating her blue eyes. Ursula was beautiful, a kind of Marilyn Monroe beautiful, but the pink streaks changed things. Now, she was beautiful, but a bit tough too, sort of punky and hard, like Debbie Harry.

There was a knock at the door, then our school principal, Sister Ignatia, came in. 'Morning girls.' She looked around the class as we parroted, 'Good morning, Sister Ignatia.'

A girl walked in behind her. She glanced at Sister Agnes then looked down at the floor. Blue ribbons were tied around the bottom of her two French plaits.

'Ah yes,' Sister Agnes said, putting down her pen, 'the new girl from Tonga.'

'This is Kalāsia,' Sister Ignatia said to us. 'She's new to our school, so I expect you to look after her and show her where to find things.'

Sister Agnes smiled at Kalāsia. 'Welcome,' she said. Looking around the room, her eyes landed on me. 'Eliza, you can be Kalāsia's buddy. She can sit next to you.'

I nodded. 'Yes, Sister.' With an exaggerated pout, I turned to Ana Babich, who sat next to me and said, 'We're being separated.'

'Torn apart,' she said, putting her hand over mine, 'like lovers who were never meant to be together.'

I laughed.

'That's enough now,' Sister Agnes said. 'Ana, take your things over to the empty desk beside Susan, so Kalāsia can sit next to Eliza.'

Sister Agnes sighed while Ana scrabbled around putting her pens into her pencil case and picking up her bag. When she finally moved away, Sister Agnes put her hand on Kalāsia's back and gently pushed her towards the empty desk beside me. 'This is Eliza,' she said. 'She'll be your buddy to help you settle in.'

Kalāsia sat down next to me. 'Hi,' she said.

'Hi.' I tried to give her a reassuring smile. 'You can just call me "Liza".'

'Okay.' Kalāsia looked towards the two nuns talking quietly up the front. 'Liza,' she said, as if practising the name.

When Sister Ignatia left the room, Sister Agnes turned back to finish marking the roll. 'Right, we'd better add your name, Kalāsia,' she said. 'How do we spell that?'

Kalāsia said, 'K', but it sounded like a soft 'g'.

Sister Agnes glanced up. 'K?'

Kalāsia nodded, her eyes fixed on her desk. She reached up to straighten a plait, her hands trembling. There were no other Tongan students in the class to help her.

When Sister Agnes got to her surname, she put down her pen and asked Kalāsia to write it on the blackboard. We watched her make her way up to the front of the room. On the left-hand side of the board, she wrote 'Hopoate'. It stayed there for a week, as if it was on detention, as if it had misbehaved in some way.

CHAPTER 4
SPACIES

At the end of school, Rewi was waiting outside the main gate. Newton Grammar was just up the road and they finished ten minutes before we did, so Rewi usually waited for me so we could walk home together.

I was a bit late to meet him, because I'd gone with Kalāsia to meet up with her two sisters. The statue of Our Lady in the school garden was their meeting point. I'd accompanied her to meet them at morning tea and lunchtime too, because she'd said she needed to see them. It was probably comforting for them to see each other on their first day at a new school. Each time, her sisters asked me questions.

Now, her older sister, 'Amanaki, wanted to know where I lived, how many were in my family and if I'd met a Tongan person before. Her younger sister, Lupe, who was thirteen, asked if she could touch my hair. My hair was browny-blonde and very thick. I found it hard to control. She ran her hands over my ponytail a couple of times. Kalāsia reached out to touch it too.

'I will plait it for you tomorrow,' Kalāsia said. 'Easy.'

'Okay,' I said. Rewi was waiting for me, so I needed to get moving. 'Which way do you walk home?'

'This way,' 'Amanaki said, pointing towards the gate where Rewi was standing.

'Same as me,' I said. 'Let's go, then.'

At the gate, I introduced Kalāsia and her sisters to Rewi.

'Are you Māori?' Kalāsia asked.

Rewi lifted an eyebrow. 'Yep,' he said, as he swapped his bag onto his other shoulder. His aunty had sewn his bag for him. It was a rectangular shape in the Rastafarian colours: green, red and yellow. She'd stitched the words, 'Bob Marley' in black thread over the yellow bit.

'We're from Tonga,' Kalāsia said.

Rewi nodded. 'Just arrived?'

'No, been here for six years,' Kalāsia said. 'Used to live with our aunty and uncle but now we have our own house near this school.'

'Hard to leave our old school,' Lupe said. 'Lots of Tongans there. Lots of Samoans. Lots of Māori kids. Here, it's mostly Palangi. Only one other Tongan family's here.'

'Palangi?' I asked.

'White people,' Kalāsia said.

'So, I'm Palangi?'

They nodded.

'Wow, I'm Palangi,' I said, which made Kalāsia and her sisters laugh.

We walked together, but Rewi hung slightly behind in case a teacher saw us. Saint Theresa's students weren't allowed to walk to or from school with boys.

When we reached the takeaway bar, I slowed down so that Rewi could join me. The takeaway bar was in a small block of shops, where students from Newton Grammar and Saint Theresa's milled around after school, even though we weren't meant to. Sometimes teachers would stand outside and tell us to keep moving or tell us off for eating on the street in school uniform. There were no teachers there today. Must have been a staff meeting.

'Wanna bore me with your company and play Spacies?' Rewi asked me. 'I'll buy you some hot chips.'

'I'll stay, but only for the hot chips,' I said. 'Not interested in listening to your drivel.'

Rewi smiled. 'You sure it's drivel or could it be that my extreme intelligence is just a bit above you?'

When we were at kindy, Mum said that Rewi and I followed each other around, smiling and copying each other. We were still a bit like that, except that now we tried to outdo each other with smart-arse comments.

Kalāsia and her sisters spoke to each other in Tongan. They seemed to be having a debate over something.

'We're going to stay here,' I said to Kalāsia. 'Do you play Space Invaders?'

Kalāsia looked over at the Spacies machine where a Newton Grammar boy was frantically shooting at Martians. She shook her head slowly.

'Amanaki, answered, 'We're not allowed. Got to go home now. Come on, Kalāsia!'

Kalāsia shrugged. 'See you later,' she said, as she walked off with her sisters. 'Tomorrow, I'll plait your hair!'

The couple who owned the takeaway bar were from China. They spoke very little English but tried to communicate with us whenever we were there. The man was extra chatty today. 'You have good day?' he asked.

'Yes,' I answered. 'You too?'

He shook his head. 'Not today. Someone run with food, no leave money.'

'That's bad,' Rewi said.

'Very bad,' the owner said. 'My wife cry.'

His wife looked up from the food she was cooking, then looked down again.

'What you want today?' he asked.

'Two chips, please,' Rewi said. 'Did you chase them?'

'No chase.' The owner looked surprised. 'Three of them.'

'Ah.' Rewi put some money on the counter.

'Here,' I said, pulling two dollars out of my pocket.

'I'll buy today,' Rewi said. 'You buy next time.'

'Did you tell the police?' I asked the owner.

'No police.'

'Don't blame him,' Rewi muttered under his breath. 'I wouldn't call them either. Y'know after I left your house on Saturday night? The police were on our street. They made me answer the same old questions.'

'Name, address, stuff like that?' I asked.

'And more. Parents' names, where I'd been, why I was coming home at one-thirty in the morning . . .'

'Because of your mum's photos?'

'Yep, pretty much.' The Newton Grammar boy had finished playing and stepped back to let Rewi in. Rewi put a coin in the Spacies machine. The game's repetitive bass line started up, like a heartbeat that speeds up as the pace of the action increases.

I wasn't into Spacies. I just came along to keep Rewi company and eat chips. Shooting aliens from outer space felt like a waste of time, but Rewi was my oldest friend, so I stood and ate chips beside him.

I was bending to pull my school jumper out of my bag when I heard someone yell my name. A car slowed down at the traffic lights. Ursula was hanging out of the window. Her pink-streaked hair flew around her, no longer in a ponytail. Josh was in the back beside her. There were older guys in the front.

'We're going to the beach!' she yelled. 'Surf's up, baby! Hey, these are my brothers, Reece and Kev. Say hi to Liza, Kev!'

The guy driving waved at me. 'Hi, Liza!'

I waved back. 'Hi!'

'Hey, Harry wants your phone number,' Ursula called. 'Shall I give it to him? Ooops, lights are green. See you tomorrow!'

She was gone.

Rewi was concentrating hard, thumbs on the buttons, firing as aliens descended. Above the noise of the machine he said, 'She's wild.'

'Ursula?'

'Yep.'

'But in a good way?'

'Don't know.' Rewi glanced sideways at me for a moment before looking back at the game. 'Guess we'll find out.'

CHAPTER 5
TAMING

Ms Jefferson (aka 'Starship') handed out copies of the Shakespeare play we were going to study. '*The Taming of the Shrew*,' she said, 'is a play about how society expects women to behave. Put up your hands if you think that sounds interesting.'

I looked around to see if anyone was putting up their hands. A few girls had. Mine was half up. It did sound interesting, but I didn't want to look like a greaser.

Once she'd handed out all of the books, Ms Jefferson moved to the front of the room. My copy was a hardback, an old one that had been through the hands of lots of students. I could see their names and the dates they'd been given the book written on the inside of the cover.

'This year, a big wedding is coming up,' Ms Jefferson said. 'Who's getting married?'

My friend, Stella, put up her hand. 'Lady Diana and Prince Charles?'

'Yes. What will be expected of Diana?' Ms Jefferson picked up a piece of yellow chalk. 'Come and write any expectations you can think of on the board.'

A few girls made their way up the front. They wrote things like, 'look beautiful', 'be polite', 'dress nicely', that sort of stuff. Ursula went to the front of the room and wrote, 'be a virgin', which made us all laugh nervously. Ms Jefferson nodded at her, and Ursula sat down smiling.

'Anyone else?' Ms Jefferson asked, holding up the piece of chalk. No one else stood up. 'Well, I think there will be expectations on Diana about the way she must behave. I'm going to add a few things to your list.' Ms Jefferson turned to the board and listed, 'do as requested by the royal family', 'only say things that are acceptable for a princess', 'hide her own feelings and thoughts', 'present a happy face to the world'.

None of us had thought about these aspects of becoming a princess. It had all seemed so glamorous on TV and in magazines.

'We're going to read a play written four hundred years ago,' Ms Jefferson said. 'The old language takes a bit of getting used to, but back then there were strong beliefs about how women should behave. I want you to keep asking yourselves how much has really changed. I want you to think of Lady Diana and what is expected of her.'

I looked at the book on my desk and put my hand up. 'Ms Jefferson, what's a "shrew"?'

'Good question. A shrew is either a small mouse-like animal or an argumentative, aggressive, bad-tempered woman.'

'So, this play is about taming a mouse or a bad-tempered woman?' I asked.

'That's right, Eliza, but, in this case, it's about taming a shrewish woman.'

I wanted to ask her about the word 'taming', because it was usually used for an animal, but here it was for a woman. I didn't want to keep asking questions though, so I kept quiet.

'Write your names in the front of the books and then let me know what number your book is when I call out your name,' Ms Jefferson said. 'Then, we'll start reading.'

Kalāsia was sitting next to me. She leaned in and whispered, 'If a woman behaves like that in Tonga, like a shrew, she sometimes gets a hiding.'

'True?' I put down my pen and listened.

'True,' Kalāsia said. 'My aunty sometimes says things my uncle doesn't like, and he gives her a smack. My dad used to stop him and tell him to go outside for a walk, but we don't live with them now. She's got no one to stop him anymore.'

'Eliza?' Ms Jefferson's voice interrupted us.

I looked up.

'Book number?'

'Ah, sorry.' I fumbled with my book until I found the number. 'Twenty-one.'

'Thanks,' Ms Jefferson said.

'Must be the same for Palangi women too,' I whispered to Kalāsia. 'A woman Mum used to work with had to stay with us for two nights a few months ago. Her boyfriend got drunk and gave her a black eye and made her lip bleed.'

Kalāsia nodded, tapping her pencil on her bottom teeth. 'Was she a shrew?'

I shrugged. 'Don't know. She seemed nice. She broke up with him then went to live with her sister in Tauranga and got a new job. I haven't seen her since.'

None of us had ever read Shakespeare before. It was like stepping into a strange land. We were given parts to read, but the language was so unfamiliar that we stumbled over it. Ms Jefferson didn't seem to mind though; she'd just explain what the characters were saying.

By the end of class, I understood that this guy likes Bianca, but he can't marry her unless Bianca's big sister is married first. The problem is, Bianca's big sister, Kate, is so loud-mouthed, rude and wild that no man wants to marry her. One guy says, 'That wench is stark mad.' Ms Jefferson said 'wench' often meant a woman who was a prostitute or a bit rough and wild.

At the end of the lesson, most of the class went outside for morning break. Because Kalāsia was going to plait my hair, Ms Jefferson let us stay in the classroom as long as we agreed to lock the door behind us when we left. My friends, Ciara and Stella, stayed to watch.

'Will you do mine?' Ciara asked Stella.

'I'll give it a go,' Stella said.

'Anything to stop her looking like a wench!' I said.

'Speak for yourself!' Ciara said.

Every now and then, Kalāsia would reach over to help Stella, pulling stray strands of Ciara's fine black hair into the plait.

'You're good,' Stella said, watching Kalāsia's quick fingers weaving my unruly hair into shape.

'Finally taming that shrew's hair,' Ciara said.

'Do you mean I'm a cute little mouse?' I asked Ciara.

'Far from it!'

'Want to look in the mirror?' Kalāsia asked, patting my shoulder. 'I've finished.'

'I haven't got a mirror,' I said, running my fingers over my tightly woven hair. 'Feels strange! I'll go down to the loos to have a look.'

'I've finished too!' Stella said.

Ciara's plaits looked a little less sure of themselves. Some parts bulged loosely out of the top or sides. She ran her hand over her head. 'Do I dare to look in the mirror with you, Liza?'

'They look good!' Stella protested.

'What do you think?' Ciara asked Kalāsia.

'Stella just needs to practise,' she said.

We laughed.

'Exactly,' Stella protested, 'I've never plaited before. Give me a chance!'

Stella and I bent down to pick up our bags at the same time. We'd slung them between the rows of desks to keep them out of the way of the plaiting. Stella saw it first. It was on the side of the desk in the next row. Her finger lifted as if about to point it out, but I'd seen it by then and shook my head at her. She dropped her finger. Someone had written in pen, 'Keep NZ white'. They'd pressed hard into the wood, so that even an eraser wouldn't get rid of it.

'Let's go,' I said, standing up. 'Coming?' I asked Kalāsia.

'I'm going to see my sisters,' she answered. 'See you in the maths classroom next?'

'Yep, the one on the top floor.'

'I know.'

'Thanks for doing my hair,' I said.

'Hope you like it.' Kalāsia disappeared down the long corridor to meet up with her sisters.

In the toilets, Ciara pulled her hair out of the plaits as soon as she looked in the mirror.

'I tried,' Stella said, laughing.

My plaits hung like immaculately woven macramé on either side of my face. 'I love mine,' I said, running my hands over them and admiring myself in the mirror.

'Ursula was sitting there today,' Stella said.

'Where?' Ciara asked, still unravelling her long black hair. 'What are you talking about?'

'Someone wrote "Keep NZ white" on the desk Ursula was sitting in during English. We should tell Ms Jefferson,' Stella said.

'We don't know she wrote it,' I said. 'Someone could've written it last week or yesterday or in period one today.'

'She's right,' Ciara said, pulling her hair back into a ponytail. 'We can't say who did it, because we don't know.'

'We should at least tell Ms Jefferson though, so she can get the caretaker to sand it off,' Stella said.

I picked up my bag. 'I'll tell her. I'll wait outside the staffroom until she comes out. See you in maths.'

As I made my way along the landing to the stairs, I looked out at the sea of girls. Some were on the field playing hockey and others were playing netball on the courts. Turning onto the stairway, I almost bumped into Ursula.

'Hi,' she said, smiling at me. 'Like your hair.'

I reached up to touch my plaits. I'd almost forgotten they were there.

'I left my jumper in our English classroom,' Ursula said, 'on my chair.'

'There's no jumper on your chair,' I said.

'You sure? I was sitting opposite you.'

'I know,' I said. 'There's definitely no jumper there.'

'Shit.' Ursula screwed up her face. 'Where were we period one? Science. I'll go and wait outside the lab. If I'm late for maths, tell Mrs Williams that I've just gone to get my jumper.'

'Okay.'

Ursula turned to run down the stairs, then stopped. 'Hey, forgot to tell you I gave Harry your phone number this morning. He lives near me and we walk to school together sometimes.'

'You never told me he lives near you. I don't even know if I want him to ring me. I never said to give him my number.'

'It's only a phone call,' Ursula said, walking down the stairs. 'You don't have to do anything you don't want to.'

I turned to walk up to the staffroom. The bell was due to go for period three. My pulse sounded in my ears and it wasn't because I was walking upstairs, but because I didn't know what I'd say to Harry on the phone. Ursula was right, though, I didn't have to see him if I didn't want to.

Ms Jefferson stood outside the staffroom door talking to another teacher. She looked at me and asked, 'Do you need to see me?'

'Yes,' I answered.

'Be with you in a minute,' she said.

I stood a short distance away, gazing out over the school grounds. Students were making their way to class. Ursula would be waiting outside the science lab. She'd only recently joined our class, so I didn't know her very well, but she wouldn't write something racist on a desk, would she? I pictured her in the back of the car with Josh, her brothers in the front, on their way to the beach after school. She just liked to have fun. She was a bit wild, like Rewi said, that was all.

LOCKDOWN

It's Thursday evening, week two of the Level Four Covid-19 lockdown. Since I started writing about my fifteen-year-old self a few days ago, I haven't been able to stop. Eva, Jesse and Ross are insisting I read to them tonight. They've put chocolate and corn chips in bowls, as if we're celebrating. I think they're relieved that I'm finally motivated by something, instead of wandering the house muttering about whether a newspaper or magazine will ever offer me work again.

Jesse and Eva are sprawled across the sofa and Ross is in the armchair. Seeing them there, waiting for me, I feel a smile surfacing, like a piece from a shipwreck floating up and bobbing over the waves. I wipe at my smudged reading glasses, which I have to wear because I'm reading under the lamplight. Eva insists that we have the big light off.

'We need to create the right mood for this,' she says, 'like a café or something.'

'Or a sleazy nightclub,' Jesse adds.

'Don't listen to him, Mum,' Eva says.

'Okay,' I say, 'let's start. You ready?'

'Put your phone down, Jesse,' Eva says.

'Sorry, it's just . . .'

'We're not interested,' Eva says. 'This is about Mum now.'

Jesse nods. 'Yep, okay. Go on, Mum.'

I begin to read the first part about being in lockdown with them. Then I read about Harry at the social and the fight and the boy with the afro. I continue to the part where Kalāsia comes to our school. After that, we stop for a five-minute break. Jesse needs to go to the loo, and Eva wants a hot drink.

When everyone's back, Jesse starts to ask me questions, but Eva stops him. 'Let her finish everything first,' she says.

I read about Rewi and the police asking him questions and Kalāsia plaiting my hair and the 'Keep NZ white' graffiti on the desk. Then I stop.

'Does Harry phone?' Eva asks.

'Yep, but . . .'

'That's all I need to know,' she says. 'Don't tell me anymore. I can wait till you've written it.'

'When will you start to write about the Springbok Tour protests?' Jesse asks.

'I guess the story begins in April of 1981, the weekend before Easter, at the social, so . . .'

'So, keep going now,' Ross says. 'It's good to hear you tapping away at that keyboard.'

'Did Grandad write about the protests for the newspaper?' Eva asks.

'Yes, he did.' I sit down on the rug and settle back against the empty armchair. 'I still remember him crying after a really violent protest.'

'He cried?' Eva leans forward. Her long dark-red hair is swept up into a messy bun and her blue eyes are fixed on me.

'It was particularly brutal. Two people dressed as clowns and one dressed as a bumble bee were beaten up badly by the riot squad.'

'Riot squad!' Jesse's eyebrows lift.

I nod, reaching for a piece of dark chocolate. 'A song called "Riot Squad" was released that year. Can't think of the band's name.'

Jesse picks up his phone and I wonder what or who has suddenly taken his interest.

'Will you write about Grandad crying?' Eva asks.

'Maybe.' I reach for another piece of chocolate. 'This tastes so good!'

'Here it is,' Jesse says, 'that "Riot Squad" song. The band was called The Newmatics.'

He switches on the TV and casts the video of the band performing the song from his phone. I begin to sway to the familiar ska beat. I never hear ska music on the radio now. Ross stands up and starts to dance. He pulls me up and swings me around, and we laugh as we copy the dance movements from the TV screen. Jesse and Eva watch and laugh too. When the song finishes, Jesse turns off his phone, while Ross and I collapse back into the armchairs.

'Talking about Grandad crying makes me think you should phone him and Gran now, Mum,' Eva says. 'See if they're alright.'

'They're fine,' I say. 'I saw Mum today over the fence. Dad was inside having a nap.'

'I still think you should just check in,' Eva says.

'Stop telling her what to do,' Jesse says, nudging at Eva's leg with his foot.

'Get your dirty socks away from me!' Eva shoves his leg away. 'And don't tell me what I can and can't say to my own mother!'

'Right,' Ross says, standing and stretching. 'I think that's the end of the reading tonight. Next instalment in a couple of nights, Liza.' He leans down and kisses my forehead, as our kids begin to push each other in a half-joking way.

'I think I'll get out of here too,' I say, grabbing one last piece of chocolate.

I go into the kitchen where there's no noise and pick up my phone. My father answers immediately, as if he's been sitting by his phone, waiting. 'Hi, Dad,' I say. 'How are you?'

He coughs. 'That you, Eliza?'

'Yep. Just been thinking about you and thought I'd phone.'

My father chuckles. 'You checking on us twice a day now?'

An image of my father crying at the kitchen bench comes to me. He'd been at work until two in the morning and I'd heard him come in. He'd been reporting on the protests at the final test at Eden Park. I'd snuck into the hallway where I could see him in the kitchen. He was stirring his coffee and telling Mum about the clowns getting bashed. Mum had taken the spoon out of his hand and hugged him. They'd stayed like that for a while. I went back to bed. I'd never seen either of my parents cry before.

'Just had you in my thoughts, that's all,' I say. 'Thought I'd make a quick phonecall.'

'Well, I've been out walking the dog. Your mum's already gone to bed, so I'm just watching TV alone. It's heaven having the remote to myself. Your mum's quite bossy when it comes to which programme we watch.'

'She's keeping you from watching rubbish,' I say, laughing.

'She makes me exercise too. We walk the dog together a couple of times a day, but at night, she leaves it to me. If I don't take him out for a wee before bed, he's likely to wee on the carpet. Really, I never wanted another dog after Sal. Still, I'm quite fond of him now, aren't I, Foxy?'

I picture Dad's fox terrier lying by his feet and looking up at him. 'Glad you have Foxy with you to watch rubbish on TV, Dad.'

Eva comes into the kitchen. 'That Grandad?'

I nod. 'Eva wants to talk to you. Here she is.' I pass my phone to Eva and switch on the kettle.

Eva widens her eyes at me as if I've done something wrong then walks to the dining room table. I guess our kettle *is* loud. She's laughing and telling Dad off about something. Then her face becomes serious. 'Grandad, you can't go into supermarkets. You're eighty-two! You're more vulnerable to this virus than younger people.'

'I do their shopping!' I say to Eva. 'Tell Dad just to put anything he needs on the list for me.'

While Dad was inside snoozing today, Mum and I talked over the fence. She kept two metres away, strictly following the Covid-19 rules. At least *she's* taking this lockdown seriously. She's not happy I'm unemployed though and said I should be looking for a job. 'Ross's salary isn't enough on its own,' she said, 'and it's not healthy to sit around all day doing nothing.'

'I'm not doing nothing, I'm writing.'

'Writing what?'

'Don't know exactly. It's about the Springbok Tour.'

'Well, that's something, I suppose.' Mum looked a bit concerned.

'As long as you keep busy.'

Eva passes my phone back to me. 'There! Don't you feel better now that you've spoken to him?'

'I do.'

'Grandad thinks it's okay to just whip in and out of the supermarket. I don't think he really gets that he's at risk.'

'He's too old to argue with. Let him do it his way,' I say. 'I'm going to bed, Eves. You and Jesse turn off the lights.'

Ross is singing the riot squad song in the shower. I put my cup of tea down on the bedside table and look at what I've written so far. Back in 1981, who would ever have guessed that the world would be staying home to stop the transmission of a virus?

I sit down on the bed. 'Nineteen-eighty-one,' I think to myself. 'Harry.' Closing my eyes for a moment, I picture his turned-up top lip and the way his eyebrow would shoot up when I said something funny. I open my eyes. It's time to write about Harry.

CHAPTER 6
THE PHONE CALL

The phone had gone a few times that night. I'd answered it each time. Twice it was for Mum and once it was for Jo, who'd spent so long talking that I almost gave up on Harry ever being able to get through. Finally, Jo stopped cackling with whoever was on the other end of the line and, at nearly nine o'clock, the phone rang again. I pounced on it, pulling the phone cord as far as I could up the cold hallway, so that Jo couldn't hear me from her bedroom, which was next door to mine. The phone table was in the hallway outside both of our rooms.

'Hello, Liza speaking,' I said quietly. Now, I was close to the lounge, where Mum and Pete were watching TV. Dad was at work. The door was closed, and the sound of the TV meant it was unlikely they'd hear me.

'It's Harry,' he said. He didn't say 'hello'.

'Hi,' I said, almost whispering.

'Ursula gave me your phone number,' he said.

'Yeah, she told me.' I twisted the curly phone cord around my fingers.

'What've you been doing?'

'This evening?'

'Yeah.'

'Um, homework.'

'Wow,' he said, and the possibility that he was being sarcastic made my cheeks redden.

'What've you been doing?' I asked, trying to shift the focus away from me.

'Well, not homework.' He laughed briefly. 'I've been watching TV with my mum and my sister.'

'How old's your sister?'

'Eight.'

'Eight?' I quickly worked out the maths. 'So, you're eight years older?'

'Yep, my parents broke up for a few years, then got back together. Sometimes Dad's still a dick, but when he came back to live with us, they had Sophie, which was pretty cool.'

I'd never heard about parents breaking up like this. Mum had a friend who came to stay for a night every now and then, after a fight with her husband. She'd turn up at the door in her dressing gown with her toothbrush. She always went home the next morning though.

In the Catholic church, divorce was a sin, but in the Anglican church, it wasn't. I knew this because Ursula was Anglican. She was only allowed to enrol at our school because there was a rule that ten per cent of students could be non-Catholic.

'Have I shocked you?' Harry asked.

'No,' I said. 'Sorry, I was just thinking.'

Harry sighed and my ear tingled. 'I've shocked you.'

I could almost see his lip turning up at the corner. 'No, you haven't.'

Harry continued, 'Anyway, now they're nice to each other for a while, but then there's another fight. Sometimes, Mum kicks Dad out and sometimes he walks out. Either way, he leaves and comes back a few weeks later when he's sick of staying with his parents.'

'That's ... hard.' The sound of laughter came from the lounge, as if in response to my hopeless attempts to say the right thing to Harry.

'It's just the way it is,' Harry said. 'Anyway, let's talk about something else. Do you want to meet up somewhere?'

'Okay,' I said. I'd wound the phone cord around my fingers so tightly that they were white.

'Want to go to the Newton shops on Friday night? It's late-night. We could sit in that new ice-cream place.'

'Johnny's?'

'Yeah, Johnny's Ice-Cream Parlour. We could sit in there, have a smoke, maybe an ice cream.'

'What time?'

'Six? Six-thirty? Seven?'

'I could be there at six-thirty,' I said. Sometimes I walked up to the shops on Friday evenings with Ciara and Stella, who lived nearby. Mum and Dad wouldn't ask any questions about that.

'See you then, gorgeous,' he said, and the phone clicked off. He didn't wait for me to say goodbye and he'd called me gorgeous.

I put the phone back on the telephone table and went into my bedroom. Sitting down at my desk, I stared at my English homework. I had to read some of *The Taming of the Shrew* and answer questions about it. Ms Jefferson said our answers would show her whether we understood the play. I stared at the refill paper in front of me. My heart was racing. It was pointless trying to concentrate on English now.

I stood up and walked over to the tape recorder on my bedside table. In it was Fleetwood Mac's album, *Rumours*, which Mum and Dad had bought for my last birthday. I pressed 'play'.

Opening the window, I leaned out into the cool night. Stevie Nicks' voice drifted past me, out through the branches of our peach tree, over the hedge and beyond the houses in my street.

Somewhere out there, the sound was breaking into fragments, her voice crumbling into tiny pieces, so that only a moth might hear it.

CHAPTER 7
PETERSON AVE

Rewi's house was in Peterson Ave. It was a long, flat street, with houses built in the late 1800s. They had verandas and porches with railings and banisters carved into looping, curved shapes. Some houses had been repainted and looked tidy and posh, unlike the old ones with paint flaking off them. Sometimes, when I walked along Peterson Ave, I imagined the houses when they were first built and the men and women in Victorian clothing sitting on the verandas, fanning themselves in the afternoon heat.

Rewi's dad had painted the Māori flag on their letterbox. He'd also painted koru along the banisters of the front veranda, which dipped and curled upward like waves. Sometimes, I'd gaze at them for a few moments and imagine a stream, birdsong and bush around me. Usually when I did this, Rewi went on inside, leaving the front door open for me.

It was about an hour after school had finished and Rewi and I were finally closer to his house. We'd been walking slowly, having stopped at the dairy for an ice cream. I was licking the last chocolate drips off my fingers when I noticed a police car a few houses away from Rewi's place. It was jammed up against the kerb as if it had been parked in a hurry.

Two police officers sat in the front. As we came closer, they stepped out of the car. One, a tall blond man, spoke first. 'Stop for a moment, please,' he said to Rewi. 'We'd like to ask you some questions.'

Rewi stopped walking. He looked sideways at me, then back at the policeman. I looked at the other policeman. He had a moustache and his skin seemed extra-red, as if he was sunburnt. As he came closer, I wondered if he had eczema, like a girl in our class, because his skin was raw and inflamed under his police cap. He had a small notepad and pen in his hand.

I felt a thin trickle of sweat down my back. It was hot and I felt like I'd done something wrong. My mouth had become uncomfortably dry and I wanted to lick more ice cream off my fingers.

The blond policeman spoke again. 'Name?'

'Rewi Matheson.' Rewi rolled his eyes at me, but I could tell he was nervous by the way he was tapping his right foot. His beige Nomads lifted and landed and lifted and landed on the broken concrete.

'Father's name?'

'You know his name,' Rewi said.

'Father's name, please,' the policeman repeated.

'Tipene Matheson.' Rewi sighed. He acted as if he didn't care about their questions, about their blue uniform.

'Mother's name?' the policeman asked.

'Mere Parata.'

'Where do you live?'

'You know where I live,' Rewi said. 'You're here watching us every day.'

'Where do you live?' the policeman repeated.

'There!' Rewi pointed at his house. 'Number eighty-nine, the one you've photographed and filmed us going in and out of.'

The officer with the eczema stepped forward. 'What's *your* name?' he asked me.

'She's my friend,' Rewi said.

'She has a name,' the policeman said.

I tried not to look at the police officer's skin when I answered him. Instead, I focused on his eyes. 'Eliza,' I said, 'Eliza Newland.'

'And where do you live?' he asked.

'Why do you need to know that?' Rewi asked. 'All you really want to know is what Mum's doing. Just knock on the door and ask to see her photos.'

'Address, please,' the officer said to me.

'Sixty-six Tawa Avenue,' I told him.

'Not far from here then.' The eczema officer looked at the blond officer. 'Tawa's a few roads away.' He wrote something down in his notebook.

The blond officer nodded and was about to speak when a voice called, 'Hey, everything okay?' Rewi's dad, Tipene, was at the letterbox. He had his hand inside it, as if frozen there, while he looked over at us.

'They're asking me questions,' Rewi said, 'the same questions as always, all over again.'

'You two go inside,' Tipene said, walking over to us. His eyes shifted from one police officer to the other. 'I'll answer any questions you have.'

'That's okay,' the blond policeman said. 'I think we have all the information we need.'

'In the future, I'd rather you didn't question my son and his friend like this,' Tipene said. 'My wife and I have answered your questions already.'

'We'll ask questions when we need to,' the policeman said, 'for the safety of the community.' He turned to the eczema officer. 'Shall we go?'

We watched them walk back to the police car.

'Let's go in,' Tipene said.

That day, I didn't stand and gaze at the koru carvings on the veranda rails. I went straight inside. The police had written down my name and address. What did they do with names and addresses?

Tipene called us into the kitchen. I usually dawdled down the hallway, taking my time with each of the framed photos on the walls. They were black and white, and Rewi's mum, Mere, had taken most of them. There were photos of Rewi, his brother, Nikau, and his sister, Marama, from when they were little right up until recently. Nikau was only eight and Marama was ten, and I loved being around them because I didn't have any younger brothers or sisters.

The photos popped out from the cream walls. My favourite one was of Nikau and Marama sitting on their nana's knee. She was smiling and Rewi was standing beside her with his hand on her shoulder. I knew they were in the countryside somewhere because there was a tractor peeking in at the edge of the photo.

Another favourite was a photo of Rewi's mum, Mere, when she was younger with baby Rewi on her hip. Her long black hair was swept up under a scarf, and she was wearing shorts and a T-shirt. Rewi was grinning up at her as she looked at the camera.

There were photos of the protestors at Bastion Point too. I was twelve when it had been on the news. On TV, we'd watched the police dragging people through the mud to get them off the sacred Māori land that the government was planning to sell for luxury housing instead of returning it to the people they'd taken it from.

Tipene called me from the kitchen, 'Liza, you need to hear this too.' With a jolt, I realised I had got lost in the photos yet again.

Rewi was sitting at the table. He bit loudly into an apple, handing me one as I sat down beside him. Tipene filled the kettle with water, switched it on and leaned against the bench. 'Listen, you two, this isn't going to stop any time soon,' he said. 'You have to remember your rights in these situations. You only ever have to tell a police officer four things: your name, address, when you were born and where you were born. Nothing else. If they ask about us and where your mum's been or what I've been doing, Rewi, you don't have to answer. You can say you want a lawyer to be present before you say any more.'

'Okay, Dad.'

'Four things,' Tipene repeated. 'Nothing else.' He put coffee and milk into a cup and stirred it. 'I'll go and tidy up the studio now. Marama and Nikau are playing with the kids next door. Be good to get my paints and brushes cleaned up before they get home. You two okay?'

I nodded. The kettle switched off and Tipene stirred hot water into his cup. I stared at the bun at the back of his head, holding his wild black ringlets in place.

'What do they do with our names and addresses?' I asked.

He shrugged. 'Don't know. I think they've got a file on our whānau. They know Mere took photos at Bastion Point that were published in a book, which didn't make the police look good. They also know we're members of HART. Probably keen to search our house but, so far, they haven't asked.'

I knew about HART. It was an anti-Springbok Tour protest group and the letters meant 'Halt All Racist Tours'. I wanted to ask Tipene if the police waited outside HART leaders' houses too, but he started to walk out the back door to the garage, which he'd turned into an art studio.

'Where's Mum?' Rewi called after him.

'At the darkroom,' Tipene called back. 'She'll be home soon. Would you mind peeling some potatoes, son?'

Rewi looked at me. 'Potatoes,' he said in an Irish accent. 'Potatoes, potatoes, fiddle-dee-dee, potatoes!'

I laughed. 'You're a spoon.'

'And you're far too cheeky for your own good,' Rewi continued in his Irish accent. 'Eating ice cream on the street in school uniform! You should be thrown out of that Catholic school. And now you're on police records!'

'Egg!' I stood up. I didn't want to think about my name and address on police records. 'Come on, I'll help you peel some potatoes, then you have to show me the photos. I didn't walk all this way just to hang out with you.'

The photos were in an album in the laundry. The album was hidden up high in a box on a shelf above the washing machine. On top of the box was a small basket of rags and cloths, so it was less noticeable. It was surrounded by laundry powder, stain remover and other stuff.

Rewi climbed up on a chair to slide the box out from under the rags. He whispered to me that none of the photos' negatives were in the house. They were hidden in the houses of friends.

'Why are you whispering?' I asked. 'Won't the police have gone?' Even if they'd stayed, they'd still be outside in the car, I thought to myself.

'They won't have gone,' Rewi said, stepping off the chair. 'Bet they're still there when you go. We never talk out loud about these photos, just like we never talked about the Bastion Point photos when that was happening.' He put the photo album down on the chair and we knelt on the floor to look at it. The photos were carefully attached to the thick, black paper in the album. There was tissue paper between each page.

'These are some of the leading members of HART,' Rewi said. 'Mum and Dad go to their meetings, but Mum's not just a member, she's keeping a record of the whole protest against the Springbok Tour, including the meetings.'

Rewi turned the pages carefully. I could see people who looked so ordinary, they could have been any of the parents from school. There were Māori, Pākehā and Pacific Island people. Some people looked like hippies, with long hair and tie-dyed T-shirts. Some had dreadlocks. There were children on knees and on hips. A few photos were closer up, showing one person speaking; others showed the whole group.

'That's John Minto,' Rewi said, pointing to a tall man leaning against a wall, listening to a speaker. 'He's the one that gets interviewed on TV most of the time. There are heaps of anti-Springbok groups, not just HART. The Auckland ones are joining up together in a big group, a coalition, called MOST, which means Mobilisation to Stop the Tour. Lots of cities are joining up small groups into one coalition like that. They reckon they'll be better organised that way. There's going to be a massive march, called a mobilisation, on May the first. They want the mobilisation to be so huge that the rugby union and the government decide not to let the Springboks tour New Zealand.'

The next pages were empty. 'Mum's planning to make it into a book, a photographic history of the Springbok Tour protests, like she did with the Bastion Point photos.'

He closed the album and stood up on the chair to place it carefully back in the box under the basket of rags.

CHAPTER 8
BECOMING SILENT

Ms Jefferson was wearing a green T-shirt with a black peace sign on it, and a long skirt with boots. She wrote up on the board, 'And will you, nill you, I will marry you (II.i.)' then she turned to the class. 'Who says this?'

'Petruchio,' Stella said. 'He wants to marry Kate so that he can have her father's money. He doesn't care if she's a shrew; he just wants the money, the dowry.'

Ms Jefferson nodded. 'And what does it mean, 'will you, nill you'?'

'Like it or not?' Ursula answered.

'Exactly,' Ms Jefferson said. 'Whether you like it or not, I will marry you.'

Ursula leaned over to me. 'Starship loves me.'

I smiled at Ursula, and she wriggled her eyebrows at me.

'Listening, Eliza?' Ms Jefferson asked.

'Yes.' I turned back to Ms Jefferson.

'But Kate doesn't want to marry Petruchio. She knows he doesn't care about her and that he must find her behaviour off-putting; she even hit him!' Ms Jefferson walked down the aisle between some rows of desks. 'Why then, does she not correct him when he tells the other men that she can't keep her hands off him? Why does she not argue when Petruchio says the wedding will be on that Sunday?'

No one spoke. It was weird that the screaming, angry Kate suddenly went quiet like that.

'Think, girls,' Ms Jefferson said.

I put my hand up. 'Maybe she's tired of arguing.'

'Yes, maybe she is. What else might she be tired of?'

'Being single?' I said. 'She says to her father . . . hang on, sorry, I just have to find it.' I flicked back a page and ran my finger down the lines. 'Got it. She says to her father that her sister, Bianca, is his treasure and must have a husband. She says, "I must dance barefoot on her wedding day."'

'Hmmm . . .' Ms Jefferson tapped her fingers on her folded arms. The sunlight through the window bounced off her hoop earrings. 'So, okay, she doesn't want to be single. Fair enough. But why Petruchio? He's rude to her, argues with her, makes sexual comments to her.'

'Maybe she likes that!' Ursula said.

The class laughed.

Ms Jefferson smiled. 'Maybe she does, but I think there's another reason she becomes silent and lets this marriage go ahead. What is there about Petruchio that's different?'

The class was quiet. Then, someone suggested, 'He doesn't run away from her, frightened, like other men have?'

Ms Jefferson nodded. 'And he says some kind things to her, which may not have ever happened to Kate. We don't know why she's become such a difficult, angry woman. If Bianca was always the pretty, prize daughter, maybe her fury grew from this. Would you feel angry if your father favoured your sister like that?'

Ms Jefferson gazed around the room. 'Petruchio is possibly the first man who says kind things about Kate. For example, in front of her, he says to the other men, "For she's not froward, but modest as the dove. She is not hot, but temperate as the morn." He's saying that Kate is *not* pushy and assertive, but quiet and well-behaved and *not* hot-tempered, but as mild as morning. These similes might be the nicest things any man has ever said to her.'

'But is that why we marry someone?' I asked. 'Because they say nice things to us?'

'Maybe that's a better option than staying in her father's house,' Ms Jefferson said. 'Her father doesn't respect her.'

'But Petruchio doesn't respect her. He's just saying those things.'

'But we all want guys to say nice things to us,' Ursula said.

'Not if it's not real,' I said.

Ursula tipped her head to the side and made a face at me. I made one back at her.

Kalāsia, sitting beside me, spoke for the first time. 'He's just lying to get what he wants.'

'You don't think he might feel sorry for her?' Ms Jefferson asked. 'He could be trying to help her get out of her unhappy life.'

Kalāsia shook her head. 'Nah, he just wants her father's money. No one would want to marry her.'

'Okay, here's another thought,' Ms Jefferson said. 'Maybe he thinks she's interesting. Women had to be so well-behaved and mouse-like back then. Maybe he's excited at the thought of life with a strong, intelligent woman.'

One of the girls on the other side of the room put up her hand. 'Ms Jefferson, is Prince Charles and Lady Diana's marriage an arranged one?'

'Well, it's not exactly arranged, but it's one that his family and society approve of.'

'Do you think she loves him?' another classmate asked.

'Maybe she just likes feeling special,' Ursula said, 'like Kate does when Petruchio flatters her.'

The discussion continued for a little longer and, even if people weren't speaking, everyone seemed to be listening. Finally, Ms Jefferson stopped the discussion and swung around to pick up some chalk. 'Write this down, girls.'

On the blackboard, she wrote: 'Petruchio is either a money-grabbing liar, who says nice things just to get his way OR he really is interested in being with a woman who shows fierce independence.' Pointing at the sentence, she said, 'I want you to think about this as we read the rest of act two. Now, if you don't have the play in front of you, get it out of your bag now, and let's keep reading.'

Later that day, Kalāsia walked home with me and Rewi. Her sisters walked behind us with their friends.

'Do you know that Liza's going on a date on Friday night?' Kalāsia asked Rewi.

'It's not a date,' I said. 'I haven't told Rewi cos it's nothing.'

Rewi shrugged and adjusted his bag on his shoulder. I noticed he'd drawn Bob Marley's face next to his name. Rewi was a good artist, like his dad.

'Who is he?' he asked.

'This guy from the social. Ursula knows him cos he lives near her.'

'That guy you were talking with?'

I nodded. 'Yep, before we went outside, before we saw the fight.'

'Is he spunky?' Kalāsia asked.

'I — I don't know,' I said. 'He's okay.'

'We're not allowed to go on dates,' Kalāsia said. 'Tongan girls can't hang round with boys like that.'

'Well, I don't know if I'm really allowed,' I said. 'My parents don't know.'

'Want me to play Spacies across the road, to keep an eye on things?' Rewi asked.

'No, it's fine,' I said. 'We're just having an ice cream! You two are making this into something big. I'm just getting to know a new friend.'

'Friend!' Kalāsia laughed. 'He wants to be more than friends if he phoned you to go out with him.'

Thankfully, at this point, Kalāsia and her sisters had to turn into another street. 'I'll come to your house before school to plait your hair,' Kalāsia said, as she walked away.

After she'd gone, I changed the topic and told Rewi about *The Taming of the Shrew*. I told him how Ursula had said that saying nice things to someone was okay, even if they were lies.

'She said that?' he asked.

I nodded.

'So, if I told you your hair looked nice, you'd believe it?' His eyebrows shot up.

'Well, that's the truth, so of course I'd believe you.' I pushed him so he stumbled slightly.

'Hey, hey, careful!' Rewi cried, laughing. 'Violence will only make you less attractive to a man!'

We continued like that, teasing and joking, and by the time we got to my house, that uncomfortable feeling was behind us.

CHAPTER 9
JOHNNY'S
ICE-CREAM PARLOUR

I tied Sal to the lamp post outside Johnny's Ice-Cream Parlour and patted her head distractedly. 'Stay there, girl. Won't be long.'

Inside, 'Bette Davis Eyes' by Kim Carnes played on the American-style jukebox. In fact, everything about Johnny's was an imitation of an American milk bar. I looked around the bright red tables filled with families and small groups of teenagers. I suddenly felt nervous that Harry might not have come. Maybe it was all a big joke. Then, I heard him call, 'Hey, Liza!'

He was leaning out of one of the booths on the side, which offered more privacy. I breathed out slowly, but I could feel my heart racing. For a moment, I pictured Mum and Dad watching Friday night television at home and wished I was with them. Instead, I sat down on the bench seat opposite Harry. 'Hi,' I said.

'You came,' he said.

I nodded. 'I'd be a bit of a cow if I didn't, wouldn't I?'

'So that's why you came, to avoid being a cow?' Harry smiled, and I noticed how soft his lips were. Some people had thin lips, like Sister Agnes.

'I'd rather not be a cow,' I said, looking away from Harry's lips, and trying to think of something else to say. My heart was still pounding. 'Shall we get something to drink?'

'Ah, yeah.' Harry slid along the seat and stood up. 'Vodka or gin?'

I smiled. 'Gin, please.'

'Coming right up.'

'Make it a lemonade.'

'Come on, live a little,' Harry said, turning to go to the counter, but I'd seen him smile. That was good. We were getting each other's sense of humour. I put my hand on my chest. Stop pounding, I said silently.

Harry came back with a lemonade for me and a Coke for him. I stirred mine with the straw and watched the bubbles move.

'So, finally, I get to have a date with Eliza Newland,' Harry said.

I looked up from my drink. 'A date?'

'Yeah.'

'But don't you have a girlfriend? You were with a girl at the social.'

'She's not my girlfriend,' Harry said. 'Not anymore. Well, she never really was. We just hung out sometimes.'

'Is she okay with that?'

'With what?'

'With not being your girlfriend?'

'Guess so. She didn't really say.' Harry pulled a packet of cigarettes out of his jacket pocket and lit one. 'I told her I was going out on a date with you and she asked me if it was serious. I said, "I hope so", so that was kind of the end of that.' Harry held the cigarettes out to me. 'Want one?'

I nodded. 'Thanks.'

He leaned across the table, flicking his lighter, and I bowed my head to light my ciggie. My hair fell forward. I had taken it out of the plaits Kalāsia had woven that morning, so it was wavy and wild. Harry pushed my hair back with his other hand. 'Careful, don't want to set fire to yourself.'

We sat for a moment, drawing on our ciggies. I tried to blow smoke out the way Ursula did, with a slightly parted mouth and a soft, smoky sigh.

'So, tell me about you,' Harry said, his green eyes on me. 'I told you about my family on the phone the other night. Your turn.'

'Um, I've got an older brother and sister. My mother's a part-time social worker and my father's a journalist at the *Auckland Star*.'

Harry blew smoke out of the side of his mouth. I recognised the next song on the jukebox — it was Juice Newton singing, 'Angel of the Morning'.

'So, will he report on the protests?'

'The anti-Springbok Tour protests?'

Harry nodded, dragging on his cigarette.

'Yep. He'll be there next Friday night.' The first nationwide protests were organised for Friday, the 1st of May.

'You going?'

'Yeah, I'm going with my friend, Rewi. He's at Newton Grammar too. Do you know him?'

'Nah, but I think I saw you leaving the social with him.' Harry looked over towards the jukebox. 'What do you want me to put on?'

'A song?'

Harry's eyes settled back onto me and his lip curled as he smiled. 'I suppose you want a hymn?'

My cheeks warmed, but I couldn't help smiling. 'No! No hymns!'

'What sort of a Catholic girl are you?' Harry said with a mock-shocked tone and waved his hand in front of his face as if to stop himself fainting.

I laughed.

'She laughs!' he said. 'I've been wondering what your laugh sounded like.'

I clamped my hand over my mouth. What did my laugh sound like?

'I'll choose a song,' Harry said. He walked over to the jukebox and stood for a few moments, scanning the list of possibilities, before placing some coins in the slot and coming back to sit down.

'So, what do your parents do?' I asked.

'Fight a lot,' Harry said. 'Nah, seriously, Dad's a mechanic and Mum's just at home. She used to be a kindergarten teacher.' He stubbed his cigarette out in the ashtray.

A song that I liked came on the jukebox. It was 'How 'Bout Us' by Champaign. 'Love this song,' I said.

'This is the one I chose,' Harry said. His eyes locked onto mine. A quiver filled my stomach and stayed there, so that my brain couldn't focus on anything else. I busied myself stubbing out my cigarette.

'I'd better go,' I said. 'My dog's outside. Can't leave her tied up for too long.' The quiver had filled my throat and my voice sounded a little unsteady.

'No worries,' Harry said. He slid along his seat. 'I'll walk you home.'

'It's okay,' I said.

'Even part of the way home? I insist.' Harry's lip did its curl and he reached down to pull me up from the seat. His hand stayed in mine until we were outside and I had to let go to untie Sal.

When we began to walk, Harry took my hand again. I'd never walked hand-in-hand with a boy before. It felt warm and comforting, but nerve-wracking at the same time. What if one of my parents' friends saw me? I kept my head down and tried to concentrate on the conversation.

We talked about school and which subjects we were taking. Harry laughed when I told him one of my subjects was Christian Living. 'You study how to live a Christian life?'

'Yep,' I said. 'It's not as bad as it sounds. We discuss stuff like the famines in Africa and how to create more equality in society. It's sometimes interesting, but sometimes boring.'

'When is it boring?'

'When we have to read parts of the Bible and answer questions about them.'

'Sounds riveting!'

'Sister Agnes teaches us Christian Living. She's pretty old-fashioned and strict, but she's kind too.' I thought of how, once, Sister Agnes had called a girl in our class up to her desk to discuss her homework. At least, that's what she'd said in front of the class. I'd walked up to sharpen a pencil over the bin, and I saw Sister Agnes take a brown paper bag out of her desk drawer and put it inside the cover of the girl's exercise book. Later that day, I saw the girl eating sandwiches from the bag. Sister Agnes had snuck her some lunch.

'Nuns look a bit scary,' Harry said. 'I try not to make eye contact when I pass them at your school gate.'

This time I laughed.

Harry stopped walking and put his hands on my shoulders, turning me around. 'Can we stop talking about nuns and Christian Living, so I can kiss you?'

I nodded. 'Ah . . . okay.'

Harry was slightly taller than me, and he leaned in, planting his Mick Jagger lips on mine. The quiver surged through me again. I'd never felt this when I'd kissed the other boys at parties. Then, it had just felt like something I'd needed to do.

I pulled away and looked around. We were at the corner of my street now. 'I'd better walk home alone from here, just in case Mum or Dad are putting the milk bottles out or something.'

'Okay,' Harry said. 'No worries.'

'Thanks for a . . . a good night.' I smiled at Harry, watching his face crease into a smile back at me. We stayed like that for a few moments.

'I want to kiss you again,' he said.

'I can't. Got to go.' I turned away, with Sal beside me.

'Hey,' Harry called after me. 'Can I come on the protest march with you and your friend? What's his name?'

'Rewi.'

'Yep, that's the one.'

'I . . . guess so. My mother will be with us, my sister too and Rewi's family. We're bussing into town.'

'Choice, I can meet them.'

'But they don't know about you. We can't . . .'

'I won't hold your hand or anything like that,' Harry said.

'Okay, I'll phone you and tell you where to meet up.'

Harry nodded and took out a cigarette. I turned away again.

When I reached the top of my driveway, I looked back. He was still standing there. I pictured the cigarette hanging from his mouth. He waved at me. I lifted my hand, then turned into my driveway, Sal trotting beside me.

CHAPTER 10
EARLY MORNING VISITS

Kalāsia arrived an hour earlier than usual the following Monday morning. Sal barked and Mum shushed her, opening the front door. Her voice was louder than Kalāsia's as they walked down the hallway to my room.

'I'm early,' Kalasia said, as I opened my door.

'That's okay,' Mum said. 'Maybe she'll get up and get dressed now. I've knocked on her door twice.' She disappeared along the hall, saying, 'I'll put the kettle on for you both.'

'I stayed up late finishing homework,' I said, collapsing back into bed and pulling the duvet back over me. 'We had so much homework!'

'Don't get back into bed, Liza,' Kalāsia said. 'Get dressed. I'll go and make some tea.'

I sat there for a moment. Sal came in and lay down on the floor with a groan. 'I know how you feel, girl,' I said, pushing myself off the bed and pulling a clean school blouse out of the wardrobe.

Our uniform consisted of a mustard yellow blouse and a brown tunic dress worn over the top of it. Mustard yellow and brown! Add to that the winter school uniform *brown* shoes. . . . Some girls wore more expensive shoes like Treks or Nomads, but Jo and I wore plain old Charlie Browns.

I could hear Kalāsia talking with Jo and Mum in the kitchen. Dad was still in bed. He'd worked late last night, and Pete hadn't come in from the caravan yet. Maybe it was a good thing that the men of the household weren't in the kitchen right now. Kalāsia had told me that, in her house, once they were teenagers, the brothers and sisters didn't stay in the same room together. 'If the boys are in the lounge watching TV, we don't go in,' she'd said.

Kalāsia came back to my room with two steaming cups in her hands. She placed them on my dressing table. 'I can plait your hair now. Bring your chair over.'

I pulled my desk chair over to the dressing table and sat down in front of it, so we could see in the mirror.

Kalāsia picked up my brush and tried to drag it through tangled wads of hair. I winced. 'I'll start at the bottom,' she said. 'It won't be so painful.'

The steam from our cups swirled upward. Kalāsia began to brush from the bottom, then up a bit more and a bit more, until she was able to separate my long, thick hair into sections.

'What made you get up so early today?' I asked.

'Had a bad dream.'

'What was it about?'

Kalāsia stayed focused on my hair, weaving over and under. 'It's stupid.'

'But if it upset you enough to wake you up, then . . .'

'It's not really a dream,' Kalāsia said. 'It's sort of the truth.'

I picked up my tea and drank some. Kalāsia did the same. For a moment, I lost myself in the sensation of hot, sweet tea in my mouth.

'So, what was this true dream then?'

Kalāsia put her cup back down and resumed plaiting. 'It happened four years ago, when I was eleven.'

'What happened?'

'We were all in bed. We lived with my aunty and uncle in Māngere back then.' She looked up at my reflection in the mirror and I nodded at her. She continued, 'No lights were on, nothing. No sound, nothing. I was sleeping with Lupe in the double bed, and 'Amanaki, was in the single bed.'

Kalāsia stopped talking and reached down to pick a hair band off the dressing table, then twisted it around the bottom of the first plait. 'There was this torch that shone through the bedroom window,' she said. 'I woke up and saw it, but before I could wake my sisters, someone banged on the door. We all woke up. I could hear my parents and my aunty and uncle and cousins getting up and speaking in Tongan to each other. "Who is it? What's wrong?" they were saying, stuff like that.'

She stopped for a moment and wiped the back of her hand over her eye. We looked at our reflections again. I wasn't sure where this story was going or what to say, so I passed her cup to her. 'Have some tea.'

She took sips in between wiping her eyes. A plait hung down one side of my neck, straight and even, just like Kalāsia's. She put the cup back down and began to plait the other side.

'My uncle opened the front door,' she continued, 'and two policemen were there, with a dog. One spoke to my uncle loudly, asking who lived here and saying he needed to see our passports. We were all out of bed then, with our tupenu and T-shirts on. The policeman with the dog pushed past my uncle and aunt and went into each room one by one. The dog sniffed everything, even us. I remember it by my legs. I thought I'd done something terrible and it was going to bark up at me and sink its teeth into my legs. In the dream, I get that feeling that I'm going to faint again.'

'So, this is your dream?'

Kalāsia nodded. 'Don't tell anybody.'

'I won't,' I said. 'What happened?'

'My parents and uncle and aunty got all the passports out of the cupboard with the important stuff in it, like bills and birth certificates. They showed them to the policeman. The other policeman had taken the dog into the bathroom. He was looking through our cupboards and behind the shower curtain. The one with the passports yelled out, "They're not overstayers!" but the one with the dog went into the kitchen and kept looking through our cupboards. He opened the back door and let in another policeman, the one who'd been outside with the torch. He didn't turn it off and waved it into our faces, even though we had the lights on.'

Kalāsia reached up again and wiped at an eye.

I looked down at my knees, so that she didn't think I was staring at her. 'Sounds terrifying. How often do you have this dream?'

'Not always; just sometimes.'

'Did they leave after that?'

She nodded. This time she didn't pretend about the tears. They were unstoppable.

I pulled out my drawer, found the roll of loo paper I used to wipe off make-up and passed it to her. With one hand holding my plait, she used her other hand to blow her nose and wipe her eyes before placing the paper in her pocket.

'Just chuck it in that bin,' I said.

'I'll flush it down the toilet later,' she said, reaching for another hairband. Both plaits were done.

'Have you had breakfast?'

Kalāsia shook her head. 'I can't eat after that dream. My stomach feels strange.'

'Let's have some toast,' I said, quickly putting on some mascara. It was against the school rules, but other girls took their chances, so I'd decided to wear it too. I smeared some lip balm over my lips.

We didn't talk about the dream while we ate breakfast. Pete came in and sat with us, and I wondered if that made Kalāsia uncomfortable, because she was quiet. There wasn't much chance to talk though because Jo ran in saying she couldn't find her hockey stick and asking if I'd used it.

'I've got my own hockey stick!' I said. 'Why would I use yours?'

'I must've left it in the school changing room after practice last week,' Jo said. 'Hope no one's nicked it.'

'It might be in Lost Property,' Mum said.

'Hmmm,' Jo mumbled, grabbing her lunch out of the fridge and stuffing it in her schoolbag. 'Got to go. Bye!' She ran out the door.

'You two had better get going too,' Mum said to me and Kalāsia. 'Rewi's probably given up on you.'

'So glad I'm not at school anymore,' Pete said. 'My first lecture's at eleven today.'

I rolled my eyes at him. 'Stop showing off.'

'Go and get your bag,' Kalāsia said.

'I'll quickly clean my teeth too. Won't be long.' I left Kalāsia picking up our plates and mugs and carrying them to the bench.

When I came back into the kitchen with my schoolbag slung over my shoulder, I realised Kalāsia and Pete were talking. Pete looked up at me. 'Kalāsia's brothers play rugby,' he said. 'They're at Saint Francis's, my old school.'

I nodded, grabbing my lunch out of the fridge. 'We'd better hurry, Kalāsia. Bye, everyone!' I yelled, as we headed out the door.

I wondered if Rewi would be waiting for us. He hadn't contacted me over the weekend, but I'd had hockey on Saturday and so much homework that I hadn't bothered to call him either. Also, I'd been unsure of what to say to him about Harry. Maybe he'd felt the same way too, so it was just easier to avoid each other.

He *was* up the driveway though, tapping his watch. 'Time, girls!' he called. 'The nuns won't be happy.'

'We'd better walk quickly,' I said. 'Sister Bernadette is on morning gate duty and she always gives detentions.'

'Better beat da feet!' Rewi said.

We began to half walk, half run.

'How was your hot date on Friday night?' Rewi asked.

'It wasn't a hot date. We just talked and drank Coke and stuff.'

'She kissed him,' Kalāsia said.

'I — well, it wasn't a . . .' I ran out of ideas and stopped trying to talk my way out of it.

Rewi looked straight ahead. 'You must like him.'

I thought for a moment. 'I don't really know him.'

'But you kissed him.'

No one spoke for a moment.

'Well, I kind of like him, so far.'

Thankfully, Kalāsia changed the subject. 'I didn't understand some of *The Taming of the Shrew* questions. Can you help me at morning tea-time, Liza?'

The conversation moved on to homework until we reached the school gate. Rewi left us there and continued walking up to Newton

Grammar. His school started five minutes later because they had a shorter lunchtime.

We'd made it before the bell, but Sister Bernadette spouted her usual words of wisdom at us: 'Greatness never came from lateness, girls.'

'Yes, Sister,' we answered.

The school bell clanged deafeningly just as we were hanging up our bags in the corridor.

Kalāsia tilted her head to me and whispered, 'Sorry about this morning . . .'

I started to speak at the same time. 'Just come over early when you have that dream, like you did today.'

Kalāsia lowered her eyes as if there was something interesting on the floor. Girls bustled around us, and the smell of strong perfume filled my nostrils.

'It's good for me anyway,' I said. 'Gets me out of bed.'

Kalāsia nodded. 'Thanks.'

'Better go in before Sister Agnes marks us absent,' I said.

We walked into the classroom. Sister Agnes was reading something at her desk and didn't look up at us. Stella and Ciara were chatting to girls who sat nearby, but Ursula was writing furiously in her book, probably using form-time to do some last-minute homework.

Sister Agnes stood up. 'Quiet please, girls. I'd like to get started. Let's bow our heads and say a "Hail Mary" together. Ursula, whatever you're doing, stop now please. Right now. There is nothing more important in this moment than saying this prayer.'

Ursula put down her pen and closed her exercise book. She looked up at Sister Agnes and locked eyes with her. It seemed she was about to argue that there *were* more important things than prayer, but Sister Agnes stared her down, so Ursula lowered her eyes, bowing her head ever so slightly.

I'd seen it though, the haughty beauty of Ursula as she held Sister Agnes's gaze. Her blue eyes, lined with black eyeliner and mascara, had fixed themselves on Sister Agnes's and, in that moment, I longed to be that daring.

The class was halfway through the prayer when I finally joined in.

'Holy Mary, mother of God, pray for us sinners. . . .' My voice seemed thin, a pale echo of a prayer I'd said daily since childhood. Now, it didn't feel as satisfying as it always had. Now, I'd begun to yearn for something more.

CHAPTER 11
BANANA SKINS

A few nights before the big march, Pete came home with a flyer someone had handed him at university. Mum, Jo and I were sitting at the table, eating, when he walked in from his late afternoon lecture. He sat down, piling food onto his plate with one hand, while pulling the flyer out of his pocket with the other. 'Have a look at this,' he said.

At the top of the piece of paper were the words 'MOBILISE MAY 1ST' and underneath was a picture of black South African people with their fists raised in the air. Under that, there was a list of events for students to attend, leading up to the march. On Thursday, the 23rd of April, there had been a meeting of Māori groups, trade unions and churches. On Sunday, the 26th of April, there had been a banner- and placard-making session. A South African speaker was attending one of the events. It all seemed so much more interesting than listening to teachers at school.

I remembered how Father Luke had said that playing rugby with South Africa was like having a beer with a wife-beating neighbour and pretending nothing was wrong. If Catholic priests believed that, why wasn't Sister Agnes organising speakers from South Africa and Māori groups to come to talk to us?

Pete stuffed the flyer back in his pocket. He told us that some students had set up a Bantu shack in the quad to show how poor the living conditions of black South Africans were. 'The shack's made out of bits of wood, corrugated iron, anything they can use. There's no running water or toilets inside, just a dirt floor.'

'What's Bantu?' I asked.

'A black South African group,' Mum said. 'Y'know how we use the word 'tribe' to describe Māori groups? Bantu are like a tribe.'

'And what's the quad?' I asked.

'It's a kind of square where people sit and talk and eat. Anyway,' Pete continued, 'I was eating lunch in the quad today, and a Māori woman was up on a stage talking about how discrimination against black South Africans should make us look at ourselves, at New Zealand's discrimination against Māori. Some young guys were arguing with her and one threw a banana skin at her as she stepped down from the microphone. It landed on the side of her head and slid down her cheek onto her shoulder. She just left it there and stepped back up to the microphone. "Look in your own back yard," she said. "It's not only South Africa that has to change." Then she stepped down, flicked the banana skin off her shoulder, and walked away.'

'That's mean,' Jo said, 'throwing a banana skin at her.'

'People have strong feelings about this tour,' Mum said, 'and past tours too, but this feels . . .' Mum sat back and frowned. She reached up and straightened a hair clip, although wisps of her hair still fell around her face. 'Y'know, I told Mrs Bindon next door that we were going on the protest march tomorrow night and she was shocked. She said the same thing so many tour supporters say, that it's just a game and that politics should never interfere with sport.'

'It's a bit late to say that,' Jo said. 'Dad told me that at the summer Olympics five years ago, twenty-nine countries refused to participate because the Olympic Committee allowed New Zealand to attend. Twenty-nine countries! Most of them were African.'

'Why didn't they want New Zealand to attend?' I asked.

'Cos we'd let the All Blacks tour South Africa earlier in the year,' Jo said.

'And the United Nations had asked countries to stop playing sport with South Africa,' Mum added.

'So other countries stopped sporting connections, but we didn't?'

I asked, sticking a forkful of potato in my mouth.

'Exactly, and we're *still* playing with them,' Jo said.

'Embarrassing,' I said.

'There are guys I played rugby with at school who reckon it's just a game,' Pete said. 'I saw some of them at the gym and they're going to watch the Hamilton game and one at Eden Park.'

'You mean *if* the tour goes ahead, they'll watch them,' Mum said. 'Your dad reckons it might get called off, because anti-tour groups are growing in size and . . .'

'I heard those guys say they're going into town tomorrow night to give the protesters a hard time,' Pete interrupted.

Mum nodded. She picked up the salt and shook it over her potatoes. 'At least today, Pete, it was only a banana skin and not a rock. Let's hope things don't get that bad.'

CHAPTER 12
MOBILISE MAY 1ST

Rewi and his family came to our house at 6.30pm on Friday, the 1st of May. His mum was already in town, taking photos of the gathering protesters. Dad was reporting on the march, so he was already there too.

As we put on jackets and made our way outside, Pete held back, standing in the doorway.

'Coming?' Mum asked.

Pete pushed his brown hair back from his eyes. He had a side parting and his wavy hair hung over his forehead. 'I was just thinking about those guys I was telling you about. If they see me . . . I mean, I don't agree with apartheid, but I love rugby. If they . . .'

'Stay home and keep Sal company,' Mum said. 'Just make sure that pile of dishes has gone by the time we get home.'

Pete nodded and went back inside, shutting the front door behind him. He'd miss out on meeting Harry, which was a relief.

Harry was meeting us outside the Central Post Office in Queen Elizabeth Square at 7.15pm. I'd decided to introduce him as my friend, which was mostly true because I didn't actually know if we were boyfriend and girlfriend yet. Neither of us had discussed whether we were going round together that night at Johnny's Ice-Cream Parlour. Of course, he wasn't like any other friend because I'd kissed him and, if he'd just been a friend, I wouldn't have taken so much time earlier to decide which top to wear with my jeans. I'd finally chosen my new, white, off-the-shoulder top, which was meant to be for going out somewhere special. It was hidden under my faded blue sweatshirt though because, even though it had been a sunny day, it was a cold evening.

There were other protesters on the bus. One group of old people had a placard with 'No Tour' painted on it. A young guy sitting by himself carried a piece of cardboard with 'Boks Go Home' written on it in thick felt pen. We hadn't made any signs.

There was lots of loud chatter on the bus. Excitement and nervousness fizzed around like a gas. If a match had been lit that bus would have exploded.

When we got off the bus, the driver nodded at Rewi's dad. 'I'd join you if I wasn't working,' he said.

Tipene shrugged. 'You got us here, e hoa. You're doing your bit.'

Queen Street was buzzing. People were everywhere. Some were just doing ordinary late-night shopping, but most were making their way down to the Central Post Office. Placards and signs bobbed up and down around us, and some people were already chanting, 'Springboks, stay home!'

Posters advertising the march had been stuck onto lamp posts, shop windows and bus stops. I recognised one because it was the same as one that had been pasted onto the rubbish bin outside the takeaway bar near school. I'd studied it while Rewi had been playing Spacies. It was grey with dark blue writing. At the top it said, 'Fight Apartheid. Stop the Tour. MOBILISE MAY 1ST'. Underneath the writing was a print of South Africans holding their fists up in the air, like the ones on the flyer Pete had brought home. Dad had explained that the closed fist was a symbol of solidarity, standing together in protest. The people holding their fists up in the air were smiling, all of them, as if something good was about to happen.

Beside me, Rewi spoke over the noise. 'Packed, eh?'

I nodded, but I was distracted by a sign that said, 'Remember Biko'. I turned to Tipene. 'What's Biko?'

Tipene was piggybacking Marama, and her chin rested on

his shoulder. She smiled at me and I reached up and tickled her cheek.

'You mean, "*Who's* Biko?"' Tipene said. 'Steve Biko was an anti-apartheid activist in South Africa, who was beaten up and killed by police officers.'

'He's dead?'

'Yep. They didn't like the way he was getting black South Africans fired up about racism and inequality. He died four years ago.'

'Steve Biko,' I repeated silently. I'd have been eleven when he died. My parents had bought me a hockey stick for my birthday that year. I'd been desperate to play hockey after watching Jo's Saturday games and, the minute I started form one at Saint Theresa's, I joined a team.

When we got to Queen Elizabeth Square, I couldn't see Harry anywhere. I scanned the huge crowd. There was a man on a loud hailer standing up on a big wooden box. He said we were going to make our way up Queen Street to Aotea Square, where there would be more music and speakers. He talked about Robert Muldoon, the prime minister, and how we had to make it clear to him that this tour was *not* wanted. People clapped and cheered when he said that.

Rewi tapped my shoulder. 'Want one?' He pointed to a container a woman was holding out. She had a white T-shirt with the words, 'Stop the Tour' on it. Underneath, there was a silhouette of a person backing away from a police officer holding up a baton.

Rewi reached into the container and took out a round badge. He held it out to me. The top half of it was red with 'STOP The '81 Tour' written in white. The bottom half was black with a picture of a heart split apart. One half of the heart was black, and the other half was white. Underneath, it said 'fight apartheid'.

'It's the HART symbol,' the woman explained.

'How much?' I asked.

'I just paid her,' Rewi said. 'Little present from me.' He took another badge out and pinned it to his black Stevie Wonder 'Master Blaster' T-shirt. I copied him, pinning mine onto my sweatshirt and trying not to think of my off-the-shoulder top underneath, which was meant for Harry, who wasn't even here.

At 8pm, the guy on the loud hailer told us to start walking, and the crowd, which was already spilling onto Queen Street, began to move in one long, wide chain past shops and pubs. People stood on the footpath, watching. Some gave thumbs-up signs and clapped or joined in with the chanting. Mum and Tipene were in front of us, but Marama and Nikau had hung back to walk with us.

'Hold onto our hands,' Rewi said to them. 'Don't want you two to get lost.'

Nikau took Rewi's hand, and Marama took mine. She squeezed it and looked up at me. 'Don't let me get lost, Liza.'

'I won't. Promise,' I said, squeezing her hand in return.

Around us, quite a few people carried signs that looked like the red stop signs on the road, except instead of just saying, 'STOP', they said, 'STOP THE TOUR'. Attached to sticks, they looked like massive lollipops.

A woman behind us carried a sign that said, 'Human Beings Against the Tour'. She smiled at me as I read it. Beside her, some young guys in rugby shirts held up a sign that said, 'Rugby yes. Racism no.' I wished Pete could see the sign. I'd tell him about it later.

'David Lange's here,' Tipene called back to us. 'Just saw him further up. No sign of Muldoon, though!'

The chanting was so loud that I didn't try to speak back to him; I just nodded and smiled. David Lange was the deputy leader of the Labour Party. Robert Muldoon was the leader of the National Party and the prime minister. He said the decision to cancel the tour was up to the New Zealand Rugby Football Union, but everyone marching thought it was his responsibility.

Mum looked back at me. 'You guys alright?'

'Yep,' I replied.

'I'm not alright,' Marama said, looking up at me. 'I'm scared we'll get arrested.'

'Why?' I asked. 'We're not doing anything wrong. We're allowed to march like this.'

'What about those people who got arrested in Wellington this morning?' Marama asked.

I looked at Rewi. 'People got arrested?'

'Yeah, they hung a banner over a motorway bridge. Is she saying she's scared again?'

I nodded.

'Marama, Dad said they only got arrested cos what they did was illegal. Remember? We're not doing anything illegal.'

Marama nodded. 'Why is it illegal to hang something from a motorway?'

'Not sure,' I answered. 'Maybe it distracts drivers or maybe they're worried it might fly off the motorway and land on a car.'

The chants from people around us were like a jigsaw of words. Some repeated, 'Boks stay home' while others shouted, 'One, two, three, four, we don't want your racist tour!' Some chants had South African words like, 'Remember Soweto'. I knew that Soweto was a place in South Africa. It had been in the news a few years back, because some black school children had been shot by the police. I couldn't understand one chant though. A group of young people, maybe university students, were chanting, 'Amandla! Amandla!' Then they said something else that I couldn't work out. I'd ask Mum or Dad about those words later.

The thought of Dad made me look around again. He was here somewhere writing shorthand into his notebook, which he'd use to write up an article for the newspaper after the march had finished.

Rewi's mum, Mere, was here somewhere too, but the only person I could see with a camera was a man on the footpath. Near him, a group of guys held up a large New Zealand flag with 'Support the Tour — Play the Game' painted across it. They were yelling at some protesters, who yelled back at them. One guy shoved another, and some police officers pushed through the crowded footpath and pulled them apart.

I swivelled Marama around, so we were facing the cinema on the opposite side of the street. 'Have you seen *Flash Gordon*?' I asked, pointing to a huge billboard showing an evil-looking guy in a swirling red cape.

'No,' Marama said. 'Will you take me?'

I nodded. 'Okay, one day soon.'

A couple of rows behind us, some women were singing a song that repeated the line, 'We shall overcome'. Even though the lyrics were hopeful, there was something sad about them too, that even though things would work out, it might be a massive struggle to get there.

When we reached the Civic Theatre, the road sloped uphill, so I turned to look back at the crowd. It still reached as far back as Queen Elizabeth Square, where we'd started. It looked like one long creature with banners and placards that swayed all the way down its spine and across its body. A shiver of excitement filled me. 'I am part of this,' I thought. 'I have joined everyone here to make this protest powerful.'

Music blared as we turned into Aotea Square, but already there wasn't enough room for everyone. People kept coming and coming though, so we all had to squish together. A band was playing that I'd never heard before. Tipene said they were The Red Flag Bush Band. I tried to listen to them properly, but we kept having to move forward or over a bit, as people nudged their way into Aotea Square, so it was hard to concentrate.

Soon, there were a few speakers. One, Mum told us, was Reverend Andrew Beyer, an Anglican minister, who led MOST, the big Auckland coalition that organised the march. 'It means "Mobilisation to Stop the Tour",' Mum said. I nodded, not bothering to raise my voice to tell her I already knew that. The reverend on stage said that the size of the march had exceeded his expectations. Everyone cheered and whistled. He said this was a call to the government and the New Zealand Rugby Football Union to cancel the tour.

Another speaker was Syd Jackson, a well-known Māori activist. He said that this march was the beginning of a battle that we would win. The crowd cheered.

It was hard to see because of the crowds, but also because Marama was on Tipene's shoulders in front of me. A guy named Tom Newnham spoke next. He said he was the national secretary of an anti-racism group called CARE, the Citizens' Association for Racial Equality. He said that this protest march was necessary because, if the tour went ahead, the world would see New Zealand as supporting apartheid.

He said that the NZ Rugby Football Union needed to realise it was destroying New Zealand's international reputation.

I didn't get to hear the rest of Tom Newnham's speech because someone tapped me on the shoulder, a firm tap, right on my collarbone. I swung around, and there was Harry, hunched under a thick, grey jacket with army-type pockets on it.

'You're here!' I cried.

Harry nodded. 'Yep!'

'I — I — you weren't outside the post office.' My cheeks were warm. I was glad he couldn't see them in the dark.

'I got held up,' Harry said. The slight curve of his top lip felt familiar, and I wanted to reach out and put my finger on it.

We were both silent. A woman was speaking now. She said she was Mira Szaszy, the director of the community department at Ngā Tapuwae Community College. She said she had been the president of the Māori Women's Welfare League. I didn't hear any more of what she said though, because Harry spoke. 'That your friend from the social?' he asked, nodding towards Rewi, who stood beside me.

'Yeah, that's Rewi.'

As if he'd heard me, Rewi turned, about to say something, then stopped when he saw Harry. 'Hi,' he said. 'Harry, eh?'

Harry nodded. 'Last time I looked.'

Rewi held out his hand. 'Rewi. Good to meet you.'

Harry took his hand out of his jacket pocket, but it seemed slow and I wanted to pull it out for him so that Rewi's hand wasn't waiting in the middle of us all like that. 'Liza talks about you a lot,' Harry said, finally shaking Rewi's hand.

Rewi's eyebrows shot up. 'Liza, talking a lot? No!'

'Shut up,' I said, a relieved smile on my face. Rewi was making things feel normal. He grinned at me under his curly mop of hair.

'Lots of pigs here tonight,' Harry said.

'Cops?' Rewi asked.

'Yep.' Harry reached out and took my hand.

I froze. What if Mum or Tipene or Jo turned around and saw? I gently pulled my hand away. 'What made you late?' I asked. 'Everything okay?'

'Not really.' Harry put his hand back in his pocket. 'Some shit went down at our house, so I've already seen the pigs tonight.'

I went to speak, but there was a huge round of applause for something Mira Szaszy had said. When the clapping and cheering finished, I spoke. 'Everyone okay?'

Harry nodded and looked up at the stage area.

'Bad buzz,' Rewi said.

Harry shrugged. I reached out and squeezed his arm quickly, then pulled away again.

The rally was still going, but Mum and Tipene decided we should head home before it finished, when crowds of people would be trying to get the bus all at once.

After we wound our way through the crowd and back onto Queen Street, I introduced Harry to everyone. Marama and Nikau nodded sleepily at him, Tipene shook his hand, and Mum patted his arm, saying it was lovely to meet him.

'You go to Newton, eh?' Jo asked.

'I do,' Harry said.

'Did you go out with Stephanie Lulich?'

'A while ago.'

'She's in my class,' Jo said. 'Thought I'd seen you around. Maybe at our school social.'

Harry nodded. 'Maybe.'

We walked through the crowds of people towards our bus stop. Harry walked beside me and Rewi. When no one was looking, he reached out and rubbed his hand up and down my back. I looked at him and smiled. It was okay because Mum and the others were walking ahead of us.

'Which bus do you get?' Rewi asked Harry.

Harry held his hand on my back for a moment longer. I hoped Rewi hadn't seen it because the thought of that made me uncomfortable. 'A different bus to yours,' Harry said, dropping his arm and putting his hand back into his jacket pocket, 'but I'll walk down to yours with you guys, then head home.'

When we got on the bus, Marama sat next to me and Rewi sat

next to his dad, who had Nikau on his knee. Outside, Harry stood watching as we took our seats. I waved at him. Marama lifted her small hand and waved too. Harry smiled.

As the bus pulled away, I turned. Harry was putting a cigarette in his mouth. The bus crawled up Victoria Street, stopping and starting to let groups of people cross the road. Harry lit his cigarette, then we turned the corner, and I couldn't see him anymore.

When I got up the next morning, Dad was already sitting at the table, looking at the newspaper and drinking coffee. Pete, Jo and Mum were trying to do things over the top of each other as they made toast or poured milk on cereal. It looked too chaotic for me, so I sat down beside Dad to wait till they'd finished.

'What time did you get home?' I asked him.

'Around one in the morning,' he said, rubbing his eye. 'You guys missed the most important part. After the speeches finished, the crowd voted to tell the Rugby Union and the government to cancel the tour. Everyone was cheering and clapping.' Dad looked at me and smiled. 'Pretty exciting!'

'It was amazing, Dad. So many people.'

'Lucky we're in a big city,' Dad said. 'In some of the small towns, the protesters marched during the day, because they were frightened of possible violence from pro-tour people at night.'

'I felt pretty safe in that huge crowd last night,' I said. 'It was almost like a party atmosphere.'

'Everyone knows everyone in small towns,' Dad said. 'There's no safety in numbers. In Taumaranui, fifty-five people marched through the main street. Bet the town knew exactly who they were.'

I nodded, then remembered the chant, the one the university students had been saying. 'Do you know what "Amandla" means, Dad?'

'It means "power" in one of the South African languages. Sometimes protesters say, "Amandla ngawethu" which means "power to the people".'

So, that's what I'd heard the university students chanting.

Mum came to sit at the table. She had toast and a mug of tea. 'We met Eliza's boyfriend last night,' she said.

'What?' I spluttered.

'Well, isn't he?' Mum asked. 'He seemed smitten.'

I glanced at Jo and Pete in the kitchen, hoping they hadn't heard, but they had.

'What's his name?' Pete asked.

'Harry,' Jo said.

'He's not my boyfriend; he's a friend.'

'Hmmm,' Mum said.

'He couldn't take his eyes off you,' Jo said. 'You know I've seen him around, eh? He used to go out with a girl in my class, Stephanie Lulich.'

'Yeah, I heard you ask him about her last night.'

'Oooh,' Pete said, 'our little Liza's got a boyfriend.'

'Shut up,' I said. 'He's just a friend.' Standing up, I stomped past them into the kitchen to put some bread in the toaster.

No one said anything. I turned to the cupboard to get some peanut butter, avoiding eye contact with any of them. Finally, I couldn't bear the silence, so I turned to face them. They burst into laughter. I folded my arms, rolled my eyes and stared at them. 'What's your problem?'

'Ah, it's okay,' Dad said. 'As long as he treats you well, and you don't let him affect your schoolwork, we don't mind.'

'Dad,' I said, 'he's *not* my boyfriend.'

'No, of course he's not,' Dad said. He looked at Mum, and they started laughing again.

I turned back to the toaster. My protestations were getting me nowhere, so I ignored them. Sal came into the kitchen and brushed against my leg as I smeared butter over my toast. At least she wasn't a pain, I thought, breaking off a corner of my toast and giving it to her.

LOCKDOWN

It's Saturday, the 11th of April, week three of level four lockdown. I'm leaning against the bench, listening to the news on the radio, and wondering what to cook for dinner, when Eva walks into the kitchen.

'Don't listen to the news, Mum,' she says. 'It's the same old depressing stuff: Covid, Covid, Covid.'

I switch off the radio. 'I just wanted to hear how many cases we have now and see what the global numbers are.'

'Yes, but it begins with that and then you're sucked into the whole news programme and, before you know it, you're sobbing into the sink.'

'What? I have not sobbed into the sink!'

Eva smiles. 'I know, but it sounded kind of dramatic. Put that in your story, Mum, your Springbok Tour memories.' Eva leans over the sink and makes a crying sound, then whispers, 'She sobbed over the sink. Would the Springbok Tour really go ahead?'

I laugh. 'That's a soap opera version!' I go to the fridge and scan what food we have. There are no fresh vegetables: no carrots, no broccoli, nothing. I had planned to go to the supermarket today, but the thought of waiting in a long queue put me off. Tomorrow, I'll have to. At least we have some frozen veggies. They'll do.

'So, what *is* the latest Covid count?' Eva asks.

'Ah, see, you want to know!' I pull the large frying pan out of the cupboard and begin to chop up an onion.

'Just the latest statistics, that's all.' Eva rips open a packet of crackers and eats one.

'Can you not fill up on crackers when I'm about to cook dinner?' I say. 'It makes me feel there's no point in cooking.' I don't enjoy cooking and I'm sick of trying to keep food in the cupboards with everyone home eating all day and night.

'Mum, I'm hungry, so I'm eating.' Bits of cracker fall from Eva's mouth. 'Oops, sorry.'

'Well, you'd better eat dinner!'

For a short time, neither of us speak. I slice up onion, while Eva munches on crackers. Onions make me cry though, and as I wipe a tear away, Eva whispers, 'She sobbed over the onions. Would the Springbok Tour really go ahead?'

I smile.

'So, Covid summary?'

I stop chopping and turn away from the stinging of the onions. 'Okay, there were twenty-nine new cases today. Fifteen cases are in hospital, and five of those are in intensive care. Lots of people have recovered, over four hundred.'

'Your memory is incredible,' Eva says. 'Are the new cases still connected to those clusters?'

'Yep, still the rest home, the wedding and the school.' I turn back to the onions.

Jesse comes into the kitchen and takes some crackers out of the packet. 'We'll be okay,' he says, 'because we locked down so quickly and closed our borders. The United States is in a bad way though. They've got almost half a million cases and they've had more than eighteen and a half thousand deaths, like Italy.' Jesse stuffs three crackers into his mouth all at once.

'Could you two please stop eating and wait just half an hour for the amazing stir-fry I'm cooking.' I gesture at the cracker packet with my veggie knife.

'Are you sure it'll be amazing?' Jesse says. 'I'd say that's debatable!' He walks over to me, takes the knife from my hand, and turns me to face him. 'Mum, there's something serious I need to talk to you about. Where's Dad?'

'Out running.'

'Okay, we can talk about it while we eat your amazing stir-fry.' Jesse grins at me. 'Come on, Mum, just a little chuckle? You know I'm funny!'

I take his hands off my arms, keeping a straight face. 'You are funny, but right now, I'd just like to get on with cooking.'

'Tell me what you need to discuss now, Jesse,' Eva says.

Jesse turns away, grabs a handful of crackers and leaves the room.

'Come on, Jesse,' Eva calls after him. 'You can tell me! Are you pregnant? Dodgy drug deal? Mafia onto you? Acne problems?'

I picture him halfway to his room, 'flipping the bird' at her, as they say now. When I was a teenager, we called it, 'giving someone the fingers'.

Half an hour later, we're all sitting down, eating. Ross is still red in the face from running, even though he's had a shower. He tells Jesse to hurry up and tell us about whatever this big thing is.

Jesse looks at Ross and me and says, 'You can say no to this, but I hope you'll say yes.'

'Just get on with it,' Eva says.

Jesse puts down his knife and fork and says, 'Y'know Adam?'

'Your friend Adam?' I ask.

'Yeah.'

'Course we do,' I say. 'Why?'

'He needs somewhere to live. Just for a while, until lockdown is over.'

'Why, what's wrong?' I ask.

'His father's a dick,' Jesse says. 'Guess you'd call it abuse, sort of. He's always telling Adam how useless he is and swears at him, calls him names.'

'I thought he lived with his mum,' Eva says. 'Why is he staying with his dad?'

'Because his grandma came to live with him and his mum over lockdown and his mum was worried Adam might be a risk to her.

He works at the supermarket, remember?'

Supermarket staff are considered essential workers, so they have kept working through the lockdown. Adam's grandma is in the vulnerable group, because she is elderly and, if she got Covid, she'd be more likely to die from it.

'So, what are you saying, Jesse?' I ask.

'He needs to get away from his father.' Jesse picks up his fork and shovels some rice into his mouth.

'Are you asking if he can stay here?' Ross asks.

Jesse nods.

'You do realise that we're meant to stay in our bubbles, don't you?' Ross says.

We all use the word, 'bubble' now. Our prime minister, Jacinda Ardern, uses the word for the people you lock down with. We're only allowed to mix with those in our bubble during level four lockdown.

'Yeah, course, but this would just mean adding one more person to our bubble.' Jesse puts his fork down. 'It's not such a big deal.'

Ross looks at me and I shrug. 'What about the fact that he's working in a supermarket and Covid can stay on clothing?' Ross says. 'He's putting *us* at risk.'

'Ross, that's a bit . . .' I say.

Jesse interrupts. 'He's already doing stuff to stop that happening, Dad. He sanitises his hands before he enters the house, leaves his shoes outside the door and washes his clothes and showers as soon as he gets inside.'

'What do you think?' Ross asks me.

I shrug again. 'He's a seventeen-year-old living with an abusive father.'

'Does he hit him?' Eva asks.

'Don't think so,' Jesse says. 'Just never says anything nice to him. He's an arsehole.'

'Jesse, we're in week three. We're nearly there, if Jacinda's right about four weeks of level four,' Ross says. 'Just tell him to hang in there.'

'I knew you'd be like this,' Jesse says. 'How would you feel if no one helped me or Eva?'

'What do you mean "be like this"?' Ross's face is still red, and it makes him look angry now. 'I'm worried about my own family. Is that such a terrible thing?'

'It takes a village to raise a child, Dad,' Eva says.

'Adam's seventeen,' Ross says. 'He's not exactly a child.'

'He's only seventeen, Ross,' I say. 'He's still at school, working part-time and doesn't have many options. Also, we don't know how long level four will go on for. Adam could end up stuck in his dad's house for another month or two.'

'So then he could be here with us for another month or two,' Ross says.

'We'd make it work, Ross.'

Ross picks up his glass of water and drinks until it's empty. When he's finished, he looks around at us. 'Seems it's three against one, so he's coming into our bubble.'

'We all have to agree, Ross,' I say. I hate it when he does this 'you're all against me' thing.

'Well, if we were in normal times, I'd be happier about it,' he says.

'So would I,' I say. 'This isn't an ideal situation for any of us. We're working so hard to keep our bubble separate, as we're being told to do, and, yes, we will have to accept the small possibility that, even with all of his hygiene practices, Adam might bring Covid into the house.'

'It's unlikely,' Eva says. 'Supermarkets make you sanitise your hands and they disinfect the trolleys. Adam will be wearing a mask and gloves, and he'll be behind those screens at the checkout counter.'

'True,' I say. 'It's extremely unlikely, but I guess there's a very small risk, and that's what's worrying your dad.'

'Tell him he can come to stay,' Ross says. 'Where will he sleep?'

'He can have my little writing room,' I say. 'I've been writing here at the dining table or outside on the deck most of the time anyway. We've got Jesse's old single bed in the garage. We can swap it for my desk.'

Ross nods. 'Okay. Just remind him that he does not come near the kitchen or any of us until he's showered and put his clothes in the wash.'

'Yep, and he can use the sanitiser outside the front door before he touches the door handle, like the rest of us,' Jesse says. 'It'll be okay, Dad, and it means Adam doesn't have to listen to his father tell him what a loser he is.'

'What a jerk,' Eva says.

'He is,' Jesse says. 'He's a . . .'

I interrupt. 'Don't say dick or arsehole.'

Jesse grins. 'I was going to say, 'He's a difficult man'.'

'I doubt that *was* what you were going to say.'

Dinner is over, and Ross goes straight to the lounge. The muffled sound of the TV filters through the walls into the kitchen. Jesse and Eva scrape plates and I tell them to clean the frying pan and rice cooker. I go into the lounge and sit down on the sofa beside Ross, who continues to look at the screen.

'Hope we don't regret this,' he says.

'We'll be okay.' I reach over to pat his hand. He doesn't respond, so I stand up and go down the hall into my little writing room. It will be easy enough to sort the room out for Adam. Ross just needs a bit of time to get used to the idea. We can't leave Adam with his dad if he's making his life hell.

A memory of a phone conversation with Harry comes to me. He'd rung after dinner one night. In a quiet voice, he'd told me about the hole his dad had punched in the kitchen wall while his mum was cooking dinner. He said his dad had grabbed a pot of veggies off the stove and emptied it all over the floor, then stormed out of the house. Harry's mum had sat with Sophie until she stopped crying, while Harry cleaned up the mess. His mum had ripped a picture of a fluffy cat out of a magazine, trimming the edges neatly so it was a perfect rectangular shape, then stuck it over the hole in the wall.

Later that night, Ross comes into the kitchen. I'm writing a shopping list, telling myself I'll get up early so I won't have to stand in a queue outside the supermarket. I look up at Ross.

'It's the right thing to do,' he says. 'Just hope it doesn't backfire on us.'

'Me too.'

He reaches over and holds my hand for a moment. 'We'll be okay.'

I squeeze his hand gently. 'We will,' I say, 'we will.'

CHAPTER 13
MADNESS

It was Monday morning and Kalāsia and I were under her umbrella. The rain fell in slants, hitting our legs and shoes. Charlie Browns were hopeless in the rain because they had decorative holes on top, so it didn't take long for my socks to become soggy and my feet to start squelching. Even though we were getting soaked, Rewi, Kalāsia and I were not rushing. I'd been telling Kalāsia about the march on Friday and how I'd been humming that song 'We Shall Overcome' all weekend.

Kalāsia began to tell us about how Tongans sang in mass. 'They sing loudly and harmonise too, so it sounds much better than the singing in a Palangi mass. You should come with me next time there's a Tongan mass, Liza. They're once a month.'

'But then Liza might join in the singing,' Rewi said, 'and that's never a good idea.'

'Hey, I can sing!' I said.

'Yeah, ah, I've heard you sing,' Rewi said.

'Around the house! That's different, cos I'm not trying to sing well.'

'Ah, and whenever I play a song on my ghetto blaster, I can't help but notice how you massacre the song when you join in.'

I stepped around a puddle and then thought better of it, kicking water up Rewi's legs. 'I have a good voice!'

Rewi laughed. His legs were soaked, and his drenched raincoat hung off him. I grinned back at him. What could he possibly do next? How could he beat that?

'You two,' Kalāsia said. 'Now you've got to sit in class wet all day!'

Rewi nodded. 'Yeah, Liza. Stop being silly and grow up. Come on, let's have a hug and make up.' He was too quick and wrapped me in his arms, his raincoat soaking into my school jumper.

I pushed him away. 'Get lost!'

Rewi let go of me. 'Oh no, you're so wet, Liza,' he said. 'That's terrible, but it was such a nice hug, wasn't it? It was worth it!'

'You're going to get it, Rewi Matheson.'

We were near the school gate now, so Rewi veered off, chuckling as he headed on up to Newton Grammar.

Sister Agnes was fiddling around in her desk drawer when Kalāsia and I walked into class. Stella noticed us first. 'You're soaked, Liza,' she said.

Sister Agnes glanced over at me. 'Silly girl. Where was your raincoat?'

'I had an umbrella,' I replied, 'but it didn't keep me dry.'

'You'd better sit next to the heater,' she said. 'Try to have a bit more common sense, Liza.'

'Sorry, Sister,' I said.

Ursula's desk was near the heater. I plonked myself down beside her, peeled off my jumper and spread it out to dry. Leaning back, I settled against the heater so that its warmth seeped through my damp school blouse.

'What happened to you?' Ursula asked, looking up from her usual frantic attempt to do homework before the bell went.

'I got into a bit of a play fight with Rewi.'

'You know what that means, don't you?' Ursula said.

'What?'

'A play fight between a man and a woman is sexual really. It's because you're attracted to each other.' Ursula tapped the end of her pen on her lip.

'That's crap,' I said. 'Rewi's like a brother to me. I've never looked at him any other way.'

'Hmmm.' Ursula stretched out her long legs, pushed her homework aside and turned to me. 'I'm going to Madness tomorrow night at the Logan Campbell Centre. Josh bought me a ticket for my birthday. He's picking me up in his mum's car cos he got his licence last week.' Ursula started to sing 'My Girl' by Madness, turning back to her homework.

Now *that* is flat and off-pitch, I thought to myself. Rewi needs to hear Ursula sing!

The bell went and Sister Agnes said, 'Stay where you are, Eliza. You need to get as dry as possible or you'll get sick.'

The wind rumbled around our old block of classrooms, and I snuggled back against the heater.

Sister Agnes stepped away from her desk and walked to the centre of the room. 'Girls, I'd like your attention, please and I'm waiting for complete silence.' When the chatter had completely stopped, she continued, 'Sister Ignatia has asked that we remind you of the school rules. Some of you are blatantly ignoring them. Please remember, you are to remove nail polish before you come to school on Monday mornings.' She looked over at Ursula beside me.

Ursula spread her fingers out and inspected her red fingernails. She had an expression of curiosity on her face, as though she'd just noticed that her fingernails were painted.

'Please do also remember that you are only allowed plain studs in your ears. No hoops, no sleepers, nothing except plain studs.' Again, Sister Agnes fixed her gaze on Ursula. 'Take your sleepers out please, Ursula.'

The heat on my back was becoming a bit much. I sat forward, peeling my steaming blouse off the heater. Ursula was still inspecting her nails. One of them was chipped.

'Ursula, I'm speaking to you,' Sister Agnes said.

'I heard you, Sister.' Ursula reached up to her ears and slowly removed each earring, placing them in her pencil case. She moved as if there was all the time in the world and she wasn't being watched by a nun and a class full of girls.

Sister Agnes looked back at the class. 'So, no more nail polish, no earrings except for plain studs and, while we're at it, no make-up.

Nowhere in the school rules does it say that make-up is part of school uniform. Follow the uniform regulations please, girls.' Sister Agnes moved back to her desk. 'Now, let's do the roll.'

Ursula picked up her pen and doodled on her refill pad. She tilted her head towards me and whispered, 'What's her problem with looking good? She should try it some time, ugly old cow.'

Nodding, so that Ursula knew I was on her side, I tried to think of something to say. I didn't really think Sister Agnes was a cow, but I wanted to reassure Ursula. 'I wear eyeliner,' I offered.

'Exactly. She could do with a bit of eyeliner.'

'Anyway, forget about her. You're going to Madness tomorrow night, your birthday's on Wednesday *and* you're having a party in a few weeks.'

'Sweet sixteen,' Ursula said.

'And never been kissed,' I said, finishing the line I'd heard people say.

Ursula's plucked eyebrows rose. 'Been a lot more than just kissed, Liza.' She flicked through her refill paper. 'Shit, I can't get this *Taming of the Shrew* stuff done by first period. Thank God Starship likes me. She might forgive me! She's pretty cool, not like this old trout.'

At that very moment, Sister Agnes called out my name. 'Eliza Newland.'

'Yes, Sister,' I answered.

Without taking her eyes off the roll, she said, 'That jumper dry now?'

'Almost, Sister.'

'Good. Put it on the heater when you get to your next class too.'

She really wasn't as bad as Ursula said.

In English, Ms Jefferson wrote questions on the blackboard. She wore hooped earrings, a flowing skirt and bangles on her wrists that tinkled against each other as she wrote. She hadn't noticed Ursula's nail polish and, even if she had, she probably wouldn't say anything. Turning towards us, she rubbed her hands together to get the chalk dust off. 'Two questions, girls. You have five minutes to discuss them with the people beside you and then I'd like to hear back from you. Off you go.'

On the blackboard, Ms Jefferson had written:

1) How does Petruchio behave in ways that are not acceptable for a wedding?

2) Why do you think he does this?'

I turned to Kalāsia beside me. From across the aisle, Ursula pulled her chair over to join us. 'I didn't do my homework, as you know,' she whispered, 'so I don't really know what happened in Act Three.'

'What were you doing last night?' Kalāsia asked.

Ursula tapped her nose with her finger. 'That's for me to know and you to find out.'

'I don't understand that answer,' Kalāsia said. 'I just tried to find out.'

'Ignore her,' I said. 'She's trying to be mysterious. Let's discuss these questions before Starship gets to us.' Ms Jefferson was walking down the aisles between the desks and listening to everyone chatting. She'd reach us in a minute.

'So, Ursula,' I said, 'Petruchio humiliates Kate on their wedding day. He dresses up in old, horrible clothes and rides a sick horse down the street. He's late for the wedding, then he swears in front of the priest, who drops his prayer book. When he bends down to pick it up, Petruchio hits him so the priest and the book fall.'

'Why?' Ursula asked.

I shrugged.

'He's trying to embarrass her,' Kalāsia said.

'Well done, Kalāsia,' Ms Jefferson said, as she passed by our desks. 'So, my next question is, 'Why?' Have a think about why he wants to embarrass her.' She moved away to the girls in front of us.

'Quick,' Ursula said. 'What else happens?'

'When the priest says they are now man and wife, Petruchio yells out for wine and then throws his wine at the sexton saying his beard is too thin.'

'What's a sexton?' Ursula asks.

'I looked it up in the dictionary,' Kalāsia said. 'He's kind of a church helper.'

Ursula nodded. 'Petruchio's a bit of a spinner.'

I smiled. 'A loose cannon.'

'A sandwich short of a picnic,' Ursula added.

We both laughed.

Kalāsia stared at us. 'I don't know what you two are talking about. You're crazy.'

'They're all ways to describe a mad person,' I explained.

'Anything else I need to know?' Ursula asked.

'He won't stay for the wedding feast,' Kalāsia said. 'He makes Kate leave straight after the wedding ceremony.'

'Why?' Ursula asked.

'He wants her to know he's the boss,' Kalāsia said.

Ms Jefferson interrupted us. 'Girls, let's hear your thoughts on this now.' She waited for our discussions to die down, then asked the class to tell her all of Petruchio's strange behaviours on the wedding day. She wrote them on the board, then turned back to us. 'Look at that list, girls. Look at it. How would this make Kate feel?'

'She'd feel ashamed and humiliated,' Ciara said.

'Yes, she would,' Ms Jefferson said. 'I would.'

'Would you marry someone who treated you like that, Ms Jefferson?' Ursula asked.

'No, I wouldn't,' Ms Jefferson said. 'I doubt any of us would. Why do you think Kate goes ahead with the wedding when we know we wouldn't?'

'She doesn't want to stay single,' I said. 'It's embarrassing to be single.'

Ms Jefferson nodded. Turning to the board, she wrote, 'Old maid', 'On the shelf' and 'Spinster'. Pointing to the words she'd written, she said, 'These are ways we describe a woman who is single. None of them are feel-good words or phrases. They all make a woman feel like she's not attractive or lovable enough to become someone's wife. So, Kate would rather be deeply humiliated and married to someone who appears to be mad, than stay single. That's how bad being unmarried feels to her.'

'You're not single, eh, Ms Jefferson?' Ursula asked.

Ms Jefferson looked at Ursula and tilted her head. 'Why do you ask, Ursula?'

'I saw your husband drop you to school one morning, and you . . .' Ursula stopped.

'Kissed?' Ms Jefferson asked.

Ursula nodded. Her cheeks were pink. She was treading risky territory discussing such personal stuff with a teacher.

'He's not my husband,' Ms Jefferson said, 'and, yes, we kiss every morning he drops me off.' She turned to the whole class and smiled. 'We're off topic. Let's get back to that final question. Why does Petruchio purposely embarrass Kate like this?'

Someone answered, 'He wants to show her he's in control.'

'Yes,' Ms Jefferson said. 'He wants to show her he holds all the power, that he actually owns her now that she's his wife. When she wants to stay for the wedding reception, he makes this very clear. Can anyone find what he says to show his ownership?'

Kalāsia put her hand up. In most classes, Kalāsia was shy and quiet, but in Ms Jefferson's she was more relaxed. We all were. 'Is it the bit where he says he's her master?' Kalāsia asked.

'Yes, Kalāsia. Would you read that bit to us?'

Kalāsia flicked over a page of the play. She probably hadn't expected to be asked to read. After a small cough, she began, 'I will be master of what is mine own. She is my goods, my chattels; she is my house. My household stuff, my field, my barn. My horse, my ox, my ass, my anything.'

'She's his arse?' Ursula said.

The class laughed.

Ms Jefferson smiled. 'Another name for a donkey is "ass", so not quite what you're thinking, Ursula.'

'So, is he saying she's his property, like his house and his horse?' someone asked.

'He is,' Ms Jefferson said. 'Different times, girls. This play was written four hundred years ago. Although, some would say that not enough has changed. I'm interested in your thoughts on this. Perhaps a paragraph on whether enough has changed for women could be your homework.'

As soon as the bell went and we were out of earshot, we talked about Ms Jefferson's unmarried status. Clearly, she lived with her boyfriend, or at least they stayed together some nights because he dropped her off some mornings.

'She'd never be able to do that if she was Tongan,' Kalāsia said.

'From a Catholic point of view,' Ciara said, 'she's living in sin.'

I thought of Ms Jefferson with her flowing skirts, peace signs on her T-shirts and kind smile. How could she be a sinner?

'I don't think it's that bad,' Stella said. 'My aunty lives with a man and they never got married. They're not Catholic though. They're on Dad's side of the family.'

'I don't think it's that bad either,' I said. 'I think she was brave telling us that, cos she could get in trouble with the nuns if they found out.'

Each time we chatted about Ms Jefferson that day, I wished I could thank her, but I wasn't exactly sure why. The way she'd chosen to do things differently felt like a door opening. *The Taming of the Shrew* and Ms Jefferson's English classes had become something I looked forward to.

CHAPTER 14
THE MOUNTAIN

We were walking up the hill near my house. It was Saturday afternoon, and Harry and I had just been to the movies. Mum and Dad had said I could only go to a daytime movie and had to be home by dinner time. I'd argued that I was four months from turning sixteen, but they'd insisted on a daytime movie only. I'd had to race home after hockey and shower quickly, so I could give myself enough time to think about what to wear and put some eyeliner on.

We went to see *Private Benjamin*, which made us laugh a lot. It was about a woman who joined the army after her husband died. She thought it would be easy, but it wasn't. It had a predictable ending: she had to learn to not give up and to work hard, and she became a good soldier, which made her self-confidence grow.

We sat up the back of the cinema. During the movie, Harry put his arm around me and with the other arm, he reached over and held my hand until it felt a bit awkward. After a while, I tried putting my hand on his knee, but it felt like a strange place to just leave my hand, so I placed it back on my lap. Harry leaned over and kissed me four times. After that, I felt more confident, so I reached over and kissed him back. The darkness of the cinema was like a cloak covering us, a place of protection where no one could see us.

After the movie, it wasn't yet dinner time, so we got off the bus one stop after my usual one and walked up the road to the mountain. It was like stepping into the countryside. There were cows on its grassy slopes and the birdsong was loud. Through the trees, the harbours edged around Auckland's curves.

Harry was telling me about how his physics teacher had it in for him. The teacher would sometimes stop mid-explanation and ask Harry if he'd like to teach the class. When Harry asked why, his teacher would say things like, 'Because you always seem so bored, so you obviously know all of this.'

'What do you say?' I asked Harry.

'At first, I said nothing. I just looked at my textbook cos I didn't know what to do. Silence didn't work though because the other day he said it again.' Harry put on a British accent. '"I presume you know all of this, Harry O'Connell, am I right? Am I boring you with what you already know?"'

'What did you say?'

'I stopped trying to be politely silent. He was like a mouse that keeps running in front of a cat. I just said, "Well, Sir, if you insist on asking me if I'm bored, I suppose I'd better admit that I am, not because I know it all, but because you're a dull teacher."'

I stopped walking. 'You really said that?'

'He kept asking me!'

'But, what did he say?'

'He told me to pack my things and go straight to the dean's office, so I did. The dean wasn't there though, so I sat outside his office and looked at the old photos on the wall. There were so many! Head boys, prefects, duxes, rugby teams, cricket teams, things like that.' Harry put on a British accent again and said, 'Such upstanding young men!'

I smiled.

Harry put his hand on his chest and gazed into the distance, as if an actor in an old black and white movie. 'I'm grateful I was sent to the dean's office, cos I learnt so much looking at those photos. I realised how much I was wasting my life, resenting school and the way teachers treated me. I realised I wanted to put all that behind me and straighten myself out, change my ways. I know it's unlikely I'll be head boy next year, but I can be head boy in my own heart.'

He patted his chest. His green eyes were wide, as if he truly believed his own words.

I laughed. 'So did the dean turn up?'

'He did and he wasn't happy about my plan to be head boy in my own heart. He told me to stop making fun of my schooling and that my negative, cynical attitude meant I'd leave school without qualifications, which was a shame. Apparently, I'm intelligent and should learn to respect myself and the gifts I was born with. I agreed with him and told him I'd start to respect my intelligence more and that I'd pay attention, not just in physics, but in all my classes.'

I watched the shape of Harry's lips as he spoke, the way they mostly worked together to make words, but the top one sometimes curled up and away, determined to do its own thing. 'So, he believed you?' I asked.

Harry snorted. 'He rolled his eyes and put me on detention and told me I'd regret not taking education more seriously.'

'That was that then?'

'Yep, that's why, if you'd passed Newton Grammar at three-thirty yesterday, you'd have seen me picking up rubbish. For being honest!' Harry stopped walking and pulled me to him. His eyebrows furrowed as he looked into my eyes. 'And so, young Eliza Newland, there's a lesson in this and it goes against everything the nuns probably tell you. The message is this: Honesty is not always the best policy!'

I reached up to smooth out his eyebrows and ran my hand down his cheek. It was an instinctive action, like Sal wagging her tail when she sees us. I watched my fingers move as if touching something fragile.

Harry took my hand before it left his cheek and kissed it, his thick, soft lips moving slowly over my palm, paying attention to every millimetre. He pulled me closer to him, still holding my hand, and we kissed. It was an exploration, slower, faster, gentle here, pressure there, a curious research of lips and tongues. We stroked each other's backs, uncertain at first, but then pulling the other more tightly to us. Our breaths merged, scattering across our cheeks like sparks, fluttering through our eyelashes.

Soon, my hands were doing things without me thinking for them.

They were around the front of him, pressing against his stomach through his T-shirt, sliding up his chest, over his Adam's apple, around the back of his neck and up through his wavy hair.

A motorbike roared past us and I pulled away, as if the world were suddenly watching us.

'It's okay,' Harry murmured. 'It wasn't a nun on that bike.'

I laughed. Maybe the motorbike was a good thing. I hadn't wanted to stop but I didn't know where I was going. 'I'd better go home anyway,' I said.

Neither of us spoke for a while as we made our way back down the mountain and out onto the street. We just held hands and walked.

CHAPTER 15
CHRISTIAN LIVING

Sister Agnes straightened her veil often. It was a habit she had. She'd reach up and pull the front of it forward so that her greying brown hair was fully covered, neatly tucked away under the white cuff of her blue veil.

Today, we were talking about the word 'charity'. Sister Agnes had written it up onto the board. She stood before us, waiting for silence, and then spoke. 'Did any of you see the news last night, girls? If you did, who do you think Jesus would be trying to work miracles for if he were alive now?'

Ursula sighed and put her hand up, as if doing Sister Agnes a favour. 'The people in Africa.'

'Yes, Ursula. Do you know which part of Africa the news item was about?'

Ursula shrugged. 'I only know it's in Africa.'

'Well, many parts of Africa are in crisis, but which part was on the news last night?'

Ursula seemed to give up and began to pull a bit of broken fingernail off. Thankfully, there was no nail polish on it.

Sister Agnes looked across the room. Ana Babich, who'd sat beside me before Kalāsia joined our class, put her hand up. 'Uganda, Sister.'

'That's right, Ana, Uganda,' Sister Agnes said. 'On the news last night, they said that around 150 million Africans don't have enough food. Over the last eighteen months, the drought in only one part of

Uganda caused the death of 30,000 people. Thirty thousand people starved to death!'

The room was silent for a moment, then Ana put her hand up again. 'Sister, my father said they need to stop having so many babies.'

Sister Agnes lifted her hand as if to point at something but lowered it again. 'Babies are a gift from God,' she said. 'The Catholic church doesn't approve of stopping babies from coming into the world.'

'It's just what Dad said.' Ana's cheeks reddened.

'Not enough rain is a problem in parts of Africa,' Sister Agnes said, 'but war is also a huge problem.'

'If Jesus was walking around Africa now, he could do the miracle with the fish and the bread again,' Stella said.

'And that would be helpful, but what about the next day and the day after that?' Sister Agnes asked. 'How can we help these countries in the longer term?'

Another girl put her hand up. 'Charities, Sister?'

'Yes, charities, and we all give money to charities, don't we? We have collections at school sometimes, where the money we make goes straight to charities. How *can* charities help a place like Uganda though?'

'Help them plant more crops,' someone suggested.

'Increase access to water,' someone else suggested.

'Yes,' Sister Agnes said, nodding, 'water is important. Crops die without irrigation and people need water to drink.'

'Sister,' Ursula said, 'if women can't use contraception, how can they stop getting pregnant? It must be hard having babies if you know you can't feed them.'

Sister Agnes turned back to the board. 'There's a method people can use to stop pregnancies that the church does allow, but I'm not going to discuss that with you now.' She drew two arrows coming from the word 'charity' on the board and wrote 'crops' next to one arrow and 'irrigation' next to another.

The direction Sister Agnes was pointing the lesson towards was being re-set by us, much as she tried to keep it on track. Susan Leighton put her hand up. 'I think another thing Jesus would be concerned about is the way protesters are behaving about the Springbok Tour. They're doing stupid stuff, like last week they took over the Canterbury Rugby Football Union and re-named it the South African Embassy for the afternoon. They lied to the guy who worked there and asked him to help with something outside, then locked the doors on him and barricaded themselves in. That's not right.'

Sister Agnes folded her arms. 'Well, there are two sides to that story, Susan. Let's think about this a little more deeply. Does anyone know anything more about that incident?'

I put my hand up. Rewi's mum had told me about the people who had taken over the rugby union office in Christchurch. She said their group was called 'Action Against the Tour' and she told me facts behind their protest. 'They did it on June 16th because hundreds of black school children in a town called Soweto in South Africa were killed by the police on that date in 1976. The children were protesting because they were forced to speak only Afrikaans at school. They didn't want to only be allowed to speak the Dutch settlers' language.'

'Yes, but it's not very Christian treating the rugby union people like that,' Susan said. 'It's not something Jesus would approve of.' Susan jutted out her chin as she spoke.

'What about police killing hundreds of black school children?' I said. 'That's not very Christian.'

'I think we should concentrate on what's happening here, in New Zealand, not what's going on in other countries,' Susan said.

'Susan,' Sister Agnes said. 'New Zealand signed an agreement with other Commonwealth prime ministers and presidents, in which we committed to avoid playing sport with South Africa. The agreement was called, "The Gleneagles Agreement" because it was signed in the Gleneagles Hotel in Scotland. We have not honoured that agreement by allowing the Springboks to come here to play.'

Everyone was silent for a moment. Sister Agnes never took sides. Maybe she surprised herself too because she quickly added, 'Goodness, we've gone way off topic.'

I didn't want to leave it at that though. 'Sister, those people who protested in Christchurch were mostly Catholic,' I said. 'They believed they were doing God's work, trying to make people aware of how bad things are in South Africa. That's a good thing, isn't it?'

'That *is* a good thing, Eliza, but I'm going to move us back to our original topic.'

Lucy Jensen put her hand up. She was very short and thin, and barely spoke in class.

'Yes, Lucy?' Sister Agnes asked, probably hoping that Lucy might get us back onto the topic of how charities could help African countries.

'My dad's a policeman,' Lucy said softly. 'He's a bit nervous about the way protesters might behave if the tour goes ahead.'

Sister Agnes adjusted her veil. 'Yes, I imagine he is,' she said. 'The tour may not go ahead, Lucy.'

'There's another huge march on July the third,' Lucy said, 'a big mobilisation like the one on May the first.'

'I'm sure your father will be okay,' Sister Agnes said. 'I think we might do a bit of silent writing now, girls. I'm going to give you the topic. Get your pens out. Right, here we go.'

On the board, Sister Agnes wrote, 'How I think charities should spend money in famine-stricken Africa'. She made her way to her desk. 'Off you go, girls. At least one paragraph, please.'

Kalāsia nudged me and pointed at Sister Agnes, who was sitting at her desk, looking down into her lap. 'She's praying,' Kalāsia said.

'Maybe,' I said, 'or maybe she's just thinking.'

'She's praying,' Kalāsia said firmly.

I wrote the topic into my Christian Living exercise book and thought of Susan Leighton's jutted-out chin. She didn't understand why those people were protesting. Kalāsia had begun to write. I watched her brown fingers holding the pen as it swept along the lines on the page. If Kalāsia and I were in South Africa, we wouldn't be sitting together. We wouldn't even go to the same school. The thought of never knowing Kalāsia made me want to grab her hand and squeeze it. I wanted to tell her I was glad she'd insisted on plaiting my hair and that she came to my house every morning before school to chat and drink tea with me. I stared at my page until the angry pulsing in my head stopped and then I began to write. After a feeble attempt at a first sentence, I glanced up at Sister Agnes. She was still looking down into her lap.

CHAPTER 16
SNAPSHOTS
IN THE LAUNDRY

Every time we passed the small shop on the way to Rewi's house, I insisted on stopping to buy an ice cream, because the grocer rolled the largest scoops I'd ever seen. Rewi complained that ice cream made his teeth hurt, but I was never sympathetic. I told him that if I could support him while he played Space Invaders, the least he could do was support me with ice cream. I told him it was good for him, because it had milk in it, so it was full of protein.

A police car was parked a couple of houses down from Rewi's house. The blond policeman was there, but the one with the eczema wasn't. It was Saturday afternoon, so maybe it was his day off. Instead, another police officer stayed in the car, while the blond one stepped out. 'Afternoon,' he said. 'Another ice cream today?'

'Ignore him,' Rewi muttered. 'He thinks he's being friendly. It's their new strategy, but we all know he's just a dick.'

We walked past the police officer and turned into Rewi's house. I didn't stop to gaze even momentarily at the Māori flag on the letterbox or the koru painted onto the veranda. I walked inside then closed the door behind me.

Rewi's mother, Mere, came out of the darkroom that she no longer used. She developed her photos at a couple of other secret locations now and kept them there so that the police wouldn't find them if they searched the house. 'Kia ora, young people,' she said, kissing us both on the cheek. 'Good to see you, Liza. Barely seen my own kids over the last six weeks, but things are a bit less chaotic at the moment.'

'The police were trying to be friendly again,' Rewi said.

'Ignore them,' Mere said. 'They're trying to engage us in conversation now, Liza, so we tell the kids to say nothing and just walk past. I guess it's an improvement on having to tell them our name and address all the time.'

'We're going to a party tonight,' Rewi said. 'Remember I told you?'

Mere nodded. 'Yes, yes.' She began to walk down the hallway to the kitchen. 'You walking there?'

'Yep.' Rewi nudged me and winked. 'We'd better eat something, or we'll get drunk.'

Mere turned around. 'Beg your pardon?'

'We need to eat so we don't get drunk,' Rewi said. He kept a straight face for a few seconds as Mere's eyes widened, then a smile broke out. 'Man, you are so easy to razz, Mum.'

'Well, I was about to say that I doubt you'd get drunk on two bottles of beer, which is all your father said you could have,' Mere said.

'What? He said he'd give me half a dozen to take!'

'You and I both know that's not true,' Mere laughed as she opened the pantry door. 'Your dad's taken the kids to see Nana and they're having dinner there. What have we got in the cupboard?'

'We can make it, Mere,' I said.

'Course you can. You could make toasted cheese sandwiches. There's some onion and tomato if you want to add them too.'

'Sounds good to me,' I said. 'Hey, have you got any new photos?'

Mere nodded, closing the pantry door and lowering her voice. 'I'm keeping the negatives and the full sets of photos at a secret address. The police follow me to a friend's house, where I leave the negatives and photos, then her grandmother, who looks very innocent, picks them up from there and takes them to another location. The dark room's in a different place altogether. It's all pretty crazy, but I have to take precautions. I could ruin things for the anti-tour movement if the police get hold of these photos.'

'But have you still got copies in the laundry?' I whispered.

Mere nodded. 'They're in the usual hiding place.' She picked up a stool. 'Come and have a look.'

Rewi and I followed Mere into the laundry. She climbed onto the stool, just as Rewi had last time, and lifted the overflowing basket of rags off the box where the photo album was hidden. Rewi took the box from her and carefully removed the lid, placing the album on the benchtop next to the sink. He flicked past the bits I'd already seen. 'Here's the mobilisation,' he whispered, 'the march we went on.'

I nodded. There were photos of placards and signs, of faces caught in a moment of yelling or chanting. There were photos of the speakers on stage in Aotea Square.

None of us spoke as Rewi flicked through these. Then, he turned a page and I said, 'Stop. What's . . .?' I leaned in to look more closely, reading the explanation underneath aloud. 'The Canterbury Rugby Football Union became the Black South African Embassy for one afternoon on the 16th of June, to commemorate the killing of Soweto school children on this date five years ago.' I looked at the photos of a black embassy banner across the scaffolding in front of the building, of people chained together in an office and of police battering through a glass panel in a door. I thought of Susan Leighton in Christian Living saying how unfair this protest had been and felt irritation swell inside me.

I turned the page. 'What's this?' There were photos of young people advancing towards people dressed in police uniforms. Then a photo of guns raised and some people on the ground. 'Is this in Aotea Square?'

'Yes,' Mere whispered. 'The students at Auckland Metropolitan College acted out the Soweto student protests.'

I turned the page and stopped. A student had picked up another student, who was pretending to be unconscious, and was turning away from the police.

'It was very powerful,' Mere said. 'I had to keep wiping tears from my eyes so I could see through the lense properly. Merata Mita will have the whole thing on film. She's making a documentary on the tour and, like me, she has police watching her house.'

'This is the kind of thing *our* school should be doing,' I said. 'Instead, we talk about charity and do nothing.'

'Well, be comforted by the fact that the churches are pretty active in the protest movement,' Mere said.

I nodded, closing the album and putting it carefully back into the box. Rewi put the lid back on and climbed onto the stool to hide it away again.

'There are church people involved in lots of small, on-going protests,' Mere continued. 'Every week there are protests outside businesses that have connections with South Africa, like Rothmans and the South British Insurance company. There was a march to Mount Eden Prison to support Māori activists, members of the Waitangi Action Committee, who'd been arrested. I took a photo of the police blocking the marchers from entering Boston Road. Church groups are involved in all of those protests, Liza.'

'It's just that we do nothing about it at school,' I said. 'We talk about poverty and inequality in countries, but we don't *do* anything about it.'

Mere put her arm around me, and we walked back into the kitchen. 'Liza, there's lots more to be done yet. Don't get too despondent. The mobilisation didn't cancel the tour as we'd hoped, but there's the July 3rd mobilisation coming up. If that doesn't cancel the tour, things will escalate and, trust me, church members will be involved.'

Rewi followed us in. 'I'm going to make toasted cheese sammies,' he said. 'Want one, Liza? Mum?'

'Yes, please,' we chorused.

'Different topic now, Liza,' Mere said. 'Show me that gorgeous top under your jacket.'

It was my off-the-shoulder top. 'I think it might be too showy,' I said, slipping my black jacket off my shoulders. My cheeks felt warm.

Mere smiled. 'Not at all.'

From the corner of my eye, I noticed Rewi look at me, then turn away to get the cheese out of the fridge.

CHAPTER 17
WOLF'S TEETH

Ursula lived at the bottom of a driveway that had houses off it in different directions along each side. As we walked down to her house, 'London Calling' by The Clash and the sound of people yelling reverberated through the night air.

People spilled out onto the driveway from the party, which was in the garage underneath the house. Inside, people were jammed against each other, yelling, dancing, drinking and smoking. Someone was laughingly shouting, 'Fuck off! Fuck off!'

Rewi reached into his Bob Marley bag, pulled out a bottle of beer, flicked the lid off with a bottle opener and passed it to me.

'Thanks,' I said.

I could see Ursula's tall, blond brothers, male versions of their sister. One of them was guzzling beer from a bottle, and the other was yelling at some people over the music. I scanned the rest of the room but couldn't see Harry.

'There's Ursula,' Rewi said, motioning over to a back corner of the garage.

Ursula was leaning over Josh, who was sitting on a chair. She had a ciggie in one hand and a beer in the other. She bent down and kissed him, then stood up and swayed to the music, puffing on her cigarette. Her tight faded jeans, ankle boots and broderie anglaise camisole top made her look like a singer in a rock band. I looked down at my off-the-shoulder top. If only I could look like that.

'Shall we say hi?' Rewi asked.

I nodded.

We squeezed past people until Ursula saw us and lifted her beer bottle in greeting, yelling, 'Hey, you two!' Her dark red lipstick had left a ring around the bottle, and her thick eyeliner was slightly smudged at the side of one eye. She was already a bit drunk, which only seemed to add to the overall Debbie Harry effect. She walked towards me and hugged me. 'You're here!'

'Yep, we made it,' I yelled over the music.

Rewi lifted his eyebrows at Josh in acknowledgement, and Josh handed him a beer.

'Harry's here somewhere,' Ursula said. 'He's been pining for you.' Her eyes swept across the room. 'There he is, talking with my brother, Kev. Come on, I'll take you over.' She began to pull me through the partying crowd. I turned back to Rewi and mouthed, 'Harry', pointing with my free hand. Rewi nodded.

'Too Much too Young' by The Specials came on, and everyone began to dance and belt out the lyrics. Ursula propelled me through to Harry, who was sitting on a stool by the wall having a yelled conversation with her brother.

Harry stood up when he saw me, called my name and pulled me to him, his arm resting around my shoulder. 'Have you met Kev, Ursula's big brother?'

I shook my head. Kev's eyes rested on me. They were glazed, as if he wasn't really seeing me at all.

'Liza's in my class at school,' Ursula said.

'Ah, little sister's buddy,' he said. 'She's turning sixteen. How the hell did that happen?'

I shrugged my shoulders, unsure of how to answer and drank from my bottle of beer.

'Look at you, drinking beer!' Harry said, as he dragged on his cigarette. 'What would the nuns say?'

I raised my eyebrows at him. 'The nuns don't know.'

He smiled at me and kissed me on the forehead.

'Come and dance with me and Josh over there,' Ursula said.

'Come on, Harry!'

We made our way back through the dancing. There were girls from Ursula's old class here. I often passed them in the school corridors and said hi, but I didn't know most of their names. Some of them were dancing in a group and pulled Ursula in to hug her as we passed, so, with Harry behind me, I kept walking over to Josh and Rewi.

'Didn't realise you brought your mate,' Harry said.

'Who?' I yelled over the music.

Harry put his hand on my arm. 'Your mate,' he said, nodding towards Rewi.

I stopped beside him. 'Rewi? Ursula invited him too.'

Harry nodded at Rewi, who said, 'How's it going?' in response.

Josh handed Harry a beer and looked at my nearly empty bottle. 'Want another one?'

I tipped the last dregs of my beer into my mouth and handed the empty bottle to Josh. 'Thanks!'

The Rolling Stones had come on and everyone was yelling the lyrics to 'She's So Cold'. The whole room was dancing. Josh and some of the other guys around us joined in.

Ursula swayed over to us and grabbed the bottle of beer out of Harry's hand. 'Give me a swig of that.'

Harry shrugged, as she guzzled his beer down. 'Finish it off, why don't you?'

Ursula laughed and play-punched him in the stomach. 'Got a smoke too?' Her words were slurred.

'You a bit pissed?' Harry asked.

'Just a bit.' Ursula laughed and leaned up towards Harry's lighter, sucking on her cigarette until it lit up. She breathed the smoke slowly out of her nose, gazing around the room.

It was like a movie: watching Ursula, feeling electric guitars claw at my eardrums as everyone danced, watching Ursula's brothers make their way through the crowd of people, talking to someone here, slapping someone on the back there.

'What's your other brother's name?' I yelled to Ursula.

'Kev?'

'No, the other one.'

'Reece,' she answered. 'Have you seen his tattoo?'

I shook my head.

'It's on his bicep, a wolf's head with its mouth wide open, and sharp teeth, like its growling.' Ursula stumbled slightly as she spoke to me. I grabbed her arm, and she began to laugh. I joined in.

The music changed to 'Roxanne' by The Police, and Sting's haunting voice filled the room. The mood changed and the wild dancing slowed. People began to sway and sing the lyrics but were coming in too early for the chorus, which I knew would annoy Rewi. I looked over at him and we smiled at each other.

Harry pulled me to him and wrapped his arms around me. I felt warm, pliable, as if everything was simple and easy and I didn't need to worry about anything anymore. I rested my head on Harry's shoulder and we swayed together. He rubbed his hand up and down my back, gently touching my shoulders, before circling back down again. I thought of my off-the-shoulder top. 'I'm wearing my special top,' I said.

'It's beautiful,' Harry said, 'like you.'

'I bought it for you,' I said.

'Thank you, but it's really not my size.'

I snorted into Harry's neck. 'You're very funny. You're like the funniest person I know, apart from Rewi.'

Harry stiffened, and I realised I'd said something wrong, something that had changed the good feelings between us. 'He's actually not looking too happy right now,' Harry said.

'What?' I lifted my head from Harry's shoulder and saw Rewi was yelling over the music at Ursula's two brothers. The wolf head tattoo moved as Reece, the brother I hadn't met, jabbed his forefinger into the air as he yelled back at Rewi. The sharp teeth seemed to reach forward, as if about to sink into something.

Both brothers looked angry. One of them pointed outside. I turned to see two young Māori guys standing at the open garage door. I pulled away from Harry. 'What's going on?'

Harry grabbed my arm. 'Just leave it!'

'No,' I said, pushing my way towards Rewi.

'They're fucken gate-crashers,' Kev was yelling.

'All I'm trying to say is,' Rewi yelled over the music, 'if they were white dudes, you wouldn't have noticed them. They're not doing any harm.'

'They *are* doing harm!' Reece yelled. 'They're not welcome here, fucken hori gate-crashers.'

'I'm Māori,' Rewi yelled at them. 'You calling me a hori too?'

'Rewi,' I said. 'Let's . . .'

'You can piss off out of here too,' Reece yelled at Rewi.

Rewi turned to me. 'Come on, let's go.'

'Tell them to piss off,' Reece yelled after Rewi, 'before I smash their faces in.'

I took Rewi by the arm and pushed through the crowd. Someone tried to speak to me, but I kept going.

When we were outside, Rewi said to the young Māori guys, 'You'd better get out of here. Some racist arseholes in there want to beat your heads in.'

One of the guys said, 'We just heard the music. Thought we'd have a look.'

'Don't go in,' I said.

They started to walk back up the driveway with us. I realised I'd left my jacket but wasn't going back in to get it. I hadn't even said goodbye to Ursula. Did she even know what had happened? I doubted it. She'd been drunkenly dancing with Josh. Led Zeppelin's 'Black Dog' blared from the garage behind us.

'Hey!'

I turned. It was Harry. He had my jacket in his hand. 'You left this,' he said, 'and, in case you didn't realise, you left me!'

'Sorry!' I said. 'We had to get out of there.'

'Ursula's brothers are pissed,' Harry said.

'And racist,' Rewi added.

'Yeah, well, that too,' Harry said.

The other two guys continued up the driveway. Rewi, Harry and I faced each other.

'I'll walk you home,' Harry said.

'It's okay,' I said. 'I'll walk with Rewi. We live near each other. I'll phone you tomorrow.'

'I can walk you home,' Harry said again.

'I think Rewi needs . . .'

Rewi interrupted me. 'Just walk home with him.'

'Let's all walk together,' I said to Harry.

'Nah,' Harry said. 'I'll let you two be together. I'll go back into the party.' He tossed my jacket at me and turned away.

'Harry, don't be stupid!' I said, as he walked back down the driveway. 'Harry, come on!'

'Just walk with him,' Rewi said again.

'I'm walking home with you,' I said. 'Let's go.'

It began to drizzle, and car lights glanced over the greasy, wet street. We didn't speak for a while.

'Knew there was something about her,' Rewi said.

'Who?'

'Ursula.'

'She didn't know what was happening.'

'She's probably just like them, Liza.'

I lifted my head and let the soft rain fall onto my face. An image of the 'Keep NZ White' graffiti on the desk came into my mind. I shook my head, as if willing it away. People don't always have to be like their families.

When we reached my house, I could hear Sal barking inside. I asked Rewi if he wanted to come in for a while, but he shook his head. 'Need to get home.'

'I'll phone you tomorrow then.'

'Yep,' he said, and he walked away.

I stood watching him grow smaller as he made his way down our street, and I didn't stop watching him until I heard Mum telling Sal to be quiet and opening our front door.

CHAPTER 18
TONGAN CHOIR

The next morning, I lay in bed until the last minute before getting up for mass. I'd been awake for hours, since before the birds had started singing and, in my mind, I'd gone over the night before a hundred times. It was like a bad dream. What had begun as fun had all gone so wrong. I remembered Ursula's brothers' faces filled with anger and hatred, the way Rewi had stood up to them, how Harry had thrown my jacket to me and turned away, but mostly I remembered the look on Rewi's face as we walked home. I hadn't known how to fix things for him, and I still didn't.

It was drizzling, but Mum insisted we walk to church anyway. She fished some umbrellas out of the cupboard in the hallway, which we called 'the messy cupboard', and told us the walk would do us good. Some of the umbrellas had spokes sticking out, but Mum said they'd do, so we headed off. The whole way, Jo and Pete debated whether Sal was dreaming when she barked during her sleep. I couldn't concentrate on the conversation, so I didn't take part.

As we approached the church, the statue of Mary looked down on me. Her gentle eyes and hint of a smile made me wish I could just gaze at her for a while, so that the sense of calm in her expression might fill me. Instead, I followed my family into the church.

Moments after we sat down in one of the pews at the back, the entrance hymn began. It was nothing like any music I'd ever heard before. I strained to see who was singing, but it was impossible to see with so many people in front of us.

Mum nudged me. 'It's Kalāsia's Tongan choir. She phoned to tell you last night, but you were at Ursula's party. I meant to pass on the message, but completely forgot.' She frowned. 'You okay?'

'Yep,' I said. 'Just tired after last night.'

'Somehow I get the feeling the party didn't go so well,' Mum whispered.

'It was okay,' I said, but Mum saw the tear slide down my cheek. I wiped it away. Mum turned back to the front of the church, but she put her hand over mine and kept it there for a few minutes.

The men's voices were deep, and the women's voices swung over the top with melodies and harmonies that filled the church. It was like biting into a chocolate éclair: the taste was so good, but it would end soon, and I wanted to hold onto the sensation for as long as possible.

When the hymn finished, Father Luke began the mass. I closed my eyes, thinking about the night before. I should have done things differently. I hadn't been a good friend. I could have stepped up and told Ursula's brothers to stop speaking to Rewi like that, so that he wasn't trying to defend himself alone. Rewi was my best friend, so I should have told them to shut their ugly, nasty mouths.

Soon the Tongan choir sang again. The longing in their voices hooked into my own sadness so that tears started again. This time, Mum put her arm around me, and I rested my head against her. If I couldn't sit with Mary outside, this was the next best thing.

When it was time for the homily, Father Luke stood up, took off his glasses and wiped them with a cloth. Jamming them back on, he flicked over a couple of pages on a pad in front of him. How many notes had he written? How long was this sermon going to be? I groaned inwardly and closed my eyes.

I wanted to drift away and think of Harry's green eyes, how they creased up as he laughed at something I'd said, but Harry was unhappy with me. The night before, he'd wanted me to leave Rewi to walk home alone, which I couldn't do. Maybe I wasn't such a bad friend. Not wanting to cry again, I sat up straight and decided to focus on Father Luke's homily.

Father Luke put his notes aside and looked over his glasses at us.

'I'm not going to say what I thought I'd say. I'm going to talk about the importance of reflecting on our own behaviour. I'm going to talk about this jolly old Springbok Tour that still seems to be going ahead. I ask you to think not just about the fact that black people in South Africa cannot vote or live with dignity alongside white South Africans, but to also think about our own country, our own back yard.'

I looked along the pew at Pete, who was gazing up the front of the church. Father Luke had used the same words as the woman who'd had the banana skin thrown at her. She'd said to look in our own back yards.

'What do *you* do to oppose racism in New Zealand?' Father Luke asked. 'Jesus stood up for people that society treated badly. He befriended lepers, and he treated Mary Magdalene, a prostitute, as his equal. What do *you* do?'

Father Luke coughed and sipped from a glass of water on the lectern. He ran his hand through his grey hair, casting his eyes over the congregation. 'I have heard something that quite frankly horrifies me. One of the members of this Tongan choir told me that he was walking at night recently, when a car of young men shot at him with a slug gun, hurling racist terms at him. This . . .' Father Luke stopped and looked around the congregation, then continued, 'this is in New Zealand!'

Kalāsia would be listening to this, I thought. She'd be sitting up the front with the choir thinking of police who come into houses with dogs and this would be another thing she'd worry about now.

'The man had to be taken into hospital to have a pellet removed from his leg. He is here today and is alive and well, thankfully, but who are the parents of these young men? They are someone's sons.' Father Luke swept his hand out towards all of us. 'I ask you again, what are you doing? What are you not doing? When are you not speaking up? When must you speak up? You are not Christian just by name; you are Christian by action.' Father Luke straightened the microphone. 'I will say that again. You are not Christian just by name; you are Christian by action. Now, let us stand and proclaim our commitment to our Catholic faith.'

I stood and mumbled the words, but I felt sick in my stomach. It was as if Father Luke had been there last night, as if he'd seen how I stood there, uncertain of what to do, trying to get Rewi to leave with me, just wanting to get away. Soon, the choir sang again, and their voices were like the sea, pulling me with them.

After mass, the choir followed the priest and altar boys out of the church, while we remained seated. The women wore fine, woven mats over their dresses, tied around their waists, and the men wore them over long black or grey material. Some fine mats were plain, but others had colour and shapes on them. Kalāsia passed me and smiled. I lifted my hand, giving her a small wave.

Outside the church, she came straight over to me. 'Did you like the singing?'

'I loved it.' I reached out and touched the finely woven mat tied around her waist.

'It's a ta'ovala,' Kalāsia said. 'I'm dressed the traditional Tongan way.'

'You look beautiful,' I said.

'You ...' Kalāsia stopped and looked closely at me. 'Tomorrow, we'll have a cup of tea and a talanoa, while I plait your hair.'

'Talanoa?'

'A good chat,' Kalāsia said. 'That's what you need, Liza, a talanoa.'

Kalāsia's sister, 'Amanaki, called out to her in Tongan.

'Got to go now,' Kalāsia said. 'We're going to my uncle's house to have food, Tongan food. I'll try to save some and bring it to your house tomorrow morning.' Kalāsia hugged me. Her hair smelled like some sort of perfume. She squeezed my hand. 'See you tomorrow.'

I didn't feel much like eating when we got home from mass. Mum asked what was troubling me, and I told her that some people had said racist things to Rewi and that we'd left the party because of it. I didn't tell her it was Ursula's brothers who'd hurled abuse at Rewi. It was like a dirty secret. I wasn't sure if I was trying to protect Ursula, or whether I just didn't want to deal with who she might be. I liked her craziness, her wildness. She made school more bearable.

Mum suggested we go over to Rewi's after lunch. Sal needed a walk, and Mum wanted to pop in to say hi to Mere and Tipene.

The drizzle had turned into rain, and we huddled under our umbrellas while Sal jogged ahead. I didn't buy an ice cream at the dairy this time. For the first time ever, my stomach rebelled at the thought of it.

Rewi's mum opened the door before we'd knocked. I wondered if Mum had phoned her to say we were coming. 'Kia ora,' Mere said. 'Come in. Bring Sal up on to the veranda. It's much nicer for her than waiting in the rain.'

We left our umbrellas outside and made our way down the hallway to the kitchen. Marama and Nikau's laughter trickled out from under their bedroom door. 'I've told them to play in their room for a while,' Mere said. 'Gives us more chance to chat.' So, Mum had phoned them!

Tipene and Rewi were sitting at the table. There were biscuits on a plate. Mere flicked the kettle on and asked who wanted coffee or tea.

Rewi looked at me. 'Hi,' he said. His eyes didn't flicker with laughter the way they usually did when he saw me.

'Hi,' I said.

'Rewi told us about last night,' Tipene said. 'Sounds like you both had a shocking experience. We're so disappointed that this happened to you.'

'Me?' I asked. 'It didn't happen to me. It happened to Rewi.'

'Yes, it did, but it must have been a shock for you too,' Tipene said.

'I didn't do anything to stop them from saying . . .'

'What could you have done?' Tipene interrupted. 'What could you have said that would've stopped them, Liza?'

'I could have yelled at them. I should have told them to stop.'

'They wouldn't have stopped, Liza,' Tipene said. 'They'd been drinking and who knows if they'd taken some drug too. They were not safe to be around, and you got Rewi out of there.'

Mere brought cups of tea to us and joined us at the table.

'But Rewi's angry with me.' I glanced at Rewi, who was staring at his lap. 'I don't blame him.'

Rewi looked up at me. 'I'm not angry with you.'

'Tell her what you told us, son,' Tipene said.

Rewi sniffed and twisted his cup one way then another. 'I feel like a dick. Feel stupid.'

No one spoke. Rewi kept twisting his cup this way, then that. The tea looked as though it was going to spill over the top, like a small tidal wave.

'You didn't do anything stupid, Rewi,' I said. 'You were standing up for those guys outside and for yourself.'

'It was embarrassing, humiliating, the way they spoke to me.' Rewi sniffed again and wiped at his eye with the palm of his hand.

Mere reached over and put her hand on Rewi's. 'It can make you feel like that, son, like you're nothing because of your race, but you know you are the opposite of nothing. You are something, Rewi. You are someone.'

Mum patted Rewi's shoulder. 'You're a huge someone to Liza. You're her closest friend, and you're part of our family too, Rewi.'

'I wish I'd yelled at him and told him to leave you alone, to leave those boys they wanted to beat up alone,' I said.

'Nah,' Rewi said. 'Dad's right. They'd have just got angrier and we might've all got our faces smashed in.'

'Stop being so tough on yourself, Liza,' Tipene said. 'You got Rewi out of a dangerous situation. That party was not the place to debate their racist opinions. We're glad you got Rewi out of there.'

I looked at Rewi. 'I'm sorry.'

'I'm sorry too,' Rewi said.

'Neither of you need to be sorry,' Mere said.

'Well, I am,' I said.

'So am I.' Rewi lifted one eyebrow at me.

'Not as sorry as I am,' I said.

'Sorrier than that.'

'Okay,' Mum interrupted. 'I think we've resolved this.'

Mere nodded, laughing. 'Back to our old selves, by the looks of it.'

Tipene stood up. 'The people who need to be sorry are the young men who were abusive to you, Rewi. Kia kaha, son.' He picked up his cup. 'Anyone for a refill?'

Later that afternoon, I phoned Harry. I'd been nervous about it all day. He hadn't called me to say sorry for pushing me to decide between him and Rewi, which is what I'd hoped he'd do. Even though it seemed unfair, I was worried he was still angry with me. What would he have done if *his* best friend had been treated like that?

Harry's mum answered the phone. She yelled for him, then the phone made a clunking sound like she'd dumped it down on a table. The phone crackled as Harry picked it up. 'Hello.'

'Hi,' I said.

Harry was quiet.

'You okay?' I asked.

'Why wouldn't I be?'

'Well, last night, you seemed angry.'

'You didn't want me to walk you home.' Harry must have put his hand over the mouthpiece, because I heard him say in a muffled voice, 'I'm on the phone, Sophie. I'll be there in a minute.'

'Do you need to go?' I asked.

'Nah, Sophie just wants me to watch something on TV with her. She's okay. She can wait.'

'I did want you to walk with me. I just wanted to walk with Rewi too. I couldn't leave him alone after what happened.'

'Was it really that big a deal?' Harry asked. 'They were just being wankers. I try to keep away from Ursula's brothers, but they seem to think I like hanging out with them. Living in the same street, I've seen them bully a few people. Once, it was an Indian kid. They threw his schoolbag into the bushes at the top of their driveway. They're just up themselves. Think they're better than everyone else. Rewi shouldn't let it get to him.'

'He's okay now, I think,' I said.

'You went to see him today?' Harry asked.

'Yeah, I was worried about him.'

'So, you see him a lot?'

My hand tightened around the phone. 'Guess so.'

'You sure you don't fancy him?'

'I don't fancy him. He's my friend.'

'Yeah, well, I've never come across a guy and a girl being friends like you two,' Harry said. 'It's pretty strange.'

My knuckles were white. 'He's my friend,' I said again.

There was a silence. I could hear a TV in the distance through the phone.

'Want to go to another movie this weekend?' Harry asked.

'Okay.'

'Friday night?'

'I'm going on the protest march this Friday, y'know, the 3rd of July mobilisation.'

'Yeah, course,' Harry said. 'Want me to come?'

'If you want to,' I answered. I wasn't sure though. I felt uncomfortable when Harry and Rewi were together. It just wasn't fun like it would be on my own with Harry or on my own with Rewi.

'Okay, well, I'll meet you in there. Same place, same time? I won't be late this time.'

'Cool.' I softened my grip on the phone, watching the blood run back into my white fingers.

'Maybe catch you outside school.' Harry's voice lowered. 'Maybe get to kiss you behind some tree or building, where no one can see us, Liza.'

That familiar quiver trembled in my stomach. 'Maybe,' I said.

'Beautiful, Liza,' Harry whispered. 'My beautiful Liza.'

A young girl's voice called Harry's name.

'Gotta go,' Harry whispered. 'Bye, Liza.'

'Bye,' I said.

I stood up and pulled the phone out of my bedroom, then put it back on the phone table. I didn't know what to do next. Harry was like a warm flame sometimes, but he could also burn so fiercely that I wanted to step away from the heat. I thought of his green eyes, his sandy hair that hung halfway down his neck, his lips. My hand stayed on the phone, as if reluctant to move.

In the kitchen, Pete was saying there was nothing wrong with eating peanut butter from a spoon. Mum replied but it was hard to make out what she was saying. My stomach rumbled. I hadn't really eaten much for breakfast or lunch. I lifted my hand from the phone, let out a long breath and walked down the hallway to the kitchen.

CHAPTER 19
THE JULY MOBILISATION

It was Friday morning. Dad and Pete were standing at the kitchen bench drinking coffee and talking. I'd been slow to get out of bed, and Kalāsia had been unusually late. She quickly whipped my chaotic hair into shape because we had only ten minutes for our morning routine of tea and toast if we didn't want to end up on detention.

Dad was telling Pete about a South African man who was doing a speaking tour around New Zealand. His name was Donald Woods and he'd been the editor of a South African newspaper. Because he was a friend of Steve Biko's and his newspaper articles were against apartheid, he was put under house arrest.

'What does that mean exactly?' Pete asked.

'He wasn't allowed to leave his house and the police were watching his every move,' Dad said. 'His phone was bugged, but other scary stuff happened. Someone posted his six-year-old daughter a T-shirt that had been laced with some sort of acid and she was badly burned. When he realised his family was in danger, they escaped South Africa.'

'That poor little girl,' I said, pouring hot water over teabags, while Kalāsia buttered the toast.

'So, what does he say in his talks?' Pete asked.

'He talks about how black South Africans live in dire conditions under apartheid and how badly police treat them.'

'Steve Biko was murdered by the police,' I said, carrying our cups to the table.

'He was,' Dad said, 'and Donald Woods went to the morgue and took photos of his beaten, battered body. The photos are in a book he wrote a few years back, called *Biko*. They're horrific.'

'Why didn't you tell us you were going to his talk?' Pete asked. 'I'd have gone with you, if I'd known.'

'It was for work, so I didn't think to tell you.' Dad took a sip of his coffee. 'Andrew Molotsane's speaking at the march tonight. He's a black South African leader, who's been really involved in the trade union movement over there. I'm looking forward to hearing what he has to say.'

'I might not go on the march tonight,' Pete said.

'Come with me to hear John Osmers talk when he comes to Auckland,' Dad said. 'He's an Anglican minister, a Kiwi, who worked in South Africa, but had to leave because of his involvement in the anti-apartheid movement. After he moved to Zambia, someone sent him a parcel bomb and he lost one of his arms in the explosion.'

'Can we not talk about this while we're having breakfast?' I said.

Dad looked over at me and Kalāsia eating our toast. 'How did we get onto this topic, Pete?'

'I was telling you I don't think I'll go on the march tonight,' Pete said.

'Again?' I said, looking at Pete. 'Why not?'

'It's just, how do I keep playing rugby and be anti-tour at the same time? I don't know so I'm . . . I guess I'm avoiding it.' Pete put his coffee down and scratched his head.

'You could stop playing rugby,' I said. 'Hato Petera College is going to pull its rugby teams out of the secondary schools rugby competition if the tour goes ahead. Why don't you do the same?'

'Hato Petera!' Pete gasped. 'Did their teachers force them to pull out?'

'No,' Dad said, 'the majority of the senior students voted to pull out if the tour goes ahead.'

'What about other Catholic schools?' Pete asked.

Kalāsia spoke up. 'Saint Francis's School is still playing rugby. My brothers haven't mentioned pulling teams out.'

'That's good,' Pete said.

'Why is that good?' I asked him. 'They're a Catholic school just like Hato Petera. They should pull out! It's not fair that it's left to the Māori boys' school to make a stand on the tour.'

'It's my old school,' Pete said. 'I want them to win.'

I shook my head at Pete, pouring the dregs of my tea into the sink. 'Pete, there's an ex-All Black who's an anti-tour protester. He's even a member of HART now. What's his name, Dad?'

'Bob Burgess,' Dad replied. 'He refused to trial for the All Black team that toured South Africa in 1970 because he was anti-apartheid. On that tour Māori or Pacific Island players were labelled as 'honorary whites' so they didn't have to follow the rules of apartheid. Burgess isn't the only one though. Graham Mourie, the All Blacks' captain, has refused to play the Springboks in this tour, and Bruce Robertson's another All Black who's pulled out.'

'But will they ever get to be an All Black again?' asked Pete.

'Bob Burgess went on to play seven tests for the All Blacks even though he'd refused to go on that tour,' Dad said. 'And I'll bet Graham Mourie will play for the All Blacks again too.'

'Give up rugby in protest, Pete,' I chipped in.

'How's me giving up rugby going to make a difference? It's not going to be in the news! It'll just mean that I miss out on doing what I love.'

'Black South Africans are missing out on a lot more under apartheid,' I said.

'Let's go,' Kalāsia said. 'We're going to be late and, anyway, you two are starting to fight.'

'Wise words, Kalāsia,' Dad said. 'You'll have to run now. You've got five minutes before the bell goes.'

That evening, I wore a second-hand lace top that I'd bought from an op shop. It reminded me of the broderie anglaise camisole that Ursula had been wearing at her party. When I'd tried it on, it looked almost as good as hers, and it had only cost a dollar. It looked good with my jeans, especially once I put on a bit of eyeliner and clipped back my wild hair. It was cold again, so the top was hidden under a sweatshirt and a big jacket. I pinned my HART badge onto my jacket.

Pete was staying home again, like he had for the first mobilisation. This time though, Mum was frustrated with him. She told him not only to do the dishes but to sweep and mop the floor as well.

'I was going to chill out and watch something dumb like *The Dukes of Hazzard*,' he said.

'Well, you can, but you'll need to do those jobs too,' Mum said.

'Do you hate me for not coming on the march?' Pete asked.

'I could never hate you,' Mum replied. 'I love you, Pete, but I'm disappointed in your decision.'

Mum walked out of the house, leaving the front door open for me, but I was still sliding my boots over my jeans, so I saw Pete after she said that. He looked as if someone had punched him. He buckled over slightly, and his face scrunched up as if he was in pain.

Harry was waiting outside the Central Post Office, as planned. He smiled when he spotted me making my way through the crowd of people to get to him.

'You made it,' I said.

'Yep.' Harry pulled me towards him and kissed me. My family and Rewi's were not too far away so, after a moment, I gently drew away. Even though they were looking in the other direction, listening to the speakers, it wasn't worth the risk.

Harry leaned over and spoke in my ear. 'I could do much more of that.'

I smiled. 'So could I.'

'I could do so much more *than* that too,' Harry said.

Heat spread across my cheeks, but thankfully, Harry couldn't see them in the darkness.

'Would you like that?' Harry asked.

'What?' I asked.

'Do you want to do more than just kiss?'

I hadn't been prepared for this question. I'd expected that it might come up some time, but we were in the middle of loud speeches and a crowd of people cheering around us. 'Ah, I . . . maybe.'

Harry took my hand. 'No pressure. Just wondering.'

'I need to go back to the others,' I said. 'They're up there somewhere.'

'Okay, let's go.'

Harry and I manoeuvred around people to get back to Mum, Tipene and the others. Rewi was the first to see Harry and he nodded at him, lifting his eyebrows. 'How's it?'

'Not bad,' Harry answered.

Mum smiled at Harry, yelling, 'Fantastic turnout.'

'Yeah, bigger crowd tonight,' Harry called back.

'Hope it's like this all over the country,' Mum continued. 'Hope protesters in small towns are okay too. They're the brave ones really, because some of those rural towns are rugby-mad.'

'Hadn't thought about that,' Harry said.

I pictured towns we'd driven through on family trips and imagined a few people with placards making their way up the main street, while others watched from the footpath, with hostile expressions on their faces.

On the stage, a young Māori woman was speaking. She looked like a teenager but was probably in her twenties. 'That's Rebecca Evans,' Mum said.

I was distracted by Harry's hand moving up and down my back. Rewi must have noticed it too, because he moved forward, next to Jo and her friends. Even through layers of clothing, Harry's hand felt warm. I wanted to turn to him, to move in closer, so I could feel more of his warmth. Instead, I forced myself to focus on Rebecca Evans, who was saying stuff that reminded me of Father Luke's sermon.

She said we can't argue for apartheid to come to an end in South Africa while ignoring the oppression of Māori in New Zealand. Her youthful face was serious, and her tone was angry. I thought of Ursula's party and how her brothers had treated Rewi. Once again, I wished I'd spoken out on Rewi's behalf. Here I was on this march, yet I hadn't challenged them at all; I'd just tried to get Rewi out of there. Rewi's parents told me I'd done the right thing, but somehow, in a deeper part of myself, I felt I had fallen short.

A tall, lean Pākehā man stood up to speak. I recognised him but wasn't sure where from.

Rewi turned and yelled, 'John Minto. Remember Mum's photo?'

I nodded. John Minto was the national organiser for HART. His mood felt urgent and serious. He said that this huge crowd sent a clear message to government that New Zealanders did not want this tour to go ahead. He added that if our government ignored this protest, it would regret doing so.

Rewi shuffled back beside me and said, 'You know what that means, eh? He's really saying that HART's prepared to protest more aggressively than this.'

'You mean, they might use violence?'

Rewi shrugged. 'Don't really know. Mum said they call it "non-violent direct action". They might disrupt the games, make it impossible for the teams to play.'

With his hand on my back, Harry gently pulled me more closely to him. I wanted to ask Rewi if he'd join those disruptive protests, the ones that stopped games, but he'd gone back up beside Jo and her friends.

Around us, the crowd was so large that there didn't seem to be a beginning or an end. It overflowed into the streets around the square. With Harry stroking my back and making comments into my ear, I hadn't noticed the placards like I had last time. Now, I studied the signs around me. Some just said who they represented, like the Auckland University Workers' sign and the NZ Public Service Association banner. One sign said, 'Tour Now — Pay Later' and another said, 'Block Boks'. A sign that stood out was 'A Night at the Racists'. Others simply stated, 'Apartheid Kills', 'Remember Soweto' and 'Fight Apartheid'.

On stage, a man introduced himself as the Right Reverend Godfrey Wilson, the assistant Anglican Bishop of Auckland.

I turned to Harry. 'Anglican ministers have strange titles. What does it mean if you're a "Right Reverend"?'

Harry pursed his lips. 'That you're not a wrong reverend.'

I laughed.

The reverend lifted his arms and waved them around as he spoke. People cheered and clapped. He said that if the Springboks came, we'd be putting a game before the basic human rights and freedoms of oppressed South Africans. The crowd roared. He went on to say that if we allowed the tour to go ahead, we would be showing the world that we signed international agreements but did not honour them if it didn't suit us.

I turned to Harry. 'He means the Gleneagles Agreement.'

'What?'

'We signed an agreement with other Commonwealth countries to say we wouldn't play sport with South Africa until they get rid of apartheid.'

Harry raised his eyebrows. 'You trying to impress me with your knowledge, Liza?'

'Our Christian Living teacher, Sister Agnes, told us that.'

'Don't get me onto the topic of Christian Living classes again!' Harry said.

I laughed.

The reverend had to raise his voice to be heard over the cheering crowd. He said that if the Springboks came, our country would be split in half, all because our government was too weak to stand up to the New Zealand rugby union. The cheers were deafening.

We started moving up Queen Street at about 8pm. There were many different groups marching, holding up banners to show who they were: people from trade unions, churches, student groups, Māori groups and women's groups. The chanting crowd surged forward towards Aotea Square.

Ahead of us, Marama slipped off Tipene's back to hold hands with me. 'Just in case a policeman tries to arrest me,' she said.

'Why, what have you done wrong?' Harry asked.

'Nothing!' Marama said, alarm in her voice.

'Just ignore him,' I said. 'He's teasing.'

In front, a group of young Māori people were chanting in te reo. I asked Marama if she knew what they were saying. She shrugged, then yelled to Tipene. 'Dad, what are they saying?'

Tipene fell back, with Nikau now on his back. 'They're saying: "Ka whawhai tonu mātou! Ake! Ake! Ake!" which means "We will fight on forever and ever and ever". They are the words of Rewi Maniapoto, one of the great leaders in the Waikato war. He was a brave warrior, who tried to stop land being stolen by the British. When he was told to surrender at Ōrākau, he said those words. They're on a banner up the front too.'

'So, he didn't win, Dad?' Marama asked.

'No, he didn't. They lost that land.' Tipene stroked Marama's cheek for a moment. 'The women were brave too, y'know. They stayed up on that pa site fighting even when the British army leaders suggested they leave. One of them, Ahumai Te Paerata, said, "Ki te mate nga tane, me mate ano nga wahine me nga tamariki", which means, "If the men die, the women and children must die also."'

'But they lost the land in the end.' Marama said. She looked up at me. 'Did you know about that, Liza?'

'About losing the land?'

Marama nodded.

'I know Māori people lost lots of land, but I didn't know about Ōrākau or that brave woman or that chief. He's got the same name as your big brother.'

Marama observed Rewi walking ahead. 'He's brave too, that's why.'

I followed her gaze. Rewi was talking to one of Jo's friends, yelling something over the music, lifting his hand in an expression of frustration maybe, or excitement. I remembered how he'd stood up to Ursula's brothers, even though they were taller and larger than he was. He was brave.

As if sensing that my thoughts were elsewhere, Harry tugged at my hand. We were turning into Aotea Square. Someone on the stage was directing people to squeeze in, to make room for the huge crowd. In front of us, Mum turned. I quickly dropped Harry's hand.

'You okay?' Mum called.

I gave her a thumbs-up sign. She turned back and said something to Tipene. He glanced back at me and smiled. Maybe Mum had seen me drop Harry's hand. My cheeks became hot. How embarrassing that they might both be laughing at me.

As the crowd pushed in together, Andrew Molotsane was introduced. He wore a long beige coat, and his eyes scanned the crowd. He was so excited at the huge number of people protesting that he ripped up his speech notes and instead spoke passionately about what this march meant. 'The great majority of New Zealand people want this tour to be stopped and, because of this, for the sake of freedom, this tour must be stopped. Muldoon must stop this tour!'

As the crowd cheered and clapped, it dawned on me that he'd never be allowed back in his own country again. I thought of Donald Woods, the newspaper editor who'd had to escape South Africa with his family. They must miss their home and friends and lots of little things too. I knew I would, like lying in bed on a summer's night, listening to crickets singing. I'd miss hearing that if I had to leave. I pictured Andrew Molotsane and Donald Woods standing very still sometimes, missing one small thing, maybe sighing at the memory, then moving on with the next thing to do.

Soon, Herbs, began to play. They were one of Rewi's favourite bands. He'd already been to the record shop and ordered their first album, which was being released in a couple of weeks. He swayed to their song, 'Azania', which he'd once explained was the original name for a big chunk of the African continent. Marama left my side to go and join everyone dancing.

'Let's go and dance too,' I said to Harry.

Harry picked up my hand and held it to his lips. 'Stay here and dance with me.'

'Let's join them. Look, it's a big party!' I waved my free hand.

'I want you all to myself.' Harry hooked his arm around my waist, and we swayed together for a few minutes before I pushed away gently. 'Come on,' I said, pulling Harry with me to join the others.

'Hey, come and boogie with us,' Mum said.

The word 'boogie' from Mum's mouth made me cringe. Then Tipene added to the wrongness by saying, 'We're groovers from way back, your mum and me!' He and Mum cracked up laughing, and I found myself grinning back at them.

Tipene grabbed my hand and twirled me around. 'You used to love this when you were a little girl. You and Rewi danced to all of our *Solid Gold Hits* albums and it was usually my job to twirl you both around.'

Harry moved away a little and watched the band, swaying slightly, unlike Rewi, who was dancing wildly with Marama and Nikau. Every now and then, the younger kids shimmied over to Tipene and Mum to be twirled around. It was as if the music had splashed joy onto our faces, and Herbs were baptising us in a new kind of togetherness that was about standing up for equality and human rights.

Harry glanced from the band to me. His face creased slowly into a smile. He made his way over to me and began to dance. Something released in me, an inward sigh. Harry was happy. Everything was okay.

At the corner of the stage, I could just see Mere, her camera in her hand. She took photos of people dancing, then clambered down from the stage, kissing Tipene and Mum and giving her kids a quick squeeze. 'Stand together,' she yelled. 'I want to get a photo of you all.'

Mum grabbed Jo and her friends, calling out, 'Photo time!'

We all huddled together, and Mere's camera flashed a few times. 'Wonderful!' she yelled. 'Keep dancing. See you later on.'

We spun to electric guitars, harmonies and the reggae beat. Herbs' music throbbed through the square, out into Queen Street and across Auckland. Maybe it reached both ends of New Zealand or even travelled across the oceans to South Africa. A school child in Soweto might have heard Herbs faintly in the wind.

LOCKDOWN

We moved down to Alert Level Three yesterday, on the 27th of April. The exact time of switching from Level Four to Three was at 11.59pm. Ross and I stayed up to mark the moment. We're celebrating with takeaways tonight, because they're allowed at this lower level.

Last night, Ross told me not to get too excited. 'There were five new cases of Covid-19 and another death confirmed today,' he said.

'Yeah, but they're all connected to the cluster groups: the rest home, the school and the wedding,' I said. 'The country's efforts to keep people away from each other seem to have worked.'

'That's true,' Ross said. 'I'm being a bit cup-half-empty.'

'You are a little.' I reached over and put my hand on his. 'Takeaways tomorrow night will cheer you up.'

'Wonder if I'll have to go back into school. I'd happily keep working from home.'

'So you can wear jeans every day?' I teased.

'Exactly.'

Under level three, some teachers will return to school to teach the children of essential workers. All other children need to stay at home. Ross's school hasn't decided which teachers need to return yet. If Ross does have to go back, at least he'll only have a few students: the kids of builders, shop workers, medical staff, that sort of thing.

Level three also means we can make small changes to our bubbles, but we've already done that with Adam coming to stay. I ask Ross if we should let Mum and Dad into our bubble now too, but we decide that Adam working in a supermarket would be more of a risk to my parents than it is to us. We'll keep the two metres distance from them until we lower to level two.

Adam's been with us for a couple of weeks now. He's quiet and keeps to himself, which is a bit unusual for our family. Jesse and Eva are loud and fill a room with their presence, whereas Adam stays on the sidelines, moving out of the way if we walk in and apologising for being at the sink when we're waiting to fill the kettle. I've told him many times now that he has to treat our home like it's his home, but Ross pointed out that it might be a habit Adam has formed after being at his dad's house. He's learned to take up the least amount of space possible.

In the evening, we have our special level three lockdown takeaway dinner. I drive to the Thai restaurant that does the best takeaways ever. I wait in the car and the restaurant phones me when the food is ready. I step out of the car and a woman appears at the restaurant door. She's wearing a mask and gloves. 'Stay where you are!' she calls to me. 'I'll leave the food here for you.' She puts the brown paper bag on a table outside the door and calls out, 'Come now. Thank you!' before heading back into the restaurant and shutting the door behind her.

There are two other cars parked near me and I assume they are waiting for a phone call to say their food is ready. It feels like some sort of dystopian movie. I swing the car out onto the empty road, keen to get back home.

We eat around the table. I want to include Adam in the conversation, so I ask him if the supermarket is doing things any differently under level three.

'Not really,' Adam says. 'We still make customers line up outside so that only twenty are in the supermarket at one time. They all have to sanitise before they enter too, and we still have those big Perspex screens around us at the checkout counter.'

'Do you wear a mask?' Ross asks.

'Most of us do, but there's one older lady who works at checkout, and she can't. She says it makes her feel like she can't breathe.'

'Fair enough,' I say. 'She needs to feel she can breathe.'

'I was thinking about breathing today when I went for a run,' Eva says. 'The air was so clean. There were only a few cars that passed me, and I realised this was how our ancestors must have lived, walking everywhere, with no cars filling their lungs with crap.'

Jesse spoons more rice onto his plate and into his mouth, saying, 'The biggest difference to our air quality is having no planes up in the air. They're big polluters.'

'Yeah, but a girl in my class's mum is a flight attendant and she's lost her job,' Eva says. 'It's good for the environment that hardly any planes are flying, but it's hard on people losing jobs.'

'I'm in the same boat,' I say. 'It's not easy.'

'But you're creating a new job for yourself,' Adam says, swallowing his mouthful before he talks, which makes me hopeful that Jesse might learn some manners from him while he's staying with us.

'Well, I don't know if you could call writing my memories of the Springbok Tour a job.'

'Maybe we're all going to do things differently,' Adam says. 'Maybe this is an opportunity for the government to pressure aviation and other transport industries to look into renewable energies so that we don't go back to the pollution we had before. Maybe, Liza, this is the beginning of your new career, as a writer of books, not just articles. I like what I've heard so far.'

This is a big speech for Adam, and I can see he's surprised himself by having said so much. He lowers his head to spoon some food into his mouth.

'I like your Springbok memories too,' Eva says, 'but I want to know more about Harry. He still feels like a bit of a mystery to me. What was his family like? Did you ever go to his house?'

'I'm going to write about that next,' I say. 'I did go there for dinner, but I'm not going to tell you about it now. Wait until I've written it.'

'That's cruel, Mum,' Eva says, her eyes narrowing across the table at me.

I narrow my eyes back at her. 'Life can be cruel, my child. Get used to it.'

'Don't try to act tough with me, Mum,' Eva says. 'We both know I can wrestle you to the ground and get it out of you.'

Jesse stops eating. 'Can you wrestle Mum to the ground?'

'I could, if necessary.' Eva flexes her fingers as if about to launch an attack.

'I'm not telling you, Eva,' I say, 'but I can tell you something interesting about that second mobilisation. The Hamilton protest was completely silent. They just walked down the main street without a sound, holding their banners and signs.'

'That would've been amazing to watch,' Eva says.

I put my fork down and have a sip of water. 'Actually, I also remember that the protesters in Eltham, a town in Taranaki, had a terrible time. There weren't many of them, and a crowd from the pub threw stuff at them: beer bottles, cans, glasses, ashtrays, that sort of stuff. There were only a few police there, and they ended up trying to protect the protesters and get them off the main street. One guy had his kids with him on the march and they were crying. He'd brought them so they could have an experience of what it was like to protest for what you believe in, but instead, he was running for safety from his neighbours.'

'Those poor kids,' Eva says. 'They'd have known the people doing that to them. How could you ever trust those people or any adults again?'

'Must've been hard on the police too,' Jesse says. 'Imagine having to go to work as a police officer during the Springbok Tour.'

'I read an article about the high level of stress-related illnesses in the police force after the tour,' I say, 'but I guess a lot of the protesters experienced post-traumatic stress too. Two of the clowns that got beaten up went to live in Aussie.'

'It should never have happened, that tour,' Ross says. 'A responsible government would've respected the Gleneagles Agreement.'

'It was an election year,' I say. 'Muldoon wanted the votes of the rugby supporters.'

'Exactly,' Ross says.

Jesse stands up and walks to the curtains, opening them a little.

'Hey, what's going on next door? Some sort of gathering. How many are we allowed to have in a group now?'

'No more than ten people, I think, but that's for funerals, tangihanga and weddings,' Ross says. 'The rest of us have to stay in our bubbles and keep doing the two metres social distancing.'

'Well, our neighbours have got a barbie happening and they're not two metres apart,' Jesse says.

'They might have extended their bubble,' I say. 'We're allowed to do that a little bit.'

Eva and Adam get up and go to peek through the curtains with Jesse. I can't resist following.

'Look at you lot,' Ross says. 'Talk about nosy neighbours! Those people only moved in a few months ago and you're spying on them.'

'Tom's coming over to talk to them,' Eva says. Tom is an elderly man who lives across the road. He's very talkative, and we all like him, but it's hard to get away from him once he strikes up a conversation.

'Tom's a pretty reasonable bloke,' Ross says. 'Close the curtains and let him deal with it.'

'He's not looking too reasonable,' Eva says.

'Woah, he's getting angus,' Jesse says. 'Angus' is Jesse and Eva's word for 'angry'.

'They're yelling at each other,' Eva says. 'The neighbours' visitors are all at the fence now.'

'Tom's stepping backwards,' Jesse says.

'He's trying to keep his two-metre distance,' Eva says.

'You two are like commentators at the cricket!' I say.

'Should we help sort it out?' Adam asks.

Ross has obviously picked up on Adam's anxiety and comes over to have a look. Voices are raised now, and other neighbours are coming onto the street. 'Maybe we *should* go and help somehow,' Ross says. He doesn't seem keen. It's the end of a busy day for him, teaching students and meeting other staff online to organise what the school's next steps are. 'Oh no, Rick's joined in now.'

Rick lives a couple of houses down and is well-known for getting annoyed when people don't agree with him. He yelled at a neighbour who put her wheelie bin on his grass verge once. She'd put it there because there was a truck parked in front of her house, and she was worried the rubbish truck driver wouldn't see it. He'd upset her so much that she hadn't spoken to him since.

'Okay, let's go,' I say. 'Let's be good neighbours.'

'We'll watch through the curtain,' Jesse says. 'Lockdown's been so boring; it's great to have a bit of entertainment.'

I shake my head at my son. 'You're . . .'

'Adorable?' Jesse interrupts.

'Wasn't quite the word I was thinking of.' I follow Ross to the front door and walk outside.

There are about eight people standing on the street talking in raised voices to our neighbours who are standing behind their fence.

'Ask Ross and Liza what they think then!' says Tom, seeing us arrive.

'We just wanted to see if we can help,' I say.

'You can tell this lot to go home and stop breaking the law!' Rick says.

'This is Lyall and Trish,' I say to Rick and Tom. 'They're our new neighbours. You may not have met them properly yet, because lockdown happened soon after they moved in.'

'Well, they've certainly met us now,' Lyall says. 'Didn't bother to introduce themselves though.'

'We're more concerned about the party you've got going on here, when we're meant to be social distancing,' Tom says. 'I've got diabetes, and this Covid-19 could kill me if I get it. I have to trust people like you to do the right thing.'

'I'm not doing anything wrong,' Lyall says. 'We've extended our bubble a bit, that's all, and we're allowed to have a barbie in our own back yard if we want to.'

'There are about sixteen of you,' Rick says. 'You're lucky we haven't rung the police.'

'The police?' Trish looks shocked. 'Why would you do that?'

'You're breaking the law!' Rick says.

'We've just joined two bubbles together,' Trish says. 'This is my sister's family and we'll be minding her kids now that she's going back to work.'

'So, who are all those adults?'

'My mum and dad, who were always in our bubble, my sister and her husband and my teenage kids. My sister's younger kids are round the back on the trampoline.' Trish sips her glass of wine. 'I feel a bit like we're on trial here.'

'Tom, Rick,' Ross says, 'let's leave them alone. They're not doing anything wrong.'

'How was I to know they'd included a whole other family in their bubble?' Tom says.

'Well, we know now,' Ross says. 'Let's leave them to get back to their barbecue.' Ross turns away. 'C'mon, Liza.'

'Enjoy the rest of your night,' I say to Lyall and Trish.

'They could at least turn their music down,' Rick says, joining us.

'Rick, come on!' I say. 'Our kids play loud music with their mates all the time. Think of the parties our kids have had.'

Rick hovers at our driveway, his hand on our letterbox. 'Yeah, yeah, I'm being a jerk. I guess this whole lockdown thing must be getting to me.'

'Hey, the cases are low and there's no community transmission of the virus at all now,' Ross says. 'If this continues, we'll only spend two weeks at level three, and then we'll drop to level two. We're getting there, mate.'

'Just glad builders can get back to work under level three. Been worried it would go on longer.'

'Yeah, you can go back to work on Monday,' Ross says.

Rick takes off his cap, runs his hand over his bald head then puts the cap back on. 'Getting too worried for my own good. That's why the thought of people stuffing it up for us pisses me off.'

'They're fine, Rick,' I say. 'Trish and Lyall are completely within the level three guidelines. There are *some* people stuffing it up, but the police get onto them quickly. Just try to enjoy the last few days before you go back to work.'

Rick stares ahead, away from us, but he doesn't move. Perhaps this is the first time he's talked about how concerned he's been feeling.

'It's been a stressful time, Rick,' I continue. 'None of us have experienced a pandemic before. All we can do is follow the rules and try to focus on the good things. You've got your kids with you and so have we, so we know they're safe. That's one good thing. You've got a job to go back to. Try to focus on what's going well.'

Rick nods. 'Thanks, guys. I'll let you get back inside.' He starts to walk away.

Inside, Jesse, Eva and Adam are sitting back at the table now.

'That was pretty uneventful,' Jesse says. 'Thought there was going to be a fight.'

'Can't fight,' I say. 'Got to keep a distance, and on another topic, do you think you could rinse out the takeaway containers and put them in the recycling, rather than just sitting around pretending they're not on the table?'

'Pretending?' Jesse shakes his head. 'I'm not pretending. I'm perfectly aware that there are dirty dishes on this table. I'm just ignoring them.'

'Ignoring, pretending,' Ross says. 'Either way, get your butt off that chair and tidy up this stuff.'

'I will,' Adam volunteers. He stands up and starts stacking take-away containers and plates.

'Thanks, Adam, but Jesse can help you.' Ross glares at Jesse, who scrapes his chair backwards and gets up to help. 'I'm going to do some marking,' Ross says.

'What about Eva?' Jesse says. 'No one's asked her to help.'

'She cooked and did dishes last night, so it's your turn to cook tomorrow night, Jesse,' I say.

'It never ends,' Jesse says. 'One thing after another.'

I can't help but smile at Jesse sighing as he picks up dirty cutlery and plates. I flick on the kettle and lean against the bench. Adam is beside me, placing the dirty dishes in the sink. He clears his throat, turning on the tap to rinse the dishes. Without looking at me, he begins to speak. 'I hate hearing angry people like that. I keep wondering who's going to lose it completely. Someone always does.'

The kettle is loud. Jesse and Eva are debating what Jesse should cook tomorrow night. They can't hear me and Adam talking in low voices at the bench. 'People don't always lose it, Adam,' I say. 'Often, people express strong feelings and leave it at that.'

Adam puts some detergent in the sink and bubbles escape into the air, tiny ones gliding past me. 'Some people don't leave it at that. Those guys could've ended up getting into a fight.'

'But they didn't. They listened to each other and realised they were all worked up over nothing.'

'I've seen it.' Adam glances at me, then looks back at the plate he's scrubbed clean. 'I've seen someone get so mad, scary mad, that he smashes things or hits someone.'

'Your dad?'

Adam nods. 'I've learned to just get out of the house quickly and stay away until it's over.'

'That's sensible, Adam, and you told Jesse, who helped you. Another sensible decision.'

'Jesse's a good friend.'

'What are you saying about me?' Jesse asks.

The kettle has boiled, and the kitchen is quiet.

'He's saying you're slow at bringing dirty dishes to the sink,' I say.

'Never you worry, dear mother,' Jesse says, picking up the dishes. 'I come now bearing dishes from the table.'

I roll my eyes at Adam. 'That boy!'

Jesse puts the dishes on the bench beside Adam, grabs the dishcloth and kisses my cheek. 'You love me, Mum,' he says, heading to the table to give it a wipe.

'Not everyone loses it completely,' I whisper to Adam. 'Most people learn that the best way to keep friends and family is to try to listen. Your dad is one person, not everyone.'

'Stop whispering, Mum,' Eva says, sitting at the table, on her phone. 'And stop wiping my hand with the dishcloth, Jesse.'

'Your fingers are dirty!' Jesse says.

'I'm getting out of here.' I throw a teabag into my cup and pour hot water over it. 'I'll leave you with these mad people, Adam.'

I walk out of the kitchen and stand in the hallway. I'd been planning to watch TV, but I feel restless after the discussion I've just had with Adam. I plonk myself down on the sofa, where I'd been writing earlier, and perch my laptop on my knees. I'm going to write about the day after that second mobilisation, the day I had dinner at Harry's house.

CHAPTER 20
DINNER AT HARRY'S

The next morning, Mum and Dad were sitting at the table drinking coffee. No one else was up, which was unusual, as I was the one who slept in the most. I'd woken up and lain in bed thinking about the mobilisation the night before and the way Harry danced, the way he laughed, the way he looked at me. Then, I realised I was hungry and all I could think about was food.

Sitting at the table, Dad held up the morning newspaper. 'Our photo of the crowd last night is much better than this one. We managed to get a really high shot, so you can see the whole of Queen Street. I told Hamish, the photographer, that I was impressed. He's new to the paper, so I wanted him to have that feedback. Not always easy being the new kid on the block.'

'You're a nice man,' Mum said.

'Say that again, go on!' Dad said.

Mum put her hand on Dad's. 'You're a nice man, you are.'

'Okay, stop, you two,' I said.

Mum and Dad laughed. 'We making you uncomfortable, Liza?' Dad asked.

'Just a bit.' I poured some milk into my tea. 'Don't forget, you're taking me and some of my team to hockey today, Dad.'

'I know,' Dad said, 'but we don't need to go yet. Come and sit down and tell me about the mobe. I don't get to experience it in the same way you do.'

Dad called the mobilisations 'mobes'. He'd started doing it after the people at the MOST meetings called them that. They were the 'Mobilisation to Stop the Tour' group that met once a week, and it included representatives from around twenty different groups, all joined together in the one large Auckland coalition.

'I'll sit down with you if you stop holding hands. Look, even Sal doesn't like it!' Sal was facing the other way, staring out the ranch-slider.

'She's looking at the pigeons, Liza,' Mum said, taking her hand off Dad's. 'Can you believe our daughter is ordering us around like this?'

Dad nudged me. 'So, how was it?'

'It was amazing. So many people, so many different groups marching, and Herbs were brilliant. We just danced and danced, eh Mum?'

'We sure did. Bet Marama and Nikau are tired today. It was a late night for them.'

'Oh, and we saw Mere,' I continued. 'She was taking photos of Herbs and the crowds, then she took some photos of us.'

'That's pretty cool,' Dad said. 'Sounds like it was a good night for getting the anti-tour message across and for having fun. Not that the government's taking the protests very seriously. Tonight's their big election fundraiser for the National Party at the Mandalay Ballroom. Muldoon's determined to get back in again.'

'Are you going, Dad?'

'I am, but I wish I wasn't.' Dad rubbed his forehead. 'Feel like a lazy night in front of the telly, but I guess it'll be good to see what they're up to. Anti-tour demonstrators will be there, so that will make it interesting.'

The phone rang down the hallway.

'Will you get that, Liza?' Mum asked.

Grumbling, I made my way to the phone. It was Harry. He said his mum wanted to meet me and asked if I'd like to come for dinner that night. 'Dad won't be here though,' he said. 'He plays rugby on Saturdays, just a social team, and they go out and have a few beers after their game.'

'I'll ask my parents. Hang on.' I put the receiver down and ran back to the kitchen.

After asking if I could go, Mum said, 'I've never met Harry's parents.'

'Neither have I. That's why I want to go.' I was standing on one leg, with the other one sort of hovering off the ground, ready to run back to the phone.

'Where do they live?' Mum asked.

'In Trainor Ave, just up the other side of school, not far from Ursula's house. He's number fifty-six.'

'Right, well, how about I drive you there and just pop in to meet his mum?'

'Do you have to?'

'Yes, I do.' Mum and Dad exchanged a look.

'Why are you two . . .?' I put my hovering foot on the floor. 'Do you think I'm lying or something? Do you think there won't be any parents there?'

'No,' Mum said. 'That never entered my head.'

'Is he waiting on the phone, Liza?' Dad asked.

'Yes.'

'Well, your mother's told you what the deal is, so why are you standing here and making him wait? Go and tell him you're coming, but that your mum wants to meet his mum. Don't stand here arguing.' Dad looked down at the morning newspaper on the table in front of him and turned over a page. He looked like he wanted to say more, but he didn't.

I turned, making a 'humph' sound and ran back down the hallway to the phone. Harry was still on the line. 'I can come,' I said, 'but Mum's going to drop me, and she wants to meet your mother.'

'That's okay,' Harry said. 'Mum'll be cool with that.'

'What time?'

'Six?'

'Okay. See you then.'

Harry was quiet, so I hung onto the phone for a little bit longer. 'Can't wait to see you then,' he said in a low voice, as though someone was within earshot.

'Neither can I,' I whispered.

Later that afternoon, I tried on five different possible things to wear with my jeans. The off-the-shoulder top? I'd worn that to Ursula's party though. The lacey op-shop top? I'd worn that the night before, and it was a bit smelly too. Finally, I settled on a tie-dyed T-shirt that I'd got for Christmas.

Just before 6pm, Mum pulled up outside fifty-six Trainor Ave. We made our way down a short pathway to Harry's front door. We didn't need to knock because the front door opened and Harry stood there with his hair falling around his face, and the moon on him, like a spotlight.

A second later, Harry's mum and sister were behind him. Harry's mother leaned past him to shake Mum's hand, introducing herself and inviting us in. 'You can call me Raewyn too,' she said to me.

'I won't come in,' Mum said. 'I just wanted to meet you, seeing as our kids have become such good friends.'

Harry's mum was tall and thin, and her blonde hair was pulled up in a ponytail. Her daughter, Sophie, was beside her. 'They're boyfriend and girlfriend,' Sophie said.

'Yes, they are.' Mum nodded at Sophie. 'And you must be Harry's sister, Sophie.'

'Yes,' Sophie said. She held out her hand to Mum, who smiled and shook it.

'You look so much like your mother,' Mum said.

'Are you sure you won't come in for a glass of wine?' Harry's mum said.

'No, I won't stay,' Mum said. 'I just wanted to say hello. Thank you for having Eliza for dinner.'

'It's a pleasure,' Harry's mum said. 'I'm glad to finally meet her.'

Mum gave my arm a squeeze and headed back to the car. She was going home, and I was to phone her when I was ready to be picked up.

As soon as the door closed, Sophie asked me if I'd like to see her bedroom. Harry took my hand in his as we wandered down the hallway.

'This is my favourite doll,' Sophie said. 'I don't really play with her very much anymore, but I still love her.' She took a barbie doll off her windowsill. 'I call her Susie, but she's really just a Barbie.'

'Sophie cut off some of her hair once,' Harry said.

'I was little,' Sophie said. 'I thought it would grow back.'

I reached out and stroked the doll's hair. 'Still looks good, so that's lucky.'

Sophie showed me her favourite books and the new dress her aunty had given her for her birthday. She was happy and chatty, and Harry and I sat down on her bed while she showed us her school books and told us about some of the kids in her class.

Soon, Harry's mum, Raewyn, called us for dinner. She spooned veggies and chicken drumsticks onto plates. 'Is this enough for you, Eliza?' she said, handing a plate to me. 'Gravy's on the table. Help yourself.'

We chatted about Sophie's jazz dance class, which she did once a week. Every now and then, Sophie stopped eating, scraped her chair back and stood up to show me a move she'd learned.

Raewyn asked me if I had a favourite subject at school. I didn't have to think hard to answer her. 'English is my favourite, but I'm not sure whether that's just because I really like our teacher, Ms Jefferson. She's really cool and different from the nuns.'

'I liked English too,' Raewyn said. 'I loved talking about the ideas in books and poems. I love reading, but don't often get a chance to talk about it.'

'You can discuss your books with me,' Harry said.

'Hmmm, I could see you switching off pretty quickly.'

'I like reading!' Harry said.

'Well, I wish that enthusiasm was reflected in your school reports.'

Harry grinned at his mother. 'There's a difference between loving reading things that I choose and having some boring book forced on me at school.'

'Fair enough.' Raewyn's ponytail hung over her left shoulder, strands of blonde hair scattering across her bony collarbone. She picked at her food: a wedge of potato here and a segment of chicken there. 'What are you studying in English at the moment, Eliza?'

I swallowed a forkful of peas without chewing them so that I could answer her. 'We're reading a Shakespeare play, *The Taming of the Shrew*. I've never read a Shakespeare play before and I thought I'd hate it, cos I've seen Shakespeare on TV and it was confusing. Ms Jefferson explains it to us though, and we have really interesting discussions.'

'What's it about?' Raewyn asked.

'A woman who acts as if she's crazy, but, really, she's just feeling trapped by society and what people expect of her. Anyway, there's this guy, Petruchio, who she marries because he's the only one who's willing to marry her. He takes her to his house and, this is the bit we're up to now, he won't let her sleep or have any food. She becomes weak so she agrees with everything he says. He's taming her the way people tame hawks, wearing her out so she has no energy left and just obeys him.'

'Maybe he thinks that's the only way they'll have a good marriage though,' Raewyn said, 'if her behaviour is so crazy.'

'That's sort of what the play seems to be saying, sort of what Shakespeare must have wanted us to think, I reckon, but it's so cruel,' I said.

'If he treats her like a hawk, maybe she could turn into one,' Sophie said. 'She could fly away from him forever.'

Harry leaned forward and smiled at Sophie. 'You have the best ideas, Soph.'

Sophie bent towards him so that their heads almost met. 'I do have the best ideas.'

They stayed leaning in like that until they both started laughing. Raewyn and I joined in. I liked how sweet Harry was to his little sister.

I noticed Raewyn stiffen before I heard someone fiddling with a key at the front door. Harry looked in the direction of the sound. 'It's not locked!' he called. His lip curled up slightly as if unimpressed that he'd had to say that. 'It's Dad,' he said to me.

The door opened and there was the noise of someone hanging up a coat, then footsteps walking towards us. A tall man entered. He looked like an older version of Harry. 'Bloody cold out there,' he said. 'Started dinner already?' He went to the fridge and took out a beer.

'You said you wouldn't be home for dinner,' Raewyn said. She picked up the salt-shaker and sprinkled some on her potatoes.

'Well, I couldn't resist coming home to meet Harry's girlfriend.' Harry's father scraped the empty chair across the lino and sat down.

'Sorry, what's your name, love? Harry did tell me, but I can't for the life of me remember.'

'Eliza, Dad,' Harry said, 'but everyone just calls her Liza.'

'Liza,' Harry's dad said. 'Call me Mike.'

'There's not much food left, Mike,' Raewyn said, going over to the kitchen bench. 'There are some roast potatoes, one chicken drumstick and a handful of peas.'

'She doesn't care about me, see?' Mike said to me. 'Didn't save me any dinner.'

'You said you'd stay at the pub with the boys after your game,' Harry said.

'I changed my mind. I don't think that's a criminal act is it, to change your mind?'

Raewyn put a plate down in front of him. 'There you go,' she said, making her way back to her seat.

'Sorry,' Harry whispered to me under his breath. 'He wasn't meant to be here tonight.'

'Did you win your game, Dad?' Sophie asked.

'We did, Soph.' Mike drank from his bottle of beer, a long, slow, gulping journey from the top of the bottle to halfway down before he put it on the table again. 'So, Liza, tell me a bit about yourself.'

My fork was almost at my mouth, but I lowered it to speak. I wasn't really enjoying the food now that Mike was here. He'd brought a different mood into the house with him, along with the smell of cigarette smoke and beer.

Raewyn looked over at me. 'That's a hard one, isn't it? Where to start?'

'You can start with how many are in your family,' Sophie suggested.

'Why is that a hard question, Raewyn?' Mike asked.

Harry's mum's knife clinked on her plate. 'Oh, I . . .'

'There's nothing too complicated about telling someone a bit about yourself.' Mike picked up a chicken drumstick and bit into it. 'Where do you go to school, Liza?'

'Saint Theresa's,' I answered.

'A Catholic, eh?' Mike grinned at Harry. Some chicken was stuck between his teeth. He nudged Harry. 'They say Catholic girls can be pretty wild.'

'Dad!' Harry said. 'Sorry, Liza.'

'I'm just saying it like it is!' Mike tipped his bottle back into his mouth, and I pictured fragments of chicken swirling down his throat with the beer. 'Soph, grab another beer for me will you, love.'

Sophie slid off her chair and went to the fridge.

'Harry might feel uncomfortable with you talking about his girlfriend like that, Mike,' Raewyn said. She kept her head down, pushing a few peas onto her fork. Mike stared at her, but she didn't look up. She mashed one pea on top of another onto her fork.

Sophie placed a bottle of beer beside her father. 'I opened it for you,' she said.

Mike broke his stare and patted Sophie's back. 'Good girl.'

'Would you like anything else to eat, Liza?' Raewyn asked.

'No, thank you. I think I've had enough.'

Mike was quiet after that. Sophie talked about a budgie she'd tried to tame, and I realised she was picking up on *The Taming of the Shrew* hawk-taming discussion. She was trying to start a conversation. I wanted to help, so I asked what she'd been trying to teach it to do.

Harry joined in. 'We tried to teach it to talk, didn't we, Soph?'

'But it never talked,' Sophie said. 'We said, 'Hello, darling' to it over and over, but it didn't work.'

'Then it flew away when we were cleaning its cage,' Harry said.

'I miss it,' Sophie said.

'I don't miss cleaning its cage,' Harry said.

After everyone had finished eating, Harry, Sophie and I rinsed the dishes. Raewyn came to join us, scraping crispy potato bits off the roasting dish. Every now and then, I glanced at Mike. He was either eating, drinking beer or staring at Raewyn, but thankfully, she didn't seem to notice.

Sophie asked if I'd like to see Harry's room.

'Is it presentable?' Raewyn asked, still scraping at the roasting dish.

'I cleaned it today,' Harry said. 'C'mon, I'll show you, Liza.'

'Thank you for dinner,' I said.

'No problem,' Raewyn said.

As we left the kitchen, I'm sure I heard Mike mimic her. 'No problem,' he said.

Harry's bedroom was the same size as Sophie's, but it felt like a different world. We'd gone from frilly, doll world to basic, bare world with a bed, a set of drawers with a big ghetto blaster and music tapes on it, and a shelf on the wall piled up with books, packs of cards, a bag of marbles, some knucklebones and a Rubik's Cube.

Harry noticed me scanning the shelf and said, 'Lot of old stuff I used to play with.' He pulled me down onto the bed and we sat, our backs against the wall and feet dangling, holding hands, while Sophie entertained us with a tour of the bedroom.

'This is Cold Chisel,' she said, pointing at one of the posters. 'They're an Australian band, and this is Bruce Springsteen and the E Street Band.' Sophie stretched up. There were two men singing into a microphone. 'This one is Bruce Springsteen.'

'What's his other name, Soph?'

'The Boss.' Sophie sighed and gave Harry an exasperated look. 'You're interrupting!'

'Sorry.' Harry leaned against me and, while Sophie moved to the next poster, he kissed my ear, pulling away when Sophie turned to speak to us. 'This is The Clash,' she said, 'who I don't like, but Harry says they're a good band. Do you like them, Liza?'

'I only know a few of their songs,' I said. 'They're okay.'

'Hmmm.' Sophie moved on to the next posters, and Harry's lips were back on my ear. I almost winced with the unbearable pleasure of it.

Sophie turned to face me, pointing at a poster of Duran Duran and telling me that they wore eyeliner and mascara and used hair gel. She crossed the room, her back to us, and Harry's tongue journeyed from the front to the back of my earlobe. He stopped the moment Sophie turned to us. 'This is Debbie Harry,' she said, 'and she's in a group called Blondie, but people think *she* is Blondie because of her hair.'

At the top of the poster, the word, 'Blondie' was in white print with the word, 'Atomic', in yellow at the bottom. In between these words was a picture of Debbie Harry in a blue off-the-shoulder dress.

Her hair was loosely pulled back in a ponytail and she was wearing thick eyeliner with bright red lipstick.

'Harry thinks Debbie Harry is beautiful, Liza,' Sophie said, her eyes searching mine for any hint of a response to this information. 'He told me that.'

'She is pretty gorgeous,' I said.

'Yes, she is,' Sophie replied in a very matter of fact way, as if discussing the weather.

Right up beside my ear, Harry whispered, 'Not as gorgeous as you.'

This ear thing was becoming too difficult for me, so I climbed off the bed and suggested we play knucklebones. Sophie was happy to leave the poster tour there and plonked herself down on the floor next to me. We spent the next fifteen minutes playing knucklebones, but Sophie dropped them so often, she decided to get her game of Hungry Hippos from her bedroom.

While she was gone, Harry reached over and took my chin in his hand, leaning in to kiss me, but pulling away when Sophie re-entered with the Hungry Hippos box in her hands. 'This is such a good game, Liza,' she said. 'It's probably my favourite.'

When Mum came to pick me up, she tooted from the road. I went into the lounge to thank Raewyn again. Mike was asleep in an armchair, snoring. Raewyn stood up, holding her finger to her lips. 'Don't wake him up,' she said. 'He can stay there all night.'

Coming to the front door with me, she waved through the fog at Mum in the car, but I'm not sure Mum saw her. Sophie hugged me and whispered that she wanted me to come back to play. I promised I would. Harry gently squeezed my hand. 'I'll phone you,' he said.

Mum drove slowly through the fog. 'Nice time?' she asked.

'Yeah.'

'Nice people?'

'Yeah.' I thought of Mike, lying back in the armchair, snoring. I didn't want to tell Mum about him. She was a social worker. She'd have things to say about it all and I didn't want to hear them. I told Mum most things, but I decided to keep this to myself.

CHAPTER 21
PASSPORTS AND VISAS

I could hear Kalāsia talking with Mum in the kitchen. I lay back and closed my eyes for a few minutes. The heavy overnight rain had eased, and now it tiptoed lightly on our roof.

I'd almost dozed off again when Kalāsia knocked on my door. 'Lazy girl,' she said in a loud whisper, 'can I come in?'

'Only if you've got a cup of tea,' I answered.

The door opened and Kalāsia entered with cups in her hands. 'Your mum says you have to get up and have breakfast.'

I sat up, leaning back against my pillow. 'Let's just relax and drink our tea quickly first.'

'I'll plait your hair while we drink it, so we're not late.'

I groaned. 'Okay, but that means I have to get up.' I dragged myself out of bed while Kalāsia carried my desk chair over to my dressing table. She picked up the brush and pulled it through my hair. 'Something bad happened,' she whispered.

'Did you have the nightmare again?'

Kalāsia shook her head, picking up my comb to tease out a particularly difficult knot. 'No, thank goodness, but I didn't really sleep much last night. Y'know how my dad works at the bread factory?'

I nodded at Kalāsia's reflection in the mirror, then gulped some tea.

'Well, on Saturday night, he was at work and the police arrived and spoke to the boss. Dad saw them talking through the glass doors. The manager came out and told Dad to get all the Pacific

Island workers to come into the staffroom, so the police could see their passports.'

'But . . . why would people have their passports at work?'

'Lots of Pacific Islanders take their passports with them everywhere now, just in case. My cousin had to show his to a policeman in Queen Street.' Kalāsia held on to the bottom of the first plait while she wound an elastic band around it. 'Anyway, some of the guys at the bread factory had to go in a van to the police station, because they had no proof that they weren't overstayers. One of them asked Dad to phone his wife to bring his passport into the station. When Dad phoned her, she started crying and said she couldn't take his passport to the police station, because her children were asleep. Dad said he'd collect it and, when he finished work at four in the morning, he went to her house and took the passport in for her. The police let the guy go in the end.'

I passed Kalāsia's cup to her. 'Drink it before it gets cold.'

She drank some, then continued to plait and talk. 'When Dad got home from work on Sunday morning, he didn't go straight to have a shower and a rest before getting ready for mass like he always does. He sat in the kitchen and when we woke up, he told us what happened. He said we needed to pray for the workers still in the police station, so we said some prayers before we went to mass.'

Mum's voice sailed down the hallway. 'Liza, you'll be late.'

Kalāsia wound a hairband around my other plait. 'Put your uniform on, quick.'

Dad called down the hallway now. 'I've put some toast in for both of you.'

We ate the toast as we headed out the door. I'd grabbed my toothbrush from the bathroom, so that I could clean my teeth at school.

Rewi was waiting by the letterbox. 'I was just about to come and knock on the door,' he said. 'Thought maybe you'd slept through your alarm.'

'Well, you were right,' I said, 'but thankfully, I have a human alarm clock called Kalāsia.'

'And hairdresser,' Kalāsia said. 'I'm very useful.'

The rain had stopped completely, and we jogged towards school, avoiding puddles from the heavy overnight downfall. At one point, Rewi ran slightly ahead, turned and skimmed the surface of a puddle so that water sprayed up my legs.

'Dork!' I said. 'Why do you always do that to me? Why not Kalāsia?'

'He'll never do it to me,' Kalāsia said, 'because he knows I'll whack him.'

'Whack me?' Rewi said.

Kalāsia lifted her eyebrows. 'Yes, whack you, so don't even . . .'

'Is your whack like this?' Rewi patted her arm.

'You wish,' Kalāsia said. She lifted her umbrella high in the air. 'It's like this!' She ran at Rewi, who ducked, laughing. Kalāsia swung at him again, and Rewi dipped away and began to run.

'You can't escape my whack!' Kalāsia yelled, chasing him, her bag swinging from her shoulder.

Rewi stopped near a big puddle and, as Kalāsia caught up with him, he skimmed his foot over it, spraying water at her.

'Man, you're gonna get it!' Kalāsia yelled, whacking at his legs with her umbrella.

'Far out,' Rewi yelled. 'What's got into you this morning?'

'She had a bad night; no sleep,' I said. 'Your pathetic humour's the last straw!'

We were close to the school gate and the rain suddenly began to fall in long spears, so cold and sharp that they almost hurt. Kalāsia put her umbrella up and we huddled under it, running up the school driveway, shouting back at Rewi that we'd see him after school.

There was a buzz of chatter as we entered the classroom, and the bell went as we sat down at our desks. I was only just making it to school on time these days, so I made a promise to myself that I'd get up earlier.

Sister Agnes was pinning something onto the noticeboard. She turned to face us, fiddling with her veil for a moment. When she was satisfied that all of her hair was neatly tucked in, she clapped her hands for our attention. 'I am the bearer of good news, girls. This poster was Ciara's idea. She suggested that we have a mufti day in a few weeks, on Wednesday, the 29th of July. It's the day after your exams finish, so you can celebrate. You need to bring fifty cents if you want to wear your own clothes to school for the day. The money will go to famine aid in Uganda.'

Ursula put up her hand. 'Isn't that the day of Prince Charles and Lady Diana's wedding?'

'It is, Ursula,' Sister Agnes said.

'So, is the mufti day a sort of wedding celebration?' Ursula asked.

'I suppose it is,' Sister Agnes said. 'We thought that date would make it more fun.'

'Are there any rules about what we can wear?' Ursula continued.

Sister Agnes folded her arms and her eyes settled on Ursula. 'What exactly are you thinking of wearing, Ursula, a bikini?'

'No, Sister, it's too cold for a bikini.'

'I'm hoping everyone will use their common sense.' Sister Agnes turned and made her way to her desk. 'Let's do the roll, girls, before we say our morning prayer.'

After form time, we made our way to science. Ursula walked beside me. 'I'm thinking of wearing my mother's wedding dress for mufti day,' she said.

'No! Really?'

Ursula's lip balm shimmered as she smiled. 'To celebrate the royal wedding. Do you think it would be okay?'

I shrugged.

'Sorry about my brothers,' Ursula said. 'They can be jerks sometimes.'

We'd been a bit distant with each other at school ever since that night, a little more polite, less open than usual. We'd never talked about what happened.

'They were . . .' I tried to think of how to finish the sentence, without saying 'racist'. I didn't want Ursula to feel attacked.

'I didn't know anything had happened,' Ursula said. 'I was dancing and then you'd gone. Harry told me about it.'

We stood at the door at the end of the corridor, looking out at the rain. Kalāsia, Ciara and Stella ran through it, yelling, 'Come on, Liza!'

'Do you think the same way as your brothers?' I asked, watching my friends as they ran towards the science block.

'I don't know,' Ursula said. 'I mean, I like Kalāsia and Rewi.'

'So, what about other Māori or Pacific Island people?'

'I think that . . . Kalāsia and Rewi are nice.' Ursula lifted her bag over her head. 'We're going to be late for science. We'd better run.'

I lifted my bag over my head, and we dashed through the rain.

In the science lab, Ursula turned to me. 'Is my mascara running?'

I shook my head.

She nudged me with her elbow and whispered, 'Hey, if I wear the wedding dress, want to be my bridesmaid?'

'No.'

'You'll enjoy it. You could carry the long bit at the bottom of the dress behind me all day. What's it called?'

'The train.'

'You could carry that round all day. It'd be a laugh. Imagine what Sister Agnes would say.'

'I'm not carrying your train, Ursula.'

'Shame. You'd make a gorgeous bridesmaid.'

At lunchtime, the rain still poured. I thought of my sister in the sixth-form common room, warm and comfortable, while Ciara, Stella, Kalāsia and I sat under the eaves of our English classroom, shivering. Next year, we'd be in that common room with a kettle, toaster and fridge. We'd be able to make soup and toast and cups of tea.

Ciara was telling us about Sister Agnes's enthusiasm about the mufti day idea. 'She said it as though I'd come up with a way to achieve world peace. It's not like we haven't had mufti days before!'

'She was trying to make you feel good,' Kalāsia said.

'Hmmm, she's a bit over the top,' Ciara said. 'It was embarrassing.'

A girl was standing beside me. I hadn't heard any footsteps because of the rain. 'Eliza?' she asked.

'Yes.'

'I'm Stephanie Lulich. Can I talk with you for a moment?'

I nodded and stood up. She was the girl in Jo's class, the one who'd been Harry's girlfriend. I followed her a few steps away from my friends.

Stephanie twirled her hair between two fingers as she spoke. 'Jo said you're going out with Harry.'

'Yeah,' I said. 'We've been going round for about three months now.'

'Is it okay?'

'What do you mean?'

'It's just that sometimes he's ... possessive. Is he like that with you?'

I shook my head. 'Not really.'

'Okay, I just wanted to check.' Stephanie stepped back. 'He might've changed. Sorry, I'll let you go back to your friends.'

At the beginning of our English class, I couldn't stop thinking about what Stephanie Lulich had said. At the last mobilisation, when I wanted to dance, Harry had said, 'I want you all to myself'. Was that being possessive or was it romantic? He'd resisted dancing with everyone and seemed annoyed for a while, but he joined in eventually, and we all had a good time.

I tried to concentrate on what Ms Jefferson was saying. 'We all know Petruchio plans to train Kate, like a hawk,' she said. 'He uses the word "falcon" when he's explaining his plan to his servants. Let's make a list of the ways he makes Kate's life hell after they get married.'

My classmates started to call out answers, and Ms Jefferson wrote them down on the blackboard.

'He beats his servants in front of Kate, and she begs him to stop,' someone called.

'Good,' Ms Jefferson said. 'Copy this list down, girls. What else?'

'He says the meat is overcooked and refuses to eat, so Kate can't have dinner either,' someone else said.

'Yes, great. Keep going.' As Ms Jefferson wrote, chalk dust wafted onto her long denim pinafore dress. 'I think it's around this point that Petruchio tells the audience that he's going to "out-shrew" Kate and behave worse than she does. He plans to make it look like kindness. He tells her that her bed and the food she's served are not good enough for her, so she never gets to sleep or eat. His plan is to weaken her strong character through depriving her this way, the same way a hawk is trained. I'll add this to the list.'

'He's showing her he's the boss,' Kalāsia said.

'Exactly,' Ms Jefferson said.

'He's torturing her,' I said. 'That's what they do to political prisoners in South Africa, but they beat them up too.'

'Don't start raving about South Africa and the Springbok Tour,' Susan Leighton said. 'We already know what you think about that.'

'Susan, in this classroom, people can say what matters to them.' Ms Jefferson turned to me. 'You're right, Eliza, that is how political prisoners are treated. They wear them out until they give in and behave the way they want them to.' She rubbed her hands together to get rid of chalk dust. 'What else does Petruchio do?'

'He makes Kate watch his servant eat her food, because she'd hit the servant when he hadn't given the food to her,' Ana Babich called out.

'Excellent.' Ms Jefferson was back at her list on the blackboard. 'What else?'

'He says they will dress up and go to Kate's father's house, but when the tailor comes to make her some nice clothes, Petruchio gets violent with the tailor, saying that none of the clothes are good enough for her and that they will just visit in their old clothes,' Ciara said. 'But she liked the tailor's clothes.'

'Wonderful. Keep going.'

'He says they'll get to her father's house by midday, but when Kate says it's already two o'clock, he tells her off for contradicting him,' another classmate said.

'Great. Anything else?'

'He tells her the sun is the moon and that if she won't agree with him, they'll turn the cart around and go back,' Stella said.

'Yes, great, Stella.'

Ursula spoke. 'A man comes along but Petruchio calls him a "gentlewoman" and demands that Kate agree that the man is a woman. She starts to play his game and calls the man a "budding virgin".'

'Well done, Ursula. You're reading the play, and you said you didn't think you'd manage it!'

'Well, I skipped some of it, but I remembered that bit because of the word "virgin".'

Ms Jefferson laughed. 'Of course you did.' She wiped her chalky fingers on her dress. 'Now girls, I want you to make your own list, a list of things people are "tamed" to do in the world we live in. How are we given negative feedback to make us change our behaviour in family life, school life, church and anything else you can think of? Do this in groups. How are we tamed, girls, how are we tamed?'

Stella and Ciara's netball practice had been cancelled after school, so they joined me and Kalāsia as we headed to the gate to meet Rewi. It wasn't often that we walked home together, because they had netball practice twice a week and choir practice another afternoon. When they were free, I had hockey practice.

We walked slowly, enjoying the warmth of the sun and being in each other's company. I told Rewi about Susan's comment in English, how she didn't want me to mention the Springbok Tour or South Africa. 'How can we not talk about it?' I asked. 'It's happening here, in New Zealand.'

'A lot of people feel the way she does,' Rewi said. 'Mum took a photo of Bob Jones, a wealthy property developer, going to the National Party fundraiser on Saturday night.'

'Dad was there too. He said he saw her.'

'Ask him if he saw Bob Jones give the fingers to the protesters. Mum got a photo of it.'

'That's rude,' Kalāsia said.

'Mum said the protesters started yelling "Shame! Shame!" at him, but he didn't care. He just strutted off into the Mandalay ballroom.'

'Susan's not as bad as that,' I said.

'Mum wasn't shocked at Bob Jones giving the fingers to the protesters. She reckons it's going to get a lot worse. Tour supporters want to see their games, and protesters don't want to play rugby with South Africa.'

Stella joined in. 'On the news, they said that the government could've solved the whole problem if they'd refused to issue visas to the Springboks, but they're letting the rugby union make decisions.'

'I'd love to see that photo of Bob Jones doing the fingers,' I said.

'I'll show you next time you're over,' Rewi said. 'Want to come to the airport with me and Mum on the 19th of July, the morning the Springboks fly in? It'll be really early in the morning.'

'Yeah okay', I said. 'Hang on . . . how early?'

'About five o'clock.'

Kalāsia made a 'humph' sound. 'You'll never get out of bed at five, Liza.'

'I might!'

'You won't,' Kalāsia said.

'She's right,' Rewi said, patting my back condescendingly. 'You won't get up that early, but I'll tell you all about it and show you the photos.'

CHAPTER 22
DISRUPTION

I'd only been home a short while, when the phone rang. Jo answered it and yelled up the hallway, 'It's lover boy!'

'Don't say that,' I hissed, as I passed her on the way to the phone. She smirked at me and went into her room.

I said hi to Harry, but he was quiet for a moment. 'I came to meet you at the gate after school, but I just missed you,' he said. 'You'd already started walking with your friends.'

'Why didn't you catch up with us?' I asked.

'Don't know, just didn't feel like joining up with all your mates.'

'I'd have loved to see you.'

'As much as seeing Rewi?'

I was quiet. The phone made a static sound.

'Why don't you like Rewi?' I asked.

'I don't have a problem with Rewi, I have a problem with him putting his arm around you.'

'Putting his arm around me?' I tried to remember a time Rewi had put his arm around me. When we were little kids, we walked arm-in-arm all the time, but we hadn't done that for years. 'I don't know what you mean.'

'I saw him put his arm around you today when you were all walking home together.'

I remembered Rewi had patted my back when he was teasing me about getting up early for the airport protest. 'Rewi was getting smart to me,' I said. 'He didn't have his arm around me; he was patting me, being condescending.'

'Didn't look like that to me.'

'Harry, Rewi and I are just friends.'

'Can you imagine how I felt, watching you acting like that with him?'

'What do you mean?'

'Laughing and joking with him.'

'I . . . I . . . He's my friend.' The static started again.

'I have to go,' Harry said. 'Mum's calling me.'

I almost said I was sorry, but I hadn't done anything wrong, so I just said bye and he put down the phone.

Later, over dinner, Mum asked how my day had been. Dad was at work, so only Pete and Jo were eating with us. I couldn't tell her about the phone call with Harry, because I knew she'd be concerned. I couldn't tell her about Stephanie Lulich either. There were a few things I wasn't telling Mum these days.

'Good,' I said. I told her about the fundraising idea and how Ursula might wear her mother's wedding dress.

'That'd be brilliant,' Jo said.

'Weird,' Pete said. 'Why is everyone so obsessed with the royal wedding?'

'I love the fact that Ursula will wear a wedding dress on the day of the royal wedding,' Jo said.

'And all the fuss about Diana's dress! Who gives a stuff about her dress? It's all a big secret apparently.' Pete rolled his eyes.

'Lady Diana's going to live a life of luxury,' I said, 'but Ms Jefferson reckons she'll have to sacrifice a lot for it.'

'Yes,' Mum said. 'I wouldn't want that life.'

'What about the dress, the build-up, the secrecy? None of it would appeal?' Jo asked.

Mum shook her head. 'No, I loved my simple wedding in my simple dress.'

'With your simple husband,' Pete said.

Everyone laughed. I tried to smile, but something heavy had planted itself in me and Harry had caused that to happen.

'Good idea to do a mufti day that day, though,' Jo said. 'Everyone will be a bit excited anyway.'

'See, that's what I don't get!' Pete said. 'What's so exciting?'

'The glamour,' Jo said, 'the fairy tale of a wedding like this, of Lady Diana becoming Princess Diana.'

'I think all that money on that wedding is criminal,' Pete said. 'There shouldn't have to be a mufti day to help the Ugandan famine. The money from that wedding could probably feed all of Africa.'

Jo put down her knife and fork and glared at Pete. 'Since when did you become so moral, Pete? You won't even march against apartheid?'

'That's enough,' Mum said. 'Let's not get into arguments. We know Pete doesn't agree with apartheid. He's just trying to think through other aspects to do with friends and rugby.'

'It's wrong to throw so much money on a wedding on one side of the world, knowing people are starving in another part of the world,' Pete said.

'I agree,' Jo said, 'but we still need romance. The world needs fairy tales.'

I thought of Harry. Sometimes, he made me feel I was in a fairy-tale romance: making jokes, laughing at things I said, kissing me with his soft lips. Sometimes though, like today, he made things difficult. I thought of Stephanie Lulich, and a headache nudged the back of my eyes. I rubbed my temples with my fingers.

'You okay, Liza?' Mum asked.

'Got a headache,' I said.

'Drink some water,' Mum said. 'Make sure you eat all of your dinner too. You might just need food and a bit of hydration. Also, can we talk about something that doesn't cause arguments? No more discussion of weddings, famine or the Springbok Tour.'

We'd nearly finished eating anyway. I wasn't on dishes that night, so I went to my room and played The Eagles on my tape recorder. Turning off the light, I lay on my bed and closed my eyes.

The phone rang, but I didn't get up. Jo answered it again. She tapped on my bedroom door. 'You asleep?'

'No.'

'It's Harry again.' She opened the door and whispered. 'He can't bear to be parted from you.' She pulled the phone into my room. The cord was long enough for it to reach my bed.

'Thanks.'

'I'm being kind cos you've got a headache,' she said as she left the room, closing the door behind her.

I put the receiver to my ear. Harry spoke first. 'Sorry. I've been a jerk. I'm a complete dickhead. Sorry.'

My fingers loosened around the receiver. 'That's okay.'

'Sometimes, I'm just ... I just love you and I think you might ...'

'I love you too,' I interrupted.

Neither of us spoke. Sal scratched at my bedroom door. I climbed off my bed and let her in, then sat back on the edge of my bed.

'I get jealous easily,' Harry said.

'I would never do anything to make you jealous.' I put my hand on my forehead and pressed it. The headache wouldn't go away.

'I know,' Harry said. 'Can we forget this ever happened?'

'Yeah, let's wipe the slate clean. Fresh start tomorrow.'

'Want to go and see *For Your Eyes Only*, the James Bond movie that's just come out?'

'Okay.'

'Saturday?'

'In the afternoon,' I said. 'I've got hockey in the morning.'

'I'll come and watch if it's a home game.'

'It's on the North Shore, miles away.'

'I'll come over after the game then,' Harry said. 'We can bus into town together.'

'Okay.'

We said goodbye, then Harry said, 'I love you' again, but I'd clicked off just as he started saying it, so it was too late for me to reply. I carried the phone out of my room and put it back on the table in the hallway.

On Saturday afternoon, we sat up the back of the cinema and, for a while, we watched the movie. Harry had been holding my hand but when he began to repeatedly brush his fingers across my palm, I became distracted. Then he kissed my cheek, my hair, my forehead, my eyelids, my eyebrows, my ear, all the time holding my hand. His kisses were soft, as if I were something precious. There was nowhere on my face he neglected to kiss. His other hand was on my back, and it moved under my sweatshirt and T-shirt, resting on the side of my waist.

On the screen, Roger Moore wielded guns, while kissing beautiful women, but I couldn't follow the storyline because of Harry's hand. It was an unbearably beautiful weight, and my breath was shallow with the tension of where it would go next. Soon, it began to slide above my waist, up the side of my body, almost to my armpit, skimming over the side of my bra and pressing gently, as if trying to smooth something out.

Whatever was happening on the screen meant nothing now. I turned so that I could kiss Harry properly, and his hand slid under my bra, brushing over and over my breast. Our kiss became urgent. My hands were under his T-shirt now, moving from his back to his chest, pulling his head closer so that we were breathing the same air.

A woman walked up the cinema aisle, feeling her way in the darkness, and stumbled a little at the end of our row. Harry gently pulled away. 'We'd better stop.'

'I don't want to,' I said.

'Neither do I, but we're in a cinema. There are ushers with torches.'

I didn't speak. I couldn't sit and watch the movie quietly. My heart raced. I wanted his hand back on my breast, his breath on my face. I leaned over and kissed his cheek, then my lips travelled to his ear and I whispered, 'I want to keep going.'

Harry squeezed my hand. 'So do I, but not here, not with people eating popcorn and ice creams all around us.'

The last part of the movie was interesting, but I had no idea what was happening. Harry's hand was on mine and when the film finished and the credits came up, we sat listening to Sheena Easton sing the theme song, 'For Your Eyes Only'. It was as if she was singing about us. I breathed deeply and put my hand on my stomach, as if to quieten something. We waited until the end of the song, then we stood up to get the bus home.

On Sunday, the 12th of July, Dad came home late. It was nearly midnight. I was still awake trying to finish some maths homework, but my mind kept wandering to the day before, to the movies and Harry.

From my bedroom, I could hear Dad's animated voice. I put down my pen, made my way to Mum and Dad's bedroom and tapped on the door.

'Come in,' Mum said. She was sitting up in bed, a book in her hand.

'What's going on, Dad? I heard you from my room.'

'Sorry, Liza. Didn't mean to wake you.' Dad took off his jacket and hung it in the wardrobe.

'You didn't.' I sat down on their bed. 'I was finishing some homework.'

'I was just telling your mum about the MOST meeting I've just been to. HART want to be more disruptive. It's only a week until the Springboks arrive, and they're frustrated that the tour hasn't been stopped. Tonight, everyone agreed to disruptive action. The plan is that there'll be protests and disruption in every city centre during each rugby game, so the police will be pulled in all directions and won't be able to focus on protecting rugby grounds.'

'So, there could be violence?' I asked.

'Hope not,' Mum said. She put her book down and drummed her fingers on the hard cover. 'Let's hope the actions just stop games and that the tour ends up being cancelled.'

'How many games will there be each week if the tour does go ahead?' I asked.

'Two,' Dad said. 'So twice a week, there'll be protests happening around the country as well as at the rugby ground.'

'So, during the first game in Gisborne, people will protest here in Auckland?'

'And other cities.' Dad sat down on the bed too. 'MOST will organise the Auckland protests, and other coalitions around the country will organise for their areas.'

'If things start to get violent, Liza,' Mum said, 'I'm not sure about you being involved in the protests.'

'Mum! I can't pull out now!'

'Well, let's see. We can play it by ear. You have mid-year exams coming up anyway, so you need to do some study.'

I stood up. 'I need to finish my maths.'

'Liza, it's so late,' Mum said. 'Why don't you set your alarm a bit earlier and do it in the morning?' She stopped talking and smiled. 'That was a silly suggestion.'

'It was! Get up earlier than I already do? You know I could never do that!'

Back in my bedroom, I gazed at the numbers in the textbook on my desk. It *was* too late. Mum was right. Maybe I'd try to do it during morning tea at school the next day.

A week later, the Springboks arrived in New Zealand, and I wasn't at the airport with Rewi and his mum. I told Rewi I had to work on my *The Taming of the Shrew* essay because it was due on Monday, and I hadn't started it. There was another reason I didn't go to the airport with Rewi though: I didn't want to make Harry jealous.

That Sunday, Mum was up early to let Sal outside to go to the loo, so when Rewi came to our house after the airport protest, she greeted him at the door.

I was in a deep sleep when Rewi knocked on my bedroom door. 'Hey, want to know what you missed out on?'

I opened my eyes. What did Rewi mean? What had I missed out on? Then, I remembered the date and fumbled my way out of bed and into my dressing gown, calling, 'Hang on!'

'See you in the kitchen,' Rewi said.

It was a grey day, but through the light rain, a streak of sunlight spilled onto the kitchen bench. 'Tea?' I asked.

'Dumb question,' Rewi said.

I filled the kettle. 'Did you see Dad? He was there this morning.

He's probably back in the office now, writing up the story.'

'Yep, saw him. It was pretty dark though, hard to see much at first. Liza, y'know how you get so angry with your church and your school? There were students and teachers from Saint John's Theological College, about sixty of them. They carried this big cross, singing hymns and praying for black South Africans. Mum took some photos of them.'

'That's cool. See? That's what our school should be doing.' I poured milk into steaming mugs of tea and put them on the table.

'Some Māori protesters stood on a wall with that banner, y'know, the one that says, "Ka whawhai tonu mātou! Ake! Ake! Ake!" The police tried to get to them, but all the other protesters joined together in a chain so they couldn't get through.' Rewi drank some tea, his eyes alive and his voice excited. I felt a pang that I hadn't gone with him. 'These other protesters were all along a tall wire security fence,' Rewi continued. 'The police couldn't see some of them cutting the wire.'

'They brought wire clippers?'

'Yeah, and when the plane landed, this guy called David Williams pushed through the wire fence and ran onto the tarmac. Other protesters joined him, but the police on the other side tackled them to the ground. Mum took photos of it all. She said David Williams is the secretary of CARE, y'know, that anti-racism group? It means Citizens Association for Racial Equality. Today, Liza Newland, the disruptions began.'

'Did you see the Springboks?'

'Nah, they went straight into a smaller plane to Gisborne for the first game. Heaps of protesters were waiting for them to come through the Arrivals area, but they never did.'

Rewi stayed and had some breakfast, then we decided we'd better do some exam study.

After he left, I went to my room and sat in front of my *Taming of the Shrew* essay. I'd only written a couple of paragraphs. I didn't want to write about the play. Kate had sold out. She'd become a servant to her husband. In the final act, Petruchio proved that she was more obedient than other characters' wives, because she did everything he asked. Kate told the other women that they were not good wives if they were not obedient to their husbands.

In class, Ms Jefferson said that she wondered whether the shrew in the title of the play was really Petruchio, because his behaviour was so bad, far worse than Kate's. She reckoned Kate was taming *him*, playing his games so he'd behave well, and she could live happily with him. I didn't agree though. I thought Kate had lost her free spirit; it had been broken by Petruchio's cruelty.

One girl in our class insisted that Petruchio tamed Kate because it was the only way he could have a good relationship with her. If she'd continued the way she had been, both she and Petruchio would have been miserable. I didn't agree with that either.

I agreed with Kalāsia. Petruchio just wanted Kate's father's money, but he knew he had to live with this difficult woman, so he was showing her he was the boss. It was bad enough breaking a hawk's spirit to train it but doing that to a woman? That was a human rights issue, like apartheid. Nowadays, she'd be able to escape to a Women's Refuge, and Petruchio could end up in court.

CHAPTER 23
DAY OF SHAME, GISBORNE

Dad rang from a phone box in Gisborne a few days before the Springboks' first game against Poverty Bay on Wednesday, the 22nd of July. Mum held the phone up so we could all hear him. He'd been at the official welcome for the Springboks on Poho-O-Rawiri marae earlier in the day.

'Remember about a month ago, that article about Sam Nikora, a Māori elder, who said that if any marae opens its doors to the Springboks, it should be burned down, because it was the same as welcoming Hitler or Pol Pot?' Dad asked.

'Who's Pol Pot?' I asked.

'He was a communist leader in Cambodia whose government caused the death of about two million people,' Mum said.

'Can we hear what Dad has to say?' Jo moaned.

'Sorry for breathing!' I said.

'Stop, girls.' Mum frowned at us. 'Dad's paying for this call and he doesn't want to listen to you argue.' She spoke into the mouthpiece, 'Keep going, love. We're listening.'

'Well, security was tight on this marae today,' Dad said. 'There was a barrier about fifty metres down the road to keep protesters out. One of the protesters, Hone Ngata, wasn't allowed to go onto the marae even though it's his marae. His own uncle wouldn't let him in. Everyone's so divided, even families.'

'Our family's not,' I said.

'Well, Pete's not exactly anti-tour, is he?' Jo said.

'I am anti-tour,' Pete retorted, elbowing Jo in the arm. 'I'm just not protesting, that's all.'

'That hurt!' Jo rubbed at her arm.

'Can we *please* listen to your father!' Mum put the phone to her ear. 'No, actually, let's abandon this idea of a family chat tonight. You three kids go away. I'll talk with Dad on my own.'

Jo and Pete wandered off, and I went into my bedroom. I could hear Mum talking to Dad. 'Give my love to Mere when you see her,' she said. 'I know Tipene's a bit worried about her, and I'm a bit worried about you.'

Dad must have said something funny, because Mum laughed before saying goodbye and putting the phone down.

I waited a few moments to be sure she was busy somewhere else before I phoned Harry. He answered almost straight away. 'I was just about to phone you.'

'Well, I beat you to it,' I said.

'Hate the way I can't see you cos of exams.'

'They'll be over soon, and then there's Ciara's party, remember?'

'We can celebrate,' Harry said. 'I can hold you in my arms and no exam can stop me.'

'Can't wait.'

'I want to do more than just hold you, Liza,' Harry whispered.

'I . . .' My mouth felt suddenly dry.

Harry laughed. I pictured his top lip curling up at my reaction. 'It's okay, Liza, we'll take it as slow as you want. Hang on, Sophie wants to say hello to you.'

The phone made a rustling sound and Sophie said, 'Hi Liza, it's me.'

'Hi, Sophie. How are you?'

'Are you going to come for dinner again when exams are over? Harry said you have to study.'

'He has to study too,' I said.

'But he doesn't. Mum said she's sick of telling him.' Sophie sighed. 'I'd better go now. Dad's told me to go to bed twice and now he's getting annoyed.'

Harry came back on the phone. 'I'll phone you tomorrow night.'

'Yeah, I'd better do some study.'

'Love you,' Harry said.

'Love you too,' I whispered. The thought of Jo hearing me say that from the room next door made me cringe. She'd never stop mentioning it.

Dad rang us every night from Gisborne, telling us about the daily protest activities. On the Monday night, he said a group of protesters gave the Springboks a hard time while they trained. The group included a HART leader, Dick Cuthbert, and a Gisborne protest organiser, Laurie Harrison.

On the Tuesday night, David Williams, who'd run out on the tarmac at the airport, jumped the fence to take part in a Springbok training session, but the police quickly took him off the field. As he was dragged away, he yelled, 'Voetsek!' which Dad was told meant 'Get lost' in Afrikaans, but Rewi's mum said it meant 'Fuck off'. Later that day, protesters in a Land Rover rammed through the fence around Rugby Park, then threw broken glass over the field. They were all arrested.

None of us watched the Gisborne game. Pete would have, but he was at university at the time. The protesters called it 'The Day of Shame'.

That evening, we ate dinner in front of the news on TV. We saw protesters crossing a golf course. At the front were young Māori women with the banner saying, 'Ka whawhai tonu matou! Ake! Ake! Ake!' Behind them, people carried a huge banner, with the words, 'SPRINGBOK THE BIG WHITE LIE'. They had a picture of a swastika beside the words.

Then, we saw protesters running up a steep, muddy bank to the fence around Rugby Park. They tore at the fence, pulling a chunk of it down. They weren't wearing helmets like the police, who hit them with their batons. Fists, feet and knees knocked the protesters backward, down the muddy slope.

I looked over at Mum. She'd stopped eating like the rest of us, and she held her fork mid-air as she stared at the TV.

From behind the fence, rugby spectators threw bottles and rubbish at the protesters. Some ran through the torn fence and attacked protesters, who fell in the mud. The camera zoomed in on protesters lying injured and bleeding, then moved to a close-up of a policeman with blood on his face.

The news reporter said that, after attempts at charging the fence, the protesters stood back, yelling and chanting from that point onwards. He added that, in Auckland, protesters had forced their way through the entrance to Eden Park.

Mum turned off the TV. 'I'm worried about what's happened at Gisborne. Wish your dad would phone so I know he's okay.'

'Hope Mere's okay too,' I said. 'She's taking photos there.'

'Those protesters just threw themselves at the fence,' Pete said. 'They put their bodies on the line.'

'Seems to me,' Jo said, 'that "disruption" means protesters are putting their lives in danger.'

Mum stood up. 'I'm going to walk Sal. Would you kids please sort out the dishes?'

I was scrubbing a pot in soapy water when the phone rang. Pete dropped his tea towel and went down the hallway to answer it.

'Dad!' he cried.

Jo and I went to join him.

'You okay? We just watched the news.' Pete turned the phone towards us, and we circled around it.

'I'm a reporter, so I'm fine,' Dad said. 'I just look on, observing and asking questions here and there. Some of the protesters aren't so fine though. I saw a woman being dragged by her hair across the mud by a plain-clothes cop. Ugly stuff.'

'Mum's walking Sal,' I said, leaning into the mouthpiece.

'Well, listen kids, tell her I'm fine and that she mustn't worry about me.'

'She'll still worry,' Jo said. 'We all will.'

'You don't need to. I'm not in the line of fire.' The phone started to make a beeping sound. 'Damn. I've run out of coins. Need to go and finish writing up stories for tomorrow's paper anyway. Love you all. Tell Mum I'll phone tomorrow night.'

After we put the phone down, we went back to the dishes. I'd just finished washing the last pot, when Mum and Sal came through the door. 'You missed Dad,' I said. 'He said you don't need to worry and that he'll ring you tomorrow.'

Mum flicked on the kettle. 'I think the protesters are going to have to play the same game as the police,' she said, 'like wearing helmets to protect themselves. The whole thing's going to escalate, and the violence will get worse.'

'Who knows,' Jo said, 'they might stop a game or the whole tour. The disruptive action might work.'

'I just don't like seeing people being hurt,' Mum said. 'I'm going to see if there's anything funny on TV. Need to get my mind off things. You go and study, girls. Exams start tomorrow.'

'I have to write an essay,' Pete said.

'Let's all study at the dining room table,' Jo suggested.

'Only if no one talks,' Pete replied. 'I need to concentrate.'

We set ourselves up with our books around the table. Every now and then, Mum's chuckling filtered through the lounge door. During an ad break, she came out to make another cup of tea. 'Look at you three! How cute!'

'What are you watching?' I asked.

'*Gliding on.*'

'Don't talk!' Jo said.

'Sorry!' I looked at Mum and she put her finger over her lips and pointed to the lounge before disappearing back through the door.

I made a special effort to get up early for my English exam. In fact, I was already dressed when Kalāsia arrived. On the way to school, Rewi put his hand on my forehead. 'Just can't quite work it out,' he said.

I shook his hand off. 'What are you doing?'

'Checking to see if you've got a fever. You got up so early!'

'You're a dork. I've got an exam.'

'If I had a thermometer, I'd stick it under your arm,' Rewi said.

We talked about the Gisborne game and Rewi said there'd been a rumour about a helicopter spraying a chemical over the rugby field. It never happened, but the police did order a plane to land in Palmerston North, which they searched. In it was Steve Bayliss, one of HART's national organisers.

Ciara joined us on the way to school, which never usually happened because we were always running late. She chatted about her party.

'Dad said it's got to be all over by midnight. He said he'll turn the music off and start playing his uilleann pipes if people don't leave.'

'I don't mind if he plays those,' I said. 'I'll do an Irish jig if he does, and the party will go on.'

'You don't have to live with those pipes,' Ciara said. 'I can't talk, watch TV, listen to the radio, study or anything when Dad's on them.'

Before we reached the school gate, Rewi put his hand on my forehead again. 'Seems okay,' he said.

'Get lost.' I shoved his hand away.

He was still laughing, as we turned away into the gate. 'Drink lots of fluids!' he called after me.

I gave him the fingers, then saw Sister Ignatia looking at me as she was heading towards the gate to catch latecomers. I quickly dropped my arm.

Sister Agnes wasn't in the classroom when we arrived, but she must have been there earlier, because the desks were arranged into single-file rows.

'I can't sit beside you,' Kalāsia said. 'Good, though, in case you cheat off me.'

'Yeah, as if,' I said.

Kalāsia sat down at the desk across from me and took two pens out of her bag. 'Just in case one runs out,' she said.

'You are the most organised person I know.'

'Well, I'm trying to help you become more organised, Liza, but it's harder than I thought it would be.'

From a couple of desks away, Ursula called to me. 'Liza, come here. Tell me which quotes I should use from *The Taming of the Shrew.*'

'Now? The exam starts soon.'

'Please!' Ursula begged.

I shrugged and walked over to her desk. She'd been drawing something on her pencil case with a fountain pen, but the ink was bleeding into the coarse material. 'Tried to draw a heart, but it just looks like a blob. I wanted to write Josh's name in it.'

Ursula opened her ring binder and flicked to a piece of refill with some quotes on it. 'Which ones should I use?'

I bent over and scanned the quotes and was about to speak when Susan Leighton called out, 'Hey, Liza, bet you were disappointed with the rugby yesterday!'

I looked up. 'Sorry?'

'Y'know, all those protesters trying to stop the game, but just getting a beating instead.' Susan was sitting with a few other girls in our class. Her eyes were fixed on me, her thick eyebrows in a frown. I turned back to Ursula's page of quotations.

'Ignore her,' Ursula said.

'Was your dad there?' Susan asked.

'Yep,' I answered, keeping my eyes on the quotes.

'So, what do you think?' Ursula asked. 'That one about how he's taming her like a falcon? That's a good quote to use, eh?'

'Bet your dad got special treatment from the police cos he's a reporter,' Susan said. 'Must be so much easier to be anti-tour when you're not actually protesting!'

'Stop it, Susan,' Kalāsia said.

'What?'

'You're being mean.'

'It's okay, Kalāsia,' I said. 'I'm not listening.'

'Those protesters are full of shit,' Susan said.

Ursula swivelled around. 'Shut your mouth, Susan. We're trying to study here!'

Susan turned back to the group of girls beside her. I could hear my name being said, but I tried to focus on the quotes in front of me.

Sister Agnes entered the room and made her way to her desk. 'Sit down everyone, please.'

'I didn't really get to help you,' I said to Ursula.

'Because of that stupid bitch over there.' Ursula motioned towards Susan. 'I couldn't care less about any of that stuff.'

'About the tour?'

Ursula nodded. 'I know you do, Liza, and that's okay. I just don't care about any of it at all.'

Sister Agnes had her back to us and was writing the times for the exam up on the blackboard.

'But how . . ?'

Ursula interrupted me. 'I don't care about rugby and I don't care about people in other countries. Well, if I could wave a magic wand to make everyone happy, I would, but I can't so why waste time worrying about it?'

Sister Agnes moved to her desk and seemed to be searching for something in a drawer.

I wasn't sure what to say to Ursula. Usually people were either for or against or sitting on the fence, saying they could see both sides of the argument. 'I'd better sit down,' I said, 'before Sister Agnes starts giving me a hard time.'

Ursula reached out and held my elbow gently. 'I know you care about all that political stuff, but me, I just want to party and have a good time.'

'I like partying too, but it's just . . .'

'You care about all that stuff, I get it,' Ursula interrupted. 'It's kind of cool, but it's not me.'

'Hurry up, please, Liza,' Sister Agnes said. 'You have an exam starting in ten minutes.'

As I sat down across from Kalāsia, the smell of coconut oil in her hair wafted over to me. I breathed it in. 'Thanks, Kalāsia.'

'What for?'

'For sticking up for me.'

'You're my friend.' Kalāsia put her hand on her heart. "Ofa atu.'

'What does that mean?'

'I love you.'

I smiled. "Ofa atu too.'

We laughed.

'That's a happy sound for the first day of exams,' Sister Agnes said from her desk. 'Girls, the bell will go in a few minutes, so let's get prepared. In a moment, I'll ask you to take out pens and refill paper, while I give out the exam papers. They'll be face down, so don't turn them over until I say so. I'll start the exam off, then Ms Jefferson will be in to check on how things are going.'

Sister Agnes moved from her desk to the centre of the classroom. She reached up, tucking any stray pieces of hair under the collar of her veil, then said, 'Before the bell goes though, I'd like to say a prayer.'

I wrote so much in the exam that I ended up with a blister on my finger. I wrote about the different ways the play could be interpreted, such as the idea that Petruchio was really the shrew and Kate had ended up managing her husband's difficult behaviour. I used quotes and examples and compared Kate to Lady Diana, like we had in class.

Ms Jefferson popped in to check that we understood the exam questions, then she left. Different teachers came in to supervise us, but I barely looked at them, I was so determined to write everything I knew.

At the end of the exam, Ms Jefferson came to get the papers. She moved around the room, checking we'd written our names on our papers and thanking us, as we passed them to her. 'Go out into this sunny day now, girls,' she said. 'Have a decent break and eat some lunch before you start studying for maths tomorrow.'

'So, we just go home now?' Ursula asked.

'Yes, you do,' Ms Jefferson said. 'You're seniors, so we trust you to go home to study.'

Ursula grinned. 'This exam thing's not too bad!'

Kalāsia, Ciara, Stella and I made our way out of the classroom, chatting about what we'd written in the exam. The sun warmed our faces as we headed home.

Ciara told us about how her big sister had a new boyfriend, who was Italian. She'd met him at work. 'Did you know that real spaghetti isn't the stuff we get in a can?' she asked. 'It's not like that at all.

Luca brought some real spaghetti over and made this thing called Spaghetti Bolognese. He cooked these long pieces of dry spaghetti, like massive noodles, in hot water. He used olive oil and poured this amazing tomato sauce over the spaghetti. It was yummy!'

'What's olive oil?' I asked.

'It's made from these small vegetables called olives. There's a picture of them on the bottle. He taught me how to do this.' She kissed the tips of her fingers and cried, 'Delizioso!'

'You should've brought us some,' I said.

'I'll bring some next time, promise.'

A car with four guys in it slowed beside us. One of them yelled out the window, 'Fucking boonga!' Another yelled, 'Coon! Fucking coon!'

'Piss off!' I screamed at them, giving them the fingers, but they sped away.

Kalāsia dropped her bag.

'Ignore them,' I said. 'They're jerks.'

She nodded.

'Wankers,' Stella said. 'Don't let it upset you.'

'I'm Tongan,' she said. 'That's not bad.' She looked down at her bag on the footpath. Tears fell onto it, sliding down the blue vinyl.

'Course it's not bad.' I put my bag down next to hers and hugged her. 'Making a new Tongan friend is one of the most interesting things to happen to me this year.'

Kalāsia's back shuddered under my hands.

'We should have got their number plate and reported them to the police,' Stella said.

'But some police would agree with them,' Kalāsia said. 'I feel scared sometimes.'

'You have us,' I said, 'and my family and Sister Agnes, Sister Ignatia, Ms Jefferson, Father Luke, so many people. Don't be scared.'

Kalāsia sobbed in between her words. 'I . . . can't . . . help it.'

Ciara and Stella wrapped their arms around Kalāsia too. 'Group hug,' Ciara said.

When we pulled away, I picked up Kalāsia's bag and handed it to her, and we kept walking.

We didn't talk anymore about that verbal assault on Kalāsia. We tried to talk about other things, funny things, like Rewi's dumb jokes and how Sister Agnes and Ursula annoyed each other, but Kalāsia was quiet for the rest of the walk home. Even when Stella and Ciara turned into their streets, and it was only us, she just nodded or shook her head in response to my attempts at conversation.

When we reached my house, I asked her if she wanted to come in for lunch and to do some maths study together. She finally spoke, saying she needed to go home.

'Kalāsia,' I said, 'people like that . . .'

'They make me ashamed of who I am.' Kalāsia's eyes were on the ground again.

'But *they* should be ashamed!'

'The whole street could hear them. They're not ashamed.'

'Well, they should be embarrassed that people hear them say that stuff.'

Kalāsia looked up. 'Maths exam tomorrow. I'd better go home and study. See you tomorrow.' She turned away.

'Early?' I called after her.

'Always early!'

I began to walk into our driveway, then stopped and turned. "Ofa atu, Kalāsia!' In case she hadn't heard it, I yelled it again, so that the whole street could hear. "Ofa atu!'

'You too,' she called back. Her voice was quieter, but loud enough for some neighbours to hear. Maybe that was better than nothing.

CHAPTER 24
HAMILTON

Saturday, the 25th of July was the day the Springboks played Waikato in Hamilton. It was also two days before my science exam. Mum went to a protest rally at Potter's Park with Tipene, Marama and Nikau. I couldn't go because I had to study. So did Jo and Rewi.

Rewi came over to study with me, so that we could keep each other focused. We made a rule that after every two hours of study, we'd catch up on the news of the protests in Hamilton then go for a walk and have a ciggie. By midday, we decided we had to change the rules, because what was happening in Hamilton was too exciting. We began to take turns checking the TV every half hour or so.

Rewi's mum had told him about Operation Everest, which was a plan to break into Rugby Park. At the same time, other protesters had bought tickets to the game, so they could run onto the field from inside. It was unbearable not to be watching the march on TV. Instead, Rewi and I concentrated hard on our science notes, even when we heard Pete yelling at the telly from the lounge.

When it was my turn to go and check what was happening, I reported back to Rewi that the huge crowd of protesters was just leaving somewhere called Garden Place. 'They're chanting "Amandla"', I said, 'making their way to the Rugby Park.'

A bit later, Pete shouted something, so Rewi and I broke our rule and ran to the lounge. 'This is getting intense!' Pete said, leaning forward on the sofa. 'Get Jo, quick!'

I yelled down the hallway for Jo. Her door opened. 'What's happening? I'm coming.'

The protesters were outside the ground now, chanting, 'The people say no!' Inside the boundary fence, tour supporters hurled abuse at them. One shouted, 'Get away from here, nigger-lovers!'

'Dick!' Rewi said.

'Wanker,' Pete agreed.

Hardly any protesters had helmets on. Through the barbed-wire fence, spectators spat in their faces, swearing at them, but the protesters ignored them. Instead, they pulled at the wire fence, hundreds of them, wrenching it away. Seconds later, the fence came down.

'They're in!' Pete yelled.

Hordes of protesters ran onto the field and the game came to a halt. Some rugby fans attacked protesters as they ran in. A few tried to pull a large cross from a small religious protest group. One yelled, 'How would you feel if your daughter was married to one?'

'Married to one?' I was confused.

'He means, "Would you want your daughter to be married to a black South African?"' Jo said.

'Those guys with the cross might be from Saint John's,' Rewi said, 'the ones who were at the airport.'

The protesters who'd bought tickets sprinted down the terraces to join the increasingly large group on the field. Red smoke rose from the grass around the demonstration, and the TV commentator said that he wasn't sure whether it came from smoke bombs or was some sort of gas. He said approximately one thousand protesters were on the field. People booed and heckled from the grandstand, while the police made a circle around the crowd of protesters.

Linking arms, the protesters began to chant, 'The whole world's watching. The whole world's watching.'

'That's Tame Iti!' Rewi said. 'He's a Māori activist.'

'The one with the helmet on?' I asked.

'Yep, he's pretty cool. There's Eva Rickard too. She was arrested a few years ago for doing a sit-in protest over Māori land that the government turned into a golf course. Mum took photos of her.'

'You know so much,' I said to Rewi. I realised I'd given him a compliment, so added, 'about some things.'

The TV camera followed lines of police coming out from under the grandstand. They wore helmets with visors and carried batons. Spectators cheered as the police ran in formation around the protesters and then moved in towards them.

'They're riot police,' I said.

Now, the chant from the demonstrators changed to, 'Call it off! Call it off!'

'There's Dad!' Pete yelled.

The camera slid across Dad who was running onto the field with other reporters. They had cameras hanging around their necks, trying to get photos and film footage of what was unfolding before their eyes.

'He could get hurt!' Jo said.

'Don't worry,' Rewi said. 'He looks official with cameras and stuff, like Mum. No one'll touch them.'

I hoped Rewi was right. Jo didn't seem convinced; her eyebrows were furrowed in concern.

'Why aren't the police forcing the protesters off?' Pete asked.

'They're trying to protect them from rugby fans,' Rewi said. 'Look!'

A few spectators were dragging a protester along the ground, kicking him. The police pulled them apart.

'Man, if they let tour supporters loose on those protesters, it'd be a bloodbath,' Pete said.

The riot police formed four rows between the protesters and the crowd in the terraces. The commentator said an announcement was about to be made. Over some sort of intercom, a man said, 'The game has now been officially cancelled.'

'Yes!' we cried, as the huge crowd of protesters cheered. We watched them throw up their hands and fists in celebration.

Moments later, rugby fans began to chant, 'We want rugby! We want rugby!'

The police began to arrest some of the protesters, taking them off the field one by one. The TV commentator said that a light plane had been stolen from Taupō Airport and that a bomb had gone off at Christchurch Airport.

'This is massive!' Rewi said. 'Stuff's happening everywhere.'

The crowd didn't leave. They kept shouting, 'We want rugby!' Some leapt down onto the field and attacked protesters.

'This isn't good,' Pete said.

Our mood changed from jubilation to horror as protesters were pushed to the ground, kicked in the stomach, punched in the face and dragged by their hair. Beer cans and crates hit heads and faces. It was like something out of a movie. Hard to believe this was happening an hour and a half's drive from us, in Hamilton.

At some point we turned off the TV. Studying was impossible now. How would we be able to concentrate? We went into the kitchen. Pete put bread in the toaster, but Jo said she needed something sweet, taking out the biscuit tin and passing round chocolate biscuits.

'Mum'll be back soon,' I said.

'You two had better run off and have a quick smoke then,' Pete said.

'What?'

Pete rolled his eyes. 'Everyone knows you smoke, Liza. Don't know why you bother pretending.'

'Does Mum know?'

Pete nodded.

'And Dad,' Jo added.

'How?'

'Cos you stink of smoke when you come home,' Pete said.

'I spray perfume on myself and . . .'

'Doesn't work,' Jo said.

'Are they angry? They've never said anything to me!'

'Mum said she was worried about your health, that's all,' Jo said.

'And Dad said smoking was a waste of money,' Pete said. 'Guess they thought you'd know better.'

'Don't act all holier than thou, Pete!'

'Well, it is pretty dumb, Liza.' Pete put some toast on a plate and began to spread huge amounts of butter on it.

'Come on, Rewi,' I said. 'Let's be dumb and go and have a smoke.'

Jo passed a handful of biscuits to Rewi. 'Take these,' she said. 'We're still celebrating the game being cancelled, even if you two idiots do smoke.'

Later that evening, Dad phoned. Mum had been waiting for his call. She'd sent us off to our rooms to study and done the dishes by herself, because she said she needed to keep busy. When the phone rang, I heard Mum's quick footsteps down the hallway then, 'Hello' followed by, 'Thank God you're okay!'

I put down my pen and went to listen in. Jo came out of her bedroom to join us, and Pete stuck his head out the lounge door, saying, 'Dad?'

Mum held the phone out so we could all hear Dad talking. 'Terrible aftermath,' Dad said. 'Fantastic that the game was cancelled, but the violence afterwards has been devastating.'

'We watched the news,' Mum said. 'Tour supporters were a danger to the protesters this time, not the police.'

'Just ...' Dad hesitated for a moment, 'just horrific. Can't think of any other word. Like some sort of horror movie, where the world's gone mad and there's no law and order, no respect for other human beings ...'

'Did the police behave well?' Jo interrupted.

'From what I saw, yes. I wasn't sure they would when the protesters invaded the field. I guess after the Gisborne match ...' Dad coughed. 'An Anglican priest, George Armstrong, was talking with the police, trying to keep things peaceful.'

'I think I saw him on TV,' I said.

'And Father Terry Dibble, a Catholic priest who's the secretary of CARE, had an intense conversation with the police commissioner, Bob Walton,' Dad said. 'Apparently, the police said that a guy called Pat McQuarrie, had taken a Cessna from Taupō Airport and was heading to Hamilton. They'd heard he was going to fly the plane into the crowd, but Father Terry knows him and said he wouldn't endanger people like that.'

'Is that the real reason they called off the game?' Mum asked. 'Because they could have removed all the protesters if they'd really wanted to.'

'I reckon the police couldn't take the risk that a plane might crash into the crowd,' Dad said. 'Also, getting the protesters off the field would have involved using force.'

'What about the bomb at Christchurch Airport?' Pete asked.

'All I know is it went off in the men's toilets,' Dad said. 'No one was in there and no one was seen running out. Made a loud bang though and shattered a bit of glass.'

'Are you okay, Dad?' Jo asked.

'Yeah, just a bit shocked at some of the things I've seen today. Some pro-tour guys seriously hurt protesters, even on the field while the police were trying to help them leave.'

'It was awful,' Jo said. 'We turned the TV off after a while.'

'I saw some young guys punching two teenage girls. One lost some teeth; the other girl fell to the ground. I saw people get hit in the face with beer cans and crates. One girl tripped in the mud, and they pulled her up by the hair to punch her.' Dad stopped speaking and coughed again. 'I've been talking a lot today. Croaky voice.'

'You need a rest,' Mum said.

'Thing is, even when we went for some food and a beer, the stories kept coming. We met up with some other reporters in the pub, who told us that some nurses had constructed a makeshift ambulance out of a Bedford van. They'd put a red cross on it and were helping injured people. When they were trying to get a barely conscious girl into the van, some pro-tour guys attacked the van, almost tipping it over, yelling, "Kill the bitch!" The nurses managed to get away, but the guys chased them, smashing the windscreen and side windows.'

'That's disgusting,' Mum said.

'Did anyone hurt you?' I asked.

'Me? No, I'm fine, sweetheart. Don't worry about me. The tour supporters weren't interested in beating up news reporters. They were after the protesters.'

'I just wanted to check before I go back to my science revision,' I said. 'Got my science exam tomorrow.'

'You go and study,' Dad said. 'Don't waste any more time chatting with me.'

'At least I don't have to study *The Taming of the Shrew* anymore,' I said. 'Hate that play. It's all about making women with opinions shut up.'

'Sounds good to me,' Pete said.

I rolled my eyes at Pete. 'Dork.'

'Okay,' Mum said, 'you all know Dad's fine. Off you go to study.'

'I don't have exams,' Pete said, 'so I'll just go back and lie on the sofa and watch TV.' He looked at me and grinned.

I rolled my eyes at him again and went back into my bedroom.

The next day, we heard that John Minto had been hit by a full beer can, thrown from the stands at Rugby Park, while leaving the field. He'd gone to hospital but, after being treated there, he was followed to a friend's house and attacked again. The people responsible also destroyed the house.

That same day, we heard on the news that the prime minister, Robert Muldoon, had flown out of the country and was on his way to Prince Charles and Lady Diana's wedding.

CHAPTER 25
NEW PLYMOUTH AND MOLESWORTH STREET

The day of the royal wedding was also our mufti day. Exams were over too, so the day felt like a celebration. We weren't allowed to wear jeans to mufti day, so I wore a long, tiered skirt that Mum bought me last summer. Each tier alternated between a pinky-white and red colour. I was running late and didn't have much time to think about what I'd wear with it, so I grabbed a red T-shirt and shoved my feet into my white sneakers.

When Kalāsia arrived, I told her she didn't need to plait my hair. 'We're allowed to wear it out for mufti day.'

'Are we?' she said, sitting on my bed, watching me pin my hair back. 'Too late. Mine's plaited, and I'm not taking it out now.'

Kalāsia wore a black T-shirt that had white flower designs on it. I asked her what the flower was, and she said it was a frangipani which smelt like heaven. 'One day, you'll have to come to Tonga with me and we'll pick frangipanis and stick them in our hair. They won't fall out of your hair because it's so thick.'

As we left the house, I thought of how girls would be checking out each other's clothes. That was the only problem with mufti day, I never knew whether I quite matched up.

At school, Ursula had been true to her word and was wearing her mother's wedding dress. Sitting slightly awkwardly, surrounded by curious classmates, she waved at us as we entered the classroom, her arms clad in long, close-fitting sleeves. 'Hey, you two, look!' She stood up and I stopped. The dress clung to her chest and her waist, then flared out down to her ankles. Her blonde, pink-streaked hair fell around her shoulders.

'You look gorgeous,' I said.

'Beautiful!' Kalāsia breathed beside me.

'Mum based this dress on Audrey Hepburn's first wedding dress,' Ursula said. 'She was an actress Mum loved.'

'It's so . . .' I reached out and ran my hand along the material. 'Is it silk?'

'Yep, Mum told me not to dirty it or rip it, so I'd better skip PE today.'

'Doubt Ms Evans'll let you off. Didn't you bring your sports gear?'

Ursula picked up the train and did a pirouette. 'Course not. I'm celebrating a royal wedding. I can't wear rompers today!' She walked out the classroom door, saying 'Watch this!' Poking her head back in, she called, 'Everyone sing "Here Comes the Bride". I'll walk in while you sing.'

We all began to sing, 'Here comes the bride, fair, fat and wide, slipped on a banana skin and went for a ride.'

Ursula had only taken a few steps by the time we'd finished, so we began again. 'Here comes the bride . . .' We began to tail off and Ursula looked at us inquiringly. 'Keep going!'

Behind Ursula was Sister Agnes, walking slowly, watching Ursula make her way across the front of the classroom, as if in the aisle of a church. Sister Agnes didn't say a word. She stopped walking, looked at us, put her finger to her lips and let Ursula keep going.

We'd stopped singing though, and Ursula realised something wasn't right. She turned and her jaw dropped for a moment before she regained her composure. 'Sister Agnes, I was just showing everyone how a bride walks up the aisle.'

'I see that, Ursula.'

Neither of them spoke for a moment.

'Well, have you reached the altar yet, or do we need to wait a bit longer?' Sister Agnes asked.

'I think I'm at the altar now,' Ursula said.

'Looks like you've been jilted.'

Ursula smiled. 'Should I faint in shock?'

'I'd rather you didn't.' Sister Agnes walked past Ursula to her desk. 'I've got quite enough to do today, without taking care of disillusioned brides.'

Ursula began to walk back to her desk.

'For goodness sake, Ursula,' Sister Agnes said, 'pick up that train or you'll have everyone tripping over it.'

Ursula reached around to pull up the train. 'Liza was meant to hold it for me, but she doesn't want to be my bridesmaid.'

'Well, I . . .'

Sister Agnes interrupted me. 'You don't need to think of a reason for refusing Ursula's offer of a bridesmaid's role, Eliza.'

Ursula carefully arranged the train to fall at the side of her chair, then eased herself down. 'Sister, were you ever proposed to?'

Sister Agnes lifted her head from whatever she'd begun to write at her desk. 'No, Ursula, I joined the convent and became a nun.'

'So, you married Jesus?'

'Well, I've never felt particularly comfortable with that expression. I committed my life to Jesus. That's how I prefer to think of it.'

'I'd like to have a real husband,' Ursula said.

Kalāsia nudged me. 'She's being a bit rude now.'

I shrugged and made a face. Sometimes Ursula seemed to be on a train that was hurtling towards disaster.

Sister Agnes put down her pen and stood up, folding her arms. 'I have seen many women in happy marriages, but I've also seen some in unhappy ones. Just remember, girls, once you've chosen a man, he's your husband for life. Choose wisely. Now, the bell is about to go. Let's take a moment to pray for the Ugandan people who are facing this terrible famine and who will benefit from this mufti money.' Sister Agnes bowed her head.

For the rest of the day, Ursula flounced through the school grounds in her mum's wedding dress. Ms Evans, our PE teacher, made her be goalkeeper in a hockey game, even though Ursula protested that it might ruin her dress. Ms Evans said it involved very little running and perhaps it might remind her to pop some rompers underneath if she ever chose to wear a wedding dress for mufti day again.

While we were at school, marchers had made their way to Rugby Park in New Plymouth where the Springboks were playing Taranaki. I had hockey practice after school, and when I got home, Pete told me that the police hadn't let protesters as close to the rugby ground as had originally been agreed. When the protesters took another route, managing to get much closer to the gates, riot police charged them, grunting 'Move! Move! Move!' They walked into the protest group, hitting them with their batons.

'And Taranaki lost the game,' Pete said.

'I couldn't care less about who won or lost, Pete.' I was hot and sticky and smelt after all my running around at hockey practice. I made my way down the hallway to the bathroom.

'Well, I care!' Pete called after me. 'Think of how you feel when you lose a hockey game!'

'I'm not playing against South Africa where black people have no rights!' I slammed the bathroom door shut. Why did Pete care so much about a game? Even though I loved hockey, I'd never put it before the wellbeing of others. I turned on the shower. My legs were filthy, covered in mud. I pulled my sweaty rompers and top off and stepped under the hot water.

That evening, I rang Harry a couple of times and no one answered. I lay on the sofa, relieved that exams were over and I could completely relax.

I could have gone to bed then, as my eyelids were closing, but Jo told me I had to stay up and watch the royal wedding with her. She and Mum sat in the armchairs near me and talked about the New Plymouth game. Mum said that the marches in Auckland and Wellington had started later than in other cities, so that workers could take part. She hadn't gone tonight because she'd had a headache all day and needed to rest. 'I couldn't face marching,' Mum said. 'Guess I get to watch the wedding now too.'

'Where's Pete?' I asked, forcing myself to take part in the conversation, so that I'd stay awake.

'Gone for a run,' Mum said.

'But I'm sure he'll be popping in to remind us of how immoral it is to have spent all that money on the wedding when people are starving in Africa,' Jo said.

'Well, he's right, really . . .' I began to say, but Jo interrupted me. 'Don't you start!'

The phone rang. 'I'll get it,' I said, standing up.

'Lover boy,' Jo said.

'Shut up!'

I tried to walk casually out of the lounge, but the moment I'd shut the door, I ran to the phone. 'Hello.'

No one spoke, but I heard a sniff.

'Harry?'

'Yep.' He was whispering.

'You okay?'

'Not really.' He sniffed again.

'What's wrong?'

'Dad's a bastard.'

'Why? What's happened?'

'He came home pissed, then lost it with Mum. He said she over-cooked the veggies.' Harry stopped and blew his nose. 'Sorry, I'm a bit...'

'Upset,' I said, finishing his sentence for him. 'Then what happened?'

'Mum said the veggies weren't overcooked and he started yelling. I told him to leave her alone. He pushed me out of the way and just kept yelling, then picked up the pot and threw the hot veggies all over the floor.' He stopped speaking, but I could hear his ragged breathing and knew he was crying.

'It's okay.' I didn't know what else to say.

Harry continued, 'Sophie started screaming, then Dad punched a hole in the kitchen wall and swore at Mum, told us we were all useless and walked out of the house.'

'That's terrible, Harry.' I tried to think of how I could help. 'Want me to come over? I can ask Mum.'

'It's alright.'

But it wasn't. I could hear Harry's quiet crying on the other end of the phone.

'I'm going to have dinner with Mum and Sophie,' Harry said. 'No veggies now. I cleaned them off the floor and threw them in the rubbish, but there's still other stuff in the oven. Don't feel like eating, though, to be honest.'

'Harry, you sure you don't want me to come over? Mum could drop me off.'

'You could admire the picture of the cute, fluffy cat on our kitchen wall. Mum pulled it out of a magazine to cover the hole. She trimmed it neatly into a rectangle to make it look even tidier, but we'll always know what's underneath it.'

Jo stuck her head out of the lounge door. 'It's starting!'

Harry said Sophie and his mum wanted to watch the wedding too, so he'd go and join them and try to eat something.

'Will he come back tonight?'

'Mum's put the chain on the door, so he can't get in. If the police come, they sometimes put him in a cell for the night, so he can't come back. They didn't come tonight though, so the neighbours obviously didn't hear. They're the ones who phone the police.'

Jo opened the lounge door again, saying, 'Come on!'

'You go,' Harry said. 'I'll be okay.'

'Phone me back if you need to.' I put my lips up against the mouthpiece and said, 'I love you, Harry.'

'Love you too.' He was still crying. 'Bye, Liza.'

I walked back into the lounge. The royal family was arriving at Saint Paul's Cathedral. The Queen and her husband were in a horse-drawn carriage, and the Queen waved to the watching crowds.

'You okay, Liza?' Mum asked.

'Just . . . Harry's got something going on.' I lay back down on the sofa, then sat up again. I couldn't relax now.

'What's happening?' Mum asked.

'He's just having a bit of a hard time,' I said, 'but it's alright.' I didn't want to tell Mum too much in case she interfered somehow.

Mum nodded and stood up. 'That's good. Let me know if I can help in any way. I'm going to make tea and get some biscuits.'

'That's very British, Mum,' Jo said. 'Tea and biscuits!'

We watched political people enter the cathedral, like the British prime minister, Margaret Thatcher, and the American president, Ronald Reagan. Royals from all over Europe were there too. The TV commentator explained who everybody was.

'They're all wearing hats, eh?' Jo said. 'We don't really wear hats to weddings here, do we?'

'Don't think so,' I said.

Lady Diana was inside a carriage, like something out of a fairy tale, with her dad, Earl Spencer, beside her. We couldn't see her face through the windows, because of her veil.

Prince Charles arrived at the cathedral first, surrounded by men in red suits on horses. Then Lady Diana arrived, and the commentator said she was 'demure' behind her veil and began to talk about her dress that had been kept secret up until now. He said it was made out of ivory silk taffeta, with antique lace trims and a long, twenty-five-foot, hand-embroidered train.

Mum came in with mugs and chocolate-chip biscuits. 'The dress, eh?' she said.

'Mum, what does "demure" mean?' I asked.

'Ah, modest and shy.' Mum passed the biscuits to us.

'Why is it that the perfect woman is always modest and shy? It's the same in *The Taming of the Shrew*, and that was written hundreds of years ago. Nothing's changed. It's 1981 and the perfect woman is demure!' I took a biscuit and sank my teeth into it.

'Things have changed a bit, Liza,' Mum said. 'We're watching a traditional royal wedding here, so it's not exactly reflecting the real world.'

'I don't know, Mum. I reckon most guys still like a woman who behaves like that.'

'Hmmm, maybe you're right,' Mum said. 'Well, I'm not demure and your father quite likes me.'

I smiled. 'Yeah, well, not all guys are like Dad.'

We were watching Lady Diana and Prince Charles saying their vows when the phone rang. I leapt up thinking it might be Harry again, but it was Dad.

'Have you heard about Molesworth Street?' he asked.

'No.'

'I'm in New Plymouth, but I've seen some of the photos and news footage. The Wellington marchers were attacked by the Red Squad in Molesworth Street outside parliament. They were marching and chanting peacefully, but the police behaved as if they were fighting off murderous criminals. Honestly, I've never seen anything like it. Old women, young people, injured by our own police force.'

'That's . . . we've been watching the wedding,' I said.

'The wedding?' Dad paused for a moment. 'Oh, yeah, the royal wedding. Forgot about that. You need to watch what's going on here, in our own country. Would you get your mother, Liza? I've still got a few coins here to keep talking.'

'Okay. Love you, Dad.' I ran to the lounge. 'Dad's on the phone. There's been heaps of police violence at the march in Wellington.'

Mum stood up. 'Is he okay?'

'Yep, he's still in New Plymouth.'

'Thank God.' Mum left us in front of the wedding to speak to Dad.

'I've had enough of this now, Jo,' I said.

Pete entered the room, showered and clean after his run. 'I've had enough of it without even beginning to watch it.' He grabbed a handful of biscuits and sat down on the sofa.

'I'm going to bed,' I said.

As I closed the lounge door behind me, I could hear the beginning of an argument between Jo and Pete. 'Waste of money,' Pete said. 'That dress alone could feed a whole village.'

I was too tired for their arguing, too tired to think about how police could beat up their fellow citizens and too tired to think of Harry and his sadness and anger. I needed to sleep.

CHAPTER 26
CIARA'S PARTY

On Saturday, after my hockey game and before the Springboks' game against Manawatū, I walked Sal up the road to the Anglican Church. There was an op shop there, and I wanted to buy something special to wear to Ciara's party that night.

Two older women behind the counter smiled at me as I walked in. A few middle-aged women were already searching through the racks of clothes. I hoped that didn't mean there was nothing for younger people.

I'd already decided to wear my denim skirt and boots. At least I had that sorted out. I just wanted something beautiful to go on top. I thought of Ursula's broderie anglaise camisole top again, the one she'd worn at her party. It was sexy. I wanted something like that. Please, I thought to myself, let there be something like that.

I went to the rack of tops. Many of them were just plain old T-shirts or tops with strange sequins and buttons on them. Then, squished between an Iron Maiden T-shirt, which looked like it needed to be washed, and a pink T-shirt that said, 'Super Mother', was a velvet and lace top. It wasn't exactly a camisole, because the straps were wider, the width of a belt, but that didn't matter. It was the colour of red wine and the edges, all of them, were lined with lace.

I took it into the dressing room, which was basically a curtain that pulled around an old mirror with a small crack in it. Pulling off my T-shirt, I shimmied into the velvet camisole. For a moment, all I

198 IN OUR OWN BACK YARD

could do was stare. The colour did something to my hair, giving the brown bits a reddish tinge and making the blonde bits stand out in contrast. It made the blue of my eyes more noticeable too. Best of all though, it clung to my chest and waist in ways that I wanted Harry to see. I loved it. There was no price on it, so I took it out to the women at the counter.

'It's lovely, isn't it, dear?' one of them said. 'I'd have kept it for myself if I were fifty years younger.'

'I love it,' I said. 'How much is it? There's no tag.'

'Oh, everything on that rack is two dollars, love,' the other woman said.

The day couldn't get any better! Two dollars! This was a bargain.

Sal must have known that my spirits were high because she trotted along with her tail up in the air as we walked back home.

I washed the top and hung it outside in the sun. For a few minutes, I gazed at it, enjoying how it swayed in the breeze, before heading back inside to tidy my bedroom.

I'd managed to clear all the stuff off my bedroom floor when Pete knocked on my door. 'Game's starting soon, Liza,' he called through the door. 'Mum's made us all toasted cheese sandwiches. Lots of protesters are wearing helmets now, and the army have been brought in to help the police.'

'Coming!' I called. I smiled as I made my way to the lounge. We'd won our hockey game and I'd bought a gorgeous top for two dollars. My stomach rumbled at the smell of the toasted sandwiches on the coffee table.

'Have to admit, I feel a bit nervous about this game after what happened at Molesworth Street,' Mum said. 'The army's put barbed wire, trucks and massive steel jumbo bins around the outside of the ground in Palmerston North. It looks like a fortress.'

I grabbed a sandwich, sat down and watched the scene unfolding before my eyes.

'A guy called Alick Shaw, the spokesperson for COST, was just talking to the protesters,' Mum continued. 'He said their right to freedom of speech was abused in Molesworth Street, so they would express it now in a peaceful march.'

'I've forgotten what COST stands for,' I said.

'Citizens Opposed to the Springbok Tour,' Mum said, 'the Wellington group.'

'Fifteen hundred police there today,' Pete said. 'They could do some serious damage to a protester.'

The camera zoomed in on a notice being handed out to protesters. It said, 'This march is to be peaceful and orderly.'

'Bet some HART members aren't happy about that,' Mum said. 'They came all the way from Auckland to disrupt, not behave well.'

Two police helicopters whirred above rows of helmeted riot squad members, armed with long and short batons. Protesters stood in front of them chanting, 'Remember Soweto'.

A Red Squad leader ordered everyone to stay within fifty yards of the police lines. A moment later, he instructed his squad to draw their batons and move forward towards the demonstrators. Protesters booed as the lines of Red Squad police advanced, thrusting their batons forward in rhythm with their steps.

Alick Shaw, from COST, competed with the Red Squad megaphone, yelling that the batons looked like machine guns in the Red Squad's hands. Their violent behaviour on Wednesday at Molesworth Street made him wonder whether they'd prefer to have machine guns. He clearly didn't want to risk any violence like that though because he then directed the protesters to turn back.

As they swung away, the protesters began to chant, 'The whole world's watching', then 'Shame, shame, shame'. The camera showed close-ups of their angry faces.

'They're so brave,' Jo said, 'walking right in front of the police and yelling like that.'

'Dangerous for them,' Mum said. 'Feels like the police are ready to baton them if they put one foot wrong.'

A huge banner with the word 'SHAME' passed under the noses of the police, as the crowd turned away. The camera zoomed in on the long baton held by a riot squad member. Dad had told us about the PR-24 batons and how they could be fatal if the person using them wasn't properly trained.

'Thank God they're all turning away,' I said.

The camera passed over a woman near the front screaming, 'Shame! Shame!' at the riot police. A man with a moustache and shoulder-length hair was beside her.

'That's Bob Burgess,' Mum said, 'the guy that refused to play for the All Blacks. He's part of a group called "MAST", which means "Manawatū Against the Springbok Tour".'

'The guy you and Dad were telling me about?' Pete asked me.

'Yep.' I stretched and picked up some dirty dishes. 'Thanks for lunch, Mum.'

'You're not watching the game?' Pete asked.

'Not interested. I think I sort of hate rugby at the moment.'

'Same with me,' Jo said, standing up.

'So, it's just you and me, Mum?' Pete asked.

'No, son. I'm going to do a few things around the house. Guess I'm having a bit of difficulty with rugby too, if I'm honest.'

'You're all leaving me on my own then?'

'Yes, Pete,' Jo said. 'You're on your own.'

In the late afternoon, Rewi, Stella and I went to Ciara's to help her decorate her garage. Kalāsia wasn't allowed to come to the party, so we'd promised her we'd take a photo of our decorations. She'd have to wait until the film was developed, but at least she'd get to see it.

At first, we just blew up balloons, breathed in the helium and talked in strange high voices to each other. Then, Ciara said we needed to stop messing around and start stringing balloons up across the walls, so we did.

Ciara plugged in her huge ghetto blaster and put on one of the mix tapes she'd made for the night. It consisted of disco songs, rock, reggae and New Zealand bands. We danced to 'And the Beat Goes On' by The Whispers, 'Stomp' by The Brothers Johnson and 'Celebration' by Kool and the Gang. We yelled along to 'Ace of Spades' by Motorhead, 'Hit Me with Your Best Shot' by Pat Benatar and 'Be Mine Tonight' by Th'Dudes.

'Are the tapes alright?' Ciara asked, pinning crepe paper across the walls.

'They're brilliant,' I said. 'You've covered every musical taste a person could possibly have.'

'Except for classical music,' Rewi said.

'Well . . .'

'And rock'n'roll,' Stella interrupted.

'Okay, but . . .'

'And there's no jazz,' Rewi said.

'Okay!' I stamped my foot. 'Maybe not every musical taste is covered, but many are.'

It wasn't long before the garage was ready. We stood back and admired how festive it looked.

'I love it,' Ciara said. She picked up her parents' camera and took some photos. 'I want to remember this forever.'

Rewi and I walked home to get ready for the party. Stella stayed to get ready with Ciara. I'd have stayed too, but my top was drying at home, and Harry was coming to my house to walk to the party together. Rewi said he'd meet me there. I wanted to invite him to walk with me and Harry, but the thought of them walking together made me feel anxious.

Harry put his arm around me as soon as we left our house. 'You look so beautiful. That top is . . . I just want to run my fingers under here.' He placed his fingers underneath the lacy bits on my chest.

'Well, I'm not going to say no to that.'

'Good,' Harry said, snuggling me to him. 'I've missed you.'

'That makes two of us. Talking on the phone isn't the same.'

'It's not. You can't do this.' Harry planted his warm lips on mine. My mouth pressed back onto his, as we pulled each other in. It dawned on me that kissing Harry wasn't enough anymore.

Harry seemed to have read my thoughts and took a step back. 'Wish we had a room all to ourselves.'

'That would be ... good.'

Harry laughed. 'Only good?'

'Brilliant, that would be brilliant!'

A streetlight lit up Harry's green eyes, as we passed under it. We held hands and continued walking. 'So, your dad's back and everything's okay?'

'Everything's back to normal,' Harry said.

I thought of the evening I'd had dinner at Harry's house. If that was normal, then that wasn't too good either.

'Want a smoke?' Harry asked.

'Is the pope Catholic?' I asked.

Harry lit a cigarette, puffed on it, then passed it to me.

'Hey, you get to have an extra puff when you light my ciggie like that,' I said. 'You're stealing!'

Harry blew smoke out into the night air, and his lip curled up. 'But you get to put your lips where mine have been, so I'm kind of kissing you.' He leaned in and kissed me. 'You also get the real thing whenever you want it.'

I put my hand in his. 'Come on, let's get to this party.'

The music was blasting when we arrived. Ciara's garage was lit up by lanterns along a top shelf on the walls, so it was dim, but not dark. Groups of people stood in huddles outside on the driveway and inside the garage. Some of them I knew from school.

I found Ciara in a corner talking with a boy I recognised from Newton Grammar. Harry knew him and they began to chat. Ciara leaned over and yelled into my ear, 'My parents keep coming outside to check on everything. So embarrassing!'

'Don't worry about it; just have a good time.' I patted her back. 'You're sixteen!'

Ciara nodded. 'Yeah, you're right. I'll just ignore them and have a good time.' She reached under the long table we'd put up earlier in the afternoon. 'I've got some rum that my brother got for me. Want a rum and Coke?'

'Okay.' I watched Ciara duck under the tablecloth with two glasses.

When she came out, she had a bottle of Coke. 'Quick, pour some on top of the rum, in case Mum and Dad come out and see us.'

Harry had two bottles of beer that he'd stolen from his Dad's stockpile in the fridge. He held one out to me.

'I've got this!' I said, holding up my glass. 'Rum and Coke!'

'She's going wild!' Ciara said. 'Hey, Liza, let's dance!'

The song, 'Funky Town', had come on. It was one of our favourites. Ciara pulled me into the middle of the garage, and we began to dance. 'Hey, Rewi's here,' she said.

We waved at Rewi, who came straight over to join us. 'Love this song!' he yelled. 'It's a sin not to dance to this.' He took off his jacket and threw it over a chair at the side of the room.

'Love your top, Liza,' Ciara yelled. 'Is that the op shop one?'

I nodded and smiled, deciding that was easier than yelling over the music.

'Well, it's gorgeous,' Ciara yelled, 'eh, Rewi?'

Rewi looked at me and smiled. 'Sure is! Almost as beautiful as this!' He took off his sweatshirt, revealing a black T-shirt with the word 'HERBS' written on it. The letters began in red at the top, merging into yellow, then into green. 'Mum bought it for me. Cool, eh?'

'Love it,' I yelled.

'Where's Stella?' Rewi asked. 'I brought a beer for her. Dad let me have two again. Only two! She said she's not allowed any, so I promised her she could have one.'

'She's there!' Ciara pointed at Stella, who was in the corner of the garage talking and laughing with a guy. 'I think she's pretty happy, and I gave her my secret rum and Coke too, so keep your beers.'

'Choice!' Rewi yelled. He spun around in a sort of Michael Jackson way, and I laughed.

'You're an egg!' I yelled.

'Complete idiot,' Ciara said, 'but we wouldn't have you any other way.'

I felt a hand on my elbow and turned around. It was Harry. 'Want a dance?' he yelled.

'Come and join us! It's Hello Sailor.' I pulled him into the circle, but he resisted.

The saxophone intro to 'Gutter Black' filled the garage, soaring out into the night. I began to sing the lyrics and tried again to coax him to join in with us.

'Just us!' Harry yelled. 'Let's dance, just you and me!'

I turned to Rewi and Ciara and shrugged, then moved away from them to dance with Harry.

After the song, we went outside for a smoke. I took my glass of rum and Coke with me, swallowing most of it at once. It was delicious. I took a ciggie out of my jacket pocket and lit it.

'Hey, you!' a voice called. Through the darkness, I could make out Ursula and Josh. 'We're a bit late,' Ursula said. 'We had something to do first.' She gave me a meaningful smile so that I was clear she meant they'd had sex. She kissed my cheek, smelling strongly of alcohol. 'Bit pissed,' she said. 'Love that top, Liza, you sexy little minx!' She leaned on me to stay standing.

'Want to sit down, Ursula?' I asked.

'Maybe,' she said.

I went into the garage and dragged out a chair for her. Plonking herself down, she lit a ciggie, sucked on it and blew the smoke out like a Bond girl. I felt a flutter of longing in my stomach. If only I could look like that.

'I'm going to get another rum and Coke,' I said.

'Get me one while you're there,' Ursula said, her speech slurred.

I made my way through the increasingly large crowd of dancers to Ciara. 'Another one?' I yelled, holding up my empty glass.

Ciara nodded and we went to the table where she did her disappearing trick underneath the tablecloth with my glass. 'Don't let Mum or Dad smell you,' she yelled. 'They'll be back in here to check on us soon.'

'Smell me?' I thought. 'Did Ciara say smell?' I began to giggle.

With a full glass, I headed back outside. Rewi was standing with a smoke in his hand beside a few of his Newton Grammar friends, so I stopped to chat. Rewi said that he was onto his second beer and then that was it. He'd promised his dad, only two.

'You must be the only person I know who tells the complete

truth to his parents,' I said.

'They're pretty cool, my parents, so it's not that hard. They don't expect me to be perfect anyway.'

Ciara's mother came out of the front door of the house and walked over to us. 'Hello, you two, well, all of you,' she said to the group.

I stepped back a bit, thinking of Ciara's command not to let her mother smell me. Again, I felt like giggling. Maybe the rum and Coke was going to my head. Rewi and I chatted politely and then Ciara's mum sighed. 'Well, looks like it's all going fine out here. I'll head back in.'

'I'm not allowed to let her smell me,' I said to Rewi as she walked away.

'I'd rather not smell you either!' Rewi said.

I laughed and elbowed him in the ribs. 'Shut up, dork. She meant smelling the alcohol on my breath!'

'Don't try to wriggle out of this one!' Rewi said.

A hand slipped into mine. It was Harry. I smiled at him.

'Everything okay here?' he asked.

'Everything's fine,' I answered. 'Do you know these guys? They go to Newton Grammar too.'

'Yeah, we know each other.' Harry lifted his eyebrows in acknowledgement of Rewi's friends. 'Want a dance?'

'Okay. I love this song.' It was 'Little Sister' by Ry Cooder.

We walked into the garage and joined the crowd of people dancing. Harry forced a smile.

'You okay?' I yelled over the music.

He leaned into me, close to my ear. 'You were the only girl in a group of guys.'

'I know those guys,' I yelled.

'I just . . . don't like it.' Harry's eyes were a bit bloodshot. Maybe he was drunk or maybe he'd smoked dope. I'd never smoked it, but I'd heard it made people's eyes red.

'They're friends,' I said.

'Just . . . don't talk to other guys, Liza,' Harry said, right up close to my ear. Normally, his lips on my ear would have made me tremble with longing but, instead, a nervous tingling filled my stomach.

I tried to make a joke. 'So, you don't want me to talk to half the population?'

'I'm serious, Liza,' Harry said. 'If you want to be my girlfriend, you can't talk to other guys like that, or dance with them.'

I didn't feel like dancing anymore, but I kept moving, conscious of people laughing and yelling around me. Every now and then, Harry and I made eye contact, but we didn't speak. I just moved to the music, forcing myself to look as though I was enjoying myself. When the song finished, we made our way back outside, bypassing Rewi and his friends and rejoining Ursula and Josh. Ursula was draped over the chair, like an exhausted movie star.

'Liza!' she said. 'Thank God you're back. Did you bring me a drink?'

I remembered how I'd promised to bring her one a while back. 'I'll go get you one.'

'Don't bother,' Ursula slurred. 'I've probably had enough.'

'Me too,' I said.

Ursula reached out and took my hand. 'Liza, you are kind and patient with me.'

I tried to smile and relax into the conversation with Ursula, the way I usually would, letting her entertain me, but something was blocking me.

'Liza, do you hear me?' Ursula said. 'I love you. Oh, just come here.' She stood up, pulled me over to her and hugged me. She was a bit shaky on her feet, so within a few seconds her hug turned into leaning on me. I helped her back onto her chair. 'Sit back down, Urse. You'll fall over.'

'See, you're kind. Some people let friends fall over, if you get my drift.'

'Some people do.'

'I think I'm going to be sick,' Ursula said. She stood up and Josh took her by the arm and led her to the hedge at the side of the driveway. Ursula vomited while Josh held her. For a moment, they both nearly fell into the hedge, which made them start giggling.

'I feel a bit sick too,' I said to Harry. I wasn't drunk but my stomach felt strange, and I felt shaky, like the nervous feeling before doing a speech. 'I need to go home.'

'Okay, I'll walk you.'

'I'll just go and tell Ciara.'

Rewi waved at me from the middle of the dancing area and I smiled. If I lifted my hand to wave back, was that like talking? I decided not to in case Harry saw and was upset.

Ciara was by the table, stuffing Cheese Balls into her mouth with some other girls from our school. 'Liza!' she yelled. 'Come and eat with us.'

'I feel a bit sick,' I said. 'I'm going home.'

'No!' Ciara dropped a Cheese Ball back on the plate and wrapped me in her arms. 'Well, I'm giving you my first hug as a sixteen-year-old.' She let go of me and grabbed a half-full bag of Cheese Balls out from under the table. 'Here, take these. They'll make you feel better.'

I nodded. 'Okay, thanks. See you tomorrow to help clean up.'

'Aw, you're a good friend, Liza Newland.' Ciara hugged me again, then I headed out of the garage, keeping my gaze straight ahead so that I didn't catch anyone's eye, especially Rewi's.

On the way home, Harry said it'd been a tough week for him, and he just couldn't handle seeing me chatting with guys on top of it. He told me he loved me, and he showed that love by not chatting with lots of girls. That wasn't too much to ask of me, was it?

I shook my head.

'You know I love you, don't you?' Harry said.

I nodded. 'I just need to get home,' I said. 'I feel sick. I need to walk faster.'

Harry took my hand. When we reached my house, I let go of it. 'I have to go inside right now,' I said to Harry. 'I'm going to be sick.'

Harry bent down and kissed my cheek. 'I'll phone you tomorrow.'

'Cool.' I turned and knocked on the door. I hadn't taken my housekey with me. Sal barked and Mum came to the door in her dressing gown.

'Hi, Liza,' she said. Then, seeing Harry on the street by the letterbox, she said, 'Do you want to come in, Harry?'

'I'm feeling sick,' I said, walking into the house. I felt cold and shivery. 'I need to go to bed.'

'Oh, that's no good,' Mum said. 'We'll see you another time then, Harry.'

Harry replied, but I didn't hear what he said. I went straight to the bathroom and was sick into the toilet. I heard Mum's footsteps behind me. 'Oh, Liza, how much did you drink?'

I retched and Mum took hold of my hair for me. 'Not that much, honestly,' I said.

'I'll get you a warm flannel to wipe your face. Hang on.' She tucked my hair into the back of my jacket and disappeared for a moment. I vomited into the bowl again.

'You used to be sick like this when you were little if something upset you,' Mum said, wiping my face with the warm flannel.

'I'm okay now,' I said, standing up. 'I only had one and a half glasses of rum and Coke.'

'I'd rather you didn't drink at all,' Mum said. 'Anyway, let's get you into bed.'

I threw off my clothes, my beautiful top lay in a heap on the floor. Mum grabbed a nightie out of my drawer and helped me into it. I sank into bed and Mum perched on the edge. 'Do you think you might have a tummy bug?'

I shrugged. In an effort to change the subject, I asked if she'd heard from Dad today. He was still down in Palmerston North.

'He phoned a while ago and said that the protests down there continued to be peaceful. He said the Auckland march to the Domain today had been peaceful too. Apparently the protesters up the front had a banner saying, "We are peaceful. Do not shoot". Isn't that powerful? As if the police were South African.'

'What else did he say?'

'Hmmm, he said that HART wasn't happy with today's peaceful Auckland protest. Apparently, they wanted to protest on the Auckland Harbour Bridge and stop the traffic.'

'Wow,' I said, yawning.

Mum stroked my head the way she used to when I was small. 'I'll let you get some sleep, sweetheart.'

'Mum, I only drank a tiny bit, promise.'

'I believe you. Now, go to sleep.'

As Mum flicked off the light, I glimpsed my new top lying on the floor. I'd carefully washed it and been so excited about wearing it. Sadness pushed against my ribs. I turned my face to the wall and let my tears soak into the pillow.

LOCKDOWN

It's early morning, Tuesday, the 26th of May. I'm sitting up in bed with a cup of tea in my hand, and the sun is pouring through the window. Ross is whistling in the bathroom. We dropped down to Alert Level Two at 11.59pm on Wednesday last week. Ross is now back to teaching full classes of students, back to his normal routine.

As soon as we dropped to Alert Level Two, Jesse and his friends went straight to Burger Fuel, while Eva and her friends went to McDonald's. I told them they were junk food addicts. Jesse's response was, 'It's been seven weeks in lockdown, Mum!'

'And it's still not over,' I said. 'Both of you make sure you keep physical distancing as much as possible and wash your hands often.'

Ross and I went to our local café for lunch. Level two rules meant we had to stay seated and the staff came over to the table to take our orders. The tables had been rearranged to allow for physical distancing. We kept smiling at other customers, who smiled back at us. I had two flat whites and they tasted so good.

None of the magazines I've worked for have been in touch with me, but my fingers are crossed that they'll make contact at some point soon. In the meantime, I'm still writing my Springbok Tour memories.

I'm listening to the birds chattering outside and Ross whistling in the bathroom, when the door bangs open and Eva plonks herself down beside me. 'You won't believe this,' she says. 'It's the most terrible thing. Look!' She holds her phone out in front of me, showing me a video clip of a white American police officer kneeling on an African American man's neck, as he lies face-down on the concrete. Other police officers are there, watching. The man on the ground says, 'I can't breathe.'

'Stop!' I say to Eva. 'I don't want to watch anymore. It's too distressing.'

'I can't watch the whole thing either,' Eva says. 'He's dead, Mum. That cop killed him.'

I shake my head slowly at Eva, trying to process the fact that a police officer killed a man in front of other police officers and in public.

Ross walks in and stops when he sees us. 'What's up?' he asks.

Eva passes him her phone. 'Watch that.'

I hear the voice of the man again, pleading for the officer to stop. He says they are going to kill him. The cop tells him to stop talking to save oxygen. The man asks the cop to tell his mum he loves her.

Ross looks away. 'I feel so angry seeing that.' He passes the phone back to Eva. 'Shit, this is going to be the talk of the school today.'

'It's huge,' I say.

'But is it huge in the States?' Eva demands. 'I mean, I'm young and, in my short time on this earth, I've heard of white police officers killing black men there *so* often.'

I put my hand on her shoulder. 'I hope it's huge in the States. It should be huge all over the world. Maybe we all need to stand up and say we're sick of seeing this disgusting treatment of African American people too.'

'Like people did with South Africa, Mum,' Eva says.

I squeeze her shoulder. 'Exactly.'

We sit together while Ross finds some socks. 'I'd better get to work,' he says. 'That piece of film might just get that cop arrested. Bloody hope it does.' He leans down to kiss us.

'I'd better get ready for school too,' Eva says.

'You students are lucky,' Ross says, as he heads out the door. 'Teachers have to get there early for staff meetings.' The front door clicks behind him.

'Mum, I don't know how to have a normal day after seeing that video, knowing that's going on in the world.' Eva stands up and walks towards my bedroom door, then turns. 'Weird stuff happens here too, like what happened to Kalāsia's boys.'

Kalāsia is Eva and Jesse's godmother. She rang me one night to say that, earlier that evening, her two teenage sons had walked up to the local gas station to buy some milk. On their way, a police car slowed beside them. The two police officers asked where they were going and why. Then they asked them to get in the back of the police car. When the boys asked why, they were told just to get in. The police drove around town with them for three hours. Kalāsia had been worried sick. Finally, at 10pm, the police dropped them outside their house. They'd never managed to buy any milk. Instead, they'd spent three hours sitting in the back of a police car.

'I mean, they did nothing wrong,' Eva says. 'They were just walking along the road at night with brown skin. The police were trying to intimidate them. Did Kalāsia ever make a complaint?'

I shake my head. 'She felt too nervous about it. I think the idea of complaining about police behaviour felt too frightening for her. Remember, she had to deal with dawn raids, and then there's what happened to her father.'

Eva nods.

'Her boys were victims of racial profiling,' I say.

'What?'

'Racial profiling. It basically means that the police expect a race to be doing wrong. So, say a teenage Pākehā boy and a teenage Māori boy are hanging around outside a shop, police would be more likely to stop and question the Māori boy. Same with a Pasifika teenager.'

'Have New Zealand police ever caused the death of people like that man in the video?'

'Not in extremely public, obvious ways like in the States, but other ways. For example, I keep reading about police car chases that end up in deaths, and Māori teenagers seem to get chased more than Pākehā. There's a well-known lawyer, Moana Jackson, who's done research into it. He says some people call it a "Māori death chase policy".'

'Why do they try to escape the police?' Eva asks.

'Police believe it's often because the driver is only on their learner or restricted licence.' I stretch and yawn.

'Stupid reason to die. Stupid reason to chase them too. Why not just get the licence plate and follow up that way, instead of making kids panic?'

'Exactly.'

'And why make getting a driver's licence so expensive?' Eva turns away. 'I'll go and wake up Jesse.'

'Thanks, Evie.' I get out of bed and head for the shower.

By evening, the murder of George Floyd by a white police officer in Minneapolis is all over the news. They show a screenshot of the police officer with his knee on George Floyd's neck. Then, they show protest marches in America, huge crowds of people chanting and carrying placards with 'Black Lives Matter' and 'I Can't Breathe' on them. After the news finishes, I turn off the TV.

'Wonder if that police officer will be charged with murder,' Ross says. 'They often get off lightly.'

'And those other cops,' Jesse says. 'They need to be arrested too. They just stood there watching.'

'Yeah, they all deserve to get slammed for this,' Ross says.

Adam, who's still staying with us, tells us about an experience he had at school earlier in the year. 'I was walking with my mate, Hemi. He wears his hair in a traditional Māori topknot. You know Hemi, eh, Jesse?'

'Yeah, we do history together.'

'We were walking to class, and Mr Grey stopped us and said to Hemi that he was only allowed to wear his hair in a bun at the back of his head. I mean, Hemi is the most tidily dressed student in the school. His uniform's always perfect. He even polishes his shoes!'

'Who does that?' Jesse says.

'You sure don't,' I say.

Jesse grins at me, and I can't help but smile back.

Adam continues. 'Mr Grey told Hemi that if he wears his hair on top of his head like that again, he'll be on detention. Our school always goes on about its commitment to the Treaty of Waitangi but doesn't allow Hemi to wear his hair in a traditional topknot.'

'Mr Grey's a dick though,' Eva says. 'Don't forget that!'

'Hemi's parents wrote an email explaining that it was a traditional Māori hairstyle,' Adam says, 'so the principal said he could continue to wear his hair that way, but Mr Grey never apologised to him.'

'If the school really wants to make Māori students feel valued and respected, maybe they need to make sure teachers understand what that involves,' Ross says.

'And management,' I say. 'Mr Grey's a deputy principal.'

'He just made Hemi feel like crap,' Adam says, 'telling him off loudly like that while other students walked by.'

'Embarrassing kids publicly like that and making a massive issue of minor things just makes them give up,' Ross says. 'I've seen it happen. It can wreck their lives.'

Jesse, Adam and Eva head off to study after watching the news, and Ross does some marking. I tell them I'll do the dishes and tidy up. I switch on the radio while I rinse dishes. A Black Lives Matter spokesperson is talking about the George Floyd murder, saying that this is yet another in a long chain of police murders. She talks about how the right to breathe has many layers. Feeling nervous on the street because of the colour of your skin affects breathing too. It makes black people feel they can't take up space and breathe in the air in the same way white people do. They are not welcome on the streets.

I switch off the radio and realise I've been holding my breath. I let it out slowly. When I finish the dishes, I sit down with my laptop. I need to write about Kalāsia's dad.

CHAPTER 27
KALĀSIA'S FATHER

The day after Ciara's party, I joined Rewi, Stella and Ciara to help clean up the mess. Rewi asked me why I hadn't told him I was leaving, and I told him that I'd felt sick.

'Yeah, I know, Ciara told me,' Rewi said, 'but you could've said goodbye to me.'

'Sorry,' I said. 'I didn't want to interrupt you. You were dancing.'

When the garage was clean and smelling of disinfectant instead of stale beer and cigarettes, we walked home. Rewi asked me if I was okay and I told him I was tired. The truth was, my brain felt slow, like I couldn't think clearly.

At home, I lay on my bed, my arm dangling so that I could run my hand along Sal's back, as she lay on the floor beside the bed. The phone went and my hand stiffened. Sal looked up at me.

'Liza,' Mum called. 'Phone! It's Harry!'

I didn't want to speak to Harry, but if I told Mum that, she'd ask why. Pushing myself off the bed, I stepped over Sal to the phone table outside my room. I pulled the phone through my bedroom door and shut the door, squishing the cord between it. 'Hi,' I said.

'I'm sorry,' Harry said.

No words seemed right. I couldn't say, 'that's okay' or 'never mind' because I'd be lying. I didn't speak.

'I was a dick,' Harry said, 'a complete dick.'

I could hear my pulse in my ears and a slight crackle in the phone.

'I drank too much,' Harry continued. 'I'm a prick when I drink. Sorry, Liza.'

Finally, I managed to say, 'Okay.'

'Please forgive me. You can talk with anyone you like.'

'I have to go now. Mum's calling me.'

'Hang on. I just want you to know I love you, Liza. That's all I want to say, apart from how sorry I am. I love you.'

'Okay,' I said again. 'Bye.'

The next few days, I tried not to think about Harry. I concentrated on my friends and school. We were getting our exam results back and going over the answers with the teachers. I'd passed everything, thank goodness, but only scraped through maths. My sister, Jo, was good at maths, so I decided I'd ask her to give me some help before School Certificate exams at the end of the year. She was my bossy older sister though, so being tutored by her could be a nightmare.

I was relieved at my English mark, because I hadn't been sure of how well I could write an essay.

Ms Jefferson was so excited by our English marks that she stopped me and Kalāsia when we were passing her in the corridor. 'I know I'm seeing you in class later in period five, but I just wanted to say you did well in your English exams,' she said. 'I've been smiling all day long. I won't tell you your marks now, as that would be unfair on the others, but I'm excited for you both.'

'I hated *The Taming of the Shrew*,' I said.

'I know you did, Liza, but it gave you lots to discuss in your essay. Well done!'

'I've never done well in English,' Kalāsia said. 'It's my second language.'

'Exactly,' Ms Jefferson said, patting Kalāsia's arm. 'You've done better than everyone else in the class for that very reason.'

'Did I get a high mark?' Kalāsia asked.

'It was seventy-something per cent, Kalāsia, which is incredible for someone who's only spoken English for the last six or so years.'

Kalāsia smiled at Ms Jefferson, then at me, and we smiled back at her. 'Congratulations, Kalāsia,' I said.

'Can't wait to tell my parents,' she said. 'I'll have to tell Dad tomorrow, cos he won't be home from work until about three in the morning.'

The next morning, the phone went at about five-thirty. Mum answered it, and I lay in a half-sleep, hearing her quietly talking in the hallway. Then I fell asleep again.

A couple of hours later, Mum woke me. She held my hand and shook it gently. 'Liza, something's happened to Kalāsia's dad, so she's not going to school today.'

My eyes opened at the mention of Kalāsia's name. 'What happened?'

'He's been arrested.'

'Arrested?' I sat up in bed. 'Why?'

'His car wouldn't start, so he walked home from the bread factory, but the police stopped him. They asked him for his passport, which he showed them, but he was carrying two loaves of bread that were out of the rejects bin, so they've charged him with theft.'

'What?' I rubbed my eyes. 'Theft?'

'It's ridiculous. Kalāsia said that the bread in the rejects bin can't be sold because it's squashed, so staff often take it home because it's perfectly good to eat.'

'So, what will happen?'

'He'll appear in court today, but I phoned your dad at the hotel in Wanganui, where the game is today, and he rang his editor, Tom. Remember him?'

'I think I met him at Dad's work Christmas party.'

'Well, Tom's going to put the story on the front page today.'

'The front page?'

Mum nodded. 'Not sure what time Kalāsia's dad will appear in court, but I'll take her mum in and wait with her. I've rung work to tell them I won't be in today.' Mum pushed strands of hair behind her ears. 'I'm going to see if Ted, our mechanic, can tow their car for them and maybe fix it too.'

'What should I do? Shall I go to school?'

'Yes, yes, go to school. I think Kalāsia and her brothers and sisters are too upset for school today, so they're staying home. Maybe just phone her before you leave, so she knows you're thinking about her.' Mum stood up. 'Right, I'll phone Ted about their car now. I won't need to come back to check you're out of bed, will I?'

'No,' I said, throwing off my duvet. 'I'll call Kalāsia after you've spoken to the mechanic.' I grabbed my dressing gown from the chair and slung it over my shoulders, heading to the bathroom to wash my face. When I went back to my room to get dressed, Mum was on the phone, saying, 'Thank you, Ted. Much appreciated. Yes, let me know what the problem is once you've had a look. Thanks again.' She clunked the receiver down and disappeared up the hallway.

When I phoned Kalāsia, she was crying. 'He had his passport,' she said.

'They were just trying to find a reason to arrest him,' I said. 'Don't worry. It's not theft.'

'My dad's a good man. He goes to church and is kind to people. He'd never do anything illegal.'

'Dad's newspaper's going to write a story on this, Kalāsia. It'll be on the front page.'

'That will embarrass Dad,' Kalāsia said. 'Everyone will know.'

'People need to know about this sort of racism in the police force, Kalāsia. Your dad's case is an example of how the police are mistreating lots of Pacific Island people.'

Kalāsia was quiet, apart from her sniffing and then an almighty blast in my ear. 'Sorry,' she said, 'just had to blow my nose.'

'I heard!'

We both laughed.

'I guess it will keep happening as long as the police keep getting away with it,' Kalāsia said.

'Exactly,' I said. 'I'd better go to school. No one to plait my hair! Guess it's a ponytail today.'

'It won't look as good as the plaits.'

'I know.'

'Where would you be without me?' Kalāsia said.

'I'd be lost without you! I'd better go and get ready. Mum might give me and Rewi a lift to school on her way to pick up your mum.'

'Liza?'

'Yeah.'

''Ofa atu.'

'You too. I'll phone you after school. See ya.'

The newspaper ran the story and a photo of Kalāsia's dad on the front page. The following morning, a university student went into the police station with a raspberry bun that he'd taken from the Yesterday's Leftovers container at the university café. He asked the police to arrest him for taking it. That afternoon, two other students turned themselves in for taking leftover raspberry buns. The editor of Dad's newspaper put that story on the front page too. The police wouldn't arrest the students. The charges against Kalāsia's father were dropped.

Kalāsia didn't remember to tell her dad about her English exam mark for about a week. When she finally told him he said he was proud of her and that her exam mark had lifted his spirits. He was trying hard to be happy for her, but she said his eyes were sad. Even though he'd done nothing wrong, he still felt ashamed.

CHAPTER 28
WHANGANUI AND THE LOWER SOUTH ISLAND

Mum went to court with Kalāsia's mother on the 5th of August, the same day the Springboks played in Whanganui. Along the road that led to the rugby ground, hundreds of protesters stood in silence. At the front, using separate placards for each letter, was a sign that said, 'NO PEACE WITHOUT JUSTICE FOR ALL SOUTH AFRICANS'. The protest was peaceful, and the police were not dressed in riot gear.

On Auckland's Khyber Pass though, a MOST protest turned nasty. It took place outside the offices of Lion Breweries, sponsors of the New Zealand Rugby Union, and Hughes and Cossar, who imported South African wines. When protest leaders tried to enter the buildings to hand a letter to the managers, the riot squad violently attacked them. I was glad Mum had been busy in court that day because she'd been planning to join that protest.

The following Saturday, I came home from hockey covered in mud and looking forward to a hot shower. Mum saw him first as she parked the car. 'Look, Liza, it's Harry, with some flowers.'

On our front steps, Harry sat with a bunch of flowers lodged between his knees. He stood up as Mum stepped out of the car.

'Are those for me?' Mum asked, opening the back door to let Sal out.

Harry looked momentarily unsure of what to say, then realised Mum was joking. 'You can go halves if Liza lets you.'

'She won't,' Mum said. 'I know her. She doesn't like to share.'

'Mum!' I said. 'That's so . . .'

'Just teasing!' She unlocked the front door. 'I'm going to make some lunch.'

Sal followed Mum inside, and I shut the front door behind them then sat down on the front steps. Harry sat beside me.

'You're still upset with me,' he said.

I nodded.

'I've said I'm sorry, and I really mean it, Liza.' Harry passed me the flowers. 'These are for you.'

I took the flowers and gazed at them. No one had ever given me flowers. It was the sort of thing that happened in movies. 'Thanks.'

'So, I'm a dick,' Harry said. 'We've established that.'

It was hard not to smile at this comment. 'You can be a bit of a dick.'

'But still charming and sexy?'

'Maybe.'

'Maybe is good,' Harry said. 'I can live with maybe for now.' He took my hand in his. Its warmth and the sudden sunlight on my face made me feel tired. I'd played a hard hockey game and we'd lost, but we hadn't made it easy for the other team. I wanted to rest my head on Harry's shoulder and close my eyes. Resisting that urge, I said, 'I'd better go and have a shower.'

'That's cool,' Harry said. 'I need to go anyway. I'm walking Sophie to her friend's party soon. Mum's got a bad headache, a migraine, so she's in bed.'

'What about your dad?'

'He's already at the pub revving up to watch Southland play the Springboks.'

'Dad's down in Invercargill.'

'Lucky guy. He's part of history, seeing the games and the protests.'

That was true. Dad was watching history unfold as he reported on the tour.

'Anyway, better go. Sophie wants me to put her hair up like a princess. Not quite sure what that means exactly, but she'll make it clear to me in her own slightly bossy way.'

I smiled. 'Good luck!'

Harry leaned down and kissed my cheek. 'Want to go to a movie later or go to Johnny's Ice-Cream Parlour for a sundae?'

A date with Harry felt too hard so soon after what had happened at the party. 'I can't today,' I said. 'Maybe next week?'

'Next week then.' Harry stood up. 'I'll phone you.'

'Okay.' I went into the house.

Mum was making a sandwich. 'Need a vase?' she asked.

'Yep, a big one.'

'Look in the top cupboard.'

'Where shall I put them?'

'On the table? Or do you want to put them in your bedroom?'

'Table's fine.'

'That was nice of Harry.'

'It was.'

The flowers looked good on the table. When I saw them filling the room with colour like that, my uneasiness lessened. Maybe Harry really was sorry. Maybe we could put the party behind us, and he'd be different from here on. I turned to Mum. 'Just going to have a shower. Don't eat all of that yummy bread.'

'I wouldn't dare,' Mum said.

I walked down to the bathroom, threw my mud-covered hockey uniform on the floor and stepped into the shower. Hockey had tired me out, but that deeper, sad tiredness was washing away down the drain with the mud. I was going to start afresh, forgive and move on. That's what I was going to do.

Later that afternoon, I lay on the sofa eating popcorn, which Jo told me was bad for my digestive system. We were watching the build-up to the Invercargill game. On the phone the night before, Dad told us that, in front of the spectators' stands, the army had placed huge coils of barbed wire. He said police must be concerned about keeping tour supporters off the field, as well as protesters. Most cities in the deep south were strongly pro-tour, he said, apart from Dunedin, with its university student population.

We'd been watching John Minto's speech at the protest rally at Queens Park in Invercargill. He said that racism had deep roots in Invercargill. News reporters stood around him and, for a moment, we thought we saw Dad. Pro-tour people threw mud, rocks and eggs at John Minto and another speaker, Francesca Holloway, who was HART's Otago-Southland Regional Officer. She was young and spoke with such anger and conviction that I couldn't keep my eyes off her.

Pete said that it looked like there were more police than at the other protests. The marchers had clearly noticed it too because they began to chant, 'Two, four, six, eight. Racist tour, police state.'

The TV commentator said that police had asked protesters not to go any closer to the rugby ground than 200 metres. They had to stick to their agreed route too, because police had blocked off any other options. As they marched, tour supporters hurled abuse at them. When they reached their two hundred metre point, riot police were there, holding batons.

'What's happened to our country?' Mum said.

'There aren't many protesters,' Jo said. 'Why are riot police there?'

'Maybe they're trying to protect them,' Mum said, 'or maybe they're not taking any chances and showing who's in charge.'

The phone rang and I went to answer it.

'What are you up to, dropkick?' It was Rewi.

'Something that doesn't include you.'

'Want to come over and destroy my will to live with your dull attempts at conversation?'

'Not sure I can bear an afternoon of your company.'

'Guess I could force myself to meet you at the shop down the road for ice cream.'

'Now that you mention ice cream, I could be interested. Otherwise, I probably wouldn't bother.'

'Half an hour?'

'Half an hour. Meet you at the shop.'

I wasn't interested in the game. Pete would tell us who won. I was more interested in the protests, and it looked like the protesters had hit a wall of riot police, so that was that. After eating most of the bowl of popcorn, I headed off to the shop. Sal trotted along beside me and I tied her up outside the shop where Rewi was waiting.

'Did you win today?' he asked.

'Lost, but we played well. They were a stronger team.'

We walked inside. 'What flavour are you getting?' Rewi asked.

'Chocolate, always chocolate.'

'You could branch out,' Rewi said, pointing at the containers of ice cream through the glass. 'There's hokey-pokey, orange choc-chip, boysenberry . . .'

'I can see them, Rewi, but they're not as nice as chocolate.'

Rewi sighed and said to the shopkeeper, 'She'll have two scoops of chocolate, and I'll have one scoop of hokey-pokey and one of boysenberry, please.'

'Disgusting,' I said.

'Adventurous,' Rewi said.

'Disgusting and adventurous.'

'Adventurously disgusting.'

We grinned at each other.

Outside, I untied Sal and we walked back towards Rewi's house. A police car was parked a few houses away from Rewi's, as usual. This time, I didn't recognise either of the policemen in the car. They didn't get out to ask our names or try to make small talk with us, which was weird, but I was so busy enjoying my ice cream, I didn't comment on it.

'Dad's taken Marama and Nikau to the park,' Rewi said.

'So just us?'

'Till they get home. Thought you might like to listen to my new album.'

'What is it?'

'Herbs.'

'Herbs?'

'The record shop phoned me as soon as it came in. I didn't tell you. Thought I'd surprise you when you came over.'

'I want to hear it.'

We went through the gate, past the letterbox with the Māori flag on it and up the steps onto the veranda with the swirling koru carvings. Rewi took the key out of his pocket, but the door was unlocked. 'What the . . ?' He pushed it open. 'But I locked it. Dad must be home.'

It was quiet though, and it was never quiet with Marama and Nikau around.

'Dad!' Rewi yelled. 'You home?'

We walked down the hallway and into the kitchen. Rewi looked out the window into the back yard, but no one was there.

'I locked the door when I left,' Rewi said, 'because of the cops and Mum's photos.' He looked at the open laundry door. 'Shit!' He ran into the laundry.

The basket of rags and the box underneath looked as though they hadn't been touched. I dragged a chair into the laundry. Rewi climbed up and shoved the rags basket off the top of the box. Rags tumbled onto the floor. He lifted the box down. There were no photo albums inside it.

'Shit!' Rewi said again. He ran down the hallway and I followed him. 'Where are you going?' I asked.

Rewi ran out onto the street to the police car. 'You don't have a warrant!' he yelled at the police through their closed window. 'You broke into our house without a warrant!'

Sal followed me as I ran after Rewi.

One of the police officers stepped out of the driver's seat. 'Think carefully before you accuse us of anything again, son,' he said.

'You broke into our house!' Rewi yelled. 'You took something that isn't yours.'

'One more time, young fulla, and I'm going to take you into the station.'

'Rewi, stop,' I said. 'Let's go. You'll just get arrested.'

Rewi stared at the policeman, and the cop stared back at him. 'I'd get going if I were you,' the cop said. 'Do as your girlfriend says.'

'C'mon Rewi,' I said. 'Let's go.' I pulled him by the arm.

'We've got negatives and more copies, so you haven't won, just so you know,' Rewi said.

'No idea what you're talking about,' the police officer replied.

Rewi and I walked back to the house with Sal.

It was hard to think about anything else. We blasted Herbs and put the rags back in the basket. We turned on the TV to see if anything else had happened with the protests. Then the door opened, and the sound of Marama and Nikau's excited chatter echoed down the hallway. Rewi turned off the TV. His dad came in and smiled at us. 'Kei te pēhea kōrua?' he asked.

'Not good,' Rewi answered. 'They entered our house without a warrant. I locked the door, like I always do, and the photos have gone.'

Tipene looked over at the laundry, then at Rewi. 'You checked thoroughly?'

Rewi nodded. He bit into his bottom lip. 'Sorry, Dad. I did lock the house, promise.'

Tipene held up his hand. 'Stop, Rewi. This isn't your fault. I'll have a wander round to see if they've touched anything else. Corrupt bastards.'

'Maybe I'd better go,' I said.

'No, play Last Card with us first,' Marama said.

'Yes!' Nikau cried.

'Okay, one game, and then I'd better go.'

When Tipene had finished looking around, he phoned the police to make a complaint. His voice grew louder and then he stopped. 'Never mind,' he said, slamming down the phone. He came back into the kitchen where we were sitting around the table playing cards. 'Just going for a walk, Rewi,' he said. 'You okay to watch the kids for a little while?'

Rewi nodded. 'You going to talk to those cops?'

'Maybe.'

'Don't get arrested, Dad.'

'I won't. Don't worry.'

About ten minutes later, Tipene came back into the house, put the kettle on and took some biscuits out of a tin. 'Room for one more player?' he asked.

I stayed for one more game, then I walked home with Sal, past the police car, keeping my eyes straight ahead.

Dad phoned us later that night, and I told him about the photos being stolen. He said that Merata Mita, the woman filming a documentary of the protests, had had trouble with the police too. Police behaviour towards protesters was also very worrying, he said. Earlier that day, at a protest outside the Springboks' hotel, a cop had slammed John Minto, head-first, into the closed door of a police car. 'Poor guy,' Dad said, 'they're always after him.'

'But they must've let him go because he was at the rally,' Mum said.

'That's right. They gave him hell though.'

I left Dad talking with Mum and collapsed onto the sofa. Jo was watching *McPhail and Gadsby*. It was funny and took my mind off the fact that some of our police officers had burgled Rewi's house and beaten up John Minto.

The following Tuesday, the 11th of August, the Springboks played Otago in Dunedin. Dad told us that the protests had begun days before. On the Sunday night, groups of protesters yelled, blew whistles and chanted outside the Southern Cross Hotel, where the Springboks were staying. The next day, they protested at Tahuna Park, where the Springboks trained.

I was at school on the day of the match. That night, I watched the news with my family. The reporter said that protesters had agreed with police that they'd march along the motorway, stopping when they were visible from Carisbrook Stadium. Approximately 500 people marched, but they were stopped by police and the riot squad before they could even see the rugby ground. Francesca Holloway led the march forward until they were face to face with the police. Then she turned the marchers around but came back again chanting, 'Christchurch! Christchurch!'

'Why are they saying that?' I asked Mum.

'They're letting the police know that things will escalate in Christchurch,' Mum said.

Inside the rugby ground, Steve Bayliss, HART's South Island co-ordinator, and about 30 other protesters, shouted and blew whistles, before police arrested them. In town, around 600 people marched silently, while around 300 protesters sat down outside the Southern Cross Hotel and, when they wouldn't leave, the riot squad came to remove them.

CHAPTER 29
FIRST TEST, CHRISTCHURCH

The phone rang just as I walked into the house after my hockey game. It was Saturday, the 15th of August, the day of the first test match between the Springboks and Christchurch. Mum and Jo were going to the Auckland rally to protest, but I was going to the movies with Harry after lunch instead.

I ran to the phone thinking it might be Harry, but it was Dad. 'Just checking in,' he said. 'I miss you all. This is the longest I've been away from you.'

'We miss you too, Dad.' I pulled my hairband out and shook my hair around me. There was mud in it. I'd have to wash my hair.

'Mum going to the protest?'

'Yeah, when she gets back from Jo's hockey game.'

'Ah well.'

'You okay, Dad?'

'Yes, yes, just wanted to tell your mum a couple of things.'

'You can tell me.'

'Well, I guess I'm a bit worried that people might get seriously hurt today. A couple of days ago, someone set fire to the main grandstand at Lancaster Park. Today, the police raided Te Rangi Marie Marae, where CAT, the Canterbury Against the Tour coalition, has been based. They were looking for guns, explosives, that sort of thing. Crazy, really.'

There was a loud whirring noise in the background. 'Is that a helicopter?' I asked.

'Yes, I'm near Cathedral Square, where the march begins. There are already huge crowds. Their plan is to get as close to the rugby ground as possible, until police stop them. They want to take over the ground from the outside and the inside, but I think the police are aware of protesters buying tickets now. It'll be interesting to see how many manage to get in.'

'Will you follow the march?'

'Yes, that's what I do every day there's a game.' Dad was quiet. The helicopter thumped through the phone. 'I have a bad feeling about today,' he said.

'Why, Dad?'

'It's just that things are getting nastier, more violent.'

'You'll be careful, eh, Dad?'

'Course I will, Liza. Don't you worry about me. I'd better go now. The march starts soon.'

After I'd put down the phone, I went to have a shower and tried not to think about Dad and how worried he'd sounded. Winding a towel around my wet hair, I threw on some jeans and a sweatshirt. It was cold today, so I'd have to wear my big jacket too. I made myself a huge sandwich with lots of salad stuff from the fridge, then went to put on some eyeliner and brush my hair.

Harry and I were meeting at the bus stop. I could see him standing leaning against a pole as I crossed the road to join him. His hair had fallen over one eye. He looked up as I approached and smiled. 'It's you,' he said.

'It's me.'

We hugged and Harry held onto me. 'Been a long time since I've hugged you.'

He smelled good and I burrowed my face into his neck, breathing him in.

The bus arrived and we sat in the middle. An elderly woman sat up the front of the bus, and two groups of young guys sat down the back on opposite sides. When I saw them, I thought of the fight at the social. One group was white. Two of them had shaved heads. The other group was brown, and one had a T-shirt with the word 'Tonga' on it.

One of the white guys said something under his breath.

A guy from the other group spoke. 'What did you say?'

I turned away. Harry took my hand in his. 'Have you seen *Arthur*?' he asked.

'The one with Dudley Moore in it? No.'

'It's meant to be funny. We could see *Endless Love* but it's sad.'

'Let's see *Arthur*.'

'Okay.'

We gazed out of the window, and I rested my head on Harry's shoulder.

'What's your problem?' someone down the back said.

'What?'

'Got a problem, coon?'

I stiffened.

'Don't look,' Harry whispered. 'Don't get involved.'

'What did you call me?'

'A coon,' the same voice said, 'a black coconut coon.'

There was movement behind us, and my heart began to race.

'You want to get your head smashed in?'

'Sit down, Tim,' another voice said. 'Sit down.'

'Fuck off. This boonga hasn't got the guts to hit me, but I might just thrash his black arse!'

A sudden violent movement behind us made me jump. I looked around. Two guys wrestled and grunted, throwing punches at each other, then fell into an empty seat.

'That's enough!' the bus driver yelled. He pulled over onto the side of the road and stopped the bus. 'I said that's enough.'

Their friends stood up and seemed to be trying to pull them apart, but then they too began to punch each other. It was fast and angry: quick, hard punches, knees in groins and stomachs and swearing and grunting.

The elderly woman got off the bus. The bus driver came down the aisle. He was stocky, probably round Dad's age, and he pointed at the open door. 'Get off this bus, all of you.'

One of the skinhead guys pulled away and said, 'Let's get out of here!'

The bus driver shoved him towards the door. 'Go on. Get going!'

The guy's mates stumbled off the bus, two were bleeding, one from his eye and the other from his lip.

'You lot get off too.'

'We didn't start that!' the guy with the 'Tonga' T-shirt said. 'He kept calling me a coon.'

'Get off the bus now.'

'They were hassling us! There were five of them and only four of us!' He rubbed the knuckles of his hand. His eye was bloodshot, and tinges of bruising were appearing around it. 'We paid for a ticket, and we didn't start that fight.'

The bus driver took a deep breath. 'Want me to call the police?'

'We've done nothing wrong,' another guy said. 'They attacked us.'

My mouth opened. 'That's true,' I said. 'I heard it all.'

The bus driver looked at me, then looked back at the boys. 'One more word out of any of you and I'll contact the police. We clear?'

The boys nodded and sat down. As we pulled away from the kerb, the guys on the street held up their fists and did the fingers to them. I couldn't see whether they did anything in return.

Harry held my hand. 'You okay?'

I nodded.

He looked out the window at the shops and houses we passed. 'There's no point getting involved in shit like that. You can end up getting hurt.'

'I was just telling the truth.'

'Yeah, but sometimes it backfires and you end up more involved than you want to be.'

'Harry, if no one got involved in stuff, there'd be no anti-tour protests. We have to get involved sometimes to stop crappy things happening to people.'

'I got involved once,' Harry said. 'A policeman took me aside at our house one night. He asked me some questions and he was so friendly and kind that, eventually, I told him that Dad had hit Mum that night. They arrested him after Mum confirmed what I'd said, but she dropped the charges against him. I think she was scared. When he came home, he didn't speak to me for weeks and told me to keep out of his way. I was eleven. I was terrified.'

'Well, that's . . . that's terrible.' I squeezed Harry's hand. 'But you did the right thing.'

'I've never done it again. Not worth it.'

We were quiet for the rest of the journey and so were the guys down the back of the bus.

At the cinema, we bought ice creams and sat in the back row. In the darkness, the violence on the bus melted away. We were safe in the peaceful, hidden world of the movies, watching a rich, alcoholic man fall in love with an ordinary woman and laughing at his chaotic life.

The cinema was full, so we couldn't kiss the way we had last time. Instead, Harry put his arm around my shoulder so that his hand could brush against my breast, while his soft lips pressed on my neck. Sometimes, his touch was so unbearably good that I had to turn and kiss him, but not for long. There were too many people around.

That night, Mum and Jo told us they'd protested at Eden Park during the Christchurch game. Some protesters had marched along the north-western motorway towards town, bringing traffic to a standstill. Another group protested on the southern motorway.

We switched on the news to see what had happened in Christchurch and saw a crowd of protesters facing the riot squad. The reporter said there were approximately 7000 demonstrators. The riot squad commander yelled, 'Visors down! Advance five!' The police advanced, jabbing their batons forward, in time with their words, 'Move! Move! Move!'

The front row of protesters couldn't escape. Batons crunched into heads and stomachs. Grunts and shrieks and wails came from the front rows. The riot squad stepped back. Maybe they were as shocked at what they'd done as the protesters. Their eyes and faces weren't visible behind their visors. Protesters who'd been hurt were assisted off to the side, and the reporter said some would be taken to hospital.

One protester wearing a white motorbike helmet walked in the space between the marchers and the police. He threw green leafy twigs down on the concrete, like a peace offering, or maybe to make the point that this was meant to be a non-violent protest.

A high camera shot showed the crowd stretching back from block to block, intersection after intersection filled with people. The camera cut to one intersection. A blockade of sand-filled jumbo bins stopped protesters from veering from the agreed route. Now, though, police at the intersections were fighting off protesters trying to get through. The reporter explained that police had been diverted from the main gates on Lancaster Street to protect the intersections. The camera cut to protesters running to the main gates hoping to get in, but police reappeared, beating them off with their batons.

Inside the rugby grounds, a reporter said that about sixty protesters had managed to get into the park and run onto the field. We could see them being beaten by police and tour supporters.

When the Springbok Tour news came to an end, Mum switched off the TV.

'Dad phoned today, before the march started,' I said. 'He said he had a bad feeling about today.'

'Did he? His feelings were spot on. I'm amazed no one's dead.' Mum stood up. 'After what happened on your bus today, and the violence we've just seen in Christchurch, I think we need some hot cocoa, Liza. Want to help me make it?'

In the kitchen, I stirred cocoa powder into a cup of hot water, while Mum poured milk into a pot. When the cocoa had dissolved, I poured it from the cup into the pot. Mum and I watched the brown liquid swirl until it mixed into the milk. I added some sugar and Mum kept stirring.

We went back into the lounge with cups of steaming hot cocoa. The TV was still off. Pete was reading the newspaper, and Jo was sprawled across an armchair, her eyes closed. We sipped the sweet, rich liquid and nobody spoke. The silence was peaceful. Sal sighed deeply, as if she too was beginning to finally unwind. Mum had been right. This was just what we needed.

CHAPTER 30
NELSON AND NAPIER

It was the last day of term two. Kalāsia, Rewi and I were in our usual rush to get to school, even though there wasn't much to look forward to. Assignments were always due on the last day and new assignments were given out to do over the holidays, especially as these holidays were the ones before our final exams.

'So, why was the Timaru game cancelled?' I asked Rewi. 'Your mum must have some idea of what was going on.'

Rewi shrugged. 'She only knows what the rest of us know, that it was cancelled for security reasons.'

'A bomb?' I asked.

'Liza, you have to believe me, I don't know. Mum doesn't know either.'

'The police must've been tipped off about something,' I said.

'You should be a detective,' Rewi said sarcastically. 'You're good!'

'Shut up!'

'Don't you two start arguing,' Kalāsia said.

'We never argue!' Rewi said. 'Sometimes I just have to let Liza know that her ideas aren't correct, that's all.'

'I'm warning you, Rewi,' Kalāsia said. 'You're going to get the whack.'

'No, not the whack!' Rewi said.

Kalāsia raised her eyebrows and nodded. 'A different whack. This time, I'll hit you over the head with my schoolbag.'

'So, if I say Liza's ideas are a bit misguided, you'd hit me with your schoolbag.'

'That's right!'

'So, if I say Liza is a bit . . .'

'You'd better watch what you say!' Kalāsia swung her schoolbag off her shoulder and held it up in both hands.

'I was just going to say that she's a bit lacking in intelligence.'

'That's it!' Kalāsia yelled.

Rewi began to run. 'It's not unkind; it's the truth!'

'Speak for yourself!' I yelled after him.

Kalāsia ran after Rewi and threw her bag at the back of his head. It was a good shot.

'Ah, what's in that bag?' Rewi yelled, laughing. 'A rock?'

'Assignments! Lots of them!' Kalāsia bent to pick up her bag, but Rewi scooped it up and ran off with it.

'I feel like I'm walking with primary school kids!' I yelled after them.

It was pure luck that neither Kalāsia nor Rewi had injuries by the time they parted at our school gate.

In our classroom, Sister Agnes was writing on the blackboard. She saw us out of the corner of her eye. 'Morning, girls. Glad you made it on time today.'

'Good morning, Sister,' we replied.

Ursula looked up from her seat, where she was inspecting her forehead in a small hand mirror. 'They made it on time because they value their learning, Sister,' she said.

Sister Agnes didn't respond, but I saw her smile as we passed.

'Hey, Liza,' Ursula said as I passed her desk. 'I've got a zit on my forehead. Not happy about it. Not happy at all!'

'It's about time you got a pimple. Your complexion is annoyingly flawless!'

'Up until now,' Ursula said.

Sister Agnes turned from the board. 'I'm just popping out to get some more chalk from the storeroom, girls. I'll be back before the bell.'

I sat down beside Ursula at her desk. 'That gives us a few minutes to chat.'

'Want to go to Cook Street Market with me one day to buy a dress for the ball?' Ursula asked.

'Yes!' I hadn't bought tickets for the ball yet, but it wasn't for another month, so I had time. I pulled the mirror out of Ursula's hand and put it face-down on the desk. 'Stop looking at your zit. When do you want to go?'

'During the holidays but only at a time when you're not studying, my hard-working little friend.' Ursula patted my arm.

I pushed her hand away. 'Smart-arse. I won't study every day. I'll ring you next week, okay?'

Ursula nodded and put her mirror away. I stood up to go to my desk, but Susan Leighton was in the way. 'Sorry,' I said, squeezing back behind Ursula's chair. 'You go.'

Susan stood there. 'Were you glad the Timaru game was cancelled?'
'What? I . . .'

'Bet that made you happy.'

'I kind of want them all to be cancelled.'

Susan shook her head at me, then pushed past. 'You think you're something special, don't you? Daddy's a reporter and your family goes on protest marches.'

'Susan, I . . .'

'Leave her alone!' Kalāsia interrupted.

Susan looked at Kalāsia. 'Don't tell me what to do, coconut.'

Kalāsia's face was still.

'Ignore her, Kalāsia,' I said.

'Ignore her Kalāsia,' Susan mimicked.

'Sit down, Susan,' Ursula said.

'Don't tell me what to do, Ursula. You don't like coconuts. I've heard you say that.'

'You're wrong,' Ursula said. 'I like Kalāsia.'

'But you don't like any other coconuts. Be honest!'

Sister Agnes stood at the doorway. The room was completely silent. She crossed the room and stood behind her desk. 'Sit down, girls!'

Susan's face flushed red as she turned to sit at her desk. I went to sit beside Kalāsia. She was drumming her fingers on the desk and whispered, 'I hate her, Liza.'

'She's a total cow,' I agreed.

Sister Agnes moved to the centre of the room, bowed her head and did the sign of the cross. 'In the name of the father, the son and the holy spirit.' She stopped. 'I can't hear you, girls. Let's start again. In the name of the father, the son and the holy spirit.' She looked up. 'Would you like to say the prayer this morning, Kalāsia?'

Kalāsia shook her head. 'No, thank you, Sister.'

'How about a Tongan prayer? Do you know the Hail Mary in Tongan?'

Kalāsia nodded. 'Yes, Sister.'

'Well, I doubt many of us have heard the Hail Mary in Tongan. Off you go then.'

Kalāsia took a deep breath. 'Si'oto 'ofa Malia, 'oku ke mohu kalāsia, 'oku 'iate koe 'a e 'Eiki, 'oku ke monū'ia koe 'i he fefine fua pē, pea 'oku faitāpuekina 'a e fua 'o ho manava ko Sēsū. Sangata Malia, Fa'ē 'a e 'Otua, ke ke hūfia kimautolu angahala, 'i he 'aho ni pea mo e 'aho foki 'o 'emau mate. 'Āmeni.'

When Kalāsia had finished, Sister Agnes said, 'Does, "'Āmeni" mean "Amen"?'

'Yes, Sister,' Kalāsia replied.

'Well, let's all say, "'Āmeni", girls.'

The class said, "'Āmeni".'

'I noticed you said your name in the prayer, Kalāsia. What does your name mean in English?' Sister Agnes asked.

'Grace, Sister.'

'Ah, 'Hail Mary, full of grace'. So, you have an extra special name, Kalāsia. Thank you for saying the prayer for us.'

On Saturday, the 22nd of August, the Springboks played Nelson Bays, but the game on my mind that morning was hockey. Ms Evans, our PE teacher had convinced Kalāsia to join our hockey team, and now she played midfield, like me. She was fast and picked up on the rules quickly. She dribbled, shot goals, tackled and passed as if she'd played for years. Whenever she lost the ball or missed a goal, she swore in Tongan, and it wasn't long before I was swearing in Tongan too.

Kalāsia's parents took us to hockey that day because Mum had taken Jo to her game and Dad was in Nelson. Kalāsia's dad was quiet on the sideline, watching with his arms folded and shaking his head or clapping every now and then. Her mum was the complete opposite. She was loud and yelled at Kalāsia constantly. 'Whack it! Run! Too slow! Think, Kalāsia! Try looking!' I'd never heard anyone make so much noise at a game.

On the way home, Kalāsia's mum asked me if my mother would be home by now. 'We've got something we'd like to give her, give your family.'

'She should be home by now,' I said. 'Jo's game started before ours.'

Kalāsia's mum talked the whole way home. She told me about how Kalāsia wanted to go to the school ball and how she wasn't sure about that. Kalāsia rolled her eyes at me. Maybe she'd let her go if 'Amanaki, went too. She said she was worried about her mother in Tonga and how she was having heart problems and that medical care in Tonga wasn't as good as in New Zealand. She told us about a woman in the Tongan choir who sang off-key but blamed everyone else when it sounded flat. She asked me if I'd ever tried 'ota ika. 'It's raw fish with lemon and coconut milk,' she said. 'Tastes good.'

'She's had some before,' Kalāsia said. 'Remember that day I brought some and left it in your fridge before we went to school?'

I nodded. 'That was delicious.'

'Ifo,' Kalāsia said. 'Ifo means delicious.'

'Well, that raw fish was ifo,' I said.

Kalāsia and her parents laughed.

'Maybe Kalāsia will teach you Tongan,' her dad said. 'Every day she can teach you a new word.'

'I can do that,' Kalāsia said. 'A new word every morning while I plait your hair.'

'One day, I might be able to speak to you in Tongan,' I said. 'Imagine that!'

When we arrived at my house, Kalāsia's mother took something out of the boot of the car. It was a wide, thick material, rolled up with string around it. Then she passed Kalāsia a covered bowl, and we made our way into the house. Kalāsia's dad walked behind us.

Mum was listening to the radio, making tea when we walked in.

'Well, this is a lovely surprise!' she said, hugging Kalāsia's mum.

'We wanted to give you this,' Kalāsia's mother said, handing the rolled-up material to Mum. 'It's a Tongan tapa cloth, a ngatu. You can hang it on a wall somewhere in the house.'

Mum unrolled the ngatu and held it up. It reached the floor and was as wide as Mum's extended arms. 'It's beautiful!' she gasped.

'You helped us,' Kalāsia's dad said. 'This is our way of saying thank you.'

'You've already thanked me,' Mum said. 'This is very special though. I'll treasure this. We all will.'

I reached out and ran my fingers down the rough bark cloth. There were images drawn inside squares. Kalāsia pointed to a bird, saying it was a dove. 'And that's the Tongan coat of arms, and those words, "koe kalauni" mean "crown". I'll explain it more to you another day when we're not rushing off.'

Mum put her arm around Kalāsia. 'We should be thanking you, really. Kalāsia gets Liza out of bed in the morning and helps her get organised for school.'

'Mum, I'm not that bad,' I said.

'Yes, you are,' Kalāsia said.

'Now, who'd like a coffee or tea and some lunch?'

'No, we can't stay,' Kalāsia's mother said. 'We're going to Saint Francis's now to watch the second half of our son's game. Another time that would be nice.'

'Here's some lu pulu,' Kalāsia said, passing the bowl in her hands to me. 'It's made with taro leaves, green onions, coconut milk and beef. It's yummy!'

'So, it's ifo,' I said.

Kalāsia's parents laughed.

'Exactly,' Kalāsia said. 'It's ifo.'

After Kalāsia and her parents had gone, I took the lid off the bowl. The lu pulu smelled good. Dipping a fork in, I tasted a mouthful and stood by the bench savouring it.

'Thought you were going to serve some for both of us,' Mum said.

Jo came into the kitchen in her dressing gown, her wet hair rolled up in a towel, like a turban. 'Win your hockey?' she asked.

'Yep. You?'

'Lost, four nil. Not a good game.'

'Want some?' I asked her. 'It's lu pulu, a Tongan dish from Kalāsia's family.'

'Smells good,' Jo said. 'Pete still at rugby, Mum?'

'Must be,' Mum said. She was reading the paper at the table and not really listening to us now.

I served the three of us a bowl of lu pulu, grabbed a section of the paper to read and sat beside Mum. Jo joined us. Then we all had second helpings of the lu pulu and agreed that eating such delicious food was a good way to start the holidays.

A bit later, we hung the ngatu up on the lounge wall and sat on the sofa gazing at it. Pete had the TV on to watch the build-up to the game and see what the protesters were doing. On the screen, a yellow 'STOP THE TOUR' banner hung from the top of Nelson Cathedral. Below, a reporter said that the Springboks had been woken many times by protesters throughout the previous night.

The camera moved to a man speaking on the cathedral steps. The reporter explained that he was Trevor Richards, one of the people who founded HART in 1969. He'd been HART's chairperson for many years. After his speech, Hone Tuwhare, the poet, stood up to speak.

I sat up on the sofa. 'We're studying his poetry at school in English. I like his poems.'

'So do I,' Mum said. 'Let's listen to what he has to say.'

The camera didn't stay on him for long though. It moved along the crowd that had filled up the main street below the cathedral. Then it showed lines of police stationed along every possible marching route, all wearing helmets and holding batons.

The protesters didn't get onto the ground that day, but they made their presence felt, chanting and waving placards and banners.

A few days later, on Tuesday, the 25th of August, the Springboks played the New Zealand Māori team at McLean Park in Napier. Again, no one made it onto the field, but Pete, Jo, Rewi and I watched crowds of protesters sit down in the streets and chant. Rugby spectators passed them as they walked to the game.

Mum was at work, but we were on holiday, eating and lying around the lounge.

'Why is a Māori team playing South Africa?' Jo asked.

'Because they love rugby,' Pete said.

'But they wouldn't be allowed to play against them in South Africa,' I said.

'Mum and Dad are pissed off that they're playing,' Rewi said. 'Lots of Māori are not happy about it. Some are protesting outside the Māori Affairs Department today.'

'Fair enough!' Jo said.

'It's the second test match in Wellington this Saturday,' Pete said. 'Dad reckons Wellington's the most organised coalition in the whole country, so protesters might get onto the field.'

I picked up a cushion and threw it at Rewi. 'Want to go for a quick ciggie?'

'I'm giving up.'

'Don't lie. You're just trying to impress Jo and Pete.'

'I might give up,' Rewi said, 'one day.'

'Okay, let's give up one day but not now.' I stood up. 'Coming?'

'She's a bad influence on me,' Rewi said to Pete and Jo.

'You are dicks for smoking though,' Pete said. 'Seriously, dicks.'

Rewi and I went out into the back yard, with Sal at our heels. Wind blew out the flame from Rewi's lighter, but we tried again. Huddled around our cigarettes, under the kōwhai tree, we puffed quickly to light up before the flame disappeared. Finally lit, we dragged deeply on our cigarettes, blowing smoke in and out of our mouths, chatting and teasing each other.

Above us, tūī squawked and sang. Below us, yellow Kōwhai flowers had scattered as if pieces of the sun had fallen on the lawn.

CHAPTER 31
SECOND TEST, WELLINGTON

It was about 10:30am when Ursula and I stepped off the bus in Queen Street and walked to Cook Street Market. The sun was out, so we spent a while wandering around the outside stalls, looking at jewellery, shoes, clothes and pieces of art and craft.

Inside, Ursula took my elbow and led me to a stall. The stallholder leafed through a magazine while we looked through the racks of clothes. Her bangles tinkled as she fiddled with one of her hoop earrings, then straightened her bright orange scarf around her long black hair.

'Look!' Ursula pulled a lacy blue dress off a rack. 'You'd look so good in that.'

'So would you.'

'Yeah, but you try it on first. If you don't like it, I'll try it.'

The stallholder pointed to a curtain, her bangles clinking. A long mirror was squeezed inside. I pulled the curtain around me and put the dress on. I felt like Stevie Nicks, with the dress falling around me and my hair out, wild, around my shoulders.

'Show me what it looks like,' Ursula said.

I pulled the curtain open and Ursula's eyes widened. 'That looks gorgeous, Liza. You've got to buy that.'

I'd done some babysitting for a couple of families in our street, so I had some money. I just hoped it wasn't too expensive.

'It's fifteen dollars,' the stall holder said. 'Give it a gentle hand wash before you wear it.'

Only fifteen dollars! 'I'll buy it,' I said.

The stallholder wrapped it in some white tissue paper and handed it to me. 'It looks good on you.'

Ursula and I moved on, stopping at the photography stall where people dressed up in Victorian clothing to have a photo taken. I had money left over and managed to convince Ursula to have a photo with me.

The man at the stall helped us choose some Victorian outfits. We changed behind the curtain, giggling at the long sleeves, gloves and hats. Even in a high-necked, buttoned-up dress, Ursula looked sexy, a demure version of Debbie Harry.

The photographer told us not to smile because photos were a serious thing in the Victorian era. He directed me to sit on a chair and Ursula to stand beside me with her hand on my shoulder. We kept straight faces, even though I felt like giggling.

He took two photos, which his camera instantly printed. He laid them on a small table, and we watched the images develop. There we were, except we looked like young women from a time past.

'We'd have had an arranged marriage back then, wouldn't we?' Ursula said.

'Probably,' I said. 'Wouldn't have been allowed to get a bus into Queen Street on our own. We'd have had an older family member with us, keeping an eye on us.'

'Makes me think of Petruchio and Kate. I don't ever want to be controlled by someone. I want to be free and wild, always.'

'Good for you,' the photographer said. He put the photos into cardboard frames and passed them to us. 'Here you go, free, wild things. One each. Keep them forever to remember. You'll never be this young again.'

Ursula found a black halter-neck dress that she liked in another stall. When she tried it on, most of her back was bare, and the young guy at the counter couldn't keep his eyes off her. He told us he was watching the stall while his mother went for a smoke.

'Do you have a partner for the ball?' he asked when Ursula paid him for the dress.

'Yes,' Ursula said, 'but if I didn't, I'd ask you.'

The guy blushed, gave her some change and watched her walk away with me.

'You've made his day,' I said.

'It doesn't hurt, does it?' Ursula said. 'Made him happy.'

We wandered around a bit more before Ursula went to meet up with Josh. I wasn't seeing Harry, because his grandparents were staying for the weekend, so I bussed home alone. The second test match in Wellington was starting soon, and I wanted to see how the protests were going. If Wellington protesters stopped this game, then maybe the rest of the tour would be cancelled. Imagine what the South African government would think of that!

At home, my family was glued to the television, barely lifting their heads to say hello to me.

'Your dad's with a group at Macalister Park,' Mum said. 'Well, that's what he told me. Although, he may move around a bit, I suppose.'

Dad had told us that the Wellington coalition, COST, had organised protesters into seven groups: Orange, Pink, Yellow, Green, Blue, Brown and White Squads. Hours before the game, each squad would block all access to Athletic Park. Later, they would push through police lines around the park itself. There were around 100 marshals, who had instructions and maps and were able to split squads into smaller groups to help with or move to certain areas. The goal was to stretch police resources in order to increase the chance of stopping the game.

Apparently, radio equipment had been installed in a house so that COST could listen to and interrupt police communications. COST was also communicating through citizen band radio in cars, so that squad marshals could find out how to support other groups or get through unsupervised spaces.

The TV showed a group of protesters walking across a grassy slope. The reporter said it was Macalister Park, where Dad was. Most of the protesters wore helmets and carried banners and placards, chanting, 'Stop the tour, call it off!' They reminded me of an army from an English battle scene, moving across the grass towards the rolls of barbed wire between them and the police. A moment later, they began to run towards the barbed wire, yelling, 'Amandla!' Some of them were repeating an 'oo' sound.

'Are they saying, "Move, move move", to taunt the riot squad?' Jo asked.

'Could be,' Pete said.

Police helicopters whirred overhead. People with wire cutters began to cut through the barbed-wire coils and fences. Tying ropes around the fence posts, they began to heave the barbed-wire fences away. When they made it to the last fence, the police started using their batons through and over the fence to keep the protesters back. A Māori group came forward and began to do a haka on the field. The police stared at them. No one moved.

The camera cut to inside Athletic Park. Some of the stands were full, but others had empty seats.

'Maybe people saw the chaos and decided to turn back and watch it at home,' Mum said.

It looked like there was a smoke bomb on the field, and the reporter mentioned some protesters had managed to get inside. From there on, the camera stayed on the game. I wanted to see what happened at Macalister Park and whether other squads had made progress elsewhere.

'We'll have to wait for the news,' Mum said, 'and for Dad to fill us in later.'

'I'm not watching the game,' I said.

'Neither am I,' Jo said.

'Show us your new dress,' Mum said.

We went into my room, followed by Sal. Mum and Jo sat on my bed. I pulled the dress out of the tissue paper and put it on.

'Wow!' Mum said. 'That's gorgeous.'

'Aw, you look like a young woman!' Jo said.

I flounced around in front of Mum and Jo, who laughed as I posed for them.

'Shhh,' Mum said, 'is that Pete?'

'What's he yelling about?' Jo said.

We went back into the lounge.

Pete pointed to the TV. 'Bloody game's been cut off. Look!'

A Polynesian fire dance was on the TV screen along with a message apologising for the interruption to transmission.

'That's weird,' Mum said. 'Hang on, the game's coming back on. It's just not very clear.'

'Why are you dressed like that?' Pete asked.

'It's my new dress for the school ball.'

'Nice,' Pete said, turning back to the screen, which had returned to normal.

I didn't want to watch rugby, so I phoned Rewi to see if he wanted to do something.

'Spacies?' he suggested.

I groaned.

'I'll jog over. Be at the top of your driveway in five minutes,' Rewi said.

He was forty seconds late, which I told him meant he wasn't as fast as he thought he was. With Sal panting along beside us, we headed to the takeaway bar.

'Weird protest, eh?' Rewi said. 'That group in the park never got past eyeballing the police and hurling abuse at them.'

'Too many police,' I said, 'and more squads kept joining them. If protesters tried to push through, they'd just get beaten up.'

'Suppose so.' Rewi lit a ciggie and passed one to me. 'Get a dress?'

'Yep, a beautiful one.'

'Females,' Rewi said, shaking his head. 'Guys just chuck on jeans.'

'Yeah, well, you can't wear jeans to a ball.'

'All the more reason not to go.'

'You're not going to your school ball? I'll be going with Harry. You have to come.'

'Not sure. Still thinking about it.'

'Do you want me to help you get a higher score at Spacies or not? Cos you're treading a very fine line! You could take Ciara or Stella as your partner?'

'You've never helped me play Spacies!'

'Excuse me! I yell when an invader is coming.'

'That just puts me off, but it's nice that you think you're helping.'

'What sort of compliment is that?'

Rewi grinned. 'Aw, you keep thinking you're helping me. That's kind of sweet.'

'Patronising jerk!' I said, but it was impossible not to grin back at him.

Later, at home, we watched the news. The reporter in Wellington said crowds of protesters had sat down on streets to stop rugby fans from getting to the rugby ground. We watched riot police barging into one of these groups. Some had nowhere to move to and were forced through a shop window. The reporter said it was Riddiford Street and the riot squad was trying to make way for rugby fans to get through. A police officer dragged a protester by his feet, while another policeman kicked him in the head. The screen was filled with riot police kicking, kneeing and hitting with their batons. There was a close-up of a guy lying on the ground not moving, but a police officer still stamped on his hand.

'My God,' Mum said. She looked at me. 'You okay, Liza? You look a bit pale.'

I felt nauseous but I couldn't look away. The camera cut to another group of protesters. The reporter said they were running through back yards to try to get into Athletic Park, but the riot squad were waiting for them. Their batons crunched into faces, helmets and hands as people tried to climb fences.

I realised I'd been sitting with my mouth open. The phone rang, and I went to answer it. Dad was on the other end.

'Dad!' I almost yelled, I was so relieved to hear him.

'Bit loud!' Dad laughed. 'I've had enough yelling and shouting for one day!'

The rest of the family crowded around the phone. Dad told us that the Springboks were sleeping at Athletic Park. They'd slept there last night too, to avoid trouble with protesters. No hotels now.

They were being carefully guarded in the rugby grounds. 'What else can I tell you that you haven't already seen on the news?' Dad said. 'The police searched HART's Wellington headquarters last night, looking for weapons.'

'Really?' Mum said. 'Anything happen anywhere else in the country?'

'Apparently some Auckland protesters cut off TV transmission from the control room in Waiatarua.'

'That's why the game stopped!' Pete said. 'That was bloody annoying.'

Dad laughed. 'I'd say it was effective if it annoyed you that much. Ah, feels good to laugh after the stuff I've seen today.'

After a few minutes, I left Mum chatting with Dad and went into my room to listen to some music. I played Fleetwood Mac and lay on my bed, closing my eyes. Stevie Nicks sang 'Dreams', and I imagined Harry dancing with me at the ball, the two of us swaying to the music in each other's arms.

CHAPTER 32
THREE NORTH ISLAND GAMES

On Wednesday, the 2nd of September, the Springboks played Bay of Plenty in Rotorua, but my classmates and I would probably always remember that day for a very different reason. In Christian Living, Sister Agnes tried to teach us about relationships.

After a short prayer to start the lesson, Sister Agnes adjusted her veil, coughed and began. 'Today we're going to talk about expressions of love, girls.' Clasping her hands together, as if still in prayer, she continued, 'Let's share some ways that human beings express love to others.'

We came up with suggestions, such as kindness, politeness, hugs, respect, kisses and holding hands, but it was just a matter of time, before Ursula put up her hand and said, 'sex'.

Sister Agnes didn't flinch. Perhaps she'd been waiting for it. 'Yes, Ursula, intercourse is one way a married couple show love.' She wrote, 'sexual intercourse' on the board.

'So, it's bad to have sex if you're not married?' Ursula asked.

'Well, God and the church bless married love, Ursula.'

'What about kissing, Sister? Does the church approve of that? Is French kissing wrong?'

'It's fine, I think, but it's best to leave it at that.'

'So, nothing else, Sister? Just kissing?'

'Well, other things could lead to intercourse.'

'But kissing could lead to intercourse, couldn't it?'

'Goodness, well, not immediately, surely!'

The class laughed. Sister Agnes was trying to be funny, which was a relief, because the tension in the room, although exciting, was nerve-wracking at the same time.

'Girls, I would say, when a man feels your breasts, sex is inevitable. There is no going back,' Sister Agnes said. She looked at Ursula, but Ursula seemed to have stopped bothering to work out Sister Agnes's views on sex and marriage. She gazed out the window, then began to inspect her nails. She'd gone the whole way with Josh, but she was probably remembering when kissing and feeling breasts were as far as she went. Like me now, she'd stopped there once.

Sister Agnes took the box of Bibles out of the cupboard near her desk. 'Let's see what the Bible has to say about love between a man and a woman. Ana Babich, you're chattering down the back. Perhaps you could hand these out to the class. Thank you.'

Walking home from school that afternoon, I told Rewi about our sex education class.

'A nun taught you that?' Rewi said. 'Did she use the word, "intercourse"? Teachers love that word, and it sounds so . . .'

'Medical,' I said.

'Exactly.'

'Ursula would be in trouble if she asked all those questions in a Tongan school,' Kalāsia said.

'Would she get the whack?' Rewi said.

'Nah, that's your special punishment!' Kalāsia said. 'But she'd bring shame on her family, talking like that to a teacher, especially a nun.'

'She is funny, though,' I said.

'She is,' Kalāsia said, 'but I sort of hold my breath when she talks like that to Sister Agnes.'

'I think the whole class holds their breath.'

'Maybe not as much as I do,' Kalāsia said.

When I got home, Pete was watching the rugby. He said that there were protesters chanting from a small hill and you could see them from inside the stadium. 'Before the game started, they showed all the barriers to stop protesters getting in. Big jumbo bins. Heaps of police.'

'Same old story,' I said, shutting the lounge door and heading to the kitchen to get something to eat.

Dad told us that forty protesters had been arrested at Rotorua Airport. He said the police had been far too rough. There'd been the usual nightly raids to wake up the Springboks too. What most struck me though, was that Dad said the Arawa Trust Board, which represented the hapū and iwi of Te Arawa people, had not welcomed the Springboks and refused them visits to tourist sites like Whakarewarewa. I thought of Rebecca Evans and Donna Awatere, the two Māori activists I'd often seen on TV. They insisted that if we cared about the inequality black South Africans faced, we had to care also about the inequality faced by Māori. I remembered the woman at university that Pete had listened to. 'Look in your own back yard,' she'd said.

On the 5th of September, the Springboks were playing Auckland at Eden Park. Dad was back home and so was Mere. Dad had gone to report on the game, and Mum and Jo had gone to the protests. Only Pete and I were at home. I wasn't going to the protests because I was going to a barbecue at Harry's that afternoon. His dad's best friend, Rob, was up from Christchurch for some work thing and was staying with Harry's family for a couple of nights. Harry told me it was never comfortable when Rob visited and begged me to come to help him get through the evening. When I suggested he come to the protest with us, he said he had to be at the barbecue, so I agreed to support him at his barbecue.

I was getting ready when Pete called me into the lounge. 'This is full-on,' he said. 'Police everywhere. Army and air force too, defending the ground like it's a war. Look! They've got freight containers and trucks now, as well as the jumbo bins, blocking off any entry to the park.'

'Dad said that MOST organised plywood shields and chest padding to give to people when they meet at Fowlds Park,' I said. 'They're expecting the worst from the riot squad.'

'Wonder if Mum and Jo are using shields,' Pete said. 'Looks like the protesters have separated into groups, maybe to try to get into Eden Park in as many places as possible.'

'Riot squad are everywhere though. They'll never get in.' Riot police twirled their batons, staring down the protesters. Apparently, people who lived in these streets were told to stay inside their houses.

The camera cut to the corner of Sandringham Road and Royal Terrace, where a large group of protesters faced neat lines of riot police, eight in each line. The reporter explained that MOST had divided the protesters into squads. This was Biko Squad, made up mostly of university students. He said the squads had been assigned marshals.

The marshal instructing Biko Squad was Norman Tuiasau. He yelled, 'Advance!' and Biko Squad, shielded, padded and helmeted, moved forward. The riot squad hit them with batons. Then Tuiasau cried, 'Withdraw!'

The reporter said this had been going on for a nerve-wracking hour or so. The protesters couldn't get through, but they were keeping their pressure on the police.

The camera cut to the rugby ground. A man who looked like a referee walked in front of the official referee just as a Springbok was about to kick off. He snatched the ball and kicked it up into the stands, near Ron Don, the chairman of the Auckland Rugby Union. The police dragged him off the field. Pete and I laughed. The reporter said that, apparently, the man was a teacher and ex-vicar, named Geoff Walpole.

'Brilliant idea!' I said. 'Can't believe he got through security to do that!'

'He looked like a referee though,' Pete said. 'Easy mistake to make.'

The rugby began, so I left Pete to it, to finish getting ready.

Harry hadn't told me why he felt uncomfortable when his dad's friend, Rob, came to stay. I'd guessed it was because his dad and Rob drank too much when they were together but, when we sat down to eat, I realised I was wrong.

Rob and Harry's dad, Mike, had been watching the rugby. The

Springboks had won, so they were a bit grumpy when they first came out onto the deck, complaining about how this or that player could have done better.

Harry told them they should be boycotting the game, and his dad rolled his eyes at Rob. 'Not this again. Ever since you became his girlfriend, Eliza, he's become an anti-tour activist.'

'I have a mind of my own, Dad,' Harry said. 'Before I met Liza, I didn't agree with the tour.'

'Yeah, yeah, if you say so, Harry.'

'Well, I'm not sure where I stand on the whole thing, Mike,' Rob said. 'I love rugby, but you have to admit it's all been a bit of a disaster really. We've got police and every day New Zealanders at war with each other.'

'Let's change the topic, Rob,' Mike said. 'Don't want to lose our friendship over this. I'm firmly pro-tour.'

Harry's dad began to cook on the barbecue, and Rob stood beside him, chatting about work and how he was trying to start a branch of his pet food business in Auckland.

Sophie asked me and Harry if we'd like to play Swingball with her. I hadn't played for a long time, so I was keen. When Harry played Sophie, he often missed the ball on purpose to let her win. Once again, I was struck by how kind he could be.

When we'd worked up a sweat, Harry's mum, Raewyn, called us to come and eat at the outside table on the deck.

Sophie and Raewyn sat on one side of the table, while Harry and I sat on the other. Mike and Rob sat at either end of the table.

At first, Sophie did most of the talking, asking me if I liked sausages. She said they were too spongy for her.

'Spongy?' I asked.

'They sort of feel squishy in my mouth,' Sophie said. 'Not like chicken drumsticks. They feel better to eat. More like real meat.'

'Sausages are made out of meat and a few other things, aren't they, Mum?' Harry asked.

'Yes, not sure exactly what else they add to the mix, but they're not pure meat.'

Sophie chatted on about gymnastics at school and how her teacher asked her if she'd like to be in a special gymnastics team and compete against other schools. She asked me if I'd like to do cartwheels together after dinner. Then she chatted about how she had to give a speech at school, but she hadn't decided on a topic. 'Harry's going to help me with my speech, eh Harry?'

'I am, Soph. You just have to decide on a topic and then I'll help you find some information on it. Easy peasy.'

We chatted about possible ideas, and then I realised that Harry's mum and Rob were having a quiet conversation of their own. Rob's head moved in towards hers, but she pulled back, sitting up straight, still listening to what he was saying.

'What's happening up that end of the table, Raewyn?' Mike asked, speaking over Sophie.

Harry's mum sat up even straighter. 'Oh, just catching up on Rob's kids and what they're up to.'

'Right.' Mike drank from his beer bottle. 'Perhaps we could all hear about the kids, then. I'm interested too. Are you interested Harry?'

'Er, yeah, sort of.' Harry smiled at Sophie. 'Want some more chicken?'

Sophie shook her head. 'I'm full.'

'So, tell us about the kids, Rob,' Mike said.

Rob began to talk about his three sons. I nodded politely as he spoke, but my attention was on Raewyn, Harry's mum. She chewed her food, her eyes on her plate, barely looking up.

'Another beer, Rob?' Mike asked.

'Why not?' Rob said.

Raewyn began to rise out of her chair. 'I'll get it,' she said.

Rob put his hand on hers for a moment. 'You sit down. Let that big oaf over there get it.'

Mike forced a laugh before heading inside to the kitchen.

Sophie leaned into me. 'Rob used to be Mum's boyfriend a long time ago. Then he went to live in Christchurch, and Dad became her boyfriend. Rob and Dad were friends. It's sort of like friends sharing a girlfriend, isn't it?'

'Guess so,' I said.

Raewyn had made a cheesecake. She placed it on the table in front of her and Rob.

'My favourite dessert,' Rob said.

'I know.' Raewyn passed him a knife. 'Here, cut yourself a piece and then pass it round.'

Mike had four empty beer bottles in front of him. Another two were beside the barbecue and eight were on the coffee table in the lounge where he'd been watching the game. I wasn't sure how many he'd drunk, but his cheeks were red, and his chin rested heavily on his hands, his elbows on the table. 'She doesn't make a special effort like that for me,' he said.

Raewyn looked at him briefly. 'That's not true.'

'Once, maybe, but not anymore.'

'Ah, stop feeling sorry for yourself, Mike,' Rob said. He spoke clearly, so only a few of those empty bottles had been his.

'She's as cold as ice,' Mike said.

'Hey, come on. This is Raewyn we're talking about.' Rob passed the cheesecake to Sophie.

'You don't know her like I do.'

'Mike, stop,' Raewyn said.

'Mike, stop,' Mike mimicked her.

'Hey, come on, mate,' Rob said. 'Let's not ruin a good evening.'

'For a change,' Harry said, helping himself to a piece of cheesecake.

'What's that, son?'

'Nothing,' Harry said.

'Let's talk about something else,' Rob said. 'Harry, tell me how school's going.'

While Harry talked about the subjects he was doing, I snuck glances at Mike and Raewyn. His eyes were fixed on her, narrow and accusing. She carefully avoided his gaze, listening to Harry and commenting that Harry's attitude at school needed to change if he wanted to pass.

Rob kept the conversation moving, telling us stories of how he and Mike had got into trouble at school. Occasionally, Mike seemed to listen in and smile at something Rob said, but his focus returned to Raewyn, while everyone behaved as if they were unaware of it.

It was getting cold, so Raewyn suggested we go inside. Mike swayed as he stood up and made his way to the lounge. When I'd finished helping bring the dishes in, he was asleep on the sofa with dribble on his chin.

Sophie, Harry and I lay on the floor in Sophie's room playing cards for a while after dinner, listening to the murmur of Rob and Raewyn's voices from the kitchen.

When Mum knocked on the door to pick me up, Rob introduced himself and Raewyn invited Mum in for coffee. From Sophie's room, I could hear Mum's response. 'That's a lovely offer,' she said, 'but I've been protesting at Eden Park all afternoon and I'm shattered.'

'Sorry about tonight,' Harry whispered to me, as we stood up from the card game. 'Dad's a bit . . .'

'Don't be sorry,' I said, quickly kissing Harry's cheek. 'It's not your fault.'

In the car, Mum commented on how lovely Harry's father was. 'That's not his father,' I said. 'He's a family friend.'

'Oh,' Mum said. 'Well, he's a friendly guy.'

I pictured Raewyn and Rob still talking in the kitchen. Neither of them had gone into the lounge where Mike lay asleep on the sofa.

At home, Jo and Pete were drinking tea and eating biscuits. Mum and I joined them.

'You'd have been amazed at the crowd today,' Mum said. 'They reckon there were about 7000 there. When we arrived at Fowlds Park, we had to join a squad. We were part of Tutu Squad, which was made up mostly of church groups. There was also Biko Squad, who were mostly students, and Patu Squad, which was mostly Māori and Pacific Island people. Rebecca Evans and Donna Awatere are key people in Patu. I like that they called a squad 'Patu'; it links apartheid to racism in New Zealand.' Mum picked up a biscuit and started to eat it.

'We had to practise things,' Jo said, 'like suddenly stopping, so that people in front of us didn't get pushed into police lines, backing away without people behind getting squashed, linking arms, stuff like that.'

'Our marshals told us we were going to put pressure on different entry points into Eden Park,' Mum said, 'and try to push through them to get onto the field.'

'If you wanted action, you were told to go up into the front lines,' Jo said, 'but Mum, Tipene and I stayed further back.'

'It was a wise choice because when people at the front did break through the police lines, they were beaten badly,' Mum said. 'Someone told me that David Williams was hit in the head and Steve Bayliss had a broken nose.'

'How can they get away with that?' I asked.

Mum shook her head and shrugged. 'Your dad phoned just before I came to get you, Liza. He's at the office now, but he said the police tried to make his photographer, Hamish, give them the film from his camera.'

'Did he give it to them?'

'No, Hamish told them he worked for a paper and wasn't a protester, but the policeman wasn't friendly. The cheek of it.'

'None of our protest squads broke the police lines,' Jo said. 'Dad said that some of Patu Squad had a huge fight with the riot squad in Kowhai Intermediate's grounds, as they tried to get closer to Eden Park. He said both sides were violent, but he saw a couple of police being extra vicious. Dad said that John Minto told reporters, even with intense police presence, protesters could have pushed through some park entry points, but it wasn't worth risking their lives.'

'I'll be there next week,' I said. 'I'll join Tutu Squad as well.'

'So will Rewi,' Mum said. 'He looked after the kids today, but next week, they'll be with an aunty, so he can come too. The only way I'll allow you to protest, Liza, is if you stay near me in the middle of Tutu Squad. Up the front is too dangerous.'

'Promise to stay near you, Mum, but I am nearly sixteen.'

'Doesn't matter how old you are,' Mum said. 'When things get violent, we're all at risk of being hurt.'

'Tipene said he might join Patu next week,' Jo said.

'Really?' Mum said. 'I hope he'll be okay.'

On Tuesday, 8th September, the Springboks played North Auckland in Whangārei. Dad said that Okara Park was like a fortress, heavily barricaded, with police everywhere. He said the protesters were loud but there was no violence, and no one was arrested.

It was as if police and protesters were conserving their energy, holding their breath, waiting for Saturday.

CHAPTER 33
FINAL TEST, AUCKLAND

The night before the final test, a group called Artists Against Apartheid (AAA) organised a march up Queen Street. The next day, the 12th of September, was the third anniversary of Steve Biko's death. To me, playing rugby with the Springboks on that date was like throwing a rugby ball into the faces of Biko's family and friends in South Africa.

We watched the AAA's march on the late news. People wore colourful outfits and costumes, and their placards were clever and creative, which was probably to be expected given they were made by artists. One placard used the slogan from the Minties lolly advertisement, except it said, 'It's moments like these you need Minto'.

There were fire dancers and a group called Clowns Against the Tour. Tall papier mâché puppets swung from poles above the marchers' heads. One puppet was of Robert Muldoon. It had blood on its white paper mâché hands. A man dressed in a Ku Klux Klan outfit beat a slow rhythm on a drum as he walked. On stage, a guy sang a Peter Gabriel song called 'Biko'.

I went to bed that night with the lyrics of the song and images of people with painted faces swirling behind my closed eyes. Tomorrow was the anti-tour movement's last chance to stop a game, to stop this tour before it was quite over. There would be confrontation and violence, but my family and Rewi's wouldn't be up the front of Tutu Squad. We'd be okay.

We didn't wear helmets. Neither did Rewi, Tipene or Harry. We stood in Fowlds Park, surrounded by people. An elderly man with war medals pinned to his jacket gazed out at the crowd. I wondered what he thought of protesters in helmets, carrying shields. Was he horrified at what was happening in New Zealand?

There were school students, university students, middle aged people, elderly people, gang members, people dressed in costumes, Māori, Pasifika, Pākehā and other ethnicities.

A small banner waved in the wind, its red letters saying, 'REMEMBER STEVE BIKO'. On top of a building, a man held a black flag with the familiar clenched fist on it, the symbol of the South African fight for freedom. Two men held up a banner that said, 'Gays for Freedom', which I thought was extra brave, because in the news, there had been cases of gay men being beaten up by other men. Also, it was illegal for men to be homosexual, so they made themselves vulnerable by standing up for the freedom of others.

Rewi nudged me. 'Look!' He pointed at people strapping cardboard padding around their stomachs and chests underneath their tops. 'They're expecting violence.'

'We don't need to worry about that,' I said. 'We won't be up the front of Tutu Squad.'

Harry reached out and held my hand and we smiled at each other.

I noticed a beautiful woman with long black hair surveying the crowd through a film camera. A blond-haired man stood beside her. 'Is that Merata Mita?' I asked Tipene. 'Dad said she's been filming the tour protests, but I've never actually seen her.'

'Yeah, that's her.'

Merata moved away to get a better view of John Minto, who was standing on a makeshift podium, speaking into a microphone. He asked people who were willing to be up the front of each squad to form a group under some trees. He told them they'd need helmets and padding. On the grass, there was a pile of plywood shields that MOST had organised, and people were taking them as they headed under the trees. Up above, a police helicopter circled.

Mum pointed to some protesters dressed in white overalls with red crosses painted onto them. 'They must be medics,' she said. 'Hopefully, they won't be needed.'

A man in front carried a placard with 'Day of Rage' written on it. The Gisborne game had been the 'Day of Shame'. It made sense that by the last game of the tour, shame had turned to rage. People seemed angrier and more determined to show it. Around me, it looked like an army preparing for war, except this would be a civil war. The police and the riot squad were New Zealanders, like us. I thought of Lucy Jensen in my class, whose father was a policeman. She'd be worried about her dad today.

We were told to separate into our squads: Patu, Tutu or Biko. Each squad had about 30 marshals and would block two of the entries to Eden Park. Our squad, Tutu Squad, was divided into two groups: Tutu One and Tutu Two. We had to block two roads that led straight to Eden Park: Bellwood Ave and Raleigh Street. They both intersected with Marlborough Ave, so we would walk there. The aim was, firstly, to make it difficult for rugby spectators to get through to the park and then, once the game had begun, to break through police lines to occupy the grounds.

Tipene told us that there were disruptions planned at other places, which would put pressure on the police force. These plans were being kept secret though because undercover police were sometimes at MOST meetings and had even joined in with the protests.

'Found out something interesting about our squad,' Tipene said, lowering his voice, so we had to huddle around him to hear. 'Some people are going to chuck a fishing net over the police, and while the police struggle to get out from under the net, they plan to get over the barricade.'

'In our group?' Jo asked. 'Tutu Squad?'

'Yeah but keep your voice down. If anyone hears, it'll ruin the plan.'

'Brilliant idea,' Rewi said, 'but it'll piss the police off.'

Tipene arched an eyebrow.

'Sorry, Dad. Bad language.'

'Yes, it is, but I was actually thinking about what you said. We could end up copping more aggressive behaviour from the police as a result.'

Dad found us in the middle of Tutu Squad before we started walking. His photographer, Hamish, was with him, but he was quite shy and let Dad do most of the talking. 'They reckon there are about seven thousand here today. Maybe more,' Dad said. He pointed to the Artists Against Apartheid group. They had a huge 'AAA' banner and lots of flags. 'They're going to walk the streets around Eden Park and entertain us all with songs and performances. I know one of the guys in the group, a painter, and he let me in on their plans. They're going to attach a banner to gas balloons so it will float over Eden Park, and they're going to fly more than a hundred kites over as well. Their other plan is to start a fire in Mount Eden's crater so that it looks like a volcanic eruption.'

'That's so cool!' Jo said.

'They're also flying a remote-controlled Zeppelin above the game,' Dad said.

'That's wild,' Harry said. 'Hope the police helicopter doesn't collide with it.'

'Hadn't thought about that,' Dad said.

'Will you be walking with us, Dad?' I asked.

'No, I'm going to be following Patu. I won't be far from you though. Patu Squad's on Marlborough Street too, but they're covering two intersections further along. There was terrible violence between them and the riot police at the game last Saturday. Hope that doesn't happen today. I hate reporting on violence like that.'

Harry pointed to a group of people carrying a coffin and funeral wreaths. They held a banner with a portrait of Steve Biko on it. 'Who are they?'

'They're the Biko Commemoration group. They don't want any conflict with the police, so they'll march peacefully around all six roadblocks placing wreaths between riot police and protesters.' Dad looked at Hamish. 'We'd better go, I guess.'

'Be careful,' Mum said, hugging Dad.

'I'm more worried about you guys,' Dad said. 'Don't go near the front. Stay back here, please.' He hugged me and Jo.

'Don't worry,' Harry said. 'I'll look after Liza.'

Dad smiled. 'She pretty much looks after herself, that girl, but it's good that you're thinking of her. I'd better head over to join Patu now. Hey, Tipene, weren't you thinking of joining Patu this time?'

'Yeah, but I didn't want to be separated from Rewi, and he wanted to stay with his buddy, Liza.'

Harry was beside me. I didn't look at him when Tipene said this. Instead I looked down at the ground and his sneakers. The toes of one foot lifted off the ground, and stayed up in the air, flexed.

Dad patted Tipene's back. 'Well, take good care, mate. See you when this is all over.' He and Hamish disappeared up the side of the crowds of people.

We began to walk out of Fowlds Park towards New North Road. People chanted and sang. A woman yelled, 'Remember!' We repeated, 'Remember!' Then she sang out, 'Remember Soweto!' and we repeated it. Police walked on both sides of the protest, which swelled out onto the road, pulsing forwards.

We turned right at the intersection into Morningside Drive. We had to anyway because huge jumbo bins blocked off the rest of New North Road. We turned left into MacDonald Street, then into Ethel Street before heading up to the intersection with Sandringham Road. These were streets I'd walked and travelled all my life, but they felt unfamiliar, filled with police, barbed wire, jumbo bins and tour supporters hurling abuse at us.

As we crossed straight over Sandringham Road into Burnley Terrace, rugby-goers watched, waiting for us to pass to get to Eden Park. Some pushed through, unwilling to wait. A group of young guys barged into some protesters near us. One threw a man to the ground. 'Get out of my fucking way!' he yelled.

Some of the protesters nearby pushed him and his mates away, which started a fight. Other skirmishes were starting up too. The police used their batons to break up the fights. Things were unravelling around me.

When we made it to the other side and into Burnley Terrace, I realised I'd clamped my teeth together so tightly that my jaw hurt.

'You can stop squeezing my hand now,' Harry said.

'Sorry.'

Mum turned to me. 'You okay?'

I gave her a thumbs-up.

'Course you're okay,' Harry said. 'You've got me here beside you.' He leaned in to kiss my cheek. 'And your best buddy. Where would you be without Rewi?'

As if he'd heard his name, which he couldn't have with all the chanting, Rewi said, 'Marlborough Street's just up ahead. Not far now. Apart from those aggro guys back there, it's going pretty well, eh?'

I was aware that, from my other side, Harry knew Rewi was talking to me. I nodded and smiled at Rewi, then joined in the chant. 'Remember!' I cried, as we turned left into Marlborough Street.

When we reached Bellwood Ave on the left, it was barricaded with jumbo bins. Lines of riot police stood in front of them, helmets on, visors down and long batons in their hands. It was the first street that led straight to Eden Park. Tutu One group broke off and stayed there. We kept walking and stopped at Raleigh Street which was also barricaded and thick with riot police. We stayed there chanting and yelling, while Patu Squad continued along to the next two streets, which turned left towards the park too.

About ten minutes before kick-off, we saw a plane coming our way. Soon, it was overhead, circling over Eden Park and away, then back over again. The cheering from the protest squads resounded along Marlborough Street. Sheets of paper dropped from the plane, wafting onto the park, before it swooped away again. After a few circuits, it dropped white powder over the field. The cheering was deafening.

'What do you think it is, Dad?' Rewi asked.

'Wouldn't be something toxic, would it?' I asked.

'Nah,' Tipene said. 'It's probably flour. Don't imagine that'll do much damage.'

'What about the Zeppelin?' Harry asked. 'Will they still fly it?'

'Doubt it,' Tipene said. 'Too dangerous with that plane up there.'

The game started. Cheers from the crowd drifted towards us. We began to boo. We could hear booing from Patu on our right and from the other half of Tutu on our left. We were all part of something special, one large, loud voice, just like at the mobilisations.

From the middle of Tutu Squad, I couldn't see what was going on up the front, but I noticed red smoke rising from down near the park. A woman near us said that it was probably her neighbour, Kitch Cuthbert, and a few other people creating that smoke. Yesterday, they'd pretended they were going to their friend, Margaret's birthday at her house close to Eden Park. The police had let them through, and they'd spent the night preparing to throw flares and smoke bombs to distract the police, so they could get into the park.

People around me started to point towards Mount Eden. Smoke poured up from it, as if it were erupting. Tutu and Patu squads cheered again.

'It worked!' Rewi cried.

We clapped our hands and cheered.

I was so busy gazing at the plane and the smoke that it took me a moment to realise something else was in the sky. It was the black AAA banner, attached to balloons, crossing over the stadium. On it, in white capital letters, was one word, 'BIKO'. It sailed across the stadium and there was silence. Everyone was quiet: police, protesters, rugby fans.

When the noise of the game started up again, we chanted, 'Boks go home!'

Harry leaned down, speaking right into my ear, 'Even when you're yelling, you look sexy.'

I turned to tell him it wouldn't be so sexy if I were yelling at him, but I heard shouting and screaming. Something was going on with Tutu One. The riot police were pushing into their front lines, and people were fighting back or scrambling to get away. Minutes later, it seemed to have calmed down.

'Bet that was cos of the net,' Rewi said.

Then, we were pressed back, forced to squish into the lines behind us. Something was happening up the front.

'Sorry!' Mum said, grabbing my arm to steady herself.

There were shouts and screams coming from the front of our group now.

'Bit of a fight,' someone said. 'Must've thrown the net.'

Thrown the net! Our group had thrown one too? I let go of Harry's hand and wiped my sweaty palm on my jeans.

An ambulance nudged through our group, so we pressed back more. Someone must have been injured, but I couldn't see who or where.

'Shit!' Rewi said.

I followed his wide-eyed stare. Battalions of Red Squad ran at us along Marlborough Street. 'Move! Move! Move!' they shouted. The riot police in front of us too, at our Raleigh Street barricade, began to charge. We were being forced along Marlborough Street straight into Tutu One.

There was nowhere to go. We fell onto each other. I saw Mum trip and I screamed, but somebody pulled her up. There was no sign of Jo or Tipene.

The Red Squad ploughed through us, their batons smashing into anybody in their way. I put my hands over my head to protect myself.

Harry pulled me towards the footpath. 'Get to a house!' he yelled.

Rewi was behind me. I grabbed his arm. We were sandwiched into each other. Some people fell and were trampled amidst the panic and screaming. The riot squad were crushing us from all sides. People shoved and screamed. We pushed through the chaos towards a house.

An elderly man ahead lost his balance near the rock wall in front of the house. 'Help him up!' I yelled at a young guy beside him.

'He's bleeding!' the guy yelled. He looked panicked, shoving people back from the man on the ground.

Rewi barged through. 'Pick him up! He'll get stomped on.' He lifted the man from under his arms.

The old man was bleeding from the back of his head. His eyes were closed.

'Get him over the wall!' Harry yelled, grabbing the man's legs.

We hoisted the man onto the rough, flat top of the rock wall. As we scrambled over to lift him down the other side, a riot policeman grabbed Rewi by the back of his T-shirt, yelling, 'Get out of here! Go on, move!'

'He needs an ambulance,' Harry cried, pointing at the old man on the wall, his arms and legs dangling either side.

The policeman looked at the old man. His face didn't move. He turned away from us and charged off into the crowd.

We'd jumped down into someone's front garden, so we lifted the man down onto the grass. I thought of the volunteer medics in white overalls with red crosses painted on them and scanned the panicked crowds on the street. There were no medics anywhere. I crouched down. 'We're getting help,' I said to the old man.

As I stood up, a policeman leapt over the wall and swung his baton at me. Rewi lifted his arm, taking the brunt of it. 'Piss off!' he yelled. 'Someone's injured here!'

The policeman prodded his baton hard into Rewi's chest. 'Little black shit!' he shouted.

We backed away from the cop, but he followed us, swinging his baton at Rewi again, hitting his arm.

'Stop it!' I screamed.

We turned and ran towards the house, but he swung at Rewi's back, making him stumble forwards. Harry grabbed Rewi's arm.

'Bastard!' Rewi yelled. He lifted his other arm to protect himself, as the cop followed, swinging again and again, until Rewi's arm fell, hanging limp by his side.

A woman stood on the porch of the house, staring out at the street. If we could just get to her, get in the house. Other protesters were in her garden, bleeding, crying or gazing out at the madness.

Harry pulled Rewi with him towards the front steps, but Rewi seemed slow and confused. The cop thrust his baton into Rewi's back, and he fell forward onto the lawn.

Someone yelled, 'Hey, leave the kid alone!'

'You'll break his back!' I cried.

The cop stopped and stared at me, then lifted his baton and jabbed me hard in the stomach. The pain bit through me. I buckled over.

'Leave her alone, you prick!' Harry yelled, stepping between us.

The woman on the porch ran down to us, yelling at the policeman, 'Shame on you! Get off my property! They're kids!'

The police officer slammed his baton down, just missing her head. 'Fuck off, bitch!' he yelled, turning and jogging out of the driveway.

The woman crouched down. 'Are you okay?' she said to Rewi.

He mumbled something back at her. His arm lay beside him at an awkward angle.

'Your arm's broken,' the woman said.

Rewi's face was pale.

'We need an ambulance,' I shrieked at her. My hand was on her shoulder, shaking her. 'An old man's bleeding by the wall.'

She didn't move.

'An ambulance!' I screamed. 'Call an ambulance!'

The woman stood up. 'I'll phone one.' She ran up the steps into the house.

Harry and I sat beside Rewi. 'It's okay,' I said, holding his hand. 'She's phoning an ambulance. Hang in there, buddy. Help's coming.'

On the street, the riot squad were still bashing protesters, and people were yelling and running, some diving into driveways, like we had. Police ran in after them too, like they had with us.

The woman came out of the house and called down to us. 'They're on their way.'

Rewi's eyes were closed. I gently squeezed his hand. 'They'll be here soon.'

Harry reached over and took my free hand in his. I looked at him. 'He's my oldest friend.'

'Yeah, but you're holding his hand.'

I pulled my hand away from Harry's. 'Stop it.'

'What? I mean, you're holding another guy's hand.'

'Is that all you care about right now, in the middle of all this?'

Harry took my hand again. I pulled it away. 'I don't feel like holding your hand.'

He stared at me, and an image of his dad staring at Raewyn flashed before me. He reached for my hand again, holding it tightly, as I tried to free it. 'Let go of my hand, Harry.'

'You'll hold his, but not mine?' Harry squeezed my hand harder as I tried to prise it out of his grip.

'Let go of my hand,' I repeated. His grip was becoming painful. I released Rewi's hand and tried to wrestle my hand from Harry's. I started to cry.

'Let go of her,' Rewi said, his eyes still closed. 'Leave her alone.'

Harry's eyes were locked onto mine. His free hand reached over and pinched the top of my hand in his grip. His fingernails dug into my skin. I pulled my arm harder. He pinched me again.

'Stop pinching me,' I said. 'Let go of me, Harry.'

'Let go of her,' Rewi said again.

Harry threw my hand down and walked away to stand under a nearby tree. I rubbed the fingernail marks on top of my hand, gulping down my sobs.

An ambulance pulled into the driveway, and two paramedics hurried over with a stretcher. I pointed to the old man by the wall. 'Help him first.'

The woman from the house joined them. Harry stayed under the tree. I told Rewi the paramedics had arrived, my hand in his while we waited.

The woman came over to us. 'They're rushing the old man to hospital. You can go with them, but we'll have to walk you to the ambulance, so we don't waste any time.'

We helped Rewi stand. He didn't speak. He put one arm around the woman, leaning on her, and we walked to the back of the ambulance.

A paramedic told us to climb up and sit down. The woman went back to her house. I didn't even think to thank her.

The siren roared as the driver inched through the protesters and riot police. I stared out the window at dislodged helmets lying on the road, people hurling rocks at the police, who bludgeoned anyone in their line of vision.

In the back of the ambulance, the paramedic placed an oxygen mask over the old man's mouth and listened to his pulse. He asked me who I was. I told him I was Rewi's friend. 'He's okay,' he said. 'Just needs to get his arm sorted out. It's this guy I'm worried about.'

I watched the pandemonium through the back window. Harry

was somewhere back there, maybe still under the tree. I'd left him there and hadn't even glanced back at him. I'd just walked away with Rewi.

At the hospital, I asked the woman at reception if I could use the phone. Pete was home. 'You okay?' he asked. 'I've been watching it all on TV.'

I asked him if Mum and Jo were there, and he said no one had come home yet. I began to cry.

'Liza,' Pete said, 'what's going on?'

'We got separated from Mum, Jo and Tipene,' I said, between noisy sobs. 'I don't know if they're alright.'

The receptionist handed me a box of tissues and left me alone at the desk.

'Where are you now?' Pete asked.

'Rewi's been hurt. I'm at the hospital with him, in the Accident and Emergency Ward.'

'Shit. Listen, as soon as Mum's home I'll phone the ward to let you know. They'll be alright. Go and sit with Rewi.'

I put the phone down. The receptionist came back to the desk and passed me a glass of water. 'You okay, love?'

I nodded, drank the water till it was gone, then put down the glass. 'My brother might phone to let me know when my family gets home.' I stood there, chest heaving, nose running and tears wetting my ears, my hair, my T-shirt.

'Take the tissues with you, hon,' the receptionist said. 'Come on, let's find you a comfy place to sit while you wait for your friend to have his arm set.'

I sat on a chair by the window, away from others. The waiting room was filling with protesters. Some were unconscious and rushed away for X-rays and surgery. There were other people crying in the waiting room now.

Soon, a nurse called out my name. 'Your friend's resting comfortably now. Do you want to see him?'

I followed her into a room with four beds in it. The nurse pulled back a curtain. 'There he is.'

Rewi gave me a small smile. 'They've given me lots of painkillers,' he said. 'Feel much better.'

'Thank God you're okay. You looked . . . terrible.' I sat beside his bed, with the tissue box on my knee.

'Thanks a lot,' Rewi said. 'You don't look so hot yourself!'

'He could've killed you.'

'I know. Thought I was going to die on the grass there in that woman's front yard.' A tear slid down his cheek. 'Are our parents alright? And Jo?'

'Don't know. Pete's going to phone when they get home.'

'What a nightmare.'

We sat together without speaking. I could hear nurses and doctors bustling along the corridor.

'You can't let guys hurt you,' Rewi said.

'I know. It's over. I have to finish it.' I put my head down on the side of the bed and cried. I didn't bother with tissues anymore. I just let the numb ache inside me pour out onto the clean white sheets.

Rewi put his hand on mine and rubbed it with his thumb, just like he used to when we were little.

Pete phoned a couple of hours later. Mum, Tipene and Jo had walked home. They'd looked for us for a while then given up, thinking we must have already left.

Tipene came to pick us up from the hospital at about eight o'clock. His cheek was bruised and there was a cut on his lip. 'Looks like we've all been in the wars today,' he said.

He dropped me home and, as I stepped out of the car, he thanked me for looking after Rewi.

'Actually,' I said, 'he stopped a cop from hitting me. That's what started it.'

'You looked after each other,' Tipene said. 'That's what good friends do.'

Mum was standing at the front door with Sal wagging her tail beside her. She took me in her arms, and we stayed like that for a long time.

CHAPTER 34
AFTERWARDS

Pete had saved me some fish and chips, so he put them in the oven to warm up. Jo was leaning on the bench talking to him when we walked in. She came straight over to hug me, a long hug, like the one I'd had with Mum at the door.

'Go and have a hot shower,' Mum said. 'It'll do you good. The fish and chips will be ready by then.'

'Are you two okay?' I asked. Mum had a bruise on her arm, and Jo had grazes on her cheek and hands.

'We weren't hit; we tripped and fell,' Jo said.

'Tipene was batoned,' Mum said. 'It was awful. He pushed the police officer off him, who lost his balance, luckily, so we had time to get away.'

'Not surprised he was batoned,' I said. 'He's got a brown face.'

'Things will change,' Mum said. 'Nothing will ever be quite the same again. This is a turning point for New Zealand. Today was . . . I still don't believe today happened. I'm in shock. I think we all are.'

I walked down the hallway to the bathroom. When I undressed, there was a wide bruise on my stomach where the riot squad guy had jabbed me. I ran my hand over it and thought of Rewi. Where were his bruises? He'd definitely have some on his back. I stepped into the shower and reached for the soap, noticing again the bruised pinch marks on my hand. Bruises and marks would heal, but I wasn't sure whether the memory of the police beating up my friend and me ever would. Then there was Harry, who said he loved me, but that seemed to include controlling and hurting me. I didn't want to feel powerless like that ever again.

I came back into the kitchen in my dressing gown. Pete took the fish and chips out of the oven. 'I'm being a kind big brother today,' he said. 'I felt sick watching that game and not knowing if you were all okay.'

Mum patted my hand, the one with the pinch marks. 'We lost you.'

'We went to help an old man who fell over,' I explained. 'His head was bleeding, and he was unconscious.'

'My Liza,' Mum said. 'My good Liza.'

'Then this cop started hitting us and chasing us.'

'It was crazy,' Jo said. 'We didn't know how to get away, which way to run.'

'The riot squad was out of control,' Mum said. 'I can't believe it.'

I didn't feel very hungry. 'I can't eat this. Thanks, Pete, but my stomach's not quite right.'

'I could've helped if I'd been there,' Pete said. 'Thing is, I don't like apartheid, but I just think rugby has nothing to do with politics.'

'We know, Pete, and you couldn't have helped,' Mum said. 'It was complete mayhem. Let's go and watch the news, shall we? I'd like to see what else was going on today.'

I lay on the sofa, and Jo curled up beside me. Pete and Mum sat in the armchairs. When the news began, the camera panned the jumbo bins lined up around Eden Park. Huge coils of barbed wire lay behind them, like steel ringlets.

The news flitted from one scene to another, while the reporter reeled off the day's events. There were protests on the Harbour Bridge, Māngere Bridge, the north-western motorway and at Auckland International Airport. There were also attempts to destroy TV signals at stations in Timaru and Dunedin.

'Those were the secret disruptions Tipene told us about,' Jo said.

'Must've pissed off people trying to get to the game,' Pete said.

'That's the whole point,' Jo said.

'I know,' Pete said, defensively. 'I'm sort of admiring them, acts of sabotage.'

'Shhh,' Mum said. 'Look, here's the Biko memorial group. They're putting a wreath down in front of all those lines of riot police. Wonderful!'

'There's Sister Ignatia!' Jo cried.

I sat up. 'With Sister Agnes! And look, other teachers. Ms Jefferson's there!'

'With a gorgeous guy!' Jo said.

'That's her boyfriend.' The camera moved off them. I lay down again. 'Sister Agnes and Ms Jefferson were there today. I can't believe it!'

The TV showed the plane circling. The reporter said the plane was a Cessna 172 and that one of the flour bombs had landed on the All Black, Gary Knight. The camera showed him covered in flour.

'Felt a bit sorry for him,' Pete said.

We then saw the police arresting the two men in the plane. Their names were Marx Jones and Grant Cole.

'I feel sorry for *them*,' Mum said. 'They'll go to prison, I'm guessing.'

The camera moved to a group of people flinging smoke bombs and flares onto the field, running between the stand and the barbed wire. The reporter said that they'd stopped the game for two minutes.

'That looks like David Williams,' Mum said, 'the guy from CARE. Bet he'll end up in court for that too.'

The reporter added that one of the protesters who ran on, a middle-aged woman, was badly beaten by tour supporters. He used the word 'vicious' when describing the attack.

The camera showed the Artists Against Apartheid group, performing and doing street theatre. It then flicked to Greg McGee, who had played for the Junior All Blacks, as he burned his All Black triallist's shirt in the middle of the street.

Then we saw scenes that were uncomfortably familiar to me. My breath stopped in my chest and I had to push it out and slowly breathe in again. A different reporter spoke into the camera. He said that this was Biko Squad, made up mostly of students. They were on Sandringham Road, trying to block rugby fans from getting to the ground. The game hadn't started yet, he said, but already the violence was reaching a concerning level.

The camera showed riot police wearing heavy coats and helmets with visors down. Long batons were in their gloved hands. Biko Squad was in front of them, equally padded and helmeted, holding shields to protect them from police batons. They moved right up to the police lines, glaring at and taunting them.

The reporter raised his voice over the yelling and chanting from the protesters. He explained that, a few times now, the protesters had used their shields to push against police lines but were beaten back. A couple of times, the riot police had unexpectedly charged into the protesters, forcing them back at least ten metres. We saw batons crashing onto helmets and people screaming, some lying bleeding on the road.

'That's too much like . . .' Jo said. She began to cry.

I sat up beside her and held her hand. 'Like us today.'

'We'll turn the TV off in a minute,' Mum said. 'I just want to see what happened with Patu. Pete mentioned something about clowns being beaten up.'

'Clowns?' I asked. 'The ones with the bumble bee and the rabbit?'

'They were bashed up badly,' Pete said. 'It was on the news earlier.'

'This is us,' Jo said, pointing to the TV. 'This is Tutu Squad.'

The TV showed people without helmets being beaten by riot police. The reporter said that because the group of demonstrators was so large, it was impossible for people to escape the riot police, who charged from a few sides. Marchers were backed up against fences, unable to move and attacked by police. Some protesters were hurling rocks at the police, which the reporter said showed how the mood had changed. Up until now, there had only been the odd case of a cracker or paint bomb being thrown. He added that protesters from this squad had been taken to hospital for serious injuries. Some were unconscious.

The camera cut to Onslow Road, showing violent confrontations between Patu Squad and the riot police. Another reporter explained that these confrontations had been constant, like an endless street fight. At one stage during a particularly violent riot squad charge, a commanding officer struggled to reign in his officers, shouting at them to get back into line.

The camera zoomed in on one man lying on the ground. He held up his shield to protect himself as a Red Squad member batoned and kicked him. Knocking his shield aside, the policeman bludgeoned him on the head. Four other Red Squad members watched. One of them told the camera operator to stop filming.

The reporter said Onslow Road had become the scene of a full-scale riot, with protesters grabbing rocks, bottles and fence posts and hurling them at the Red Squad. The camera zoomed out to show protesters forcing the police back down Onslow Road and the police pushing them back up. Then it zoomed in on protesters kicking in an empty undercover police car. 'It's got batons in it!' a guy yelled to the reporter.

They bashed in the windows and pulled a door off its hinges. Heaving the car onto its side, they rolled it over again, so that it was upside down. Protesters cheered.

Police reinforcements arrived and, finally, the riot squad forced Patu Squad out onto Dominion Road, and protesters ran in all directions. Police charged round the corner after them. The camera panned the scene. Then it stopped, and a reporter spoke into the camera. He said three students, two young men dressed as clowns, and a young woman dressed as a bumble bee had been violently beaten by riot police. The camera cut to the bumble bee. She was unconscious. One of the clowns lay on his back, trying hard to breathe. He opened his mouth like a goldfish, his eyes closed. The other clown lay crying, with his head bandaged.

We'd been watching in silence. Mum turned off the TV. 'My God,' she said. 'That girl, the bumble bee.'

'They hit her on the neck,' Pete said. 'Were they trying to kill her? If she's not dead, she could be brain damaged or paralysed.'

'I'm scared I'm going to have nightmares about this, like Kalāsia,' I said. 'I'm scared.'

'Sweetheart,' Mum said, coming to sit beside me, 'we're all going to need some time to get over this. We'll talk about it and we'll help each other.'

The phone went. For a moment, my heart leapt that it might be Harry. Then, I remembered that I could no longer be Harry's girlfriend, and loss filled my chest, thick and heavy, like concrete. I wanted to lie down again, to curl up and close my eyes.

'Who could that be at this time of night?' Mum said. She went to get the phone. I listened to her talking in the hallway.

Pete went out of the lounge and came back dragging my mattress with him.

'What are you doing?' Mum asked, following behind him.

'We're all sleeping in here tonight,' Pete said. 'I'll sleep on the sofa. Jo, I'll get your mattress now.'

'What about me and Dad?' Mum asked.

'We can only fit another single mattress in here, Mum,' Jo said, 'so Liza and I can share one and you and Dad have one each. I'll grab the mattress off my old bed in Liza's room.'

'I'll sleep on anything tonight,' Mum said. 'By the way, that was Tipene. He asked if we knew about the clowns and said that Rewi wants you to come over tomorrow, Liza.'

That night, we slept to the sound of each other's breathing. If any of us woke, we knew we weren't alone and soon fell asleep again. At one stage, I heard the front door open, which made Sal whine. Mum took her out to the kitchen, and Dad and Mum's voices filtered down the hallway into the lounge.

I crept out, trying not to wake Pete or Jo. I stopped at the kitchen door. Dad was crying. I'd never heard him cry before. My fingers stiffened on the door handle. I opened the door a little, so I could see through the gap.

Mum was hugging Dad, while he told her how the paramedics had placed the bumble bee girl in a neck brace and taken her away on a stretcher. 'She was small,' Dad said. 'and they beat her until she lost consciousness. When I arrived on the scene, another journalist was yelling, "You're going to kill her!" The cops ran off, and that journalist went to inform a policeman, who seemed to be in a position of authority, but he wasn't interested in following it up.'

Mum told Dad we were sleeping in the lounge and that she'd taken his pillow in for him.

'I'll just have a coffee,' Dad said. 'Will you sit up with me or are you too exhausted?'

'I'll stay with you,' Mum said.

I went back into the lounge and lay down beside Jo. She mumbled something in her sleep and rolled over. Pete snored softly on the sofa, while Mum and Dad's voices drifted down the hallway. Beside my mattress lay Sal. I reached over and put my arm around her and eventually fell asleep.

I woke again when the birds started singing and the room was beginning to lighten. I lay there thinking about Harry. I'd never kiss him again. I'd never sit in a movie theatre and feel the warmth of his hands again. I wouldn't laugh at his jokes. Sadness trudged back into my chest. How could someone I loved be so difficult and painful?

I drifted off to sleep again and when I woke, Mum and Dad had gone. Jo and Pete were still asleep. My stomach hurt and I ran my hand over the bruise. The sadness felt worse. It filled my whole body.

Mum and Dad came back with fresh bread from the dairy near church. They'd been to mass but had decided to leave us to sleep. We sat at the table together. I still didn't feel much like eating, but I did have a piece of the soft, chewy bread with honey.

Dad talked about the previous day. His leg jiggled as he spoke. 'I saw that bumble bee girl and the clowns before the police hit them. They were squished up against a hedge, avoiding the riot squad running down Dominion Road. Three riot police ran at them and the rest is history. We couldn't stop the police. There were people in our way. Hamish and I were there too late.'

'It wasn't your fault,' Mum said.

'The world went mad yesterday,' Jo said.

'And some of it's been a long time coming,' Dad said. 'The police have a bad history with Māori and Polynesian people. I could see hatred in some of their faces. Same with the police officers.'

Mum put her hand on Dad's. 'Father Luke was right today at mass when he said we have a lot of healing to do.'

The phone rang and I stood up. 'I'll get it.' I was expecting a phone call from Harry. This time, I wouldn't huddle behind my bedroom door, listening to his voice and imagining his lips and eyes. I would never again smile at his whispered messages of how much he wanted to kiss me or hold me.

At first, he said he was sorry. He didn't wait for me to respond, telling me that he'd stayed up late talking with his mum. She said she was worried that Harry's jealousy and insecurity were because of how he'd seen his dad behave. 'She's leaving Dad. That's what she was talking about with Rob at the barbecue. We're going to move into a flat that Rob's friend owns, and Mum's looking for a job. She's going back to kindergarten teaching. She hasn't told Dad yet cos he'll lose it.'

'That's good. She'll be much happier on her own.'

'Do you forgive me?'

'I forgive you, Harry.'

'Can I see you today?'

My hand squeezed the phone, my fingers turning white. 'I can't see you anymore, Harry. It's good you won't have to live with your dad now, and your mum's probably right about your dad making you feel insecure. I'm glad things will get better for you now, but . . .' My voice wobbled. 'I have to finish with you.'

'Please don't.'

'I don't want to,' I said. 'I have to, cos I worry too much about you getting angry. I feel panicky when you get annoyed with me. I don't want to feel like this anymore.'

'I love you, Liza.' Harry's voice was a whisper. He was crying.

'I love you too. You're the first boy I ever loved. I have to go now.'

'Please don't go,' Harry said.

'I have to,' I said, gulping back a sob. 'Bye, Harry.'

I hadn't realised Dad was in the hallway behind me. He had some folded washing in his hands. 'Just putting some clean stuff away,' he said, 'but I overheard . . .' He put the clothes on the telephone table and hugged me.

Later, when I went to Rewi's, there was no police car parked on his street. I stood outside his house and gazed at the swirling koru on the veranda. Closing my eyes for a moment, I imagined native trees and bush, tūī chortling and the sound of a stream somewhere nearby. I opened my eyes and took a slow, deep breath.

When I knocked, Marama opened the door and hugged me. 'Rewi's in the lounge,' she said. 'Dad's hired a video player for all of today and tonight. He said we need a treat, and Rewi's arm's sore so he has to relax.'

'That's cool,' I said. 'What are you watching?'

'*Scooby Doo Goes to Hollywood*.'

'I love Scooby Doo,' I said, following Marama down the hallway to the lounge.

Nikau was sprawled across a beanbag on the floor and Rewi was sitting on the sofa, his arm in plaster lying on the armrest.

'You look a bit better today,' I said. 'Thank goodness.'

Rewi smiled. 'I feel better. I was trying not to pass out from the pain yesterday.'

I sat down on the sofa beside him. 'Your face was like a ghost.'

'Are we going to watch the rest of Scooby Doo?' Nikau asked, climbing up on the sofa beside me.

'You two keep watching,' Rewi said. 'I'll go and talk to Liza in the kitchen.'

'You'll miss out,' Marama said.

'I know, but you can tell me what happens.'

'Where are your mum and dad?' I asked Rewi as we made our way into the kitchen.

'They're somewhere. Don't know. There, hanging out washing.' Rewi pointed at his parents out the window by the washing line. 'Tea?'

'I'll make it. You sit down and rest that arm of yours.' I filled up the kettle, switched it on and turned to Rewi. Leaning back against the bench, I said, 'I was scared you were going to die yesterday. That cop was crazy, I mean, insane. He just kept hitting you. I couldn't stop him.'

'You did stop him, but he ended up hitting you.'

We looked at each other.

'I'll never forget it, Rewi. I think I'll be re-living it for a long time.'

'Me too.' Rewi tapped his fingers on his plaster cast. 'Hey, there's some cake in the cupboard. My aunty brought it over.'

'Is it chocolate?' I asked.

'Yes, it is.' Rewi put on a school-teachery voice. 'But it wouldn't hurt you to branch out and try other flavours.'

'We're not in the ice-cream shop, Rewi.'

'No, but it's the same issue. You need to stop limiting your taste experiences the way you do, Eliza Newland.'

I put the mugs of tea on the table and cut a piece of cake for Rewi and then one for myself. 'Does this broken arm mean I'm going to have to do everything for you for the next month?'

'Probably.'

We didn't speak for a few moments because we were busy eating cake. For the first time since yesterday, I actually felt like eating. Being with Rewi and seeing that he was okay gave me a small appetite. It probably helped that it was chocolate cake too.

'Heard from Harry?' Rewi asked.

'Yep. I told him it's over.'

'Must've been hard.'

I put the cake down. It was suddenly difficult to swallow. I drank some tea, trying to think of the right words. 'My stomach, chest, head, everything hurts when I think of him. I . . . I've lost him, Rewi.'

'You had to let him go,' Rewi said. 'His shit was starting to mess with your head.'

'I know you're right. I know it's the right thing to do, but I'm so sad.'

'He hurt you.'

'It was pinching.'

'Whether he punched you or pinched you, it's still wrong, Liza.' Rewi put down his cup. 'Last night, I was thinking that he's a bit like the problem with South Africa. He wants to have all the power, but it hurts people. If you stayed with Harry, I reckon you'd stop seeing friends just to please him. You'd definitely have to stop seeing me.'

'I know.' I pushed some cake crumbs into a small pile on my plate with my finger. 'I know.'

Rewi leaned forward. 'You've got all of us to help you get over him, Liza.'

'Thanks, Rewi.'

'Want to watch the last bit of Scooby Doo?'

'Okay.'

Mere and Tipene came in with the washing basket as we stood up. Mere asked me if I'd seen Rewi's bruises. She pulled up his T-shirt. His back was a landscape of purple-black shapes.

'One day, you two,' Mere said, 'books will be written about this Springbok tour. Photo books like mine will be published. Merata Mita's documentary will be in cinemas. Kids will study them at school and learn about a time when Aotearoa's people stood up to racism here and in South Africa. You're those people who stood up. We're those people.'

LOCKDOWN

We moved down to Alert Level One on Monday, the 8th of June. Life's back to normal now, except for the strict border controls. Added to that, a magazine has contacted me to ask if I'll do a monthly column for them. Things are looking up.

Today is Sunday, the 14th of June, and there are Black Lives Matter marches in Auckland, Wellington and Dunedin. There was one on the 1st of June, but I didn't have the courage to go, because we were still at Alert Level Two. Eva and Jesse went though. I stuck masks in their pockets telling them to please wear them. I doubt they did. The news showed thousands of mostly young people with no face masks. They carried placards saying, 'I CAN'T BREATHE', the words George Floyd said to the police officer whose knee was on his neck.

We're all going to the march today, although Eva and Jesse are going with their friends. Adam's going with them too. He's moved back to live with his mum and grandmother now that we're in Alert Level One.

We're eating breakfast. It's been a slow, lazy one, with the Sunday newspaper spread across the table. Jesse made pancakes, which is so rare that we're overdoing the compliments, in the hope he'll do it again.

Eva has finished reading my Springbok Tour writing. 'Did you and Uncle Rewi ever, y'know, get together?'

I look up from the newspaper. 'No, never.'

'Are you just saying that cos Dad's here?'

Ross puts his paper down. 'Should I leave the room?' He laughs. 'Eva, your mum and I know all about each other's exes.'

'Really?' Eva asks.

'Fascinating,' Jesse says. 'Complete honesty . . . or is it?'

I laugh. 'Rewi was never my boyfriend, and that's the truth. I loved him and still do, but the way I love Kalāsia.'

'So, you never even kissed?' Eva asks.

'We talked about it once when we were seventeen. Rewi said, "Liza, if I ever drink more than my two beers and try to make a move on you, punch me. It'd ruin our friendship."'

'Wow, so sensible,' Eva says.

'We had too much to lose. If we'd gone out together and then broken up, we'd both have lost our best friend.' I stand up and go to the bench to rinse my dishes.

'What about Harry?' Jesse asks. 'Did you ever see Harry again?'

'Sometimes, walking home from school or at a party. We always said hi to each other, but that was it.'

'So, you never had a proper conversation with him again?' Eva asks.

'It felt too hard.'

'Weren't there counsellors in schools back then?' Jesse asks.

'No, I'd never even heard of a counsellor.'

'Ever heard what happened to him?' Jesse asks.

'I ran into someone from Newton Grammar, who told me he's married with kids.' I close the kitchen window. 'Let's lock up and go to this march.'

There are many people here in Aotea Square. Most of them are young. I gaze across the crowds of people around me protesting at racial injustice. Here we are, nearly 40 years after the 1981 Springbok Tour, still protesting against violence towards black people.

There are some people yelling, 'All lives matter' from the side lines. Some protesters nearby start having a debate with them.

After a karakia and a mihi whakatau from Ngāti Whātua artist,

Graham Tipene, a few people get up to speak. There are young Somalian and Ethiopian people, who talk about the massacre of Muslim people by a white supremacist in Christchurch last year.

Young Māori and Pasifika speakers remind us that it's not just police in the USA who behave like this. They talk about violence towards their own people here in Aotearoa. It reminds me of the woman Pete heard at university long ago, the one who said we had to look in our own back yard.

A man named Will 'Ilolahia speaks. He was one of the guys who set up the Polynesian Panthers group in the 1970's. They were sick of police doing Dawn Raids, forcing their way into Polynesians' homes to hunt for overstayers. As he speaks, I think of Kalāsia and her early morning visits after bad dreams.

Will 'Ilolahia tells the crowd to be actively anti-racist, not to just stand by and witness it. He says that racism is a white, Pākehā problem. My mind flicks back to the memory of Ursula's brother yelling racist names at Rewi. I didn't stand up for Rewi. I wasn't actively anti-racist. If I could go back in time, I would tell him to leave my friend alone. I'd tell him to get his knee off my friend's neck.

After a few more speakers, we begin to march down to the US Consulate, chanting 'Black lives matter' and 'No justice, no peace'. A truck plays music and some people begin to dance. I sway to the music, gazing out at the hordes of people around me. That's when I see him.

He's spotted me first from the other side of the crowd. His hair is still sandy blond, cut short now though. He lifts his hand and waves, smiling at me. There's a woman beside him and three teenage kids. He points at them, showing me.

I wave back, then point at Ross. Eva and Jesse are somewhere in the crowd, so I can't show them to him.

'Why are you pointing at me?' Ross asks.

I don't speak. Harry and I stare at each other, smiles stretching from one side of our faces to the other. For a moment, we are all there is, no crowd, no music, no protest. Just Harry and me, looking at each other.

'Who's that?' Ross asks.

'Harry,' I say. I give Harry one last wave, then turn to Ross. 'I think it's time to go home.'

At dinner, we talk about the march. I say that the march has got me thinking about people like John Minto and Dick Cuthbert, who gave up their professional jobs to devote their time fully to HART. 'They should be given some sort of public honour now.'

'Like a Queen's honour?' Ross asks.

'Not sure that'd be their thing,' I say. 'Some other kind of public honour, because what they did to fight against racism here and in South Africa was huge. There were others too, Māori activists like Ripeka Evans, and so many others who should be acknowledged.'

'Do you think things have changed in New Zealand since then?' Jesse asks.

'I think so,' Ross says. 'When I was reading your Springbok story, Liza, you mentioned the slogan, 'No Maoris, No Tour'. Now, there'd be a macron over the 'a' and no 's' to show a plural. Te reo is understood and spoken more widely. It's become normal to hear it on TV and on the radio. More people seem to be committed to learn about Māori culture.'

'And that statue in Hamilton's been removed,' Jesse says. 'You can't have a statue of a man in a public place if he killed lots of Māori in the Waikato wars.'

We finish dinner, but we keep talking. The day's been long, but it's filled us with energy rather than exhaustion. We talk about the riots in America since George Floyd's murder.

'I loved how people took a knee in honour of George Floyd at the march today,' Eva says.

'Funny how pro-tour people said politics shouldn't mix with sport in 1981,' Ross says, 'but it was sportspeople who started taking a knee.'

I get up and put the kettle on. Taking a deep breath, I tell the kids I saw Harry at the march. I tell them about his wife and kids. Eva says it's nice that we smiled at each other, and Ross and Jesse agree.

'Did he look different, Mum?' Eva asks.

'He was a bit far away for me to see clearly, but he mostly looked the same, maybe just wider. He's broadened. He's a man now.'

'Didn't you want to go over and talk with him?' Eva asks. 'Didn't you want to know what he's been up to all these years?'

'I . . . no . . . it took me by surprise.'

'Hey, did you end up going to your school ball?' Jesse asks.

'I did,' I say, relieved that we've moved on from Eva's question. 'We went as a group: Rewi, Kalāsia, Ciara, Stella and me.'

'Uncle Rewi went to the ball!' Jesse says. 'Thought he didn't want to go.'

'I promised him that we'd dance all night, and we did.' I turn to get a cup from the cupboard. I don't want them to see the tears in my eyes, so I fiddle around with cups on the shelf and continue to speak as normally as I can. 'I think Rewi felt sorry for me. I'd already bought the ball tickets and the dress so, even though he hates dressing up, he came.'

'He's still kind like that,' Eva says.

'He is,' I agree.

'And Jacinda Ardern says we should all be kind,' Eva says, stacking the plates, 'so Jesse and I will do the dishes, Mum. You and Dad relax.'

Jesse shakes his head at her. 'Can you *not* offer my services to other people?'

'Well, you never do, so I've got to do it for you.'

'I do offer. You're just a control freak and . . .'

'Let's get out of here, Liza,' Ross says, standing up.

We sneak out of the kitchen, into the lounge and turn the TV up loud, so we can't hear them arguing.

It's midnight, and everyone's gone to bed. I'm sitting at my laptop. The plan had been to read over my Springbok story, but I can't concentrate. It was the first time I'd seen Harry in nearly forty years.

Even though I wasn't up close today, there are things I know about that man in the crowd. I know his eyes are green and that his lip can curl up in an unsettling way. I know he can be funny, warm and kind. I know these things because he was my first love.

I save the file. The story is there now. The things that happened in 1981 and the people who mattered to me, they're all there. I stand up and rest my hand on my closed laptop. I've told the story, because some stories have to be told.

ACKNOWLEDGEMENTS

First and foremost, I'd like to thank Louise Russell at Bateman Books for deciding to publish this novel. When I phoned to ask her whether she'd be willing to look at the manuscript, it wasn't long before my fingers were firmly crossed, in the hope that this warm, insightful woman would say 'yes'. Throughout the publishing process, I have felt incredibly grateful that Louise was steering the ship. Thank you also to the other creative and hard-working people at Bateman: Paul Bateman, Bryce Gibson, Samantha Guillen, Keely O'Shannessy, (who created the wonderful cover), Tina Delceg and Lise Clayton. I also wish to thank Jo McColl from Unity Books, who wisely suggested I contact Bateman Publishers.

Nicola McCloy performed magic on this novel with her skilful editing. I am grateful for her depth of feedback, sensible suggestions and wonderful sense of humour. Some of her comments made me laugh out loud.

I'd like to thank my very special writing group: Thalia Henry, Helen McNeill, Nina Tapu and Dave Moore. They have generously given their time to critique this novel from its early stages to its completion.

Other writing friends who have gifted me their precious time and insights are Jacqui Tisch, Emma Harris, Tracey Sharpe, Meg Knott and my sister, Beth Kayes. Thanks to Annie McKillop for book-cover discussions too. A special thank you to Trisha Hanifin for kindly inviting me to join her writing group some years back, an important first step for me.

Huge gratitude to my 2014 AUT Master of Creative Writing lecturers, James George and Siobhan Harvey, who continue to support me as a writer through generously giving time and advice whenever I ask for it.

Under level 4 and 3 lockdown in 2020, libraries were closed. I wanted to locate specific books for research, so I asked the Mt. Albert Community Facebook group if anyone owned copies. The responses included not only offers to lend books but suggestions of other information sources. I borrowed some books from Mirla Edmundsen, whose father protested in 1981 and features in a photo in one of the books. I phoned Paul Smith, who chatted with me about his memories of covering the anti-tour protests as a journalist at the *Auckland Star*. Robin Kearns suggested I contact John Minto to see if he might be willing to fill in gaps and recall his experience of events. I hadn't dreamed of doing that up until then.

When libraries opened under Alert Level Two, the staff at the Auckland Library Research Centre were supportive, helping me locate anti-tour posters, images and newspaper articles.

I wish to thank the *Auckland Star* and the *New Zealand Herald* for their coverage of the 1981 Springbok Tour. There are two journalists I'd like to thank, in particular. One is the late Pat Booth, who showed that journalists can change the world, one wrongful arrest at a time.

The second journalist I'd like to thank is Pekka Paavonpera, who worked for the now defunct *New Zealand Times*. Paavonpera witnessed the attack on the students dressed as clowns and a bumblebee, and his recall of this traumatic event, although disturbing, was a useful source of information.

The books and documentaries referenced below made for riveting research. The authors' meticulous, lively accounts of the 1981 Springbok Tour protests gave me a rich source of facts, stories and perspectives to weave into this novel.

One of the documentaries referenced below is Merata Mita's *Patu*. This film continues to inform generations of New Zealanders forty years later. It is a national taonga borne of courage and determination. Kia ora, Merata.

I'd like to thank my father and my siblings for their loving interest in my writing endeavours. I wish to acknowledge my very special mum, no longer with us, for all she gave to nurture my creativity and love of stories. Huge appreciation to my husband, Steve, and adult children, Flynn and Sarah, who give me space to think, research and write and often give me feedback and suggestions. Special thanks to Sarah, who proofread the book alongside me and the team at Bateman, so that we had an extra pair of eyes.

I wish to express my admiration for the people who threw their bodies on the line to protest against the unjust treatment of black South Africans. I was incredibly lucky to have a long phone chat with one of these people, David Williams, who generously shared memories of his involvement in CARE and the anti-tour protests.

I'd also like to acknowledge the Māori protest leaders, who insisted that the oppression and injustice imposed on Māori through colonisation and on-going systemic racism be put under the spotlight alongside the plight of black South Africans. Some of these women and men are mentioned in this book. Their hard work and bravery wedged open doors, inviting all New Zealanders to have more honest conversations.

Lastly, I wish to express my immense gratitude to John Minto, who responded immediately and graciously to my request for information and clarification on certain events. I am deeply grateful to John Minto, not only for his unflinching commitment to the 1981 anti-tour movement, for which he was often verbally and physically assaulted, but for his kindness to me. This novel is better for his involvement.

References

Chapple, G. (1984). *1981: THE TOUR*. A.H. and A.W. Reed Ltd.

McCredie, A. (1981). *THE TOUR – Photographs*. Athol McCredie.

Mita, H. (Director). (2018). *Merata: How Mum Decolonised the Screen*. [Documentary film]. Arama Pictures.

Mita, M. (Director). (1983). *Patu*. [Documentary film]. Awatea Films.

Newnham, T. (1981). *By Batons and Barbed Wire – A Response to the 1981 Springbok tour of New Zealand*. Real Pictures Ltd.